A NOVEL BY STEPHEN DIXON

FALL
&
RISE

NORTH POINT PRESS · SAN FRANCISCO · 1985

Part of this book has previously appeared in
slightly different form in the *Chicago Review*

To my wife, Anne

Fall & Rise

The Party

I meet her at a party. It's a large room I first see her in. I was one of the first guests to arrive and I thought I was late. The host lives on the top floor. It's a four-story building, small for what I know of most of the city but not for her neighborhood. Red brick, narrow width, low ceilings in all the apartments but the two on what was originally the parlor floor, with a steep stoop outside of about ten steps. It was raining. I took the subway down. I didn't know what to wear. I haven't many clothes. One pair of shoes I shined the previous night. A corduroy sports jacket, couple of wrinkled dress shirts, three ties—one a bow—which I never like to put on and are a bit stained and out of date. Really only one pair of what could be called dress pants if I don't want to wear my good blue jeans. Good meaning the jeans that are still reasonably new and rough and dark blue instead of light and smooth from lots of washings and wear. Black corduroys. They needed a pressing. It was too late for that now. I had thought of it earlier. The day before. Then thought if I wear these pants I can't the jacket, since the jacket's a faded olive green and of a wider wale and wouldn't go with the pants. To me if one wears corduroy pants and jacket together it has to be a suit. I also thought, more than a week before, of getting the shirts laundered and pants and jacket cleaned or pressed, so I'd have one or the other garment and either of the shirts ready for the party. I knew I was going to it, knew some interesting and successful people would be there and a few in my field or close and that most would be well dressed and some even in elegant clothes: skirts or gowns to the floor, dark wool suits with vests. I didn't know she'd be there. Nobody had ever spoken of her to me even in passing. "Oh, maybe eighty or so," the host had said a month ago when she phoned to

3

invite me and I asked how many people would be there. And rather than meet her at the party I saw her there and later met her on the landing outside the host's front door. Diana's. One large smartly and no doubt—unless she inherited most of it, and judging from what she's told me about her genealogy and bringing-up she probably did—expensively furnished living room and an adjoining room with only an enormous armoire and dresser and big brass bed and whose lights were usually off and louver doors closed. Both rooms overlooking a small square park with joggers running around it even at night and in the rain. Even till very late, Diana had told me and several others this summer when we were having drinks outdoors and watching the sun set over some mountains or hills of upstate New York. The setting sun reminded her of the sunrise or latter part of it she can see from her apartment during the winter and spring months, and that connection led to a number of other things she sees from her windows. That sometimes she'll get up for something at three or four in the morning and see joggers and occasionally a cyclist doing several laps, or at least in the time she looks, and once even a unicyclist, though she only watched him till he reached the corner because it took him so long and she had become bored. I could see joggers and pedestrians from her windows at the party but no cyclists. It was mostly raining when I looked out her windows, raining when I left my building uptown. Black corduroys, I decided on—unpressed. Sweater instead of jacket, still smelling from the natural waterproof oils the manufacturer had left in the wool, and which I'd take off at the party when I took off my coat. I had no iron, though could have asked the landlady on the first floor to loan me one. She's loaned me things like that before. Vacuum cleaner, dishes and candlesticks when I was having eight people for dinner once. That was a year ago. May was there, slept over, made the pastry and bread in my stove. But I didn't want to go through the chore of pressing the pants without an ironing board or carrying the board up and down two flights if I also borrowed that, and thought the pants being black wouldn't look too unpressed. Long-sleeved blue cotton shirt, in the rugby mode, with a tan collar that didn't look quite right with the rest of the shirt or the pants. The shoes were the best-dressed part of me, only a month old so still with good heels and soles. I took an umbrella. Not the one someone had left behind several months ago. A woman I'd met at a PEN symposium on the rights of the translator and minimum rates he should receive, and who stayed the next night at my place. Came when it rained, left when it was sunny and mild. I cooked us dinner, made her breakfast, phoned the day after and she said she'd changed her mind and would rather not see me again if it was all right. I asked was it anything I did or didn't and she said no, everything was great in every way. I said I'd call back in a couple of weeks and maybe she'll have changed her mind. She said I shouldn't bother to call, nor even bother her with my phone rings. I said then how can I get the umbrella back to her, since it wasn't the contractible kind that were fairly simple to mail. She said she had plenty of umbrellas that people have left behind at her apartment so why don't I keep it for a rainy day. Used those very words. What was my reply? I said goodbye, though wanted to say "You think I'd use an umbrella that has a gilded mermaid handle and a canopy that's hot-pants pink?" Took my regular folding umbrella to Diana's party. Looked out my window, saw there was rain. Couldn't see how much rain because I live in back and all my windows face either an air shaft or alleyway and are two stories down from the roof. So I dialed Weather and a man said periods of heavy rain tonight and possible sleet and snow but no measurable accumulation. When I got outside it seemed as if the rain was coming down in printed periods. Hundreds of them every square foot per second. It rained buckets of periods except beneath the streetlamp where it poured cats and dogs of diagonals and double primes, and I was glad I'd also worn my fake fleece-lined raincoat. Not nippy enough yet for my muffler, I thought upstairs, or watchcap or double socks. I don't have rubbers and the rubber boots I have don't take shoes. I should get one or the other and will this week if I remember to and the price isn't too high. In the meantime I applied, half an hour before I left, mink oil around the shoes' stitching and seams and hoped they wouldn't get too wet. I headed for the subway. The periods and diagonals drummed my umbrella homophonically. Theoretically, the party had started. "Eight," Diana had said when she invited me and I said "Eight? Seems like an in-between hour to start a party: so soon after most people have just sat down to or finished their dinners." "No, when I say eight, people will know I mean nine and that's when they'll start coming, only a little after because no one likes to be first, and to only eat a light supper beforehand because I'll have lots of food there. Now if I had said nine, they'd begin coming at quarter to ten and then the party wouldn't end at one when I want it to but around one forty-five, and I have to be at work noon Saturdays." It was now half-past eight. Entire trip to her place shouldn't take more than forty minutes if there isn't an inordinately long subway station wait. There are good bookstores down there so if I get downtown too early to be late I'll browse around in one and maybe even buy a book I've wanted a long time and was only recently remaindered to a dollar or two or turned into a moderately priced paperback. Insert my umbrella into one of those stands or leakproof cans by the door, for I worked part-time in a bookstore this year when I couldn't, in spite of my various salaries, honoraria and advances, pay for both my rent and food, and know what damage a leaking umbrella and umbrella can can do to the books and floor and salesperson or customer who slides along it and maybe sprawls and then what that customer can do to the store. But finally outside, showered, shaved and brushed, perfectly hairless face except for the long graying sideburns and one or two hairs curling out of my nostrils and also the small clumps in my ears, which seem to get a bit thicker each year, stiff straight still-wet mostly ungraying side and top hair so right now not a filament or strand out of place. Raining tadpoles and diagonals, sheets and dogs. Three-block walk to the station, salute to the ornate neighborly Central Park West doorman who tips his hat to me with a white-gloved finger while he whistles with a whistle for a cab. Flower stall under a Sabrett's frankfurter stand umbrella by the subway entrance and I think Why not? and ask how much and for two bucks no tax buy five chrysanthemums and a fern frond, which he wraps in paper and then staples the top and bottom of when I say I'm going to Jersey by way of Amtrak. Downstairs, get two tokens and change and give my thanks and get skeptical eye contact back, though most times I don't. Second flight down, shaking the closed umbrella as I go and spattering the graffito on the tile wall that's calling our attention to the forthcoming carnage and war in Puerto Rico and El Salvador and how we must drive out all Hispanics and Semitics and gigolos and whores from New York. Not many people on the platform so could be a good ten-minute wait. Space for a slim-hipped and almost no-buttocked person on the one bench there and I almost sit. But the young woman I'd be sitting next to on one side is cracking and snapping gum which I can't stand the sound, smell and sight of and the man I'd be sitting thigh to thigh to seems asleep and the type who might take offense at our nearness if he suddenly awakes and thinks it's because of my dripping flowers or umbrella or something libidinous I did. Farther along the platform a man walking a ten-speed bike to what will be the first car, woman pacing back and forth carrying a typewriter case with I suppose a typewriter inside judging by her shoulder slump from the weight, a midget or someone I think would be considered a midget with that kind of forehead, hairline, face and height and whom I know as the efficient but sometimes belligerent cook of a Columbus Avenue coffee shop I've gone to on chillier days for coffee and soup, leaning against a pillar reading a weekly newsmagazine. The last person on the platform alternately looking at her wristwatch and the continually pouring whiskey clock above the bench that's about twenty minutes late, till she sees me stick the flowers to my nose for a sniff and smiles to herself and drops her watch hand. Nobody looking potentially menacing, a thought I've had here before since the night two years ago I was mugged for the first time in my life under the same squeaking clock. I start to pull a book out of my coat pocket, but with two cumbersome things I'm carrying and both wet, push it back, look to see if the train's coming, with my foot break up the puddle my umbrella's making till it takes on the shape of a dinosaur, walk along the platform reading some of the things scrawled on the wall ads: "Lenin is the tool of the Marxistplace—Free the Soviet Block 11!!"—shouted out of the mouth of a once-famous jockey who's promoting smart betting at OTB; "This ad makes asses of women by exploiting their asses"—ballooning out of the behind of a young woman modeling skin-tight designer jeans. I hear the rumble, look up the tunnel, see the beam, step behind the pillar the cook's leaning against on the other side. As the train pulls in, my mouth makes the motion of a hello to him while his fingers are in his ears and he acknowledges me with a vacant nod. We get on. Sleeping man's awake but stays on the bench. I keep the closing door open for a man running downstairs yelling "Wait, important date, hold the doors." Stand till the express stop and though there's an express waiting, catch the time on the cook's watch and sit rather than change since I'll spend the extra minutes I can afford to waste on this slower train. Across from me a woman's bawling out two young girls. Nothing they do is right. The older one puts her finger on her nose and tries to look at it cross-eyed: not right. Younger girl plays with her shoelaces without untying them: not right. Older girl skims her fingers over the woman's knuckles and then twirls the woman's pinky ring—slap, "Act your age, you're so pitiful dumb!" I'm reading one of the books of the Japanese poet's poems I'm to collect and translate from but with all that commotion I can't concentrate. Then the woman orders the girls to stand and they hold her jacket pocket-flaps and all go to the door as the train pulls in at Thirty-fourth and the woman sticks her head past the door and yells "Red." A man says "Way to go," and runs to the door and jumps on just before it closes. The woman's smiling, kids look sullen, man's laughing and shaking his head. She presses two hands of fingertips to his lips, man says "You're all looking good," and points to some seats and they sit, girls perpendicular to the woman and man. She says "I thought I'd miss you." He says "I told you I know how to work the subway. How the beauty queens been?" "Fine," "Fine," the girls say. "They been awful and don't let them convince you different, but now that you're here they're really going to be fine. Isn't that so, girls?" and they say to him

"Yes," "Yes." She puts a hand on his knee, other hand holds his two, her thumb rubbing into his bottom palm. He laughs and says "I know, me too. What's it been, a week?" "Three days," she says. "Three? Shoo. Miss you so much, feels like three weeks." "Don't exaggerate." The older girl's looking at my flowers and says "Mommy, can I ask that man what he has in his paper?" "It's flowers," she says, still staring at the man. Train goes. "I know, but what kind—live or dead?" Woman looks at me. "No, honey, you don't want to be disturbing him. He's studying." My book's closed and in my lap. "Mister," the girl says, "what's in there, flowers or a plant?" "I told you," the woman says. "Now be good and be quiet and sit up like a grown girl," and looks back at the man and rubs his palm. "Six weeks," he says. "It's okay," I say to the woman. "They're cut chrysanthemums," to the girl, "so I suppose you can say they're dead though they're still very fresh." "I know that, but what color are they?" "Yellow and red." "Can I see them?" "Can I see them?" the younger girl says. "Tell them no," the woman says. "Those kids will hound you till you hand them over to them." "It's okay. —And I'd like to show you the flowers," and they leap up, oldest one first, and come over to me and sit on either side, "but I'm going to a party and they're for the host and I want the paper to stay stapled so when she opens it she'll be surprised." "What's a host?" the older girl says, touching the paper on top, and I say "The woman or man—" "You don't have to explain to them," the woman says. "Don't worry, I like children. —The woman or man, though a woman can also be called a hostess, who gives the party, such as the woman who's giving the party tonight." "Can I come?" the older girl says. "Can I?" the younger girl says. "No, but"—"Did you hear that? Can they come," the woman says to the man—"maybe if I open the paper a little you can smell the flowers even if you can't see them." I tear open a hole on top and they put their noses in it and take deep breaths and the older girl says "It smells real good, just like yellow and red flowers would." "They do," the younger girl says, "—real good." "Do something to get them back here," the woman says to the man. "I have no control over them sometimes." The man takes out a roll of mints and says "Look what I got here, girls." The girls run to him and each takes a mint he's unrolled, sticks it into her mouth and puts a hand out for another. "So soon?" he says and they smile and nod and he starts peeling some paper back on the roll and the older girl says "No, I want to do it for you. What kind are these?" as she peels the paper back. "Mints," and she says "But what kind?" "Why why why, what what what," the woman says. "You always want to know so much till you wear everyone out including that nice flower man.

Just accept they have a flavor and a hole in them and that should be enough." "But there's lots of kinds. There's kinds I don't like." "Do you like these?" "Yes." "Then these aren't the kind you don't like." "Manure mint," the man says to the older girl. He seems annoyed. "What's manure mint?" she says, giving the second mint she's unrolled to the younger girl. The train's pulling in to the Fourteenth Street stop. "No more questions," the woman says. "We have to go." She stands, grabs the girls' hands, man says to her "I'll shoot upstairs and look first. Wait for me at the bottom here." "You're the boss," and kisses the back of his coat on the shoulder and the door opens and steps are right there and he runs upstairs. Doors close and train goes, girls staring after me as I move backwards. Must still be raining or was till a minute to a few ago, hats and hair wet of the passengers who just got on. Train stops between stations and starts, stops, lights flash off and on, goes slow. I'm glad I'm going to a party. Haven't been to one in months. Eats, drinks, best place to meet women they've been, maybe elaborate canapés I'd get nowhere else. Maybe Russian canapés and Iranian caviar because lots of Diana's friends are Russians traveling here from abroad or Eastern Europeans or recent émigrés or Americans of Russian descent, so various confabular and linguistic concoctions I also enjoy. But one quick final line to walk with, as the train pulls in and I open the book without knowing what page it's to and read in instantly translated Japanese "Storm-colored God who laughs a great deal as in children's games." Not a poem I was thinking of including in my collection but I read some more and think I just might. Title's "Supernal Underground," which will stay and maybe in the translator's forward or the introduction to the poet and his work I'll say where, when and how I chose this poem. *West 4th St. station, loitering train dawdling to a stop* or *tottering to a halt* or a mixture of those and I put the book into my coat pocket, stand at the door with the cook who's reading another newsweekly, other slipped into a briefcase on the floor where I quickly saw inside a clipboard, scissors, rolled-up pair of socks. "The Iffy Decade," the article's headline says, which doesn't make me want to read more: too broad. We get off, I race upstairs, turn around, he's reading while limping and I see his right foot has a four- to six-inch platform to even his height. I jot down those introductory notes into a memo book, forget what I thought after "dawdling to a halt," though remember it rhymed with "jot" but it was "stop," and write the word down followed by a question mark. I go through the revolving exit gate. Token booth's boarded up, its exterior vandalized. Urine smells so bad in the passageway to the street staircase that I hold my breath. At the bottom of the steps a woman wrapped in towels and with a styrofoam cup with no coins in it by her feet says "Sir, I could use a dollar or two for a hot meal." I'd stop to look for a dime if it weren't for the smell. I shake my head, start upstairs, shoelaces on one shoe flick against the steps. I lean the flowers and umbrella against the stair wall, tie the laces, drops land on my head but not much, long as I'm in this position other loosely tied shoe could be untied and tied tight too. "Sir," from below, twisted face, shaking hand with the cup reaching up to me. Maybe some of it's an act. I feel in my pockets. I could say "Here, catch," or walk down and drop it into the cup. All I turn up are two quarters and a subway token. "Sorry." Her look says look some more. "I have to go—good luck," and run up the rest of the steps. Rain's nearly stopped. Cook puts something into her hand and says "All I can spare," and she says "My babies bless you." I open the umbrella, look at the library steeple clock. Twenty to eleven or ten to seven? What'd the optometrist say that trying-on day last month? "You want to see long distances, your eyes aren't in your head anymore but on your nose." I put them on. Five to nine, so still some time. I head for a bookstore around the block. Bank's time and temperature clock says 9:12 and 43 degrees. More like it. Cleaning store clock says quarter past. So it's so. Should've left sooner. Now I won't get to talk much with Diana. Sidewalk so narrow and crowded with people, parking meters, trashcans and trash that I walk in the street most of the way and every other store selling shoes and western boots. New books in the window I might want to borrow from the library. Then one I at first can't believe I'm seeing. Same title, different cover, my name at the bottom, little dust already on it. *New Asiatic Women Poets* I collected and translated, or for the languages I didn't know, put into verse other people's interlinears, and which was published in hardcover last year but no one told me was coming out in paperback. The store's door is locked. Manager I've talked to before and who asked me to sign one of the two clothbounds the store bought—"Don't want to get stuck with more than one copy"—waves my hand away from the door handle and points to the clock I can't see from here. I point to the book he can't see at the window corner. He taps his watchband and says "Nine" and slashes his hand through the air. I hold the flowers out to him and say "Please" and he bows and smiles as he shakes his head and reaches under the cash register and must touch the switch that shuts off most of the store lights at once. I get down almost on my knees to see who the publisher is, but with the window lights off it's too dark. Monday I'll phone the hardcover editor of that anthology at half-past ten. She never gets in before that. Her assistant will answer and say she's not in yet and who's calling and I'll have to explain who I am again and why I'm calling and he'll ask for my phone number and spelling of my last name and say she'll get my message when she comes in. I'll call at eleven and she'll be away from her desk her assistant will say and maybe she didn't see the message he left and he'll make sure she gets it when she returns. I'll call at quarter to twelve and the assistant to the editor in the next office will say my editor and her assistant are away from their desks this moment and since both their coats are still there she's sure they haven't left for lunch and is there a message and name and phone number I'd like to leave? I'll call a few minutes after noon and she'll be out for lunch her assistant will say and she got my last message and in fact got all of them but she's been extremely busy today, but he will tell her I called once more. I'll call at two and she'll be in an editors' conference. At four she'll still be in the conference. At five Dolores will pick up the phone and say she was about to call me. Didn't the rights people contact me about the paperback sale? Didn't the paperback people send me a questionnaire? Didn't I even get her note about the sale? The mail these days. Worse than the subways. Check my contract with them, even if she's sure we both have a good idea what it stipulates, translators getting the worst shake of anybody in publishing other than their senior editors, and that's that I signed all my rights away to hardcover royalties or a paperback sale when I sold them the manuscript for one not-so-gainful flat fee. What about the movie rights to the book? I'll say and she'll say it's always enjoyable and a rare experience indeed to talk to an author with a sense of humor about his livelihood and with so little bitterness about the treatment of his book, but to be serious, with my next manuscript I should get an agent to handle the contractual details. I'll say all an agent's ever told me is I can probably sell poetry anthologies better than any agent, probably because my heart's really in it, they usually say, and that they don't like handling translated poetry of individual poets or any poetry for that matter when the poet isn't a novelist, because there just isn't enough money in it for them for all the time spent. Anyway, I'll say, who's calling about possible royalties or paperback fees? All I want are a few contributor copies to help fill up my barren bookshelves. She'll say I'm a lot more than just a contributor with that wise and important book and she thinks some comps can be squeezed out of the paper people and if they can't she'll send me one of her own. I'll say does she think each of the contributing poets can get one too? and she'll say with them she doesn't know, since the poets will be getting paid again for their poems in the paperback but have nothing in their contracts about complimentary books. But they do owe her a favor for a

very successful cookbook she sent them first and they bought, so she'll look
into it and get back to me soon. And then how much she's looking forward to
my next anthology of contemporary poets from remote regions like Outer and
Inner Mongolia and Pago Pago and Tierra del Fuego and our own and Green-
land's and even Eastern Siberia's Eskimos, but without an agent she can't
promise my contract will be any better with that book. As for the Japanese
poet I keep raving about and whom she knows I'm plodding away and counting so hard on, no matter how great she and the Asiatic experts eventually say
he is she only hopes her house will think he can sell well to universities and
libraries, because they've just about given up trying to push a poet's poems on
chains and ordinary bookstores. And we'll have lunch one of these days, she'll
say, when she's not so bogged down with the spring list and already another
dozen authors for next fall, and I head for Diana's building, rain still thin,
wondering what paperback house took my book, which should do me some
good in placing future manuscripts, someone recumbent in an empty refrigerator carton in the entrance of a closed sandal shop, around the corner, up
her stoop, bell at the top, voice says "Yes?" and I say "Dan Krin" and there's a
pause, static crack, "Excuse me, I'm not used to this elaborate set," and I'm
buzzed in. I keep the door open with my foot, shake out and close the umbrella, start unbuttoning my coat as I climb the first flight. Have to pee. Don't run
or think about it. "Hello." Diana, staring down the stairwell. "Hi," I say,
putting my glasses into the holder inside my pants pocket and she says "Oh, it's
you. Ringer who rung you in said it was my niece Andy. She didn't come in
with you?" "No." "You're one of the first. Come on up. Of course come on up.
And of course you're coming up. Still, you, of all people, Daniel, excluding
Andy, I thought would come sooner. Shame on you both and I hope we get
time to talk." "Funny, but that's what I was thinking just before, though not
about Andy," as I round the landing and start up the next flight. "How you
doing?" and she says "Unready, and you?" "Couldn't be better. But guess what
I just saw in the Eighth Street Bookshop window?" and she doesn't say
"What?" Maybe she didn't hear me. I'm now on her floor. Her door's open.
People chatting inside. Coatrack with three coats and a hat. Pair of man's
work-boots on the other tenant's doormat. "Same boots were there the last
time I was here," and she says "They're there permanently to scare off undesir-
able trespassers, and extra extra-large. He's petite." "Strange." Rubbers and
rubber rainboots and umbrella by her door. She's staring at me. Man in her
apartment saying "Say it again, Jane, and this time I swear by what's his name
in heaven I'll laugh." Still staring at me. Nodding approvingly. Wry smile

arising. She's about to give me a compliment. I'm about to deflect and if possible squelch it. I look over my shoulder. "What are you looking at?" she says. "Nobody I guess. Thought maybe someone who you were, for what were those 'my isn't it nice oh boy' nods and look for?" "You of course, if you have to ask."

"Telephone, Dee," a woman says from the door. Attractive, blackhaired, shiny black dress with several silver chains of various widths around her waist and neck. Bracelets, fingers full of rings.

"Is it an accent?"

"Pronouncedly Slavic."

"Have him—no, I should take care of it."

"You're busy. I speak the lingua messenger. Have him what?"

"Cibette, this is Dan. —Tell him the address and directions here right up to the fourth floor and where we're situated in relation to the top step, and just to come, you hear—no excuses, but speak extra intelligibly and have him repeat everything back." Cibette goes inside. "Some of the newer émigrés. So bright and talented. But the language is such a problem, they get lost or are spooked by our subways and have no money for cabs, besides getting cheated by them. I should have spoken to him. But you, that's who. Marble of surprises, you look practically impeccable. Or does that sound incredibly mean? It does suddenly to me."

"No. You mean, well, that you've never seen me out of my bathing suit, bathrobe, assorted worn-down T-shirts and jeans. But wait'll I take off my coat. Almost the same old summer ho-hum clothes."

"Now now, don't be so unduly. Whatever. Been hitting this nutritious green wine a Hungarian friend sent over and I think too much. But that you wore shoes instead of sneakers is a positive sign of nattier garments to come."

"How fancy," touching the aluminum coatrack. "Yours?"

"Rented, as is the fur coat you see on it, to make the best impression on my very impressive guests, though I'm not impressed. Your umbrella isn't that ratty to embarrass me, so leave it in the holder, though I can't guarantee it'll be there when you leave."

"I'll take another then."

"Don't you dare. Only the guests I don't know or who can afford it are allowed to be thieves."

I stick the umbrella into the holder, hang up my coat while she's looking me over and nodding at my pants and shaking her head at my shirt, and hold out the flowers. "For you."

"But I have no spare vases."

"Hardly the gracious way of accepting."

"I'm sorry. I'm sure they're beautiful, few and smell nice too. But the person who plans to present them should think beforehand of the harried hostess and myriad problems she's apt to have with her party and that all her vases and hands will probably be filled. But what are we indulging in all this small hallway talk for? Usually you just kiss and are quickly in the room for a drink and by now my time should be too occupied for even a lingering hello and I'm getting worried it's not. Ah, there's the bell. Give a kiss, then get in there and ring them in. First left in the kitchen, and before you get a drink. First press the button marked T. Ask who's there. Then release that button and listen while you press the L-button and then ring the R-button to let whoever it is in."

"What should I L for?"

"Just if someone says it's Harry, David or Andrei. If he says he's a crazed razor-blade wielder who's going to slice up us all, don't ring him in. But go. Quick. Kiss. They're ringing again. And find anything but an empty apple-sauce jar for your beautiful flowers," and she gives them to me and I kiss her cheek and go inside. Bell's ringing. I press the T-button and say "Hello?" and release it and listen and don't hear anything and bell rings and Diana yells "What are you doing, Dan?" and I press the button and say "Yes?" and release it and press the L-button and a man says "Velchetski and friend," and I ring him in. I take my sweater off, put it on top of the coatrack and see Diana leaning over the banister. "Grisha, how are you?—up here," and I suppose it's Grisha who says "I can't see you but can only imagine your loveliness face from below and I feel simply great. Send me the elevator."

"For two short flights?"

"These are not short. Only my legs and breath are, which make the stairs long. But you have no elevator car, don't lie to me," and something in Russian, "but I will still walk upstairs."

"Dan," Diana says, "you must meet this madman, but first plant those." I didn't know I still held them. Maybe I put them down, picked them up when I came out here. I go into the kitchen. Bell rings. I press it, put the wrapped flowers in a tall glass of water, get a glass of green wine at the bar, go to the cheese table and slice a piece of brie and introduce myself. Phil and his wife Jane. Bell rings. "Translate," I say. "I'll get it," someone says near the kitchen. "Sculptors," Phil says. "That so? What do you sculpt, or what with?" "Rubber," Jane says. "Plastic," Phil says, "but I really hate those questions, for my own idiosyncratic reasons, but understand why people ask them." "Because they're interested I guess," I say. "But you actually sculpt with those materials?" Bell rings. "Oh no," Jane says. "Molding, twisting—you know." "Something like that for me too, but it's too difficult—and again excuse my idiosyncrasies—for me to explain." "Some art forms are tougher that way I suppose," I say.

Someone uncorks and passes around a bottle of green wine. First glass I drank too fast. Doesn't taste much different than the cheap American chablis I buy for myself by the jug. Room's crowding up quickly. Coughing, smoking, phone and intercom ringing, somewhere a glass breaking, most people seem to know one another and a few exchange big hellos and hugs. "Yes, top floor, you just had to follow the noise," Diana says on the phone, forefinger in her other ear. "Excuse me," I say to Phil and Jane, "but I've done something wrong." I go into the kitchen, unwrap the flowers and bring them in their glass to the cheese table. "You brought them for Diana?" Jane says. "How nice. Not even three months since summer and you really begin to miss them," and she puts her nose into one of the corollas, closes her eyes and breathes. "Smell them, hon. Remind you of something?" Man at the table says to me "And what school do you teach at?" and I say "Me? No place. Would if I could but not much room for what I do. Except if you count junior high school here on a per diem basis, and in some subjects I know as much of as my kids," and he says "For some reason I thought you said you taught in New York," and he puts some cheese on a cucumber slice and leaves and I look around the table for a vegetable tray, don't see any and say to Jane "I could really go for a carrot or celery stick," and she looks at the table and says "I don't think she'd mind much if you raided the icebox." "Alan," Diana shouts to a man walking in. I recognize him from his book jacket I've home. I think he's wearing the same book jacket jacket and the same or similarly designed striped tie. Does very well. Front-page reviews, interviews on TV and in magazines and the news. Recently in the photocopy shop down my block I saw him on the cover of the free *TV Shopper* and read the article about him inside and learned what neighborhood restaurants and stores this "famous Westsider" likes to go to. Diana quickly introduces him to a few people and he says hello and waves to several others he knows and she leads him over to us. "I want you to meet two very dear old friends of mine, Jane and Philip Bender. They're both incredible sculptors." "I know their work, you don't have to tell me," Alan says. "Fact is I almost owned one of them."

"Which one of us did you almost own?" Jane says, shaking his hand.

"I'm sorry. I just came from another party and my communication processes got bottled up. Which one of you works in plastic?"

"Didn't he just say he knew our work well?" Phil says to me and I shrug and look to the side. Someone's cigarette smoke's coming my way. I hold my breath and look back. It's broken by my head, a little of it goes in Jane's face.

". . . didn't say 'well.' And if your wife or you hadn't adopted the other's surname, I'd know which one of you works in what much better."

"Excuse me, sir, I didn't—I hope you don't think I was saying it aggressively. Just my sick sense of whatever you call humor again, which likes to work against me."

"Same here—unaggressive, though no one could ever accuse me of humor. And whichever of those two media you do work in, let me say I admire it tremendously."

"Thanks. And I think I can say the same for us for your work too—in all your literary forms."

"Even the porno novels?"

"You don't write those that I know of."

"See? Told you I had no sense of humor." They all laugh. I smile.

"And this is Daniel Krin, Alan," Diana says, "before you get into an endless trialogue about art buying and inflated reputations and phalli and pornography. But if you are thinking of buying someone, you'd be wise to scoop up these two soon. Value of some of their older work has quadrupled."

"She'll say anything for a friend," Jane says, "and because she knows we're dying to go to Machu-Picchu."

"Will she? —Hello, Mr. Krin."

"How are you?" We shake hands.

"I'm fine thanks I guess, and you?" and laughs.

"Just an expression. 'How goes, adios, I'm well, thank the Lord, by Jove and gum.'"

"Of course. My bottled-up processes—this time the incoming. Seriously now," to Phil and Jane, Diana nipping my elbow and slipping away, "and all pornography and priapic testimonials to the rear for the time being unless you're lusting to discuss them, which one of you works in rubber?"

Diana's greeting some people at the door or maybe they're leaving. That can't be her. She's at the other side of the cheese table, behind a tall unused samovar, brushing crumbs off the cloth into her palm, taking my bouquet to the bar, dumping the crumbs into an ashtray and accepting a sip of wine from a man and sticking one of the flowers minus most of its stem into his lapel.

Diana have a twin? I put on my glasses. Woman who doesn't look like her much. Hair the same though. Graying, snipped short, shampooed sheen, and an almost duplicate purple turtleneck jersey. I listen for another minute, say "Pardon me, folks, I think I see over there my long lost brother," and walk off. "What was his name again?" Alan says and Jane knows but Phil forgets. I meet her, though not yet. She was standing in the center of the room where I am now. I don't know when she came in. I doubt she was here yet. Room's very noisy and crowded now and was probably like that when she got here. I think I would have spotted her right away or soon after. My glasses were back in my pocket but she wasn't that far away when she did come nearer where I needed them to see her. White coarse blouse buttoned to the neck, Russian-type blouse's stiff inch-high collar, lace where the cuffs end and as a collar fringe, large unobscured forehead, lots of fine kind of copper-colored hair knotted on top of her head, long neck, bony cheeks, big wide-awake eyes that later turned out to be a sea-green, taller than most of the women there, long skirt, so I couldn't see what sort of shoes she wore, but around five-nine. I suddenly get the call and set my glass on the bar and make my way to the bathroom, saying as I go "Personal emergency, please, in a rush," relieved to find it free, also combed my hair in there and splashed water on my face and dried it, for it had become uncomfortably warm in the living room, won't be too long now before I see her. Maybe she was at this moment approaching the stoop or climbing the steps. I didn't ring her in. Didn't ring in anyone since the beginning of the party. She must have rung the downstairs bell though. Or someone leaving or entering opened the door as she was coming up the stoop or about to ring and let her in or maybe the door had been left open intentionally, forgetfully or because of some door-check failure. By then there must have been too many umbrellas in the hall for the one holder. I wonder what Diana thought when she took my bouquet off the table and put it at the back of the bar away from the bottles and glasses. Glass he stuck them in is okay and more than enough if maybe too much water. But why'd he place it where hands on all four sides reaching every which way could easily spill it? Coatrack must be filled by now. Rubbers and boots lined up or strewn around the hallway floor and wall. Probably around this time that someone wrapped a woman's coat around mine and my sweater got knocked to the floor or put some other place, which could be what helped me forget when I left that I'd come with one, being quite high by then and not automatically seeing it on the shelf above my covered coat. Don't know why remembering I had an umbrella presented no problem, though probably because the holder was right outside the door. Bell rings. One every minute from the time I got to the party it seemed. Just about now I said to a man by the bar something like "You know, these recurrent bell-rings remind me of a Japanese play I recently read where the single principal in it is from start-to-finish answering ten different doors for hundreds of imaginary guests and talking to himself about who's probably ringing and what person and group and then troop he just let in and found an unoccupied space for. And whom, if he sees her at the door, he's going to do everything short of shooting to keep out." The man I said this to, after relighting his pipe and looking as if he thought over what I said, says "I saw a play like that once. A short one, on a long double bill, and both by the same famous Rumanian, who I think became famous because of that play. But this one had two characters in it who talked to each other continuously."

"Mine's got to be derivative then, since its world premiere was last year. I know the play you mean, unless there are two famous Rumanian-born Frenchmen who wrote very similar plays. In mine there are no chairs in it. The setting's one empty room eventually packed so tight with guests that by the end of the play many of them are sitting on ceiling crossbeams and hanging from wall hooks, while the doors are still being opened by this one principal on stage."

"The actor."

"Or actress. Because in the book of this playwright's selected plays the role of 'principal performer'—as she called it—is supposed to be played by an old man and young woman at alternate performances, though the sex and age of the person he or she wants to keep out stays the same."

"I'm sure my play didn't have those instructions. But what did you mean before by 'imaginary guests'?"

"Actually, it's the ringing that's imaginary, the guests only conceivably. The audience sees them or at least sees what the principal performer thinks he or she's seeing."

"I think I heard about that play. Is it the one where the actor or actress finally asks the audience to get out of their seats and then out of the theater so the guests who are pouring in can have somewhere to sit and stand?"

"Not in my playwright's play, though it'd be a better ending. And now I've lost what I was originally saying."

"The intercom ringing. Leading to the absurdity of most modern drama-turgy. But there's another one. You heard it. I know I did, if I'm not imagining us at this wonderful party and the bell ringing repeatedly. No, we're both here and the bells are real and the party's wonderful. You know Alan Merson there?"

"I know his work."

"Fine fellow, fine work."

"I don't want to say anything. Undoubtedly he's a fine fellow."

"But you are saying something. Excuse me, I see someone I know."

He goes over to a well-known painter, they clap backs and begin talking. The *Times* Sunday magazine did an article on the painter not long ago. I like a lot of his work but don't consider it art. I consider it what? Illustrations. I said that to a couple of people at this party and before it. Nobody agreed with me. One person bristled and said "Where do you come to say that?" and I said "This might sound mindless and maybe makes no sense, but I like what I know." She said "It makes no sense or not enough for me to want to think any more about it," and the conversation stopped for a minute while we both, when we weren't looking at the other looking at our feet, looked at our feet. Diana has several of his works on her walls. All inscribed to her, one from thirty years ago. It says "Sleep sheepishly Dee," which could mean a number of things but has no connection from what I can see to the illustration, which is more like a child's cartoon, and with its colors from play crayons, of the Staten Island skyline during the daytime and about ten ocean liners lined up to go out to sea. He's taller than his photographs. Could that be correct? Taller if his photographs were lifesize and he was standing in them erect. Balder also I notice passing him on my way to the couch, with what seemed to be real hair in his photographs being real hair combed over his head from the back.

I sit and take a carrot stick off an end table plate. Diana sits beside me and says before I can put the carrot into my mouth "You can't sit on a couch at one of my parties or even in one of the easy chairs so early. If you were elderly, lame or a single to multiple amputee and one of those amputated parts was a leg or foot or even recently one to so many toes, yes, but now I want you to move around and mix. Or stand in one place and have more cheese. What's wrong? You're not having fun."

"If I don't I won't be invited to the next one, that it?"

"Don't be silly. To me you're practically an honored guest."

"Honored guests rarely get the same honor twice."

"I can honor them once and practically honor them another time and then invite them when others are actually and practically honored. But now you can honor me by getting up and socially enmeshed."

"I just want to sit here and draw attention to myself and look around. You've a very interesting attractive group and Jane's a doll though Phil's a bit too driven, ass-kissing and affected to become a real artistic success."

"Phil has every right to want what he hasn't quite won but has long earned. The rest are everything you say but don't want to be looked at just yet by someone sitting on a couch. Timing's very important for a good party. Someone sits and stares before the right time comes, he makes people uncomfortable or close to it. Also, the right person or couple must usually be the first to sit. A stranger sits, particularly one who doesn't come with a big rep or hasn't yet made a terrific hit, the more frequent guests get the impression he's not enjoying himself, which makes them doubly uncomfortable: his staring and apparent discomfort. Right now everyone here—if he's to be stared at—wants it to be done by someone standing up and, allowing for variations of shyness or boldness and height, face to face. I wouldn't expect you to know this, being part social animal but mostly hermit."

"Hey, take it easy, for what am I doing that's so wrong? You said someone will have to sit on the couch sooner or later, so why not me? Some people are the first in space. Others in the hearts of their partymen. Someone might be the first to get drunk tonight, another to break a valuable plate. I don't want to be any of these, and even if I did want to I couldn't be the first in space. So isn't it better if I'm to be the first in anything—"

"You've a smooth protective and circumventive sense of humor, which could be a first-rate unctuous one if you did more to thwart people from detecting how protective it is. I'll be back in two minutes. If you're not off the couch by then or joined on it by anyone more than my cat, I'm moving it into the hallway and you can sit out there for as long as you like."

"Deal." I hold out my palm for her to slap. She looks at it and leaves. I bite off half the carrot stick. Someone sits on the couch's other end. An actor I've seen in lead roles on public TV. He's also worked in theater and movies. I smile and say hello. He nods, sets his glass down on the cocktail table, spills a little of it, "Shit!" He gets up for what I suppose is a napkin. "Here, use this," taking out my bandanna handkerchief.

"I have one of my own, thanks very much."

"I didn't mean I'd think you'd use yours. Excuse me," removing a scrap of chewed carrot off my lip, "the carrot. Because believe me, I'll have to wash it some time after I get home, since I already wiped something up with it tonight, and wine leaves a nice smell."

"Does it? Wouldn't think so. What it does leave is a gorgeous stain, at least the piss I usually drink. I'll get a paper towel," and leaves.

He's a good actor though I've never seen him in a movie or on the stage. He goes to the bar, gets a fresh glass of wine and a napkin for the bottom of the glass. Movies and TV have to be different than theater: many takes and the entire part doesn't have to be memorized. I don't see him anymore. Maybe they're tougher than theater just because of those many takes and that the scenes aren't filmed and taped in sequence. I don't know much about those fields really, but can surmise. Accessible to so many women, but all those casting calls and waits. Bell rings. Cat weaves around lots of feet as he heads for the bedroom. I put on my glasses. Can't see the cat but bedroom door crack widens an inch when nobody's that close to it, so must be him going in or a draft. More people. Four to five greeted by Diana at the door. Just popping by, I overhear, on their way to wherever it is people go these days in evening dress, one saying "Rain's frozen me stiff—what I need's a drink," and makes for the bar, tapping shoulders, poking triceps, startling some people when they see him in a tux. Maybe now she's somewhere around. Coat hung up, umbrella snugged beside mine in the holder perhaps. It was, so there had to be some room left in it, and seeing her take out hers when she left is another reason I didn't leave mine behind, or maybe only she tried squeezing her umbrella into the holder or someone leaving had just taken out his. Actor hasn't come back. If they'd met, which they might have, and arranged to meet another time, they'd make a very handsome couple, though I doubt she'd enjoy knowing him after a week. That And-who-might-you-be? look and no smile given back, though could be he thought I was gay and he's demonstrably or questionably not. I hear him from across the room. "'It's outrageous,' he said, 'and I simply won't stand for it,'" and a moment later everyone around him laughs. I don't know why. Wasn't an impersonation of a notable politico let's say. Maybe he made a motion to sit. That's an old slapstick shtick that could always do it, though I might be underrating his intelligence and overestimating his age, and I didn't hear his entire remark. My glass is empty. I bring it down from my lips. Frozen man's reaching below the bar where I suppose he knows or assumes the hard stuff is. I don't remember emptying my glass. When I watched the crowd around the actor laugh or frozen man poke his way to the bar? I put the actor's glass on the end table, wipe up the mess he left with my handkerchief and smell it. He's right. Don't know why I said it'd make a nice smell. Stupid, but something more. Policemen and performing celebrities as well as psychiatrists at parties and maybe even brain surgeons or all doctors and also scientists doing encephalic research make me uneasy at times and overeager to please. What else can I do for you, like your shoes and socks shined? Wine's left a white cloud on the wood that won't wipe off. Not my fault but someone who had only watched me when I wiped it might think it was, but I'm sure Diana or her cleaning women will know how to get it out. Should I tell her? I look at my lap. No matter how large in the crotch I buy my pants or how dark they are, my genitals still show through. Maybe I wear the wrong kind of underpants. This isn't much fun. Should I get up and if up go to the door or bar? But I don't want to go so soon. A woman might still come in whom I'll want to meet and what do I have cooking at home? Bell rings. And drink his. In the Himalayas maybe one can still get a liver-eating amoebic disease. I pour his wine into my glass.

"That was smart, taking two with you when you sat," woman sitting down on the couch says.

"This? It was someone else's and I didn't want to waste it."

"Someone you know I hope."

"No, but I trust him. I figured—one of Diana's friends? How contagious could he be?"

"What if, and this is just a what-if, it happened to be a friend of her friend's—someone he just picked up at a bar? I don't mean that, since I'm sure everyone here is more than all right, but only as an example to be more cautious other times?" and drinks from a mug of beer.

"Oh, beer. That's what I should've got. I didn't see any."

"In the refridge. Mugs in the cabinet above. Like some of mine?"

"Sure you'd want to drink from it after I took a swig?"

"You're an actual friend of Diana's, aren't you? Or at least not someone she picked up at a seedy bar minutes before she put this whole thing together, and naturally I don't mean it, and you look clean."

"Very clean. And hand-invited, that's me. But shower a day. Obsessively clean. Believe me, I change my teeth at the very minimum once a week."

"Maybe we ought to drop the subject."

"Right. Sometimes I never know where my mouth's going to go."

"That doesn't have to be a bad thing. And if you want some beer you'll get your own then, not that I'm worried I'll catch anything from you."

"No, tainted wine suits me fine and the alcohol in it kills the—but I should stop that. Honestly, thanks for the offer." I turn to the party, figuring she no longer wants to talk and not being that interested in the conversation either.

"Who are you," she says, "besides Diana's friend if you are?"

"I am. From summer camp."

"From hundreds of years ago when you were both counselors or campers there?"

"I'm sorry, I shouldn't have assumed everyone knew that reference. An artist colony upstate."

"That place. With the signed Tiffany windows and where she went this summer. You must be a painter. You look like one."

"Nope, a translator. And before you ask—you were going to?"

"I'll have to now."

"For the present a not, in English, very well known contemporary Japanese poet. Name's Jun Hasenai."

"Never heard of him. But I'm not familiar with most poetry. My husband's the one."

"That so? What's he do?"

"Forget about him. I always talk about him when I sit on couches at parties. I want to know about your work. Your poet's very good?"

"Believe me. But most translators, when they choose what they're going to translate out of love or whatever you want to call it—"

"Certainly not money."

"Money? Money? What's that? Some new form of currency? No, that's not funny. Anyway, they think all the previous translations of it aren't good enough, though with Hasenai I've been lucky since there's almost been nothing in English and not one book."

"I'm excited, a terrific new writer I've never heard of. Can you quote some of it?"

"In English or Japanese?"

"You speak Japanese too?"

"Now who's kidding whom?"

"I'm not. I thought it might be one of those transliteral or what do you translators call those translations—where you translate from the less meticulous and poetic translations of the originals?"

"That's close enough. Now don't call me a chauvinist, at least the malevolent kind, for I could give you a list of my kindred and unconsanguineous sisters who'll swear I'm not, but I bet you picked that up from your husband who I bet is a lit professor who I bet has writ tomes of published poems."

"He is and has."

"Well, that's a good profession. No, I do the entire thing. I even write the poems for Hasenai in the original and let him take all the credit." I take off my glasses. "I have to take these off and put them in their holder and the holder into my pocket or someplace safe so I know they won't fly off my face and break or holder flop out of my pocket and get stepped on, when I recite one of Hasenai's peppier poems. 'Night is a moon and then it's cigarette-yellow and done. Christ, I can't go on. The evening's reached its peak and the coyote is gone.'"

"That's good. And the whole poem I wager. And who would have thought they have coyotes in Japan, or is that your word for a similar animal there that has no exact counterpart in English? Of course the poem's probably better in the original."

"I just now made it up."

"Translated it?"

"No, it's my own."

"That's mean. You fooled me."

"Or maybe I'm a good spontaneous poet, how about that?"

"You're not being very nice."

"Why? Suppose I now said it was Hasenai's and I worked days on it and had only said it was mine to momentarily fool you? I don't usually do that and wouldn't know why I would, but I'm capable of it."

"No, you're smart enough to know what your motives are. As for the poem, I'm no hypocrite. To my uncultivated ears—hubby's poems or not, and I plead guilt to not reading them all and those I do I mostly don't understand, a problem no one else seems to have—what you recited seemed quite good."

"Thanks. And I was being too playful—maybe prematurely playful—with you. You already admitted you didn't know or care much for poetry, so where'd I come off trying to fool you? And it was my poem alone. I don't know if it was whole. I've even forgotten what I spontaneously wrote, but since I didn't put it on paper or memorize it—you don't remember it, do you?"

"Except for a coyote in it, no."

"Anyway, I can't say it was written. And probably everything I'd spontaneously compose is influenced by modern Japanese writing and these days especially, Hasenai's, so you're right if you also thought it sounded somewhat Japanese."

"Since it had no Japanese references in it, it didn't particularly sound like anything to me."

"Okay. Just don't if you don't mind tell Diana about this or she'll never invite me back and then we'll never meet again."

"I've a big mouth too sometimes so I can't guarantee what will happen." She gets up. "Excuse me. I'm not going to the powder room or to take a breath of fresh exercise or anything. Enjoy yourself."

"Please. No apologies necessary. Just mine." She leaves. I get up for more cheese. I also don't want to be sitting here when she starts talking to someone about me. "That man there. On the couch, to the left. I don't want to turn around but he—there's nobody there? I'm referring to *his* left. He's sort of disinterestedly dressed, hair gushing out of his chest, a varicose nose? There he is. Well him. Talk about a man being mixed up?"

Jane and Phil are talking to each other at the cheese table. Now there are hard sausages on it, creamed herrings, sliced vegetables, an egg and chicken salad mold with a dollop of caviar on top, pâtés and dips. I dip a zucchini stick into a dip, bite it while I slice off some pâté, put the pâté on a cracker, add a piece of cheese to it, put the rest of the zucchini into my mouth, cheese falls to the table, while I reach for it the pâté drops to the floor. I pick the cheese up and put it into my mouth, pick up the pâté with a paper napkin, can't find a used plate or ashtray to put the napkin in so I put it into my back pants pocket, but I might sit on it by the time I get rid of it so I put it into my side pocket, eat the cracker and look at Jane and Phil. They've been watching me, resume talking. "I'm not so sure," Jane says. "You're not so sure? Good God, if Shakespeare could mix metaphors and get away with it—"

"So what did Alan have to say?" I say and Jane says "Wuh?" and Phil looks at me curiously, skeptically, some way that way that makes me feel I shouldn't have interrupted or that I might have said something before that should have discouraged me from speaking so openly to them now. I think. Jane was nice, Phil not so much. "Nothing really," waving them back to their conversation and I take a glass of wine off the table and am about to drink it.

"That's my wine," Jane says.

"I'm sorry, I thought it was mine." I hold it out to her.

"I don't want it now. I'd just rather not have anyone else drink from it."

"I can understand that." I put the glass down, see a full glass of wine at the other end of the table, look at the people near it and they all seem to be holding a glass of something. "There's mine." I reach over and grab it. "Same kind of glass and green and full, just like yours. And don't worry, I'm not drunk," I say, drinking. "Just a little uncomfortable. All these big makers here and everyone knowing one another and all that or whatever it is making me uneasy. I'm also not in any kind of therapy as that must—that remark must— those last remarks must make me sound like."

"What?"

"Why do you say that?" Phil says.

"You referring to her 'what?' or to my being uncomfortable?"

"Since I was looking right at you, I think I meant you. And about your thinking you're sounding as if you're in therapy."

"Really, I know nothing about therapy."

"Come on . . . what's your name: Scott?"

"Dan," Jane says.

"Everyone knows something about therapy. Either we've been in it or have read scores of books about it or know scores who've done one or both. But forgetting that if you don't want to talk about it, why do you feel especially uncomfortable here?"

"Not 'especially.' A little, and because I've made a couple of people uncomfortable. If I also made you two uncomfortable, then more than a couple. Perhaps three or four. Definitely three or four if I've made you both uncomfortable, but now that I think of that pipe-smoking man over there I talked theater to before, it's more like five. But really. I'm being silly. A bore. I can tell when I'm being a bore. Been a bore before for sure and a boor to boot. A boor-bore or bore-boor. You see? Still a bore but not necessarily a boor-bore or one to boot. Too much to eat, that's the problem, and possibly too much wine rushing too suddenly to my head or wherever wine rushes to, and green, for whoever heard of green wine even on Saint Paddy's Day? Beer, sure, but—I should go."

"Why? Calm down. Let's talk."

"I'm calm. And thanks. That's very nice."

"Why's it so nice? If we're here for anything on this gosh-darn globe, which is just what Jane and I were having it out about before—"

"Time out," a man says to us, holding his hands up to make a T. "This is a joke."

"We know," Jane says.

"Good, you know, you love jokes. But this one is not intentionally meant to offend any ethnic or national group and any similarity to such is purely coincidental. The Polish army purchased ten thousand dilapidated bathtubs from an Italian scrapman—"

"You told us it."

"How they refurbished the tubs and used them as tanks to invade Russia?"

"And I told you it wasn't a very appropriate joke for this party and as far as jokes go, not at all droll."

"Play ball," he says, dropping his hands and walking away.

"Who let that guy in?" Phil says.

"I kind of liked it," I say. "Not the joke so much but the 'Time in, play ball.' Takes a certain amount of guts and it's something I might do—the preambular apology."

"It takes stupidity, not guts. I think he's an idiot. You know Milikin?"

"Seen his illustrations all over the place but never met him."

"Genius, man, genius, and where I come from you'd get strung up for using that word for his work. I wanted to find someone to introduce us. Diana's busy."

"Just go over to him, say 'Hello, how's by you, what's new, the family, and I wanted to meet you.' He'll like the attention, especially from an artist."

"That's what I told him," Jane says. "I'm in no rush to meet him myself, although I do admire the regard and prices he gets. I'll speak to him of course, but first I want Phil to introduce himself. Do it, Phil. Everyone has to humble himself to someone at times, and he has thirty years on you, so you have nothing to feel competitive about."

"It's not that. There are people talking to him."

"You want a few more drinks first? Because you know you're going to go over before the night's over. But then you'll be too sloshed to make any sense to him and for him to appreciate your going over to want to do anything to help push your work."

"You know that's not why I want to talk to him."

"Hey baby, this is the itsy old art lady you sleep with, so don't be giving me that shit." "Then speak like a lady, act like a lady," and he gives more reasons why he can't, shouldn't, won't introduce himself to Milikin and when she tells him to stop being a child and particularly with a voice so loud the whole world can hear, he says much lower that he's not a child which she should know by now if she sleeps with him as she says and if she hasn't been then he's been having one hell of a ball with someone else the last ten years. But all kidding aside. If she has anything like that to say to him, say it at home. Then I see Helene. Of course I didn't know her name at the time. Looking at me when I first looked at her. I'd lifted my head. First I turned my head away from Jane and Phil while they caviled about what each had just said, looked around the room, saw the woman from the couch, man with the pipe, Alan making a point, Milikin nowhere about, Cylette I think her name was being offered a light, looked at the rug, raised myself an inch or two on the balls of my soles, raised myself an inch or two on my heels, seesawed back and forth a few times like this, sipped some wine, set the glass down without looking away from it, then lifted my head while Phil told Jane how in many ways he's more honest than she despite anything she might say, but none of it loud enough it seemed for anyone else to hear, and found myself looking at Helene looking at me. Well what do you know I told myself—hello, hello. She was standing between the food table and bar, about seven feet from the bar and seven from me. A crowd stood behind her, crowded around the bar, and there was an opening between us a foot or so wide and while we looked at one another people moved past it but nobody blocked it. She was being spoken to by a man whose whole body her whole body faced, but her face was turned sideways to me. She held a wineglass with two hands. Only the stem and lip of it showed, so I couldn't tell what color wine she drank. We looked at each other for about ten seconds. Then I turned my head back to Jane and Phil while she was still looking at me. That's when I said to myself Well what do you know, hello hello. I don't know why I turned back to Jane and Phil. The position—body facing one way, head the other—could have been making me physically uncomfortable, but I don't think that was it. If it was and I'd corrected it by turning more of my body to her, she might have construed that move as too open and provoking. I suppose I also didn't think it right to look too long at someone looking at me whom I didn't know, though she did to me. Jane said something to Phil about iguanas and sausages. Phil said "What do you think about that, Dan?" I said "About what?" "Damn if he wasn't even listening when we figured out the key to his past and present and all his future configurations but swore on our children's heads to say it only once to him and never again. Tough luck, fella." "He's better off," Jane says, "and you're an awfully slick liar. Now let's drop the subject, darling, okay?" "J'agree, mon queen—to anysing." She grabs his hand and yanks him closer to kiss him. I turn my head and more of my body this time to this woman. She's facing the man with her body and face, listening to him engrossedly it seems. "We'll saunter up to him en duo," Jane says. "It can't hurt. Speak to you later, Dan, unless you want to join us," and I say "No thanks, I'll save your place," and turn back to the woman. She's still listening. He's using the words "quiddity," "tendentious" and "rhetoric" in one sentence. If I look at her long and hard enough without looking away I bet she looks at me. Seconds after I think this she turns her head to me. It never worked before. It didn't work now. She just turned to me again, or turned this way, not realizing I was still here, and last time I tried that trick I was probably in high school. We look at each other. She starts to smile, sort of smiles, then smiles because I smile or maybe I smiled because I felt her full smile about to appear and we smile at each other like this and I bob my head once and she blinks her eyes once, more a reflex than a signal I'd say, and turns to the man who has stopped talking to her and might have been looking at us looking at each other since she turned to me but is now looking at her, and raises her empty glass and he says "Not yet but it could stand some filling up," and they go to the bar.

Blouse, neck, hair, breasts, forehead, cheek, collar, cuffs, skirt, can't see her shoes. She squeezes through the crowd that came together behind the man who squeezed through first. Her back's to me. She seems to have a large round rear and small waist. I picture her ironing one of those cuffs and me moving flush up against her rear, arm around her waist, other hand cupping her breast, fiddling with her nipple, neither of us in clothes. She's behind some people now and all I see is her hair, then what seems her hand pouring wine from a bottle into a man's glass. Go over, say hello or if she's still with the man then stay close to say hello when he momentarily looks away or talks to someone else and maybe even leaves her. I head for the bar, turn to the food table, I wouldn't know what to say. "Hello, how's by you, the family?" Might be original enough to tickle her but I doubt it. A funnyman she might think, one who isn't afraid to make a fool of himself, but I doubt it. Earnest approach then. "I wanted to meet you, plain as that, what can I say?" She looks earnest herself but the approach might what? Put her ill at ease or touch her in some not too positive way and then she could silently blame me for her sudden awkwardness or whatever it might come to when before she was feeling so good. Just go over. Say and do nothing. Or say nothing but do something. Pretend to want more wine. Just want more wine, since when do you have to pretend, and while there look at her and if she's not looking at you continue to look at her and if she then looks at you, maybe then you can make one of a number of moves. But finish your wine first. Or go over with it. She'll know the real reason you're coming over, but if she's interested, and for an intermittent minute she seemed to be, she won't care what's the excuse.

I drink up and start for the bar. "Excuse me, excuse me." She's still talking to that man. What did I expect? And if she was talking to anyone, what did I tell myself to do? I look for Jane and Phil. Nowhere around. I told myself to get near her and at the right time strike. I go to the food table, put my glass down, slice some cheese, but too much cheese tonight, too much food for now. Sit down. I head for the couch. "Excuse me, excuse me." It's filled. Look for a chair. All filled. Diana's talking to someone. Seeing me she lifts her eyebrows as if saying still not having a good time? You look lost her eyebrows say. I smile, hold up my hand, thumb and index finger joined, indicating the obvious. She smiles. I turn to the bar. Woman's not there. Good. Could mean she's by herself somewhere where I could get to meet her. Good also means I can go to the bar now because she's not there. I need to? Not that I'm high but I might be slightly. No, I need something to hold. Some people smoke. Others jingle change. I go over, "Excuse me, excuse me," and pour a glass of red wine. Woman at the bar's pouring a thick liquid from a decanter into what looks like a silver thimble the size of a double-shot glass. "Vodka? Is it for someone special or can anyone have it?"

"Since it isn't hidden, I think everyone." She gives me another silver glass off a tray. Hieroglyph-like characters scratched into it that are probably Cyrillic. "You don't think a problem mixing spirits and wine?"

"My first," setting the wineglass down. "Never even tasted it."

"Then pour it back if it can be done without spilling."

"I don't know—won't people mind? And judging by the wine bottle neck, I think I'd need a funnel."

"Funnel and people indeed. Take chances." Holding the decanter and her glass in one hand, she pours my wine into the bottle with the other. A drop runs down the neck but never reaches the bar. "Hold ready. It's real Russian and ice-cold," and she starts filling up my silver glass.

"Half will be fine."

"The custom in Russia is to pour all the way up. But you want to stop half with such beautiful vodka, you must be much better man than I."

"You can say I'm a man at least. Ah, pour all the way."

"Please, you have to excuse me, but try as I have I can't be my equal in English." She fills my glass and holds up hers. "To the Western Wind. May it blow and blow." We clink and drink. "Pretty good, yes? We never saw this good there in all my years. You'll forgive me?" As part of the crowd breaks for her I see that woman by the food table, alone it seems and looking at me and then at her fork coming off her plate. Wait a moment so the woman I just spoke to doesn't think I'm following her and then go over, say prosit or how goes it or nas zdorovie if I can remember how to pronounce it or just hello and after her hello show her the glass and ask if she knows what the Cyrillic letters mean or if she thinks the snowy troika and onion dome scene also tooled-in is just for foreign consumerism. No, no plotted approach and she might be married, in love, living with the man she's married to and in love with and who's here or coming later. But if so why'd she look at me way she did?

I finish my drink. Another? One more like that and I'll be slurring through my nose. Maybe she just wants to have something extra to talk about later with her husband, lover, whatever, on their way home or just home if he didn't come with her and won't be here or on the phone if he's out of town or lives alone and phones her at home later. I pour a quarter of a glass and will just sip. "Did you talk to anyone interesting?" she could say. "Not really," he could say if he's here or on the way, "you?" "A translator. Daniel Krin—ever hear of him? But whoever hears of translators or remembers their names, except for what's-his-name again who does the famous German with the shaggy mustache and the other who only does prize-winning Latin-American novelists who if they haven't received a prize yet get one soon after he translates them. He came over, for a while prior was flashing his eyes. I couldn't just walk away, mouth filled with my fork and all those eatable edibles still on the table. Besides, he looked fairly interesting and I wanted to have something unusual but juicy to talk about with you other than those exotic foods. And he was fairly interesting, simplifying the supposedly inexplicable difficulties of translating this intricately simple Japanese poetical work. Then because I wanted a long uninterrupted answer from him so I could dish out more food for myself and chew it slowly, I asked if he also wrote poetry and if not what was stopping him and if it was a block what was he doing to break it and so forth. He said he used to but gave it up when he found he was short one minor gift and that was the real raw talent for apparent intelligence and cleverness to make up for the major one, or something with that twist. But because he still loved poetry, which he said most poets suddenly don't once they give up writing it, he decided to do the next best thing to creating poetry which was translating it."

I put my glass down and excuse myself through the crowd to the food table. She's not there. I look around. Still. Maybe in the bedroom. I open the door. No light's on and only the cat's there lying on the dresser and eating what looks like a sock. Maybe she left. I close the bedroom door and see her coming out the front door. Her coat's on. Her fur hat. She's going over to Diana. As she goes she glances at me. She's alone, though her companion could be in the hallway, struggling with his rubbers. I'll keep my eyes on her from this ten-foot distance. After she says goodbye to Diana and maybe others I'll catch up with her on the stairs. I'll say "Wait." She'll say "What?" I'll say "I'm sorry I waited so long to speak to you, to introduce myself to you, those are what I'm sorry for. You can't believe the number of excuses I gave myself for not going over and speaking to you and the conversations I imagined we had here and you'll later have about me, even one where you'd now say something to me like 'I've no idea what you mean.'" No. I'll say "Wait." She'll say "What?" I'll say "You're obviously going, that's obvious, and I only wish I'd spoken to you sooner." "Same here," she might say. That'd be great. Or "Excuse me, sir, but do I know you? Because when I saw you staring at me before I thought maybe I did from some time back or that you were just putting on the make." I move to them. Diana says to her "Oh no, not so soon." "What can I do? I told you about the other party." "Delay it." "Wish I could." "But this one's really just starting. People'll see you leave, they all might go. You speak to any old friends? But you haven't time to talk. I'll call tomorrow." "If you don't, I'll get in touch with you." "Actually, do that, since I'll probably forget by the end of tonight everyone I promised to call tomorrow. Goodnight, Helene. I'm sorry you couldn't stay." She called her Helene. They kiss cheeks and Helene turns to the door without seeing me. I start over to her. She walks to the door. I continue after her. We're going at the same pace. Someone says "Dan." I turn around. It was to another Dan. I continue. She's out the door and heading for the stairs. I'm about ten feet behind her. "You're not going also, Dan," Diana says. Helene, snapping her fingers, steps back and reaches for the umbrella and sees me. I turn to Diana. "No, excuse me," and then to Helene "Hold it, please wait." "Me?" she says, pulling out an umbrella. "Yes, don't move, at least not off this floor. I want to speak to you. It's important. Someone we both know."

"I'm a bit in a rush."

"It'll only take a second." I turn back to Diana. "No, I was only going to speak to Helene."

"You know her?"

"No."

"But you know her name."

"I overheard it."

"Want to be introduced?"

"Um, I don't know. Yes, could you? No, it's okay." I look past the door. She's holding an umbrella, eyebrows raised as Diana's were before but hers wanting to know how long she must wait and what for. "Listen, Diana, I'll be right back."

"That's good. I don't want all my guests leaving so soon after the party began, even though I know Helene has to."

I walk into the hallway. "Excuse me. I was looking at you before."

"And I was looking at you. You're apparently a good friend of Diana's."

"Probably not as good as you two are. I met her this summer."

"At Yaddo?"

"How'd you know?"

"I knew she went and Diana always meets two to three new people there who become her good friends. Half the people inside are from there."

"That so? You too?"

"Maybe half's an exaggeration, but quite a number of them."

"And you?"

"They don't take people in my work."

"Oh yes? What's that?"

"Whatever it is, what did you want to speak to me about? Someone you said we both know?"

"That was a lie or fib."

"I thought it was." She's taken her gloves out of her coat pocket and is putting one on.

"You're in a hurry."

"A hurry hurry. As a matter of fact I'm already late. I wish I hadn't had this engagement from so far back. But I did, so I really went out of my way to spend an hour here."

"That's how long you've been here?"

"About. But I'm really in a hurry. I don't mean to sound curt, but was there something in particular you wanted to say?"

"No, nothing. I just thought it'd be nice to speak to you. I have since I first saw you."

"Thank you. I'm not sure, but, well, I have to admit I thought something along the same lines about you."

"Good. Where are you off to now?"

"A wedding reception. A very dear friend's."

"That's nice. I like weddings and receptions."

"I don't especially. Are you married?"

"Never been."

"At your age? How'd you escape it? But I just don't like those big catered and structured affairs like that and this one seems especially unnecessary, since they were married last summer and have already gone on two honeymoons. I was the matron of honor or as close to that title as a woman with my marital history can get, and the whole dopey idea of it makes me question my friendship with her somewhat and just a little sick. But she wants me there tonight and so I have to be going. It's only right. There's a special seat for me."

"May I speak to you another time?"

"If you want to phone me you can. I'm in the Manhattan book. My name's Helene Winiker with an i-k-e-r. I'm the only Helene in it, and my service will be home if I'm not. Your name is what?"

"Daniel Krin."

"Okay, Mr. Krin—pleased to meet you." She takes a glove off and shakes my hand. "Now I have to scoot," and she goes downstairs.

CHAPTER TWO

The Park

I go back in, squeeze past some people by the door, push my way past some people a little ways past the door, try to squeeze and push my way across the room to get to one of the two windows overlooking the street, someone says "Excuse me" as if I should have been the one to say excuse me to her, and she's right, someone says "Excuse me" as if it's his fault the room's this crowded and he's in my way when I push past him, I say "Excuse me" to several people including the few who for various reasons said excuse me to me, one man says "I'll say," another says "Have a heart, commander, that's my only back," a woman says "Louis, you made me spill my drink," and he says "No, it was he," till I reach the freest window.

It's snowing, though lightly, not sticking except on the grass and a little on the tops of parked cars and trees, actually looking more like sleet. I want to open the window and look down to see Helene leaving the building and walking down the stoop or already heading some way along the street, but I know it'll be too cold. I could make up excuses to whoever's near me. "It's very stuffy in here," "So much cigarette smoke I can hardly breathe," "Maybe some people would appreciate a little cool air in the room because of the congestion and heat," and I say to the three people talking together next to me "Mind if I open the window?"

"Might be a bit drafty," a man says.

"The temperature's supposed to be dropping rapidly tonight," the woman says to him.

"If you do open it," another man says, "what do you say to only a tinkle?"

35

"No really, it's very stuffy in here, I can hardly breathe because of the congestion and heat. I'm serious. Too many cigarettes going. You can barely see the food on the food table being contaminated by the smoke. And I'm allergic to cigarettes that are lit. Not only my respiratory track but for some organismic reason or another, they also in heavy doses make me irritable. I'm sure some other guests must be suffering the same discomfort and so won't mind a momentary jolt of fresh air."

"I'm really not sure," the woman says. "But if you are going to, give me a chance to get to the other side of the room?"

She pardons her way past several people with one of the men behind her holding her hand the European way while I pull the bottom part of the window all the way up and stick my head and chest out and look down, feeling that by now Helene will be at either end of the block. She's standing on the top step having trouble opening her contractible umbrella. She gives up trying to open it by hand and bangs the handle end against the iron railing a few times and the umbrella pops open. She walks downstairs with the umbrella over her head. I want to call her name. She reaches the sidewalk and goes right. I think don't, it's stupid, but yell "Helene." She stops, looks around at eye level: stoops, first stories of buildings, both ends of her side of the street.

"Helene Winiker—up here."

She looks across the street as if I'm in one of the taller park trees.

"You're getting warmer, but wrong direction. Turn around a hundred eighty degrees to your left or right and look—no, now about ninety degrees to your left or two-hundred seventy to your right and look at the wet snow snowing or sleet sleeting past the red brick building you came out of and then at the middle window of the apartment you were in three flights up, which is the only top floor apartment of that building facing the street, and if your eyesight's all right and you can also see past the snow or sleet and remember who I am, you'll come to recognize me. Mr. Krin."

"It's very cold," a man says.

"Freezing," a woman says. "Could you lower the window, sir?"

"Yes, that's a terrific idea," another woman says. "Don't you think you should listen to it?"

"Hey, what's going on there, shut that window," a man says. "My wife just got over a bad cold."

"Who opened the window?" Diana says from across the room. "Even if no one did, could someone please close it?"

Helene's looking at the window now. I wave and smile, then take my glasses off and wave them at her and smile. She shakes the umbrella in my direction, didn't and doesn't smile, walks on.

I close the window, rub the lenses of my glasses against my sleeve till they're clear and dry, put the glasses away and stare outside. Give what you did time to subside before you turn around, but why'd you do it? Little high, feeling good, really am quite stupid, meeting a new desirable woman who also might be a potential mate could have had something to do with it. I want to ruin all good things from the start? Yes, yes, no, maybe, absolutely not. I'll phone her later next week. Don't see why by then I shouldn't be able to explain it. If her number's not in the book it could mean she never intended to speak to me again, which might have stopped me before but now I've this other reason to call. "Something came over me. Was so unlike me. I needed some air, threw open the window, saw you and thought what the heck. Oh hell, it was just an expression of joy."

I turn around. "Opening the window so high really was a foolish thing to do, wasn't it?" I say to one of the women who complained.

"It's over."

"Actually, though, contrary to what a lot of people might think, an open window, even if the air is cold, is a much better way of preventing colds and other virus-caused illnesses in a crowded room than a closed window. The viruses thrive in the warmth and some other reasons I read in the *Times* Science Section one of these previous Tuesdays. Keeps the viruses circulating, the cold air does, and breezier the better, and also more engaged in staying warm and alive than attaching themselves to us."

"If that is the case," a man says, "then I'd think a shivering tired virus would want to hide inside someone's warm suit or up a sultry orifice than just faint to the floor with a death of a cold and nobody inclined to help it."

"That could be true. It was the lead article and long and I tend not to finish them in that section. And I do apologize for making you so cold," and I look around for Diana. She's across the room, stacking used plates and laughing to herself. "Diana."

"Was it wise opening the window that far?"

"Sorry. Got carried away though have since made my apologies to the respective parts, but that's not what I wanted to talk to you about."

"You want to know more about Helene."

"I've known you for nearly five months. I speak to you on the phone about fifteen minutes every other week. We've had four to five cheap Chinese and Greek restaurant dinners since we've been back and ate at the same table upstate every evening for a month and we've almost always talked about a lot more than what's new, who's who, movies are phoo and whew, and the rising price of cottage cheese and beef, so how come you never told me about Helene?"

"I never told her about you either and I've known her for years and speak to her about twice the times and double the durations as I do you, even if I at the last moment at the door lost my head and said I'd introduce you. You're not suited for one another, that's what I thought. Or I didn't think it though do now. But I'm busy. There's ice to untray, trayed food to unrefrigerate, glasses and plates to wash or throw away and replace, more bells to answer, opened windows to tell people to shut, and everyone wants to talk. If you do while you're helping me, be my guest."

We go into the kitchen. "Besides," she says as she takes food platters out of the refrigerator and removes the plastic wrap and I empty a bag of ice into a bowl, "though I've kept it a stately secret from everyone we both know, I was vaguely interested in you myself. Why give away a relatively good thing, or till someone comparable but more attracted to me comes along? I was never that generous even as a girl. And that ungenerous spirit goes back to my months as a fetus, if you can believe me and I can believe my mother, when I more than most overgrown embryos wouldn't let her eat, sleep and make love and as a result was more than any one thing instrumental in wrecking their marriage. And because I lived with her and hardly saw my father, I created my own abject dependence on male acceptance and affection and till recently loathed my mother, who I thought was the one responsible for driving my father away from me at such an early, impressionable age. Overfill the bowl with ice so I won't if you're not around have to send someone else to refill it so fast. But now that I see you're not interested in me and probably never were except for perhaps the first few minutes after we met, nothing I can do about it. Besides, I'm inchoatively drunk, so don't believe most of what I say other than overfilling the bowl and later if you see it empty or low, getting more ice. I mean a bit tipsy, not inchoatively, and liable to say ridiculous tipsy thinks like 'inchoatively' and 'tipsy thinks' and that I was interested in you once, all of wish would be a thundering lie. You're okay and amusing to be around but to me not that attractive. I just never thought of Helene and you as a twosome. Not even as two people to talk together for any extensive length of time."

"We didn't."

"There. So forget her. If you can't talk from the beginning, you're through from the start—that's my motto or somewhat. I also know she prefers men a lot more established, stable and scholarly than you."

"More stable and established? I almost never leave my apartment or for that matter my desk seat. And there must be a couple of people who'd consider me scholarly. Geez, I speak the Emperor's Japanese without ever having been to the Ryukyu Islands or Japan. Who in this room even knows of the Ryukyus or at least its most recent cession and if they do then the exact date when, or can read, speak, write and translate almost flawless Japanese without in fact ever having seen the Pacific?"

"There's a Japanese weaver here and his potter wife who are visiting the city for a year. They can do all those except say they've never seen the Pacific and translate Japanese into near perfect English and the reverse, though he does have a profitable sideline translating Japanese plays and verse into Korean and Chinese."

"Oh yeah? Where? I should speak to him. What's his name?"

"Don't and let's not mention his name or allude too loudly to him till they leave. He doesn't like your translations and introductions. He specifically requested I not think it appropriate for you to meet. It's his opinion, and one he says shared widely in the Japanese literary world, denoting a fame I never knew you had, that you've done more harm than anyone in any English-speaking country to stop English-speaking people from appreciating modern Japanese poetry."

"Oh, I see him, unless you have other Japanese friends here. I should corner him and do what I can to change his mind. But nuts to him, not that I won't defend my right to object to his beliefs. First tell me about Helene."

"What's to tell?"

"Is she married, and if so, living with her husband? And if not, how long's it been since the trial separation or divorce? And if so, living with any male now in a faithful relationship? And if not, so serious with any male now that there'd be no chance of a nonmarital separation or divorce?"

"She was, once, maritally tried and divorced, and currently unattached but not loose and teaching American literature in a college upstate. She also has a book coming out not from a university press but a real live and hearty trade publisher that actually gave more than a five-hundred-dollar advance on the short stories of twentieth-century American writers. She believes, something I scolded her for because of the counterreaction it might start against my literature professor friends, in brief plain-speaking critiques and short un-gossipy biographical sketches with plenty of humor and active verbs and few adjectives or big words or discursive turgid sentences. It's her objective—I think because she was brought up hardworking and poor where every morsel, minute and cent meant something—to say in ten thousand words per author what most scholars manage to do in a hundred thousand or two, which could put a few of them out of business or force them to reduce their paragraphs, sabbaticals and requests for grants. She's also very sweet, decent, modest, sensitive, even-tempered and with the most thought-out high virtues and lived-out public and private morality of anyone I know, besides being one of my best friends. Is any of this coming through to you?"

"All. It's everything I like. If she asks, you'll slip in a good word for me, and if she doesn't, you'll volunteer?"

"The truth is you're not good enough for her. For me, yes. I prefer single-hood and no kids and my minor escapades that don't interfere with the well-paying fulltime work and month-long vacations I love, so I'll accept much less. But she needs and can maintain while carrying on her other major pursuits an equally right-minded child-wanting youngish dean of a highly regarded semiexperimental college who also teaches a freshman writing course twice a week and is adored by all his students, envied by most of the faculty, sought out by the most prestigious eleemosynary institutions and do-gooding organizations for his intellect, integrity and class and who also sails, skis and runs besides owning a woodsy home with fireplaces in every kitchen and den and a green thumb, bluish blood, purple passion, red back-ground, pink glow and lots of lustrous hair-locks and stylish tidy clothes. Something of that agglutination, but you just won't do, which she'll let you know soon enough if you're still so foolish to pursue her, since she's also intently though unbrutally frank. Please put the bowl on the bar before the cubes dissolve and try to stay up till midnight when the party starts to end and a group of us is going to eat Chinese, compliments of a Soviet-supported Russian poet on tour whom I think I just heard resonate through the door."

She leaves without the platters. Some have to be heated and I light the oven, hold the platters over my head to see if they're ovenproof, and stick them inside. I take the ice to the bar, pour another vodka, take the cold food platters to the table, see the poet, buoyant and big-voiced and coat over his shoulders, thick cowlick falling over his cheek which he keeps remedying with a quick hand sweep or flip of his head, go back for the heated food and two hot plates and potholders and serving spoons, bring them to the table, potholders on the platters' ends so the first people to take from them will know they're hot, look around for someone to talk to, forget where I left my drink, elderly man in tweed and scholastic keys whom Helene had talked to, say hello and he says "How are you, sir?" and I say "Fine thanks, but weren't we introduced?" and he says "That could be true in so rowdy a room, but my memory's still tolerably good, so I doubt it. Wheeler Smith's the name. Do you also work alongside Diana on that unlucid magazine?" and I say "No, strictly on my own, not that I'd snub an article-writing slot with free medical insurance if I could land one. Daniel Krin." I extend my hand and we shake. His is mostly meaty and cold and when I glance at mine when I take it away I see it has ink stains on it from this afternoon or maybe from a memo I wrote on the train. "Nice party," and he says "That it is, Mr. Krin."

"Daniel or Dan. Diana gives them a lot?"

"Once a year around Thanksgiving, give or take a Friday. I often think it's the one good thing I've to be thankful for around this time, not being a fancier of sugared cranberries and dried-out turkeys and parades promoting Macy's and the advent of frenzied Christmas buying."

"So you know Diana for a while."

"If I were an artfully addled old man I'd say for how long. I was her dissertation director when she was finishing the city's youngest Ph.D. in fifty years. You're a pleasant new face here so I'll conjecture you met her at that colony I'm a trustee of."

"We lived in footboard to footboard rooms and shared the same bathtub and can of Ajax. I noticed you talking to Helene Winiker. You direct her too?"

"Wish I had. She wasn't the youngest but without question was one of the brightest, aside from being an aesthetic and colloquial treat. Seeing and speaking to Helene here is the second entry I'll put on my list of things to be thankful for this time of the year. But you haven't said what you do, Mr. Krin. It could be your work was sent to me last spring and I voted on your colony stay."

"I translate."

"I only get fiction in the original. One of the Slavics?"

"Japanese, and if I have some help from a sinologist, a bit of Chinese."

"An admirable underpaid profession and if you could excel in the latter language you'll be in the coming wave. Well. Seems the line to Gurygenin has declined so mind if I say goodbye for the time being to attend to the amenity of shaking the great man's hand?"

"Is it?"

"Surely the shaking one is if that's the hand he writes with. If I were a speculator in men's fortunes and careers I'd say he'll receive a Nobel in the next ten years if his country can keep its nose relatively clean."

"Then I'd say someone a lot more deserving would be out about two hundred thousand dollars for better world politics."

"I doubt you'd think that if you translated Russian. Much success to you, Mr. Krin."

Gurygenin sighs when he sees him and kisses his cheeks and says what seems like a ribald remark in Russian in Smith's ear. They laugh. Some people near them laugh when Gurygenin repeats the remark in English, which I don't wholly hear. Something about old appetites and young women and the time it takes to complete the feast and how when a man is young and just as hungry he would pass up a steaming savory-smelling four-course supper for a cold snack. I look around, no one I know, see my glass, dump the vodka into a large glass and add tomato juice to the top, see a woman Helene had said hello to spreading caviar on a cracker. I go over, slice a piece of brie, hold it up between two fingers and say "Ah, just as I like it: boiled for two and three-quarter minutes and then quickly rolled over ice and rushed to the diner's plate," and she says "Leave it to Dee."

"For Diana? And Helene. Is she H?"

"You know Helene? I was in the bathroom scrubbing my ugly face and looking forward to a chat with her when all of a sudden she disappeared."

"Went to a wedding. Had a previous commitment to it for months."

"Anybody I might know? And listen, stop me if you see my arm reaching for another chunk of food. Anything here but the lettuce garnish—clip me on the wrist, even, okay?"

"I will. And I've been sworn not to say whose wedding it is. The bride doesn't want any gate crashers or some reason like that Helene said. Or any gates crashing. That was it. Too much noise. She doesn't want the ceremony disturbed. Because suppose the groom later contends that the wedding should be nullified because he didn't hear all the nuptial words being said. Because at the precise moment the bride was saying 'I do' or whatever they say today that legitimates the marriage contract, the gates were crashing away. No, that can't be, since the wedding was this summer. Helene never said anything to me except that she was going to the reception."

"Is that so."

"Of course she said a few other things. 'How come fall's falling so fast?' 'If you're going to the bar, could you take back my glass?' But you seem dubious of my even saying why Helene's not here."

"I shouldn't be, and for several good reasons, the best of them being that you didn't stop me from stuffing myself with more food?"

"Actually, I only met Helene tonight. Right here. No, over there where that man and woman smoking black cigarettes are standing, though our positions by sex reversed. I came over and said. She looked at me and said. Later I said and she said and then she mentioned the reception. Didn't the crashing. Did the bride, though would a bride after so many months still be a bride if the reception's her wedding's? Never said a word about gates. Yeats, yes. Maybe also mates. Traits and fates only just conceivably when we got into a hot conversation about weddings and receptions, but about beddings and conceptions, nothing. You know, I never till now realized how effortlessly so many words come to mind that rhyme with gates and also relate to it. Sates. Straits. Grates and greats, the last with an e-a-t because of Yeats, and even that e-a-t now I see relates to the ate in plates and pates if you want to pronounce and spell pâté that way, besides the past tense of eat and so on. But yes, let's. No, you won't allow me to allow you to, though I'll have some more." I hold a knife over the brie and my expression says "Would you, despite your not wanting to, like me to slice you a piece?" She shakes her head, squeezes what doesn't seem like a lot of flab on her waist.

"May I ask your name?" she says.

"It's one I'd like to forget tonight."

"My, you're feeling sorry for yourself. That the reason you're acting the bizarre way you are? The wordplay gibberish? The Helene gate business ridiculousness? If it's the drink, you shouldn't. Not my affair and far be it from me to try to stop you when you didn't my nervous eating, but you really shouldn't drink anymore tonight even if it isn't the drink. It can't make you better. I know. You're looking at a former walking bottle of alcohol. Walking? Hah. And I like a slight amount of seriousness with those I speak, so if. . ."

"Ten thousand years," and I clink her soda glass on the table with my glass and drink down my drink. "That's banzai in Greek."

"That's not funny in any language." She takes her glass, breaks off a couple of blue-cheese crumbs and puts them in her mouth and says "Really, at a party I love nothing more than to schmooze around, so it's no shun if I say I'll see ya?"

"Wait, you're right. I am feeling sorry for myself tonight and I didn't just say that to agree with you. I've been going on also. Running. The mouth. I'm not always like this. Rarely. Sometimes I'm even self-effacing, deferential and shy. I've made potential enemies here. I must be self-destructive. Just using the word 'made' instead of 'encouraged' and 'enemies' instead of 'adversaries'—or more accurately have said, since the examples I gave make little sense, 'I caused or prodded people to be hostile to me'—maybe illustrates that fact. Someone once said that about me. About being self-destructive. Someone? I can be a liar too. Meaning that that's what I can also be—I didn't mean you. Several said it. All women I was very attached to, though I doubt it was ever as evident as now, and not my attachment to them but my self-destruction. Look. I think I felt I had nothing to say before so wanted to make up clever and controversial things to say so I'd seem interesting. That sound true? I might have just said it to seem interesting, but I don't think I did and I'm pretty sure it wasn't. Excuse me. Still running. That I wasn't even able to give my name to you? Saying and doing all those socially asinine things I don't feel proud of I can tell you. Even what I've just been saying: this uncappable self-spill. At my age, coupled with my inferior income and no security, to be such a schmo sometimes is hard sometimes for me to believe and take. Oh fuck. I acted and am still acting the way I did because I don't relate, or for those or additional self-destructive reasons think I don't, to anyone here except maybe the host. So I'm provoking and annoying people and saying ridiculous and wretched things just to what? Don't go yet. That can't-relate feeling-sorry-for-myself outcast and -classed self-destructive argument I guess, though 'argument' not used in any contentious sense but in the manner of reasons induced and concluded I think, wouldn't you say, or am I now being self-destructively unclear?"

She's been doing other things but looking at me most of this time. Studying a wall hanging, snapping her wedding band, looking at the food, biting a live cuticle. Now she says "Then go home if you feel you don't belong here and work it out some other day. That's what I'd do," and picking what I suppose is the chewed cuticle off her tongue, she touches my shoulder for me to step aside. I do and she passes.

"Diana," I say, going over to her while looking at my shoulder to see if the cuticle was left there. It wasn't, or fell off, and Diana's introducing a Czechoslovak novelist to Gurygenin. Now his work I like and I wouldn't mind talking to him. "Pardon me," I say to the men. "I don't mean to bust this up, but may I plunder Diana for a moment and then maybe return with her?"

"Sure," the Czech says, "go ahead. But don't—what did he say?—plunder her to the point of making it not possible for her to come back to us to stay. This poet man. He may not have something to say with me and then I'd be bored to stand here."

"Speak English," Gurygenin tells him. "We're among friends."

I take Diana by the arm and walk her to a free corner. "You needn't explain," she says. "I overheard enough of what you said to Sally and another guest told me much of the rest. What's wrong with you? These are nice people. Intelligent, some of them gifted, and my friends. You're my friend also, so I'm trying my best not to say that if you want to stay my friend, as well as at the party, and I'm probably going too far with that to a friend, don't insult anyone else here to his or anyone else's face. I also think you've had plenty to drink already, and now I know I'm going too far with a friend, but okay?" and takes the glass from my hand.

"I am feeling a bit too self-pitying for one jerk tonight and deservedly disliked. In a way it's related to you-know-who."

"Oh please. Let me go back to my friends."

"You know so many people. I don't know how you do it."

"I work at it, not against. Take a lesson from me. That's what my mother said to me when I was a wearisome kid and what I'm passing on to you. Be tolerant, be kind, be warm, and if others can't get along with you, they'll be in the wrong. Now as far as Helene's concerned—"

"From what I can tell, just someone like her is what I meant, but because of some ineluctable eternal puke in my nature I can never get. Would I try to be getting away with too much if I said can't we just say I'm drunk and be done with it and start anew? Nah, because I know I've screwed it up entirely with you and all your friends, haven't I?"

"I wouldn't know. And you haven't been listening. And didn't we run through this before? And why make everything sound worse by allying yourself with puke and the eternity? And are you sure you used ineluctable right? And these days everyone in everything has to settle for less. And really, come nearer . . . you're behaving so intemperately besides nonsensically besides in the most mawkish pea-brained way that I don't know if I care anymore. If it'll make you feel any better, and this will be my last heroic act, sleep it off in the bedroom till the party's over, though keep half the bed free for the cat, and maybe we should forget about eating Chinese."

"No, got to go." I kiss her hand, start to leave. "Hot fool, hot fool," I say, pushing through.

"Dan," she says behind me. I'm out the door. Collect my umbrella and coat and put it on and umbrella under my arm and wait for her a few seconds I'm not sure what for and go downstairs. Young man just buzzed-in and running upstairs says "Party breaking up so fast?" and I say "An international star-cast of nyet."

"Tar cast of net?" and I say "Sorry, I meant yep, yep yep, yep yep yep."

"Hey, watch it with your umbrella," nearly speared, dodging past.

I look back and see him and then only his banister hand rounding the staircase. "Zeke," Diana shrieks, "you old son of a Z, where have you been, my big man?" and their lips smack.

"Who was that guy I—" before I'm out of range.

Outside I don't know whether to go right or left. I go straight. Wind and cold feel good and clear. Through the park on a path. Man sitting on a bench says "Excuse me but is there any way possible you can help me to get something to eat?"

Snowing. Covered his hair, shoulders, shoes, bench. Snow's on the ground. Dog tracks. Someone not long ago slipped a few feet or intentionally slid: Yippee, look at me. Several lampposts away a figure's cutting across the grass on skis. "By God it's snowing," I say, feeling my hair and accumulated crunch.

"I know and I believe I froze," still with his head leaning over his knees and staring at his feet.

"Seriously?" His eyes close. I look around. Nobody's around. Snow's become sleet and light rain. I open the umbrella, touch his hand. "Still warm, almost hot," holding the umbrella over us. "Maybe that's a sign of frostbite—the first, only and last. But what do I know about frostbite? That if the affected skin stays hot but you can't feel it—can you or my touch?" Eyes stay shut. "Then probably is or close and you should get to a hospital for it. Get into some cover at least. Don't just keep your eyes dry. And gloves. You have to see to yourself. You could also lose your nose."

He puts his hands into his jacket pockets and says "Excuse me but is there any way possible—"

"Stop repeating yourself." Rain's become sleet and then sticking snow and I close the umbrella. "Not that I don't appreciate that you at least saw to your hands, and your polite tone. No, that sounds flossy and patronizing. But craziness—this is what I'm driving at—isn't going to get or keep you well. You'll catch cold. Pneumonia. Don't let me be your mother. Here." I take some change out. "All my change, token's in there too." I hold it out. It's already wet from the rain. I open the umbrella and hold it over us. "Take it, I have to go."

I try to take one of his hands out but it won't move. Around the wrist I touch is one of those hospital identification bands with a clamped clasp. I drop the coins into that pocket. Snowing. "Thank you," he says, body same way.

"Yes, I'm a terrific son of a bitch, aren't I?"

"I own thoughts, sir."

"Then get cover. Listen, for all the money I shelled out I've the right to bark orders. So arf. Arghh arf arf. That means shelter, health, gloves." Doesn't look up. "All right. Just remember the change is in there and a token, and take it easy."

I turn around, lit storm clouds eclipsing the top of Empire State, start out the park way I came in. What's this? Feel sick, stomach cramp and cold head sweat and chills, rest against a lamppost, try to close the umbrella, can't, try, too weak to and it drops out of my hand, I didn't let it go, wind drifts it a few feet off the ground a few feet, lets it go, rolls on its rib tips along the path several cycles, off it to I-can't-see-where when I hear its handle hit up against a tree trunk—if that's it. My nose itches and I close my eyes, open my mouth, suck in air, can't sneeze. Cramps, chills, sweat and weakness are gone. Feet freezing, shoes and probably socks steeped through, turned-up cuffs caught some snow. I empty them. Strange night. Helene, my divisiveness, this weather, my seventeen-second flu. Jogger. Sloshing past in tank top, cap and shorts adding his or her part to it. Wouldn't be surprised to look up and see the sky full of stars and unfettered moon. Un what? Where these words come from sometimes? I suppose I meant of clouds and unfetid might be better. Must have picked it up from one of the hundred or so Hasenai love poems I went over the last two days. *Unchalked, unmoved, unrefined, storm cloud.* Those last two lines weren't it and I'll change "storm" to "rain" and would now or maybe to "snow" if my notebook wouldn't run, but close enough to be the source. And my divisiveness tonight? Some other time.

I look up, grateful to be well again. Snow that stops right before my eyes, a last flake, which I blow at to keep aloft. Then rain. I go after the umbrella. For the use it'll give me after the time I find it, weighed against how much wetter I'll get during the search, it'll be worth it. But must have been blown farther in or annexed in neutral territory, since it's not where I thought I heard it land. "Anyone around here—" No, nobody would say for a variety of reasons. It was a cheap umbrella, bought in front of a subway kiosk during a torrential downpour, May waiting inside for me to rescue her and bring her home partly dry, better or different days. Oh dear, so many women, so many girls, such a long life with them and most times just servicing for us while being one of their boys. I don't know, but got about a dollar thirty-five a year use out of it and May's great smile and approbation for being a sport. But get home and to bed or at least to a—

"Pardon," gray beard, man says, hand out, no hat, also soaked and unseasonably clothed and by the sound his feet make against the water running off the path, though I don't want to look, barefoot.

"Sorry but I already have with my last change to that guy on the bench there and I'm feeling a bit sick besides."

"A dollar would help." Oh would it my answer looks. "Thought it being around Thanksgiving time—" Sympathy my head shakes. "What's a buck these days anyway and I'm awfully hard up." A buck's something to me my finger points. "No problem," and as if it isn't raining and hasn't been and sleeted and snowed, walks into the park, is barefoot but on the other just a sock, stops at a trashcan, picks around, I don't want to watch anymore but my mind walking away with me sees him digging deeper till out leaps a rat with cocked teeth.

Pay phone at the corner. Now I can say with some authority as they say why most of the street booths have been removed and can assume that all will be replaced with these reasonably soon. Only enough cover under this one for one's head and hands and I run to it, thinking I have to have a dime or its nickel equivalent somewhere, but don't. Do a dollar as a woman passes, plus the napkin with pâté. "Excuse me," wrapping the napkin tighter and putting it in my side coat pocket, "but can you change a dollar bill for me?"

"No," keeps going.

"It's very important. My child in the hospital. I have to see about him. We're split, my wife and I, and my kid who lives with her got hit—"

Has slowed down, stops, pauses, turns around, starts back.

"By a bicycle."

"I'm sorry. A bike might sound like a comical thing to get hit with but I know it can be bad. I bet it was going the wrong way."

"No, my son was, but the bike was going very fast and never stopped."

"Hit and run? That could also be a joke if nobody had been hurt." She's dressed right for the rain, sleet and snow though all have stopped. Feels inside the quilted coat pockets while I look around for a trashcan nearby for the pâté, unsnaps a pocket off the coat and shakes it out into her palm. Keys, coins, candy or antacid mint and three tissue-wads roll out. "Didn't think I did and I seem to have lost my little koala bear keyring. Here's a dime." Throws the mints into the street and turns the pocket inside out and back again. "Darn. In fact take both dimes in case the phone company bungles your first call or you need to talk more."

"Take the dollar."

"No thanks." She resnaps the pocket to the coat with the keys and wads back inside. "My good deed and all that and maybe it'll get back my bear."

"Then what's your name and address so I can repay you, in just stamps."

Smiles. "Think I'm crazy?" Crosses the street, seeming from behind in her raised attached hood to ankle-length hem like a jaywalking sleeping bag or sleeping jaybag or some converse figure of speechlessness, though neither of those. I dial Information, give Helene's borough and name and last four letters in it and get her number, think I shouldn't, won't, but can't help myself tonight which true is a flimsy and untruthful excuse, but go on, what's the harm? might even help in several unexplainable ways I haven't time or mind to try to explain right now why I think they're unexplainable or even why I haven't time or mind right now, dial Information and give the same information and say "By the way, that's Stuyvesant Place she lives on, right?" and he says "I've only one Helene Winiker and it's on West a Hundred-tenth, still want it?" and I say "That's right, she moved," get the number, repeat it once to him and several times to myself, dial and a woman answers with the last four digits I dialed but combines them into two numbers, something I should have done to simplify memorizing the whole number.

"Ms. Winiker's answering service? Or Mrs.? Miss?"

"Winiker will do. Any message?"

"She's no doubt out. I don't know why I invariably say that to answering services. Most likely my initial surprise, expecting the person I dialed to answer or some surrogate of hers I know, though she told me of you."

"Who's calling?"

"She'll know what I mean by the following if she remembers who I am. Sure she will, if she contacts you in the next few days. Will she?"

"Up to her. Your message?"

"Tell her . . . That I wanted to reach her before the newspapers hit the stands?"

"That it?"

"No. Give me time to think."

"Tell you what. Call back when you have it, but I'm very busy with other calls flashing and even one on hers." Hangs up.

Who'd be calling her now? None of your bizwax and so forth. But obviously someone who didn't know she was going to a wedding tonight, if she was telling me the truth. Was she? Hardly your affair, etcetera. Tend to your sodden pants, waterlogged socks and now soaked raincoat. Could I tell by her face though? Goddamn this man never gives up. Seemed truthful enough. Seemed more than that. Seemed truth-filled, overflowed, true-blue, tried and true, true to life and to type, whatever that means, trueborn and to form and the like, though do go on: straight-out, girl scout, foursquare and forthright forsooths ago and still going strong, and so did her voice, which was mellow, intelligible and calm, and her hair, which has nothing to do with truth but which I'd love to be able to portray in a poem to her she'd appreciatively receive in the mail and repeatedly read. Maybe she had a date or wanted to go to a movie alone or felt so disconcerted and repelled with my systematically surveying her and parts unknown that I sort of forced her to set off earlier than she'd planned to. That's the case she could be home soon or home now but not answering the phone for fear I'll phone or no fear but has someone home with her now and doesn't want to answer the phone because she's or they're in the middle or start or end of something she or they don't or he doesn't want to interrupt. "True-tongued, homespun, abundantly gummed and lipped, not that I caught all of it," Hasenai says with the aid of his transgressive -lator, "jest saying, past paying, moon's out, so's this lout, wood woofs, whelp in the wild and weep in a while, Jun (his first name), same as his son (I write only semidocumentary poems), go home!" Or a man phoning to get the message she left as to when she'll be home and where's her doorkey this time: left with the elevator man or taped to the side of her doorjamb or under her stairway handrail but surely not under the doormat. Or a friend or relative saying a good friend or relative's very sick, so and so suddenly or after a long illness died, car-pool driver—if that's how she gets to her school upstate and Monday's one of her teaching days—saying he or she can't make it and she'll have to find another ride, or rider, if she's the one who drives the car-pool car, saying he or she can't make it, or friend, relative or mate of the rider or car-pool driver saying he or she's sick, can't make it or died. Or just a new or relatively new to recently old lover calling to say if she phones that he's coming by tonight, which he can do because he has his own key and knows it's all right. Or even Helene, phoning to see who might have called, learning that an anonymous indecisive man was just on the line.

I dial Information, hang up before I get it, wipe the rain and melted snow off the telephone stand shelf, set up my notebook and opened pen on it, dial Information and give the same information plus her street number and get her building and phone numbers and write them down, dial and the woman repeats the last four digits. "It's the same man from before," I say.

"What man from when before? So far tonight I've answered a couple of men's voices for this number and one woman's which might have been a man's."

"The nameless semistranger who couldn't make up his mind five minutes ago."

"You know, in every holiday season, which I think I can say we're already in—someone's blinking window wreath I can see from the slit they give us to see out of here— Well I don't want to talk about tough nights, but if you've any plans to annoy me further and nothing else puts you off, I will."

"I don't plan it. But if you think you've had a tough night—"

"I don't want to talk about it either, for that's exactly what some of the tough calls were on. Depression, rejection, help me to reach him and what'd she say when you gave her my message or told him from me to take gas, and more of the same, no?"

"No, but okay. Just tell Winiker I called. Daniel K-r-i-n. From a pay station or phone booth or one-legged stand you can't stand under even with one leg, and that I was an incredible fool Friday night, but outside of this call and the last one I made, won't be anymore."

"You're asking me to write all that down?"

"You don't have to include this booth or stand or anything about legs or even my previous call."

"Think it wise saying any of it?"

"It's not what you think. There's this carefully plotted though harmless meaning behind it all. So no matter how surprised Winiker might be when you first give her the message, you'll suddenly be surprised when she all of a sudden understands."

"Fine. Krin. Bye."

"Maybe you're right. You are right. You still there?"

"Why?"

"Please erase all I said starting from the beginning of this call. Beginning before even then. Don't even say I called this time or the last. Don't even recall I called. Put my name and namelessness and existence out of your mind. I never called either time, okay? If you wrote the message or started to, tear it up. It was dumb of me—child's play—my acting the way I did. I'll probably see her later tonight anyway, so I'll tell her myself, but don't even tell her that. I mean phone her tonight, I probably will, or one day soon, though nothing of that's to go past us too, not even an allusion to my musing about it. No, it's hopeless. Got myself into a nice hole with this one. You'll no doubt give her the message and my musings no matter what I say, since that's your job. And maybe after a couple of years of your becoming overprotective and communicationally involved with your clients, you think she should know even more so that I called, whether you wrote it down yet or not."

"Believe me, Danny, it's easier for me to rip up a message than slot and give it, so that's what I'll do if you want."

"I do."

"Then done." Hangs up. Now begin worrying about it. Not just what she'll tell Helene, but why I said it. Why did I? Not just this call but the last. Not just all of what I said to the phone and before her to the loan woman but most of what I said and did tonight starting with the party or an hour into it and how with Helene I just about ruined it. Did I? Worry about it. Useless to, since what can I do about it now and so on? High, that's why I acted the way I did I can say, first time in my life or in a year I got anywhere near to being so inebriated, which is a lie, but no reason I can't use it to try to swing things around a little my way. "You see, Helene, for some reason—no, that's not the truth. Yes it is, only I'm almost too ashamed at my behavior that night to recount and explain it, but I will because what more, since it's also in my self-interest, can I tell you but the excuse, I mean the truth, which is the reason I called, or one of them. For you see, Helene, I didn't think you left Diana's for a wedding but because I'd chased you from it with my slobbering attention from afar and series of unsuccessful passes close up, which is the reason I thought you'd be home the first time I called. As for my second call, if your answering service told you of it, and if it didn't then I don't remember making any second call, I've no excuse except that I was still high and had begun to act like a fool and was also trying to undo the damage of my first call, if you were told of it, and if you weren't then I only made one call—the second one—to leave an innocuous message that I'd called and would try to get back to you soon, but because of my highness I got carried away. Anyway, now I feel lousy about it and want to apologize for any discomfort I might have caused you by chasing you away from Diana's if I did, and also through you to your answering service for my foolish and perhaps disturbing calls to it via your number, and also to you again for my having misrepresented myself to your answering service and possibly embarrassing you because of it by intimating I was your friend or knew you better than I did. No, that's confusing and tumescent, just as that phrase was when I could have more accurately and less clumsily said 'affected and bombastic,' though I'm still being vocally showy, and even still with that last adverbial phrase, and even still by saying I know what form of speech it is, when I could have more briefly and plainspeakingly said 'flip, windy, labored and imprecise,' or to be even more plainspeaking, 'not precise,' but all of it said, including the last two revisions, in what I'll truthfully say was a laughable and ludicrous endeavor to impress you, and for that, and also for that last flashy phrase, I humbly apologize. Not humbly. Nor so dumbly. No humility, stupidity, apologies, amphibologies, metatheses, paronomasias, lapsus linguae and anglicized or any foreign or lexiphanic or high-falutin words and phrases. Everything I've said to you so far has been out-and-out dishonesty if not downright lies, not that I can particularize that difference. I'm sorry. There it is. That's all I had to say. Sorry for lots of things:

my phone calls to your service, my antics and aggressiveness at the party while you were there and after you left, and most of all for what I said to you on the phone tonight, or today if it's not tonight. Listen. Let me begin again if I can and may. May I? Because I can. Not too late? No reply? I should take that as an okay? Okay. I was quite simply—not 'quite' but just simply and maybe simperingly and simplemindedly—no, just simply. Plain and simply. I was simply high that night, though it actually does sound much better saying 'quite simply high that night,' for otherwise I do sound simpleminded, and that's my excuse. Not simplemindedness but highness—now that's the truth. Which is truly the truth but no real excuse because I have to be responsible for myself and my actions, sober or soused, unless I were a certified lush, which I'm most certainly not, so...no. Where was I? Got confused again in this endless excuse. You see, Helene..." Won't work. Yes it could. What else I got? "Drunk, stupid, pretentious, insensitive, insouciant, translucent, unseemly, unsociable and other -ent's and -ant's and trans'- and in's- and un's- like -conscious and -questionably -conscionable, because first time anywhere near to being pickled in a year, so sorries all around: service, operator, you, Diana, guests I spoke to about you at the party, because really, all I usually like is a glass of white or two every night, and not a big glass but a regular red or white wineglass, three and a half ounces and not filled to spilling level at the top, so it must have been all that seemingly innocent enough social drinking and that hundred-proof Russian rotgut." That's what it'll be. Knew I'd eventually find my excuse. "The ice-cold Russian vodka. Not because it was ice-cold, though that could have contributed to my cyclopean high, but because it was vodka and a hundred proof and also Russian and straight and I wasn't used to that hooch any old way and surely not when they filled my double- or triple-shot glass or cup all the way up. I drank it like water but without water, ice, juice or even a peel. Then before I knew it I was rude to everyone in what was left of my sight and made my dumb phone calls the same night, even though that does show an underlying social problem and perhaps at first view an overriding congenital mental disease, but please don't believe that or make more out of things than they already are. Maybe when someone's only used to the softer spiritous stuff, a certain quantity of hard liquor, particularly when it's distilled so differently and to this person is alien to his physical system in almost any amount or form, would do that to just about anyone including a European with a history of hard drinking or even a Russian who's lived and drank most of his life in the same freezing regions where that liquor is made, not that I'm trying to exonerate myself for my actions and so forth. So you see, Helene, that's my excuse. I'm sorry, apologize, you, Diana, answering service, party guests, phone calls, so forth, and hope you'll forgive me, could kick myself for what I did, pray you don't think that night or even this phone call is anything but faintly related to my normal behavior, and would like to try to make up for all I aberrantly did by inviting you for a drink somewhere, maybe that nice new, so it won't be too inconvenient for you, wine bar I heard opened up last month on some second floor above a Lebanese deli around your way, though I'd understand if you refused. You won't? You will? Meet me for just a brief drink and snack? And there is such a place? Armenian, not Lebanese? On the east side of Broadway between One-hundred-eleventh and -twelfth? See you there tonight at eight? Great. You remember what I look like? Forgivably stewed as I was or whatever the word or expression in Russian—'Vodt a dumpkin!'—I remember you."

I put my pen and notebook into my pants and coat pockets and head home by way of this street west and then left on Sixth to the quicker Seventh Avenue subway, approach, pass and start back to a bar I'd been to with May a few times over the years when it had a pianist playing mazurkas, polonaises and études, which the overturned stand-up sign outside still says it does, and go inside for old times' sake and such but more realistically or whatever I should call it to dry off and have a coffee or beer.

CHAPTER THREE

The Bar

Not the same. Lot less light. Piano music though piano covered and keyboard cover locked. Before the place always so jammed. One customer at the bar and behind it a barmaid with her mouth right up to the mirror picking her teeth with a toothpick. She reams, she digs. Got it her face seems to say throwing the toothpick away. Before when there probably wasn't so much rain. When there was and we were down here we'd get a cab or on a subway and go to either of, or a bus if we didn't mind the long ride, our apartments to be dry. To drink wine or shot of warming this or that and maybe a snack and maybe read awhile or watch—or do both—part of a television movie in our undies or nude. Or one in her or his undies and the other nude, depending if the temperature outside was mild and if it wasn't then if the heat inside was still up. And chances are one or the other of us after we'd fooled as May liked to say with one another would climb—but stop. On top of the other and get not climb or side by side each other or both of us on our knees facing one of the bedboards. But why bring all that back? I don't know. You can try. "Lost like a dog, dark like a roach, dumb like a goat and almost half as hot as a cat it'd be too rudimental and simplistic to say, those are four of the foresown fates of man—Hasenai, it's not safe: grab your son and bone and race back to your flat!" he says in his poem "Autumnal Ordinal Poems." And disinfecting smell from the john, music from the jukebox. Not jukebox but whatever those big blinking modern record-playing machines are called and which I don't think was here before. Debussy I bet.

"Debussy," I say to the barmaid, walking over bobbing my head at the jukebox as she turns puckering her lips from putting on lipstick in front of the mirror, but not taking a seat.

"Could be. Like something from the bar?"

"Sounds it. The little piano tinkle. Like rolling leaves, like falling trees. I mean rivers and leaves. The high keys. Rivers rippling, little leaves flipping in the air or on the ground briskly tripping. And ridiculous those descriptions. Not descriptions but likenesses or pictures of whatever they sound like or are depicting. Maybe depictions. But you probably know music so do you know . . . ?" snapping my fingers. "By the same composer. Not Le or La Mer or The Valse. No, that was someone else. Piano pieces all in a series by Debussy that sound like this and maybe is. I bet the pianist knows. He on his break?"

"Vacation."

"Oh, vacation, lucky stiff. But I bet he's playing twelve hours a day on a resort ship or at a Nassau hotel or one on one of the Keys. Say, that'd be the right spot. But the sign outside— Never mind. I'm not nosy and I'm sure you have your good reasons."

"You're not very thirsty either and the reason for the sign is it's not my idea. The reason is it's my boss's. To keep music lovers coming in while the pianist's away. You see what luck we've had. Sure, the freaky weather, but people are a lot smarter than he thinks. And the wind which keeps knocking it over could be God's way of saying don't pull the wool over the public's eyes too much."

"You believe that?"

"If I just said 'politics and religion,' you'd like a light know what I meant."

"Go ahead. I never get upset over those two subjects."

"But you should or you're not human. If you were a Jew and I called you a Red kike, you wouldn't mind? Anyway, you still don't want anything to drink if you never did? False advertising, so I'm not holding you to stay here."

"No, I'll have something." I take off my raincoat and hang it on a wall peg. "My sweater."

"Yes?"

"My sweater. No wonder I was so cold. I was at a party before and left it. Ah, it's too ratty for anyone to take."

"People will do that at them—leave things. I've done it plenty. Once even my year-old baby."

"You have a baby?" sitting at the bar.

"Now she's not."

"What happened?"

"She grew up."

"At the party I mean, and I didn't mean anyone would take my sweater at mine. She was later taken home and raised by someone else?"

"I went back for her after I got halfway home without."

"And, fretful the whole trip back, found she was the life of the party when you got there."

"Close. She couldn't even walk a step then but was dancing without holding on in the middle of the room. People don't believe that when I tell them. She never knew I was gone, so it had no lasting effect on her, and now she's old enough to have a baby herself."

"I know I'm supposed to think I'm supposed to say this, but it doesn't seem possible she could be that old."

"If she was like me at her age she'd have had her first by now and leaving it at wild parties too—but with her brains, forgetting where to go back for it. Fortunately, I've kept her a child."

"Probably a good idea. I'd both love and hate to be a father today, maybe something else I'm supposed to think I'm supposed to say."

"Why? And you were never a father?"

"Did I say that? Even if I did, it's true. And you're about to say something like how I'm missing the best—"

"You are. And if you were a father but the right kind, you'd have it with someone else to help bring it up, which I never had the luck to have. And unless you're ten years younger than you look, you shouldn't wait."

"You're right, I will. The right woman, she gets proposed to right away, no time-wasting, from me and our future child."

"If you're laughing to yourself, you're making a big mistake."

"I'm not. I've just about made up my mind. No, I've made it. This second. All my women and no women before—the heck. I'm getting too old. I'm beginning to taste the grit between my teeth. I don't know what that means. But yes, I met a girl—a woman—I'm sure she's a good seven or eight years younger than I—tonight—at that party—one with the left sweater—left and right, both sleeves—that, who I'm going to pursue to try to marry and have a child by. I will. The woman. Will and try."

"You could be a little high now, so don't jump to quick decisions. Girls still say yes to marriage proposals even if they keep their maiden names, and get depressed if the man suddenly backs out."

"No, I've decided. I'm tired of living alone. Being—etcetera, and getting old, gritty teeth. I want a kid under my feet. By my feet with a little silky head to pat and a wife sitting on the floor with her arms or head on my knees or lap, all while I'm seated in an easy chair, or any but some hard wooden chair, just enough lamplight over my shoulder so as not to coarsen the scene with its glare, and a rug so my wife doesn't bruise her knees while reclining beside me and my child doesn't get hurt when it falls. I mean it. Carpet or rug. And me even in a hard wooden fold-up chair if that's what it has to take to succeed. I'm game. So done." Same piano piece comes on after a half minute being off. "You didn't have a jukebox before. Not a jukebox. What's that machine called again?"

"Jukebox, what else could it be?"

"All right, jukebox. But music to my ears. Before, remember when I snapped my fingers? Well it's not like me to forget a famous piece's name that I also love. It's something like études, though I've always associated those with Chopin. Preludes, that's what they are and I'm sure this one is. Deedle leedle lee. Like that. Deedle leedle leedle lee, leedle dee. Like leaves, rippling trees. You hear it?"

"Sort of. So what drink will it be?"

"Goddamnit," slapping my head. "Brahms. An intermezzo, for piano— one in B? No, I always forget the number and key. I know Chopin's Waltz C-flat in D-minor or something, but this which she played as much? I used to love to unlock the door to her place, woman before the future mother of my child to be, and with my own keys, ones that go in the holes, when she was practicing this piece—coffee?"

"Saving it for my Irish coffee and serious Black Russian drinkers and it's been sitting on the hot plate so long it'd be too bitter to drink straight. I know I could make more, but I'm too lazy."

"I've done time behind counters. I could make it."

"Strictly you know what. Maybe you should go to a real coffee shop."

"Can't. I'm here, drying off. Running across some hitherto unseen but intriguing things about myself, and it's still drizzling and now that I know my sweater's gone I'll be even colder on the street. And if it's just the tip, I'll give you as much as for those sickening mixed drinks."

"Okay, I'll be honest." She empties an ashtray and wipes it clean though it only had a broken swizzle stick in it. "Though the boss is at his busier place he might drop in and see your coffee and how much your tab is and that you're not a regular to do favors for like that and say to me how come I'm not peddling the drinks better even with this weather and the pianist away? So how about it? An Irish coffee would warm you up quicker than anything and the bitter coffee in it sober you up a little also if that's what you think you need, or keep your high even. And I make them with real whipped cream I whipped myself, so you get some food value from it too just when you might have to use it."

"Make it without— I was going to say 'without the whiskey and cream,' but I know about bosses and I'm no wiseguy." She looks at me as if I am. I look at the mirror and see her still looking at me. A sign on the mirror says Guinness is good for you. "Good, that's what I want to be and the weather and your business to be like—so a Guinness please. It's supposed to be healthy besides."

"Ad's an antique, and as for the medicinal qualities, all the health Guinness gives is the runs. Closest thing to any brew Irish or English we have is Molson's Ale."

"Then, Miss, after you give me some jukebox change, I'd say you've made a sale." I give her a dollar.

"Hurray. And the place even makes extra cash from you too."

She gives me four quarters and steps on the pedal to open the lowboy refrigerator. Light-blue light illuminates her body when she squats to get the bottle out. Thin, tall, too-tight shirt to cast aspersions, I mean call attention or dramatize her very large compared to her tiny waist and nearly nonexistent hips, breasts, or whyever a woman would wear a shirt so tight with no garment beneath that the color and contour of her aureoles show and nipples push through and is probably unhealthy besides. To sell more drinks and get bigger tips, but doesn't excite me, I think mainly because it looks so damagingly tight. And somehow, in recent years, two. . .three, and I don't believe because of any libidinal decrease, the breasts of strangers even with the nipples erect and whatever age and size. . .I prefer the woman I love or am in the process of or think I will when she's taking off her clothes and making no show, except maybe a parody of one, but just those.

She pours my ale. I taste, say "Ah, real great," put a five-dollar bill under an ashtray in case someone suddenly comes in with the wind and go to the jukebox at the end of the bar. "Brahms Intermezzo," it says, but not who's performing which one. I stick a quarter in and press "Slow Movement Mozart Concerto," figuring it'll be piano and the romantic movement used as the musical theme for a popular Swedish movie years ago, but it's violin and Prokofiev.

I try opening the door to the men's room near the jukebox; it's stuck or locked. "Excuse me," jiggling the doorknob, "anybody in there, and going to be long?" No answer.

"Is there someone in the men's room," I yell to the barmaid, "or do you keep it locked for your own reasons?"

"Is this fiver minus your drink all for me?"

"No why, how much is the ale?"

"Two."

"You being funny then? Take a dollar. But the john here?"

"Probably the clean-up man. Give him a good knock. He could sit in the shithouse all day."

I knock, not good, and a woman says "Please, I don't feel too well. I won't be out soon. Go next door."

"This is the men's room, ma'am. You can't use the ladies'?"

"It's too filthy. Please, nothing I can do now, and I won't talk anymore."

"How filthy is it?" Doesn't answer. "Mind if I use the ladies' room?" I say to the barmaid. "Men's is being used by a woman and, if you'll excuse me, I have to go bad."

"She's in there? Wondered where she went. Thought she ducked out on the check when I was doing my nails and I truthfully didn't care she looked so sad. Be quick, will you? Not just the boss but the whole city health force frowns on the mixing of washroom sexes. And the mayor himself still keeps his rent-controlled apartment around here and a minimum of twice has stopped in to hear."

"What's he drink?"

"It was only told to me—probably to hype business—never seen."

"I shouldn't be long," and I open the ladies' room door slowly. It's not filthy at all. Floor mopped, no wall cracks or remarks, mirror, commode, sink and pipes shiny and clean, vase of fresh flowers over the toilet's water tank and above that an oil painting of beach grass or machine reproduction of one down to the smudged signature and raised brushstrokes in an oak or imitation oak frame. Seat seems to be clean, and I pull down my pants and sit. This is going to be a long one; should've brought a book. I look around: nothing much else to see. Alarm tape bordering the small barred window, so it also can be that kind of place. I try to smell the flowers from where I'm sitting. But I can't smell, if they do smell, anything but what I've so far in bulk, liquid and gas expelled and don't remember smelling anything but cleanser and disinfectant when I came in here. "Please for poor ole Petie's sake don't take posies from WC or vase to your home or to throw away on the street," notice on opposite sides of the vase says. My mother, far back as I can remember, always had flowers on our water tank, fresh or dried. Except Christmastime when she put a holly branch in and middle autumn when it was twigs with different colored leaves from the park. Not in a vase but an old cough-medicine bottle that can now only be bought at a flea market or antique shop. The bottle was still on top of her tank last time I was there. I don't know how we never broke it. I guess the bathroom was the one place in the apartment my sister and I never fought or played, since we couldn't roll around on top of one another without clunking our heads on the sink pedestal or one of the tub legs. Or maybe we did break it and she had a supply of these bottles we never knew about, though there wasn't much room in the two-bedroom apartment where she could have kept them hidden too long without our finding out. I should call her and ask, or go see her. Just call her to see how she is, or go see for yourself. Why am I always putting it off, not being a good son, because how long would it take? Hour out, drinks, dinner and talk, which could be illuminating and fun, hour-plus back, ladened with enough of her breads and overcooked food in plastic containers to fill two large shopping bags and feed me for a week. Not tonight go, though I don't think it's too late to call and haven't for two weeks.

There's no toilet paper. No tissues, hand-towel paper, cloth towel or even the paper holder on the wooden spool in the wall the toilet paper comes on. My handkerchief is in my raincoat as is the napkin with the pâté. I could use my fingers, but there's no soap. My briefs have several small holes and frayed places in them and the elastic's about to go. I start taking my trousers off. But as long as I'm going to dispose of the briefs I tear them off my legs by pulling at one of the unfabricated holes and chewing through the band, blow my nose in it which I have to do, rip the briefs in two and wipe my behind with the smaller part and drop it into the bowl and flush, hoping it all goes down. It does. I throw the other part into the can under the sink, then think I should have looked in or behind the can before I tore up the briefs for little pieces of soap or what could have been clean to semi-clean paper of any sort and also saved the clean part of the briefs for a possible emergency later on.

I splash water on my face, dry it on my sleeve and hands on my pants, check the toilet to see that none of what I flushed came up, look in the mirror at my face and say "'Now as Hasenai says in his humorous poem "Optics in Inner Space" would be a well-chosen moment to reflect on myself and place in the luminous race,'" want to pull a hair out of my nostril but because of the impending pain which has stopped me about one time in four, push it back in till it stays and go to the bar.

"That was an excellent selection that beautiful piano music you played before," man at the end of the bar says as I pass him.

"You mean my concerto came on?"

"No, a solo, soft and sweet—delicious, unless they have concertos for just one instrument and no accompanist or orchestra. You know what it was?"

"The Brahms intermezzo? Much as I love it it wasn't my choice. I put on that screechy violin piece before, though paid for and chose a slow Mozart piano concerto movement."

"Must be mine then," the barmaid yells over. "Just threw in money and with my eyes closed, pressed."

"Your own money? Doesn't seem practical with so few customers and such lousy tippers like myself."

"Not real money. Sure, real, but with red nailpolish on it, which means it's the bar's and the gorilla who collects for his company gives it to us back. You have to have music in here, but why classical? Neither of you answer me that. It's a classical music bar, so people expect it. But I don't like it and aren't afraid to say so."

"What does she know?" the man says low. "She's ignorant. She likes disco. She likes hip-huggers and guys with safety pins in their lobes and roller skates. She's not supposed to but she wears those new kind of wheels in back of the bar. You see them?"

"I don't believe so, though I don't see how I wouldn't have heard them."

"They're the new silent kind I said with something like polyurine wheels that make no noise. She knocks our music but thinks those things are the ultimate creative achievement of Western mankind till now, along with every single movie made. She's pathetic."

"I don't know. She seems sort of nice. And if the owner doesn't mind her skating or he's not around to see, I don't see why I should."

"You're right. That's what I should think. I should mind my business and not be so critical of people. Thank you for telling me that. Thank you."

"Excuse me, but I didn't say you were wrong or even imply what you should think or do."

"You don't understand. I'm thanking you. Take the compliment you deserve when someone gives it because you may have to wait a long time for the next one to come," and he sips his drink and looks at the bar mirror. I go back to my stool but don't sit.

"Can I open you another one?" the barmaid says.

"Not yet. Hardly touched this one. By the way, he says you wear roller skates, so if I peer over the bar at your feet it's just for that, okay? Oh that's stupid."

"Roller skates?"

"No really, forget what I said. I'm embarrassed by it. Trying to be provocative or something with my silly talk. Sorry. I'll shut up." I put my hand over my mouth and say through it "I've shut up."

"He said it though, true?"

"He didn't mean anything by it."

"But he said it."

I take my hand away. "What do you want me to say? If I said he said it he said it."

She shoots him a dirty look, puts her sneakered foot on the counter next to my glass. "Other one's like this one down to the broken laces. So whatever his reason for saying it, and I can tell you why but I'm a much nicer person than he, you could be an even bigger fool for believing him, not that I meant that as an insult to you—just to that troublemaker."

"Look, what are you getting so riled up about? I'm sure he was kidding me. Playing around, man to man—you know. Besides, right after he told me it he apologized and said your roller skates were none of his business, so now I don't know what to think. What does it matter anyway? And I'm the one who started the trouble, so blame me."

"Maybe you have your own reasons for wanting to take everyone's blame, but that bastard started it this time, not you."

"And maybe you're only looking to fight with him over nothing and for your own reasons and using my stupid roller-skate remark as the excuse."

"And maybe you don't know what you're talking about. You're only a first or second timer here and know nothing about what goes on around. Because that guy—yes, I'm talking about you," she says to him and he says "Huh? What? Me? I can't hear so good from so far away. Bad ears and I also can't read minds or lips."

"Sure you can't. Oh, go back to your drink," and he says "Anything to help keep cemented relations, but I'm still not so sure what you said," and he looks at me and raises his eyebrows and shoulders, then looks at the mirror while he sips his drink.

"Anyway," to me, "he's always doing something like that about me with new customers. One time he told somebody I was a man in drag. Another time that I put laxatives in the drinks of customers who don't tip. Those are jokes? Maybe if you don't take them seriously, but both times those stupes seemed to believe him and who knows what else he says when I'm not around. I ought to really tell him where to stick it."

"You just didn't? Could I have change for a phone call please?" pushing one of the dollar bills at her.

"You're just changing the subject."

"No, I have to make an important call to my—and oh, before I forget. There's no toilet paper in the ladies' room. And I'm not saying that to change the subject from your saying I changed the subject before either. I didn't then and am not now and there's no paper. Just thought you'd like to know."

"That's the truth?"

"About the paper and everything else, I swear."

"Henry," she yells to nobody I can see in back. "The girls' room needs paper." Man's still looking in the mirror and sipping his drink.

"No hand towels either or soap. Face towels. Whatever they are."

"All kinds of paper, Henry, and soap. I hope you didn't have to go too bad," she says to me.

"Just number one. And those papers in the pull-down metal container are hand or face towels, aren't they?"

"Just paper. If they're cloth, they're cloth, but now we're talking about a long linen roll."

"Okay, gorgeous," a man shouts from the back. "Toiletries and roses for the heavenly bodies. Thy will is mine done."

"And you," she says, going over to the man at the end of the bar. "You I want to have it out with now."

"Please, my change," I say. "I need it for my phone call."

"What'd you say to her about me?" he says.

"I'm sorry. The roller skates. But I told her it was a joke and nothing and my fault. It was nothing, Miss, nothing."

"Don't tell me—I know what it was. And if you're not that keen on me," she says to him, "and have to keep making these vicious cracks about me here, then I don't care if you're our best customer ever and also the chief muck-a-shit of New York. I'll have to demand that you leave and never come back while I'm tending bar and you can run to my boss and cry about it to him all you please."

"I will," he says. "I'll have you fired and get him to put a girl behind the bar who at the very least, if she has to manually drop ice cubes into the drinks, cleans her fingers once a week."

"You drip. Get the hell out of here now."

"I'll go when I'm good and ready, sister, and not a second before." He finishes his drink. "I'll take a refill if you don't mind."

"Henry," she yells.

"Then whatever comes out of this thing then," and he reaches over the counter for what I think's called a soda gun and squirts water or tonic or soda water into the sink and then into his glass.

I grab my two dollars off the bar, get my raincoat and start for the door.

"Thanks a lot, fella," the man says, holding his glass up to me in a toast. "I'll do the same for you with my fat ratting mouth any damn day you want and then worm out when it gets most ticklish too."

"Any trouble up front, gorgeous?" Henry says when I open the door.

"Half of it's on the way out now."

I turn around. Henry's tall and burly but not mean looking and is holding a roll of toilet paper and package of paper towels and a broom. "Look," I say, "let's settle this amicably. Because I'm the cause or indirectly so of this big absurd whatever you want to call it harmless to-do and I can't just leave knowing this man might get his head bashed in over it."

"I think, if intellectual wisdom's to be king, that you be better to leave now," Henry says. "No harm shall come to no one at the bar I'll here say."

"But if you think you've a good grievance against him or she does and he doesn't want to go, call a cop. At least that way you're assured nobody will get hurt."

"As you said, so I say—no man shall, long as the gentle Hen's here."

"We don't want cops when it's not necessary," she says. "They're hard at it with a lot worse than him and don't like coming in on things we can easily fix ourselves. Now close the door behind you. It's getting cold and the landlord's a cheapo with the rent. But if you want to do the most good, take with you your creepy friend."

"Thank you," the man says to me, his hand cupped behind his ear. "I didn't catch all you said, but you spoke up, that was grand, and from now on I can handle myself dandy."

"Don't handle anything. They don't want you here. I'm not wanted also— that's also clear—but not wanted not as much as you, if I got those nots right, and there's nothing to be learned or gained or anything from talking back to bartenders and so on. So be smart and pay up and leave with me and we'll have a drink or coffee down the street so long as it's not a tough dumpy joint and talk about why there's no sense talking and fighting back at bars and being big men and strong and all that hooey and stuff and pride and so on and knocking heads and losing teeth and standing on your own two feet and later blacking out after making great fatuous points, though maybe there I obviously speak for myself."

"Fine, if I agreed. But I don't because this is a public place licensed for such and no discrimination of any kind, so not somewhere you can be tossed out of indiscriminately. It's also like home to me or become one I've been coming here so long, something pretty Marjorie's going to learn from her boss Mr. Witcom very soon."

"Then you might end up getting hurt," I say and Marjorie says to him "I'll learn, all right, will I ever learn," and Henry says "What in the good name are you all mouthing on so much for? The Hen's got work."

"If I am then I am," the man says to me, "because I don't pretend to be a tough strong man like these two here."

"Uh-oh," I say looking up and Marjorie says to him "You calling me a man again?" and Henry says "Now will someone please tell the Hen what he just said to make that man say that about him? Someone. Please. The Hen's open-minded. So tell him."

"Oh, did I say that?" the man says to her and smiles for a few seconds and drinks from his glass.

She grabs the glass from him, a lot of what's in it spills on the bar and their clothes, and throws the rest of it in his face. He stands, takes out a wallet, slaps some bills on the bar, kicks his stool, it's wobbling on two of its four legs when he kicks at it again and misses but it still falls, grabs his hat and coat off a peg while Henry picks up the stool and slides it back to the bar and Marjorie raises a chair leg she got from somewhere and bangs it against something metal like a cabinet or sink and yells "Get out of here before you get your ears nailed—I'm not fooling with you, get out, get out!" and bangs the metal again and he rushes through the door I didn't know I was still holding open and outside puts on his hat and coat.

"Don't go if you don't have to," she says to me. "But if you do, I hope no hard feelings to the bar."

"No really and I only came in for a single coffee or beer," foot keeping the door open as I put on my coat and think never again in this place even with the pianist playing and a friend.

"Hey," Henry says, "the Hen's got a terrific idea with business booming this great."

"We can't," she says. "There's still the lady in the gentlemen's can and what if Witty—" but I've let the door go and step outside.

CHAPTER FOUR

The Street

Rain's stopped. That I saw from the door. But sky seems clear, even a bit of moon to be seen, and feels ten to fifteen degrees warmer than when I went in, almost too much for this coat, unbuttoning it. The man's wiping his face with a bunch of napkins. "I don't know—how'd all that happen so fast?" I say. Looks at me, shakes his head commiseratively: more my fault than his; in fact it's all your fault his pointing finger says, throws the napkins into the street and heads downtown. Napkins quickly picked up by the wind and hover a few feet over the street before four drop and one soars three flights more till I can't see it anymore. There it is—no, just a pigeon if my fading vision's not mistaken, and I take out my eyeglasses case. "You—catch it!" Wind also must have blown his hat off because here he is hatless chasing one down the sidewalk toward me. I jump to my right, glasses sliding out of the case same time I stop the hat with my foot, pick it up and my glasses and brush it off where I stepped on it and hand it to him. I hold the glasses up. "Oh no." One of the lenses seems scratched. I smear a little spit on the lens, wipe it dry and put the glasses on. "Oh nuts. It'll cost a fortune to get fixed."

"Why? They don't look cracked."

"One of the lenses got scratched through both bifocal parts."

"So? They buff it down in a jiff and say give me five bucks."

"When was that? Shit. Instinct—didn't think. Should've known they'd fall out. But if I'd stopped to think I wouldn't have been able to stop your hat from rolling past."

He turns the hat around in his hands, scratches the dirt off the brim, puts the hat on. "Lose this honey and a lot more than five bucks. Two new pairs of your glasses I could buy with it and a thorough eye exam, so you have my gratitude for a change and what else? My regrets for your spectacles and monetary loss."

"Thanks very much." He's adjusting the hat to his head. I put on the glasses to see how well I can see with them scratched. Other lens has little nicks in it which when I close my eye behind the scratched lens makes me see spots in the distant-vision part and mostly a blur in the near. Both eyes open I can't come up with a quick comparison, but my vision through both sections is even worse. But so what? No backups at home so nothing to do but get them fixed soon as I can. Tomorrow to the optician's: one of the first things before noon. No: get angry, become miserable, curse his hat and the wind and Marjorie and he for doing what they did to make me leave the bar sooner than I would have perhaps and her boss for ordering the sign put out if she wasn't lying and the rain also because if there had been more customers maybe the man wouldn't have paid so much attention to me and Marjorie to him and just my deteriorating eyes in general and small savings in particular and Brahms and whatever and whoever influenced him to compose that piece and why not while I'm at it the jukebox manufacturer and whatever brought me into the world besides, plus lots of other things: in general the world, in particular the whatever. No reading to very little for a few days though when I have to I'll strain my eyes and give in for as long as I can to the pain. No: first thing tomorrow after the quicker-than-usual postreveille rituals and no *Times*, and if the optician says he can't have them till next week, insist you want them fixed by the end of the day at the latest since your work depends on it, and if he still says he can't have them, acquiesce, though tell him day after Tuesday is out of the question and you'll have to take them somewhere else, which you'll then have to.

"Well, so long," the man says.

"Offer to talk's still open you know," I say.

"What for? I don't buy anyone drinks."

"Now that you asked, I'm not sure. No place to go but home right now I suppose, not that a lot of people wouldn't be happy with just that. But because I haven't another pair of these"—putting them in their case—"I can't really read and don't feel"—putting the case into my coat pocket—"like going to bed yet and—oh shoot," my fingers going through a soggy part of the napkin in my pocket, "I still have the pâté," and I take out the napkin, lick my fingers where they touched it—"Excuse me a second"—don't see a garbage can around, thinking of throwing it into the street, wrap the pâté up tight in the napkin and put it back into my pocket—"but maybe I will when I get home."

"What was that in your hand?"

"Some pâté inside from a party."

"That napkin? Give it here."

I do. He throws it into the street. Pâté stays inside.

"You shouldn't have done that." I get it out of the street.

"What are you doing? This is Pig Avenue. Some of my closest associates are garbagemen and the ones who work this route all tell me that. Pig Avenue we're standing on, and that at the corner going into it is Pig Street."

"I don't like contributing to the mess, what can I say?"

"Then give it back. I don't mind contributing. Everyone else is a pig, why not us?"

"If I gave it back I'd still be—"

"Then put it in your pocket and squash it without knowing it and send your coat to the cleaners for ten bucks and still not get out the stain."

"I'll find a garbage can one of these nights."

"Good for you. But bed? You were saying something before about bed? You're still too young to climb into one alone, or young enough after you got old enough to go to bed alone. Get yourself a chickie for the night or what's considered life. I've had them—plenty, too many, but you don't have to believe that and presumably won't. But five wives and a child from each of them, none of whom—wives or kids—want to see their boo-boozing me-thuselahing ex-husband and pop, if you'll allow me such verbal abuse, for I'm obviously with a very cultured man. And now I'm too old to remember what I was saying to you, so I'm finding a cop and going back with him to retrieve my lawful bar seat and maybe create a trifle more excitement in that godawful boring place," and starts downtown again. He stops at the corner, hand holding the hat to his head, waits for some cars to pass or light to change. Light changes and cars stop at the crosswalk but he goes down the sidestreet and once past the corner building is out of sight.

"Out of my way, you dumb humpky," I hear him say. "I've had a tough enough night for one drunk and also don't have a cent to my name."

Derelict comes out of the sidestreet looking back at what I assume is the man. Sees me and limps over. Has shoes. "Say you—"

"No really, wish I could help, have a good night," turning my back on him.

"Same to you and God bless you," and I say to him "Same to you and God bless you too," and go, uptown, thinking I had that last guy wrong all right and that I haven't said God bless you to anyone for many years except occasionally when someone sneezed, when in front of me I'd say a couple of blocks away there's this metal and glass crash: two cars, two trucks and a car or something like that, though I doubt a motorcycle or bike was in the crash because of the type of loud tire shrieks and all that shattered glass, and right after I hear it I throw my arms up to my eyes and spin around shoulder slightly raised so with my arms it also protects my face and see the panhandler looking as if oblivious to the noise stopping a woman who's peering past me to where the sound of the crash was and maybe what she now sees: a car aflame, smoke or human torch in the street, turns to him as if she didn't see anything unordinary and unlatches her shoulder bag. I turn around and don't see or hear anything but what I'd think would be normal vehicular traffic for this weather, time and day, though one person is leaning out of a second-story window in the direction of the crash.

"What was that crash?" the woman says.

"Something smashed, dear?" he says. "The ears. They don't hear from anywheres faraway." His hand's out. She puts in it a pamphlet from her shoulder bag and says "Do you mind if I speak frankly, sir?"

"Speak the way you please, dear. I'm a scandal, I'm a dungheap."

"Not whatsoever. But in this small tract are the world's wisest and most helpful words—"

"That's so, dear?" turning it around and over several times, walking away reading it and saying while his finger jabs the air "Mat, flap, trap, frat, aspeduty three, crap tract four, roger, roger." She sees me looking, I turn thinking "That's so" for "That's true" might be better I think, in a few seconds she's behind me saying "Pardon me, sir, but may I interest you in a timely article on why we're here eternally and what we've to expect?"

"Sure, if just for a minute, but you get around, right, so you've any idea why there are so many derelicts, panhandlers and crazies on the street tonight?"

"I believe it's every day; they've let them all out. But if you're concerned about them, you'll be concerned about this." She gives me a pamphlet. I look at it, say "I broke my glasses before so I'll have to get to it later," fold it to put away, she opens it in my hand and says "I neglected to mention," and points to the price on the cover. "My eyes again," and I give her a quarter, she already has out my dime change, I say "Really, I'm sure it'll go to a good cause," she says "We're taught to get what we're paid for too," I say "Truth is I can probably use the dime for a call later on," and put it into my pocket and she says "Good, already you're rewarded and I am by your having been. But as an added reward to us both, promise you'll read the cover article which continues on pages nine and twelve. It's a warning, from God Almighty, and is perfectly written, no zigzaggy ideas, and ministers to all, rich or poor, sick or well. If there are any questions about it or life that trouble you, there's a telephone hotline which you can use anytime of the day with your dime, or night"—she turns the pamphlet over and points to the number and address—"and this center to come to for a twice-daily meeting of our society and a free hot lunch."

"That's very generous, but it seems—what is this word, 'Brooklyn'?—a little out of my way."

"If you need a ride, we've the Bible bus. Door to door, no fare and always a seat and a very congenial group of passengers aboard and nothing required inside the center but decorum."

"Thanks again. I'll think about it, really. Goodnight." I put the pamphlet into my coat pocket and pull out of the same pocket the notebook and from my pants my pen. It's just, well, more accurate vernacular and suitable for that section of his poem: "That's true that the universe or burst goes slow while we trump and rump along so fast, but aren't we all or almost trying to make up or do for our own undivined lust time? Oh Hasenai, paltry maker of mephitic fishy poems when you would rather be or could like your dada or older breaders who trained you a rather rich unsolipsistic baker of fish-filled bisquits and pungent buns, crucify those last lines," though I don't know about the additional rhymed links or any of them in that linkage of lines. Not in the original for sure. Change it. Keep it. Rearrange it. "Thanks you very much," the woman says to another man she stopped when he let the pamphlet she gave him fall out of his hand, and she picks it up, blows on it and goes. Just think about it then but jot it down now so you don't forget and send Jun an aerogram asking if all these liberties with his work will be all right. But he's already said in a recent Christmas card something like "Do your damndest bestest, Misty Dan, and then some and once more again my favoritest friend who isn't a fabulist or Japanese, and then any way you sayest dost goes, even to the deez and doze. Hey, I play with your linguini also but not too well, so what about that Joe? And here convey big season's greetings much too early I know, but Christmas has become a temporal event in Japan also and the post lines in the ensuing weeks are the one lines I want to avoid."

I write in the notebook "That's so for that's true in <u>Last One in is Out, Jun the Souring Shout—Let's Croak</u>, antepen stanz, and call mom, see and be with her too, and don't just says, damn yous, dooz!"

Sirens—police, fire or ambulance—heading my way though not necessarily to the crash. I look, still nothing, stop at a florist's a half-block up I always seem to stop at down here for its original window displays on seasonal or topical themes. This one has a row of Pilgrim's buckled shoes on the floor with flowers and earth in them and ceiling track-lights highlighting each one. The quick slide changes behind it, from a projector I can't see but believe is behind the screen, are of the various stages of a turkey: from two mating, to the birth of one, I close my eyes to the slides of a headless turkey running around, to one roasted and dressed on a festive table. Most of the shoe flowers I've seen but can't name though once made an effort to. Exotic, must be from more Southern states at this time—perhaps the florist's birthplace—or else I don't get the point. Obsequial? Delphiniums: think that's them. In the next shoe some sort of orchid: lady's nose, girlie's big toe, something close. Someone once started to teach me about them and trees and birds and their songs and leaves, but who? Yes, effort, once did, forgot or got stopped by that old chainsmoking translator what was his name, died of a long-windedly named kidney disease a month ago. Saw the obit and photo. Two columns and a sampler and appreciation of his work and list of the many writers he'd translated and often almost recomposed. Always a relatively poor and brusque though noble and articulate polyhistoric fellow. Loved Iceland for its cheap airfares, migratory birds and heroic prose. His name though. Slivern? Slappern? Slade? Once heard him read at the Y and nearly had to leave because it was in that last-leg delivery so many poets seem to favor when his real voice, when it wasn't raucous before or after an outpour of cigarette coughs, was sonorous and strong. Like something unguent oozing through, but I was never adept at similes or even much esteemed their use. "A good simile," Hasenai says in his poem "Look Alike," which if I don't find one weaker will be the weakest of all the poems I choose, "is like a computer readout compared to an acceptance letter, meaning rhyme and poetry are better and like acceptance letters can't be written on a word-processing machine, or so it seems to me." Deep forehead crease he once in an unusually puckish mood hid a toothpick in or two, but how's it possible I forgot his of all translators' names? Snipper, Switter, Stade? Drove a red Rambler I remember with its fenders held together by picture-framing wire and with no reverse or door handles outside or in. "Jump over," he'd say when he drove us to our walks, or open the door on my side with a screwdriver and I'd sit on what looked like hay. Invariably cigarette ashes on his lap, vest and sleeves, which is such a characteristic cliché, and which he never—and this too—seemed to notice or whisk away, so they'd just float off or fall. And gaunt, worn, tall, with thick rich brown hair, which several people said he dyed, but he was never vain in that way, and close-cropped, and never in need of a shave. "I look like a toy goy in a boy's play convertible," he said, "but I doubt they ever fabricated one with a ravaged backseat replete

with Flemish newspapers, Praenestine glossary, field guides, Audubon post-
cards and Low Franconian journals." And tweeds. Even at breakfast at the
colony I met Diana at several years later and where I started to accompany him
on what he called his "quotedium post-scrambled egg and prune juice prome-
nade." And a tie. Rumpled, same one, college stripes and soup spots, shirt
collars he ironed without removing the stays. Must remember to attend his
memorial service at Columbia next week. Heard that many of the serious East
Coast translators will be there instead of anything resembling a family. Lived
alone, in a two-room Bronx apartment over a Syrian bakery which before that
made bialys and before that Irish sodabread, "which tells you how long I've
lived there and what rent I pay, place always toasty, except on the respective
Sabbaths, even when it was a cold-water flat." Because he refused to teach,
which almost he alone of us got offers to, saying he was as driven to translate
poetry as his poets were in delaying to create them, no students at the service
except maybe a few who might have read him and venerated his dedication
and work. A number of those other translators are what's been discouraging
me from going though I'll go, but not to talk about possible literature positions
anyone might know of at some not-too-distant school and the latest translating grants and awards which Switch, it is, Simon Oliver Stritch, in fact, often
got, though far as I know never went to memorials, literary functions and
parties to make contacts and get references and inside dope, but what is it I
started out to say? Right. Stritch urged me to hold off any but the most
utilitarian interest in fauna and flora till I got to around his age and had
nothing better to do with my nontranslating time than take trips to bird and
seal sanctuaries and go on long art colony nature-walks. He even, after a
while, wouldn't let me accompany him on one and also checked out every
colony library book on the subjects, so much did he want me to finish a large
body of work before I was forty when he said most promising translators get
restless and tired and need to get permanent addresses and partners and,
because of their sinking incomes and no eventual pensions, comparatively
easy tenure-track teaching jobs. "Send me your next book," he said when I last
saw him, which I did and then another copy care of his publisher, but he never
acknowledged receipt. On both I wrote my inscription for that time: "From
the poets and me or I," and added a lie: "To the contemporary master of us all,"
hoping he wouldn't see through the compliment and that he'd write back he
essentially liked my translation and would do what he could to get it reviewed
and in the future boost my work and grant chances and maybe even help me
get a university appointment or let me know of an opening of one, but why

couldn't I remember his name? Shame maybe, that I also thought to use him. More likely some different kind of slip, one with lots of answerable or to some people logical problematical possibilities predicated on something I don't quite understand now though as far as I'm concerned—But what do I mean by logical possibilities, if I didn't mean probabilities, or even answerable or problematical or possible or predicational ones? And how can I defend "different kind of slip" when I know damn well when it comes down to it—What I mean is that when I get to the deepest truth of it or something like that the possibility can't be, what? Just drop this or go back a bit. Shame. That I forgot his name. Simon Oliver something or another—oh shit, can't believe it— spit, slip, snit, shift, Stritch.

"Like a nice flower, mister?" boy's voice behind me. I turn. Foot shorter, slim, around fourteen, dark-skinned, seems like black hair, olive skin more like it, Mideastern, smiling, insincerely, continuously, tiny chipped front teeth, gypsy could be, seen plenty but much more aggressively and usually choosing to go after a man holding a woman's hand or two men doing the same, holding out to me a carnation and I say "No thanks, just window-shopping."

"Yes, from me," and sticks it in my hand, closes my fingers around the stem, "Looks nice," and I say "Christs, what do I do with you?" and he says "Buy it," and I say "Maybe just to get rid of you," and think quarter? two? and he says "A dollar please."

"A dollar please? Thought you were giving them away at first, though figured pretty quickly once it came back to me what city I was still in that— forget it. I've really nothing against this city. Don't want to make generalizations about it either and no doubt because this city doesn't make it easy to make them, though I knew soon enough I'd have to cough up something to you, but a buck?"

"No, not giving—selling. Beautiful red rose. One no more anywhere like it in the city. True. You shake no but flower is fresh, like new. Smell it."

"I know what it smells like. And it's a beautiful red carnation—at least one of those in the caryo I think it is family—and not wilted but certainly not new. But okay. Let me smell one again. I can use a big lift." I sniff. Nothing much. Harder. I smell car and bus exhaust. Even deeper. Trace of burnt coffee from someplace, but didn't May say that was toxic to noxious petrochemical fumes drifting over the ridge and river from New Jersey's gasworks? "Gorgeous. Never smelt a flower that smelt so much like a flower before. Seriously, I've a cold in my nose, but thanks," and I try giving it back to him.

"No, true. Brand-new. And cost me not a dollar each but close."

"Come on, kid, what do you take me for? This is my city. I used to shine shoes on these streets when I was half your age, but only in the daytime."

"So what do you say to me this for?"

"So what am I saying?" He nods. "I'm saying, you work this late, it's not healthy for a kid your age. I'm also saying, up and down Brooklyn's biggest boulevards I went with my wooden shoeshine box my dad made me pay him back for on time payments, so I'm saying I've known the price of things and value of a nickel and dime. So if you paid twenty-five cents, I'm saying finally, for one of these flowers, it was a lot, not that I'm saying anything bad or angry against you, remember that."

"No, wrong. Ten dollars a dozen to me. Maybe I was cheated, because they tell me where they sell them that Mexico flower fields where they grow are drowned by rain all year. Still, give it to a beautiful lady. Wish her on it. She make you her first mate."

"Now that's what I'd like, no horsing around there, but not a dollar. Let's say fifty cents, since you sure ain't looking at a pile of money, my friend. And just for the smell and to have held it, because right after I pay I'll give it back for you to sell to someone else."

"No, you pay for, you keep. That's the fair bargain, so a dollar," and smiling again he sticks out his hand. Hungarian or Basque or even Berber letters though familiar numbers except for what looks like an upside-down nine are tattooed on his palm.

"What language is that?"

"Of what?" Closes his hand.

"Those letters and numbers mean anything? No harm in telling me. Numbers aren't, except for at the top and bottom of pages, but written words are my business."

"You want to know?" Opens his palm, presses it over his right eye and closes the left eye. His smile widens. Carious too. Lights flash off them, move. From streetlights, headlights. "They say things only my people know."

"And what's that and who are they?"

"Plenty." Presses the same palm against his left eye and closes the right. "Always many different things to many different people on many different times of the nights and days of the years in the ways only we have in our heads of telling, so only we can say. But they go back thousands before the Roman and Etruscan gods, and no two messages in all time to any two people or to the same person the same." Takes his hand away, right eye stays closed. "You pay for what it will say to you, only one more dollar, and I am allowed to tell."

"You're not saying what language it is then?"

"I haven't said? Our own. But what people me and my language is from I can only say for that one more dollar, so two."

"Your people have a poetry?"

"One we talk to only to ourselves and the wise wings of the night and the wolves."

"You mean real wolves in whatever country you and your language come from, and those wise night-wings are owls?"

"I mean no poetry but what is written into our hands and heads, like everything else in our language. Newspapers. Whole-day tales. You think that funny?" He opens his eye.

"I'm not laughing, I'm listening. This smile's my regular look."

"So, also my aunt's books for cooking too. In the hand and head. Everything. Some on and on on their arms when these words go on too long. Histories. Travels. Lives. But you pay this hand," which is out again with the letters and numbers on it, "two dollars, one for your message for which and other the language of what and who they are from."

"Just for the message." I give him a dollar. "I think I've memorized enough of the language on your hand to find out which one it is."

"Never unless I tell you. But fifty cents more for the flower or language and people then. I'll do that now. I want to get home soon."

"Really, I'm just about broke." I give the flower to him and he drops it into a shopping bag with other flowers. "It's ruined now, you should pay, but okay. Now for your dollar." He looks at that palm. "Tonight's November Twenty-something in your language. I know what day of. Friday. By us, a special alone dog day, one where the tail is down and can't wag. But you've how much age?"

"Forty-two. No, I had a birthday, July. -three."

"And you lived many years here you said since your shoeshine box a half a boy my age ago, even if I guess now and then you moved. Say it's not true."

"Is true."

"That's all I must know. Not your father's name, not your mother's." Closes his eyes, presses that palm to his ear, mumbles, opens his eyes on the palm. "It says for you this night in the city you were once very young in that you will stay young in for a while and will stay here for years and make it to be a big long life for a long time, but for now these next five weeks you will make or one time soon—let me count. One, two, three," with his eyes closed and opens them on his palm. "Make the one, love, two, lot but not that lot of money, and three, keep the head and body strength you have if you still want it to do what work you like to and do best and succeed. But, it says, you must look and good and hard for all three in these next five weeks and not stop till you find, for they will not come out to look and find you. You know what all that means? I don't so much. I only repeat what I read and now unless you remember it, is gone."

"That's it?"

"Not enough?"

"No, more than I ever hoped for."

"For you don't like it, I give your dollar back, because I don't know what else you could wish for. Life forever? That goes for nobody, but if someone like me reads it in his palm for you or says 'Never sickness,' tell him he lies."

"Really, it's okay," when he puts his hand in the pocket he put the dollar in. "I thought you were great."

"Neh, maybe there's more. I don't want you to be unhappy with me or think I'm lazy and maybe left some for you behind." Holds his palm up to his nose and shakes it. Puts it to his forehead and closes his eyes and his lashes start fluttering. Makes a fist, opens it, closes it, opens, closes, opens and opens his eyes, lashes stop fluttering, and looks at it. "If anything is hiding in there it needs sometimes to shake it apart or unlock." Holds his fist to his ear, says "Wait, I hear, it's getting closer—here it is I think," and looks at his palm. "Yes. And it still says it won't be easy what that message from my hand and head called out to you, but it gives words of advice how to go out and get them and again in numbers of three. One, be not as strong as young teeth, not as weak as old bones, not as quick as quick lips with swift tongues, but someplace inside each of these: easy and hard, fast and slow, throw and catch, the in-between." He looks up. "That's all I can say. Even for many more dollars from you, because all there was of the message I read. Now I must go. Time is late. I'm not afraid, but sisters and mother who wait up for me are. And you don't want beautiful red flower, others along the way might. Goodnight," and he picks up the shopping bag and goes. "Night," and get home safe if home's where you're going, though bet he can handle himself on the street better than I, and take out my notebook to write down the letters and numbers that were on his palm, but have forgotten everything but a reverse S and the upside-down nine.

Uptown. Shoes and socks seem nearly dry. Shoeshine box. Bit of a lie. Went out a number of times with one my father bought originally for the home, though he wasn't against me trying to make some money on the street and I was probably around twelve. Said I had to be home before dark and if I broke any part of the box I had to pay for it and also for the shoeshining supplies. But almost everyone I shined for said I gave a lousy shine and most didn't tip and a few wouldn't pay the dime. Smeared and maybe stained too many socks and skin and cuffs above them with shoe polish and a few men said something like "You know what the cost of a new pair of socks is compared to this stinking shine?" Soon gave up shining with that box except at home for my uncles and parents' friends, though free for my father, and later for myself and my father when he was in bed convalescing or in his wheelchair eating or watching TV and I'd take a few pairs of his shoes out of his closet shoe rack and say "Just doing it because the leather's cracking and for when you'll be up and around wearing them again," and in front of him also to have something to do in front of him gave them a good shine.

I go over to two attached pay-phones. Receiver of one hangs by its cord below the shelf. Other's on its stirrup and I lift it. Operational tone so so far the phone's fine. I put my dime in and wait for the dial tone. None comes. Dial? Don't. I start to, stop. But what I got at first was probably the dial tone, even if the sign on the phone says to wait for the operational tone before putting a dime in. I punch out the remaining numbers. Man's recorded voice says "Your phone requires a ten-cent deposit before dialing. Please hang up and—" I hang up. Coin's not returned. I press the coin-return lever and coin comes. Other phone? Something tells me the odds are better with this one, and my coin was returned. I try again. Same thing. Same man's voice imparting self-confidence, forbearance, anyone can make a mistake, next time please try to read the instruction plate first, I am a man who makes his living through his diction and believable tone, lever repeatedly, coin comes. I leave the receiver hanging below the shelf, lift the receiver of the other phone and press its stirrup. Dial or operational tone, dime in, dialing dial tone, punch out the numbers to my mother's home. Phone's ringing. Most people I wait a minimum of four rings. My mother, because she might be resting or sleeping or on her breathing machine any time of the day, I usually hang up after the third ring, when she answers with a hello.

"Mom, it's me, how are you? I have to drag you to the phone?"

"Oh, Dan. I was wondering who'd be calling me so late."

"I shouldn't have, right? But I felt I really owed you a call and I tend to forget— Actually I almost never tend to forget, got a memory like a you-know-what, but thought you might be up because you've said your hours are so erratic. But did I get you out of bed or from any place inconvenient? Because if you hadn't answered after the third ring—"

"It's all right, and good hearing your voice. How are you too? You sound fine. We have no heat you know."

"Because it's past eleven?"

"Because we never had heat. For two days. On Thanksgiving, imagine?"

"Thanksgiving? Yesterday? Christ—never called to see what you were doing."

"I went to your cousin Bernard's and Dotty's as I usually do. They again asked if they should invite you but I told them you'd never come. They picked me up and sent me home by hired car."

"That was very nice of them. How are they?"

"Fine and their kids are wonderful. You eat out last night?"

"Nope. Bought a thick veal steak and a good bottle of bock for the occasion. But your heat."

"Boiler oil shouldn't run out. Not at the average old age of the tenants in this building. It's the landlord who should run and keep running till we never see him again. I wish it weren't so, but sometimes everything people I don't normally listen to say about landlords turns out to be true."

"You used to speak very highly about the ones who owned the building before the current guy. Mrs. Innerstein for instance."

"She lived in the building so went through what we all did, and think she would jeopardize her cats' health? Cats like a hot place. Maybe the expense of oil today would make even Mrs. In greedy. They say it's regulated by computer, the amount of oil the building needs. But either he's draining our tank to heat his buildings till twelve where the apartments go for more, or he's finagled with the oil company to once a month let the oil run out on the two most freezing days it takes to bring in a delivery. But do I sound too caustic and paranoid? I try not to be, it's unhealthy, but occasionally in this building it's impossible not to. Who knows? Maybe this time the landlord has a pardonable excuse."

"You sound plenty reasonable, so don't worry. It must be very uncomfortable without heat."

"Where you calling from? It sounds like noises on the street."

"A pay phone. I went to a party and was walking home."

"It's safe? You don't want to take a subway at night, but why not a bus or cab?"

"I'm walking to get air."

"You drank too much at the party?"

"Mom, will you stop it? I drank a little. Maybe even more than a little, but I'm all right."

"Thieves see a drunk on the street, they see a target. You have to be careful everyplace today. No matter how big you are, they come at you two and three at a time and can knock and keep any man down. I worry about you alone at night. You're too quick to leap in if you see any trouble. Maybe yesterday that was okay or you'd end up with only a bop on the nose, but today you can get killed. If they start chasing you and they're young, they'll win."

"Believe me, with all the exercising I do I'm even stronger than I was, but I no longer jump in. I'm as wary as the next guy."

"Too much exercise at your age and you could be setting yourself up for a heart condition. You ought to do only light things like yoga."

"Maybe you're right. I'll check into it."

"You're not just saying?"

"No. I'll get a check-up, have a stress test—whatever."

"Good. How long you think we've been on the phone?"

"Three minutes. More?"

"I'm surprised the operator hasn't cut in. Maybe I should call you back before she does."

"Leave it. So we get a break from the phone company for once. But if I know them they'll ring me as soon as I hang up, and if you know me you know I'll pay. But where were we? That you must be very uncomfortable without heat for two days. See how I got a memory?"

"I never doubted. And this time I don't care how good his excuse is, I'm going to a good hotel and charge them for meals and tips too if this lasts another day."

"Don't go to a hotel. My apartment's small. But if it ever came to your being warm or not and you wanted to avoid the hotel cost, you could always stay at my place alone for as long as you want and I'd find someplace else to stay or you could stay there with me."

"On the floor?"

"I'd sleep on the floor or in a chair. It's not bad. I have a sleeping bag, or I'd buy a cot, and I'd come get you."

"Your apartment must be very small. Anyway, thanks but if I didn't go to a hotel I'd go to Bernard's. He also asked me and it's nearer and roomier. Because I can't take the cold, Daniel. Nobody here can. I wore three sweaters and would have worn a fourth if I had one. Get me a good wool cardigan for Christmas if you're thinking of buying me anything. I never asked you for a gift before, but that's what I need and I don't know when I'll have the time to look for a good one. What do you need?"

"For Christmas? Nothing."

"For anytime what do you need? Don't say socks."

"It's true, socks I can always use. Socks and size thirty-two jockey briefs, next style up from what they call bikini, but not white."

"They show the stain, I know."

"I told you? Or you're getting very bold."

"You did tell me after I gave you several pairs of white. Black or red, right?"

"Any dark solid color. Size thirty-two or thirty-four. I can get into both. For some reason thirty-two stretches to a thirty-four and thirty-four doesn't to a thirty-six. Maybe I'm a thirty-four and don't want to admit it."

"Get measured."

"Let's just say thirty-four."

"I already have it. Regular dark solid-colored jockey briefs but not the old-man kind, preferably thirty-three if they carry odd sizes, and no artificial materials in them except in the elastic band. Same with the socks? Not the knee-high kind and I know no whites, but what about argyles? They used to be your favorite."

"In college. But anything. Cotton or wool or a wool blend, they're all fine. White too, don't bother yourself about what kind, but not all-nylon if you can avoid it of any design."

"Like dad used to wear."

"I find them itchy and ugly."

"You still have his after all these years?"

"The last pair's just wearing out."

"Dad also didn't spend much on clothes, but look how those socks lasted and some of them didn't come to you new. Six years."

"I thought eight."

"Six. I waited two years before I gave away any of his clothes. You thought that peculiar."

"Not peculiar."

"Peculiar, peculiar. You wanted me to throw them on the street or give them to Goodwill, but I couldn't till after two years. And you finally took his socks and also his bathrobes, and those robes were Viyella, expensive but durable and warm. I bet you still have them."

"You can't wear them out."

"I bought them for him. But let's not talk about it anymore if you don't mind. You're not too cold where you're calling from?"

"I've a coat. One thing before I forget. What color cardigan?"

"Something bright. Blue heather or heather blue. Or a pretty shade in the red family. Red makes me feel warm when it's cold. And size thirty-eight. Cardigans have to be loose."

"Good. But you feel fine otherwise and there'll be heat by tomorrow?"

"This going to be a much longer call? I'm enjoying it, but the operator not coming in worries me. And you didn't just call to say you'd be stopping by tomorrow or the next day for dinner and then got carried away with all this clothes talk?"

"You want me for dinner tomorrow?"

"It's been a long time, not that I want to coerce you."

"No, I want to. Tomorrow."

"We could make it the following day."

"No, tomorrow."

"Good—around five. What should I prepare?"

"If you're giving me a choice, fish would be fine. Simple—broiled. I could pick it up on the way."

"You can't get fresh fish where you are like we get here. But I was thinking of a roast chicken if not a meatloaf. I have both in the freezer and one of these days soon I have to defrost it."

"I don't like roast chicken—maybe the only thing of yours I don't. The idea of it, looking like something I don't want to be reminded of. I know it's my problem, but I'm sorry."

"I'll cut it up. The carcass will be gone before you get here."

"Fine then, for what am I going on about?—chicken. I liked it best when you boiled it I think and then I don't know what you did with the parts— baked or broiled them plain with a little paprika and a single onion slice on top. Just don't make a big deal. Don't bake pies. Don't start cooking early tomorrow morning."

"Why not? If there's no heat to very little, it'll keep the place warm."

"I'll bring the wine and bread."

"Only for you to drink—my system can't take it. I only have my vodka or two and that's sufficient. Are we going to speak another minute or more?"

"If you want to. It must be freezing sitting there."

"I have a bathrobe and blanket around me, so I'm almost warm. Another of dad's robes you said was ugly, but this one, and am I grateful, you didn't take. The heater's on too, so it's not that bad. I complain way too much. But what was I saying? Nothing. And I hate the operator interrupting, so if we are going to speak a while longer, give me your number and I'll call back."

"You have to be sure you want to."

"I do. I'm feeling very peppy tonight and I love it."

"You have a pen?"

"I have a memory."

"Two-four-three, ninety-one twelve."

"Don't let anyone take the phone from you. It might get too cold for me waiting if they do. But if you don't hear from me in a minute it means I forgot your number, so phone back. Bye, dear." Hangs up. Phone rings a few seconds later.

"Mom?"

"The operator. There's a ten-cent overtime charge on your last phone call."

"You never came in and told us."

"If one of us didn't, that's an error on our part, but I have registered here an overtime charge of ten cents."

"I only have a quarter."

"We'll reimburse you by mail."

"It'll cost you a twenty-cent stamp, so really wouldn't be worth it, and I am expecting a call. In fact probably owe you twenty to thirty-cents overtime for the time I talked." I put in the quarter. "Thank you, ma'am," and she says "Have a nice day," and I hang up. Phone rings several seconds later.

"Hello?"

"Where were you? I asked you not to let anyone use the phone. I also got worried thinking something was wrong—a fight in the booth and the phone turned upside down. Crazy, huh?"

"It was the operator. A bargain: only wanted a dime. But what else is new with you? How's Goldie?"

"Actually, I am suddenly feeling tired, Daniel, so just tell me how your life is going in other ways, if you don't want to save it till tomorrow, and then I'll have to say goodnight."

"I'll tell you everything tomorrow."

"You meet anyone at the party you were at?"

"There were plenty of interesting people there."

"You know what I mean. Because you should. I don't want you to be alone all your life. I hope you're at least still looking."

"I haven't been alone. I've known many women."

"A year here, six months there. You're alone now. And that last one, May. She was very nice, and sweet to me as they come, but for too long I knew she wasn't your type and you weren't hers and that it was a lost cause from the start."

"Funny, but I didn't think so. And it is strange you ask about tonight, since I did meet someone."

"Bring her along tomorrow."

"I only met her briefly."

"We can postpone dinner a day or two. You get her number?"

"I'll be calling her. Anyway, it's too early to talk about and surely too early to invite her for dinner with you."

"Why? If a woman likes you, nothing's too early. You once called me a lighthouse, so listen to the light. If you call her early tomorrow, say you're going to your mother's for the first time in months and would she like to come along. That way she won't from the start think you're a momma's boy, which you're not. And when she does see us together she'll like the idea of someone being so joking and outspoken with his mother, and if she's from out of town the idea of going to a good family dinner way out here might appeal to her too. A lot of people have heard of this neighborhood and think it's special."

"She's from the city. Anyway, I want to see you alone so we can talk."

"What will we say that we haven't tonight?"

"My work. What you've been doing. Politics. Plenty."

"How is your work going?"

"Fine. But tomorrow. Anything else I can bring? In fact I know exactly what. An electric blanket."

"You have one?"

"Two. Could you use the extra?"

"They're supposed to keep you warm for relatively little electricity, so if it's not your only working one."

"I don't have one good or bad but I'll get you one tomorrow. I knew you'd say no if I said I'd buy it."

"I don't need one."

"I'm bringing it, but ripping up the label and receipt before I get there."

"Then you should have kept me fooled. The whole thing was too calculating for you."

"Come on, will you, that's what I am."

"No you're not. Think more highly of yourself. When it comes to qualities— But before we hang up, what's this new woman's name?"

"Helene, but for who-knows-what reasons she might not want to see me or be able to for weeks or months. It's happened. So enough about her unless something materializes, since I don't want to be explaining for the next year about what ever happened to this woman."

"She'll want to see you. If she gave you her number, she will, and I bet in a hurry, and she'll take to you too. Everyone does."

"You're my mother, so you're saying this. And the truth is I think I sometimes need that kind of talk, much as I go out of my way to say I don't. But don't get your hopes up there'll be any new woman in my life. What I'm saying is that if I was really feeling bad about myself now, which I'm not, then I'd say that if there's any way to ruin it with any new woman I meet, you can be sure I'll do it instinctively or find out how."

"Then I shouldn't get out my chiffon gown yet, that it? As you wish. Goodnight, dear."

"Wait. Oh jeez. I sound like a moron sometimes, don't I?"

"No. Who said so?"

"Then I didn't make you feel awful just then?"

"No, and you didn't plan to, did you? So stop worrying. But I am very tired, so I hope to see you tomorrow. Thanks for calling."

"Thanks for what?" but she's hung up.

Walking up Sixth I think I shouldn't have said a lot of the things I said to her about myself and also should have told her of something I read in the paper this week about how anyone seventy-five or seventy and older shouldn't have his room thermostat set lower than seventy or seventy-five degrees. Which? She's over and her apartment temperature's much lower, but over seventy on the thermostat for anyone under or over any age other than for someone, let's say, seventy to seventy-five days or ill in a number of different ways sounds too high. Maybe I'm wrong about that, but the reasons the article writer gave for the warning were something about the gradual deterioration and collapse—but I'd only be making up most of that about the effects on the various body organs and tracts. But something like "Contrary to current scientific and popular layman belief and recent federal guidelines for residential and office buildings' air conditioning and heat, any temperature lower over a prolonged period. . . acute hypothermia. . . very elderly and infirmed. . ."

I haven't another coin. Easily enough achieved, considering the mission, but what would she say? "Please—the *government*—let me sleep." No, that's what she'd think. She'd say "What is it, darling, something you forgot to say that couldn't wait?" I'd say "Damn, woke you up again," and she'd say "Anyone else I might mind, but I'm sure coming from you it's for a good reason," since she knows I want nothing more for her than to be healthy and safe. Content too, of course, but there's just so much an only alone son with a weighty workload and in another borough and with a welter of excuses and all those outside willful and fortuitous abuses can do. Damn landlords sometimes. Damn city. Damn geographical location, figmental extrapolation. Damn countries and oil and gas companies and international bickering and national trickstering and so on. Too tangled for me to understand. My damn density and dumb damnedness sometimes too, and all right for me to dig-in during this kind of crisis, but my mother? I don't want her going to—

Car shrieks, startling me. Pedestrian almost hit. Leg inches away from the bumper, exhibiting her fist. Standing in front of the cab at the corner, fist shaking, pigtails waving, boot raised to boot the bumper, stumps the ground. "You shit." Cabby waits, seems to me resignedly. No fare in the cab, for her to finish and go away. Sits back, pushes his hat back, scratches his back, ah that felt good, tugs on his nose and looks behind him, can't back up and then go around her because a truck's there. "You goon," she says. Records on his clipboard. Let me see: Fiftieth to Broome and West Broadway, next pickup on Prince to Greenwich and Sixth— Truck honks, he points in front and honks back. You back up, then I can back up, because she won't back up, and we can both go. "You dope. Yes, dopo, moronico, maniaco, cause you won't be happy till you run over some poor dildo which you've no doubt done a hundred and 0 times before. At least say the fuck you're sorry." It'd seem he was in the right, had the light, maybe driving too fast, that I didn't see, but she was walking against it. Light turns red for him. "Suck," and smacks his hood and crosses the street. He opens his window, wouldn't I love to with you honey, hell with her, closes it, truck and cars behind him honk. Raises his arms without turning around: what do you want me to do, be as dumb as that broad and run the light? Lights up a pipe and puffs on it. Match must have stayed lit where he threw it on the floor, for he suddenly ducks below the dashboard. Green, cars honk, trucker just shakes his head not believing this, cabby pops up, oh the light, what do you think but the light? honks, beeps, from farther down the street my dog has fleas, makes a left, truck and cars behind him, where was I? Woman seems stoned. Nursing home. Don't want my mom in one. Shaking her fist or waving a kerchief at the cab as it passes, for my eyes can't focalize from so far. Her getting chronically sicker and weaker, one of my worst fears. Like my dad his last two years: incontinent, sometimes defecating in bed, "Looked like afterbirth," my mother once said, "Bedsores muffins could fit in," nothing she or the visiting nurses could do about them, her worst fears too.

How could we afford it for one thing? Not foremost but one. For another I just don't want her in one of those homes even if we could afford it or through Medicare or -caid, whichever gives the applicable aid, nor do I ever want to visit her in one, though if she had to be there I of course would. But what would we do or say? Walk her around the halls, sit in the solarium sun, how's the food, what'd you do today? Me, what could I be doing here that's new? Nothing's new. Please drop me in the nearest grave. "Whatever you do," she once told me, "don't stick me in one of those old-age places. I didn't to your father, and he never even asked me not to. Fact is he told me to do what was easiest for me with him, but what could I do but help while I still had my strength and health, and taking care of him I also have to admit gave me something very useful and engrossing to do and improve on. The second most urgent thing I'm asking you to do if you can't the first is just before you send me to one, give me all the sleeping pills you can lay your hands on that it'll take to kill me in one night. You won't have to be home. Just give me them and say goodnight and I'll take them alone." I told her not to think or say such things and she almost screamed at me that she was serious so what was I going to do? I told her I'd have to think it over and she said "Think about it quick—one never knows." I said "Why, is there something about your health you just found out that I don't know?" and she said "No, it's up and down as ever, but let's be realistic—at my age and condition anything can go to pot overnight," and a week later phoned and said "You remember what I asked you about promising me something extremely important to do?" and I said "No, wait, what, afraid I forgot, sorry, but how are you?" and she said "You remember— you got a head screwed on you tighter than a vise and certainly for something like that, but maybe we should drop it till you tell me you remember or want me to help retrieve your memory for you—do you?" and I said "Sure, if that's what you want, but better another day, because right now—well, I had to have a translation in by noon if I wanted to get paid, so I stayed up all night and am now feeling sick from it besides very tired—anyway, how are you?" and she told me how she was and Goldie and Ray and that was the last time she spoke to me about sleeping pills.

I wait for the light. Other night I dreamed. Car beeps, big-dog barks from far off, someone scraping a metal garbage can along the sidewalk, waterlogged car transmission squeaks. Of my mother and jarring that dream, as I start to cross the street.

"Watch it," a man says, Walkman wires in his ears, running against traffic and nearly clipping me.

"You should've," I yell and he gives me the finger as he runs. "At least get a bell. And if you do, ding the damn thing, you dumb id—," because he still has his finger in the air, but forget it. In one and out if he can even hear me and why start trouble? He could come back, but being a runner I doubt it, as others have when I went on too long. Light's green. What was it I dreamed? Seemed important, one with both my folks. Jolted me out of sleep and kept me sitting up and thinking about it till I thought it had seeped in deep enough for me to go back to sleep and bring it back easily when I woke for the day. Often told myself to keep a pen and pad— Anyway, the dream. She'd locked herself in the bathroom. "My hair is white," she said through the door, "overnight," when in real life it's steel gray. And something about her bones pushing through her face. "My weight's down to seventy-eight"—her age? "My back's so bent I can never again stand straight. I just saw my image in the light." Apartment was dark. Crack under the door showed the bathroom was black. "Don't stare at me," she screamed from behind the closed door. Maybe she was talking to herself. "I'm ancienter and mangier than our goldanged race," though at the time I felt she was talking to me. I said something like "Get yourself something to read, Ma, that's all you need. I'll find a good book if you open the door." Good book could be the Bible but what would that or the rest of what I said mean? We were never a religious family. Ceremonial dinners once or twice a year and inexact observances of the high holy days. They let me fast for a day and skip school those holidays because the other Jewish kids did. But it wasn't till my sister got very sick that she put a cloth napkin on her head once a week and lit memorial candles and mumbled a prayer. Bible at funeral? I tried the doorknob but it was locked. "Don't! I'll open it at my own speed." Knob turned from the inside and door creaked open an inch. Creaking part from old ghost movies I saw as a boy and radio mystery shows. *Suspense Presents*—one of those. "Not yet," I said. "Wait till I get you that book." Said that because I was afraid to see her so old, decrepit and sick. In another room my father rose from a coffin on his hospital bed and stretched. He was naked and scrawny, his room dark and stuffy, only a little light from somewhere on him and his hair hung as it never did over his shoulders from only a few places in his head. He released the railing, climbed out of bed and lumbered to me dragging strung bones and a long iron chain. "Drag something imaginative," I said. "And put something on, for crying out loud," and covered my eyes and opened them on him wearing a loincloth opened at his genitals and dragging the bones and chain. In real life he died in his sleep in a hospital gown in a hospital bed in the apartment my mother lives in now. In the dream his testicles were twice their normal size and low-slung and swung as he walked and his penis peed like a horse's. "Come quick," my mother said when I came into their apartment as I did almost every morning to see them and give him his shot and help her in any way I could, "I can't get from dad a single heartbeat or breath." Bathroom door was wide open and there was daylight on her from a bathroom window she doesn't have. Rattling and clanking from the bones and chain got louder. My mother looked as she'd said she would and said to me "Where's your book? Don't lose your eyes. If anyone should be reading," pointing to my father coming into the room completely naked but done peeing, "It's him. Sol, you need a cover. I love you. Sol, you need to be fed and dressed. Your son will assist you, but come to me first, you big clown," and she went to him with her arms out. He spun around once, looked lost, dropped the bones and chain, defecated as he stepped toward her but the excrement which had smeared his thighs and was heaped on the floor, disappeared, fell to one knee and she took him into her arms. His eyes stayed shut through all this. I sniffed hard and wondered how come no shit smell. He was wearing an old bathrobe that I now own. It was open below the waist and his testicles rested on the floor. Scrotum, my thought then, looking like a sleeping white Chinese-porcelain cat squeezed up for warmth. She smiled when she first hugged him, was crying, lips on his brow. His hair was now thick, bouncy and brown. That's all I recall. It could have ended then. Awoke in a sweat, sat up fast. If my mother ever got, how should I put it, incapacitatingly sick or was declared terminal, if declared's the term medical people use, and asked me to take care of her or her doctor did and it was possible for me to, I think I'd do it till I couldn't anymore at her apartment or mine, with a visiting nurse or without, depending what the governments could afford, because what else could I do? I'd work at home while I nursed. Live partly off her Social Security if I couldn't earn enough on my own. That wouldn't be wrong, since I've nothing but a few hundred saved. Maybe for the first time look for book reviews to do if it took that to manage it without dipping into her funds, but ones that pay reasonably well. So it's all resolved? "Mothers grow old and sick, fathers die, I don't like it one bit," Hasenai says in a poem I chose, "but I'll try." I know what he means? Thought so then. If I'm still uncertain tomorrow I'll write Hasenai for advice, since I always make sure to get the author's meant intention if it's anything but pure sound, which in his case I've tried but can't duplicate.

I jot down in my notebook: "Last stanza for clarity's sake 'Old Folks Leaving Home.' Include in collect whatever you do even if it takes phone calls & transpacif cabes to make it precise, & maybe even make concluding poem, since that's how deep you feel about it & good you think it is at least now. Listen. Ambulanc passing op way other emerg vehics passed half hr ago. Just looked but am now back to jot down this nite of Di's part, meeting Helene, snow-rain-umbrel blown out of my hand, woman walking like a sleeping bag, no perf word-words for it so far color Helenes hair, Hel looking at me at her across room and then thumping her umb open on Di's steps, shortorder dwarf no sport intended intentionally reading unrecognizing me on the sub & tho ironic what he read I forget what, dresser-cat feeding on a sock, dont forget dinner with mom tomor 5 & bring elect blank & if poss bot of one of the best foreign vodks, broke-soaked poor guys in Wash Par & tif over unclean fingers was it in class music bar & berber-basque boy or so with wrong roses & now on my way to my apar (cant see exact what streets Im between because my pocketed scarred specs but somewhere in the teens) & falling on my face before & not jus the snowrain (t for the) & jus for t Jun sound of it now my lack also befor of something/another grace (no that didnt work), tho now thinking so jettisonly-clear, wha? & someone on t cot inside & someone in white seated beside & whirling red atop making wet images etc on t st & siren whining moo-mah moo-mop prob like dont say it yl regret it t incoming inpatients heart & for a sec jus now making me recolect t halfdoz emerg times rushed pop to hosp. & my decis about work & nurs mom if disabled or selfunable becaus of her ilness old or new &/or age (o for or) & realization (cdnt think shorter word on t spu o how to contract rlztion) about pure sound when I duplicate in Juns o realy any japanes poets case almos impos to translat, tho aboutface thos at(e)s. So now—tho how you rlly feeling now pal? Huh? Come on, once in yr life, heres yr chanc, rly tel. Whys it impor & whats this onc biz for Ive sporadly told? Never on memo. Thats ridic. Then nevr to friends. I hav, much of it. Then nev to me. Tha cd be tru I think but who ar u? Thn to complet this diar of yr nite & one so memorabl. T diar? T nit? Wha maks it so & who writs thos? U shld so whn u get back home—wel u kno, look bk whn u gt bk yl think bk 'Oh so thas wha happed & I rly felt tha partic nit so memobl becau so many eventfl events & all t dif things I fel, I remem now.' No, for deeper reas. Wha? Reasons, deepr, on paper, so mayb som of t sam of wha u said, but whas rly trubling me & mayb somethings i dint kno o wdnt excep thru my probe now wer there, y not? & mayb nows t tim to do it for now Im thinking of it so mayb now I shd, rt? So cmon thn, out wit em, no mor excuses, digresons, questons o jokes—how u feel, whas deep insid, not jus yr mom & work but yr soco lif too, want to mak lov? Me, wit u? U kno wha I mean & I said no mo digres, ques o joes. Sur think, u bet, tho hope nobo ever sees this notebo, not tha I cnt rip it up, rt? tho I want mo than mak lov, now thas t tru. Yes? Yes, tis so. So? So yes, ok, no mo digres, caus here comes, penpal gt yr undrlining pen set: so lonly, longing, yernng, me, hart smartg, partly frm litl work recgniton & almo no doe, but deepst down mos trublng me is Im alo, wan to b wit He or somone lik her—o, o—wit a fe bod in bed tonit & me screeng in betwee, liqidy syrpy ros petl lips—who 1st wro somthg lik it?— strapy wrapy legs, arms al aroun, ruty souns aboun, to hold, to clutch, to click, 2 nuz, 2 dic, 2 lov, tug & kis, 2 cover b covrd, 2 b flatend by her flat 2 big brests (2 for to forget), 2 jus agreebly b wit for a nit, 2 go 2 sleep wit for 1 nit, 2 wak up wit nxt morng as I wnt 2 slee wit, as befor wnt 2 sle wit is wha I ment wit, meang talkg lovg befor wnt 2 sle wit, holdg/jokg wit, serious/unseros wit, 2 jus b simply o simly b wit a responsv xcitg mind as wel as bod is wha I mos want 2 b wit tonit & if pos 4 a long lng tim, tho Im sur I hvnt made myslf clear here, but anythg els wit? Tot wit perhaps in tim, but mayb I mentond tha, tho not here. Marag wit perhps, tho tha too tho nt hre. But anythg els wit? No nt rt now tho wha I jus wro wasnt awful enuf? Nt 'awfl' tho if awfl thn afl meang banal, sily, imatur, nt so muc thos but u kno, tho wha? O u kno or (no mo o for or now but jus fo oh) can fil in tomor or whaevr tim if I kee this tha lng, so now cn clos ths joebo & cap pen wich, caus I dint refil befo I lef hom cd b runng dry, I mt latr nee fo mo impo thngs, meang relatd 2 trnsltd, 2 writ (& mt fo mite). But enuf, genug & yah. Hu? Wel, tel me whoevr sd I mus ma sens 2 myslf—who? Nu? O Go, stop go, tho whas tha supo 2 mea tha OG, sto go? Ju 2 sto wrtg rt no, go ho, lo at ths tomo, thn ter it ou of t memobo and up. I mea '& up.'"

I put away the notebook and look up. Something's doing on the next block. Take out the book, look at it, put it away. Car commotion, people in the street, but what was I looking for second time I opened the book? Did it so quick I forgot to look for what I started out to and now I forget what that was. Memo to someone—myself? An anagor—somewhere, whatever the word is? Realization, reclamation, recognition of my own situation, nature and character—something like that? I take out the book, look at what I wrote. Last stanza, include whatever you do, even to concluding with, etcet etcet, snow and rain, dinner at five tomor, pop in hosp, what the heck's hart smarting? and I cross it out with my pen till I can't read it. Here and now feelings, meeting Helene, just to be with someone tonight, etcet etcet— makes sense but's nothing new. I cross out all those too, worried someone one day might see what I wrote and wonder what was with him. I write "Anorisis or anagisis or some other an-isis or -asis—look it up. Word's in Web's 3rd." First stumbled on it when? Was looking up anagoge not long back, fourth time it

seemed in as many weeks. Some words are like that with me. Heuristic's
another—why can't I remember what it means? "Anagoge & heuristic," I
write. "Lk em up & how to pronounc anagog again." Pen runs dry on "n". I
unscrew it, squeeze the bladder, nothing inside. Ink's one of the only things
one can't borrow from a passerby. Plenty of things, but I know what I mean. I
put the pen away. Strapy wrapy legs—oh so po. My eyes already ache. Ruty
souns aboun is abysmal, abominable—quick, which, if forced to make an
instant deadline printing decision between those two, would read better and
would I choose? I close the nobook—abandonable—and put it in my coat. Of
course. What I wanted to do and was in that book was that love buzwax,
marag, tot. Maybe then, with an adjective adjective woman, one who makes
trenchant observations about me I've been unable to hit upon on my own,
things would change for me somewhat. Woman who unscrews me, presses my
bladder, I don't know if the latter act works, till I run dry. Who holds me and
let me hold her while I sleep. No lets, we just do: hold each other going into
and in sleep and when we wake up. To know when I've awakened that I've held
her and am holding her. Of course I'd know I'm holding her because I'd have
waked up. But that's what I want or something like: woman and bed simultaneously. Right now. This sec. I want to snap my fingers and open my eyes
to it. I believe in miracles? Will if this one now comes true. I snap my fingers,
close my eyes, say to myself, but maybe I should have first closed my eyes,
snapped my fingers, said to myself, anyway I close my eyes again, snap my
fingers, say to myself "Me with Helene in Helene's bed what I want right now,
please." Forget the please. Too much like when I used to pray to God out of fear
every night before I fell asleep. God please this, please that, God please keep
my mommy well, sister unsick, daddy making money and alive, God no awful
war, enemy soldiers landing ashore, please God I beg, wish, swear I'll be a good
boy from now on and pray to you as much as you like, and please if there's
anything I'm doing or not doing you're not pleased with, please let me know.
Close my eyes, snap my fingers, say to myself "Me with Helene in really any
nice clean bed right now," open them. I liked it when she used the word scoot.
And way she moved. As well as what she didn't say and do. What do I mean
"way she moved"? She moved normally, naturally, unaffectedly, but athleti-
cally, though not muscleboundly, as if as a girl she used to seriously tap dance
or take some after-school classical or modern dance or early-on had exceptionally agile legs as if she'd run and won or second-placed in dashes and
long-distance races in grade school and beat when they let her compete most
boys her age, and also how she flew downstairs at Diana's so sure she didn't

even think that flying down so fast she could have fallen on her face. Or just fallen, forget the face. Tripped but not gotten hurt. And "as well as what she didn't say and do"? So subdued. That's not the word. But something I liked. Not edgy, testy, overpeppy, sloppy, noisy, coarse, raucous, smoky, talky, scowly, mousy, so on. That she whacked the umbrella open: in notebook too. "Okay, Mr. Krin, now I must scoot." "I've got to." "Now I got to." Or "have to." But definitely "scoot." This one I truly mustn't ruin. Meaning she: I shouldn't. Though with those phone calls? No, lots of apologies as I said. "Um, just joking, I was, but not the best jest-joking, no?" No, no more jesting in joking. "I didn't think my call would wreak so much harm." Or truth: "I was a little high. Not a little. Let me tell the truth: a lot. But you also should know that's unusual for me to get so high. No it's not. Truth is, if I'm gonna tell it, or going to, cause that's, I mean because that's or those are just another language affectation or digression I use to direct attention to what I say and away from what I do: I get high. Don't want to but I do. No, truth, I do want to, because lots of times I've nothing else to do or think I don't or just don't want to think about doing anything else, so about once every three weeks I get high, but not as high as I got that night, is the truth. Usually by myself high. A solitary tippler mostly. I don't like it though do when I'm doing it or planning to. If things changed for me in ways I've gone over with myself, I'd probably change that drinking habit as well as stop drinking a little too much almost every night of the week while I read and often just to get to sleep, and that's also the truth. Doesn't interfere with my work though. Wake up, regular time, no alarm clock, exercise, coffee, newspaper, maybe a shower and in an hour I'm ready to go, or almost, though ten to fifteen times a year or so when I get high the previous night, mornings till around noon will be slow. And God knows why I feel compelled to tell all this in my first call to you when you certainly didn't want to hear it, right? Look: right, wrong, truth or not, and maybe half of that was, since I tend to distort as well as affect and digress—well, maybe not as well as, though I am a pretty effective distorter too—just see me, okay? You've no reason to even speak to me I guess, but what but an hour or less do you have to lose? Meet me I mean, not see, for coffee, tea or even a drink, because what I didn't want you to think before, and I swear I'm not trying now to affect, digress or distort, is that drink's any kind of problem with me. Those ten to fifteen mornings-after a year perhaps, but usually when I start work late I work later into the day than I usually do, and because I'm so tired from having worked late and maybe also from the evening before, that late day is usually one of the ten to fifteen days a year I don't drink or hardly at all. And meet not

tonight if you don't like. Now that I think of it we can't, since tonight, and
what I'm going to say isn't going to be said so you'll think something like how
nice that he's such a good son, I'm going to visit my mother, but maybe in the
coming week, so what do you say? Even a couple of drinks or dinner or both for
two on me. You can't? You won't? You never will? You'll meet? Great. Time
and date and see you at yours or you at mine or just at the meeting place." I
want to hold her face in my hands and bring it toward mine and lean over the
two to three inches I think it'd take if what I'm remembering now is right about
her height and if she doesn't raise herself on her toes to kiss. I want to. Yes.
Very much. To open my eyes and find hers closed. Then open them again and
find them open. Hers. Her to smile when I find her eyes open when I open
mine. Her to take my face in her hands and bring it down to hers and kiss my
lips. Want to. I. Lie my head on a pillow beside hers on a pillow or both ours on
the same pillow and our lips almost touching but not speaking and then
touching and our eyes closing, though I don't know why not speaking. Sure
we can be speaking. Softly, moderately, I suppose any way but loudly, crudely,
though even there too. So we're kissing and holding and possibly speaking and
possibly crudely but not loudly and doing the rest. Doing the best. To have
done the rest. To shut the light and her to turn over and face away from me or
the light's already off and we've done the rest and her to turn over and I press up
from behind while my nose is in her hair or lips are on her shoulder or neck and
penis against her behind or between her thighs. I'm sure I can get out of that
window scene and calls to her service some way. Lots of apologies. But not to
act oafish on the phone. She's a bright woman. She'll probably respect the
work I do. She looks like she likes poetry. Courses she gives. Plenty of poetry
in there and that she'll respect what I do I didn't mean makes her bright. But
all could be so nice. Live at her place if it's big enough if first we worked out.
Two bedrooms, one for her to work in, I'd set up and tear down the living room
table every day or some other unused day space. I'd mind but adapt. All I
need's one drawer and a long shelf. Two incomes, not rents, how else can a
representative couple like us afford to live in this city without a struggle, and
600 block of West Hundred-tenth could be along Riverside Drive or close.
Maybe she overlooks the Hudson. Tugs would pass. Summertime Circle Line
trippers. Columbia area may be near as she can safely live to City College did
Diana say? If so my alma I'll tell her next time we speak. Pre-med, then
pre-dent, but I'd frequently feel queasy when I entered the bio and chem
buildings because of the formaldehyde and rotten eggs smells and couldn't
learn the formulas and laws or dissect the baby pig or earthworms. Wasn't a

smart student—I can get part of this into the phone call some way, maybe just to say I thought she taught at City but then remembered it was a college upstate. Now makes me wonder why she lives around Columbia: went there or to City for her postgraduate work and got a cheap flat and stayed? Someone cut them up and labeled the parts for me and in exchange I took the requisite swimming test for him in gym under his name. Never got a post-B.A. I'll say. Not boasting of course. They wouldn't believe him when he said he sinks when he jumps in. Got interested in Japanese language and lit through a deeply moving Japanese movie about Japanese prisoners of war when I was nearly thirty and waiting tables at a beach resort. But more from the book it was based on that I later read and took a quick Berlitz thinking that would be it and then private lessons from an elderly Japanese businessman I taught English to and cooked dinner for in return. He also taught me the sake and tea ceremonies and how to disembowel myself and make paper insects and birds. Started translating poetry on my own and for a while brought my literal translations to this man. "Hasenai," he once said, pushing my other poets aside. "I buried his grandfather's sister. He be the one you should assist and do. What if I say without saying why or when of then, if you'll allow me, that I owe his grandaunt a grave favor," and by heart he recited in Japanese the end of one of Jun's earliest poems and first I ever heard: "Juvenile, goose-fed, young junk, halfcocked bloom. Pardon me, exceedable fathers, but I've got to make rot and humor and doom." She might appreciate some of that. An ill-mannered autodidact. Hardworking, a bit self-deprecating, humble origins, funny-boned. Had enough of her stuffed pedants, pedagogues and preppies and might be drawn to a literary roughneck. But I'm not that ill-mannered or much of a roughneck and her men friends probably aren't pedantic or stuffy and I'd love to get a pedagogical job. I want to say goodnight to her from behind while she lies on her side and she to turn her face toward mine and barely be able to reach my lips and turn away from me again and my face in one of those places I mentioned and hand on her breast, hip or thigh and other arm under a pillow or holding her shoulder or hand and to fall asleep like that, penis pressed, legs and chest. Sure there'd be problems but. Two bedrooms, not two beds. Two of us working in the same apartment. Two typewriters going at the same time but a door or two closed between them to shut out the noise. Two pens or minds or pairs of eyes going at the same time and the doors to shut out the quietness. Only one living room and bedroom and when she passes me on her way to the kitchen for coffee or tea, what? To brush her hand across my shoulder or head or back of my chair. For the phone to ring and both of us to go for it. Door or doors to her bedroom suddenly opened to get the phone in the living room. Or if it's in the bedroom her phone, for her to say "It's for you, Dan" or "Sweetie, it sounds like Dick or Jane—the phone," and for me to go to the bedroom and touch or brush up against her or her chair and smile at her when she hands me the receiver if she didn't leave it on the bed. Or she might have a long extension cord and bring the phone to me from the bedroom or even past the living room to the kitchen where I could be boiling water for coffee or tea. Or it could ring and I could answer it and it's for her, her mother or last lover, her colleague or student or friend, and I'd bring the phone into the bedroom where she's working. Or just for her to be in the kitchen around noon and say "I'm toasting a roll, want me to toast one for you too?" Or come in crunching a carrot and say "Want me to peel you one too?" Or hold a carrot or roll up and say "You want one too?" Or hold both up and say "You want these two too?" Or to hear her chewing or crunching a carrot or radish or celery stick in the kitchen. She's in the kitchen, I'm in the living room. I want it to disturb my work enough for me to say "You make a hell of a racket with your crunching" or "chewing," and she could say "Why, does it bother you?" or "Why does it bother you?" but she'd say "I'm sorry, does it bother you?" and I'd say yes and take the carrot or what's left of the radish or celery out of her hand and even out of her mouth if the carrot or celery's sticking out of it and bite into it loudly or take all three if she's holding them and bite into each loudly and chew more loudly than she and she could take back the carrot, radish or celery stick, though I doubt anything would be left of the radish by then, or even the toasted roll or a toasted or three-day-old bagel and bite into it or two of those three and we could chew loudly simultaneously. I've done things like that. Or I want to have egg salad on my lips after taking a forkful from a bowl of egg salad she just made and to look at her and suddenly want to kiss her and she could say "This is a childhood fear I once had—to have a boy with egg salad on his lips try to kiss me." Something like that happened to May with chicken salad I think, but I want something like that to happen to Helene with me. That's silly but true but I want much much more to. To go to France with her for a month to drink, eat, serious sightseeing and sleep and especially for a week the prehistoric caves. To go back to my roots—wrong. To return, at least in my mind—skip it. Or to spend, if we didn't have the loot for France, a couple of summer months in a remote bay area of Gaspé let's say. Way up. Northern lights and deep in woods. Fireplace going every night. Fog, some days I want plenty of fog and most nights sky swarming with stars clear as whatever simile and for a while during that time not only northern lights but meteorites clear as that same simile too. And even if I heard and saw them all before I want her to tell me which star is which and when combined their constellations or parts and yarns. She looks a lot like a woman I knew who knew a lot about stars and sailed. Also with a cheery bright face, long full frame, long white neck, straight bright teeth, long light hair, but wavy and blond, not red and I think straight, long strong legs and little feet, which with Helene's long skirt I couldn't see, little to no makeup around the eyes and on the lips and cheeks, and who nuzzled and made love only when it was most expedient to and it seemed had little to do with me and wrote poem after poem on beach after beach, but shortly after I last saw her on one wrote she's turning me loose and giving up writing poetry and living off her family to just write critically for the time being and study, read and teach. But this time with Helene or someone much like, meaning with a bright full mind, hard worker, no snob, someone I'm sexually drawn to and who's similarly drawn to me, and with substantially a cheerful disposition and strong sense of fairness and constancy, I want it to be much different than the rest and to start happening soon. I want to love and be loved and be called my love and beloved and make love with my beloved and call out love love love while we do. To take long beach walks and bike rides and go berry-picking along country roads. All that and then some I want unabashedly. Berries. Together. To pick. Rasp-, straw-, black-, blue- and even cran- and goose- in a mutual quart-basket or two, one for me, with the black-, straw-, rasp- and blue-, two for it, gibt here ein kiss, fourth for you, something I once did too. Was when? Eight or so years ago with a woman where? Coastal Maine and someone other than May or that star-and-sail woman whose name I can't recall and did that for a week and fell ears over heels for her for several days and she a little with me she said, though we both later said it could only have been because of the sea, fog, stars, fresh vegs and berry pickings and knew beforehand I was only bussing up to escape the hot city and make lots of love with someone and she at the time was the one woman I knew who, just as she'd said on the phone she'd been alone too long with her foxgloves and Muscovy ducks and wanted someone to bike, beach, pick and make love with too, "So come come come, it's a long trip but not much fare and I'll go in half on it and if this is any inducement, I'm as sticky as your city and as needy to be relieved." I want to rowboat out with her or canoe which I did with that Maine woman too. Her name was Lale, star-and-sail woman Sue. Want her to catch a fish from the boat's aft with last night's fish as bait while I paddle or row. Want her to troll. Want to get blisters on my hands first time I row and for her to say next day "You've blisters, I'll row, you troll," or

"I'll paddle, you fish," but this is too ridic. Even if it is. What I want. To sit facing her in the boat and look at her tightened thighs spread apart in her swim bottoms or jeans and that bulge where's the vulv as she struggles against wind, current or tide. Want her to wear a sun hat out there and her hair to hang salty and loose. Want to make afternoon love. On a sunny porch or on top of a sleeping bag beside the fired-up fireplace with all our clothes but her socks and watch off if there's rain or cold fog. Want to make love before breakfast on a quilted bedspread just after we get up and start to dress. Want it to come to us like that. Slap-bang, I want to, you do, down again. Want to take the hook out of a fish's mouth first time for me and maybe gut the fish with her instructions and fry my fish whole with its eye looking up at me adverbially first time for that too. I don't know why I want all those but I do. Watch because it's racy. Want to lie there after with my ear unwittingly near her wrist and listen to its tick. Want to nudge those socks off with my big toes. Want the crazy colors and cushiness of the quilt. Sleeping bag so we can be sloppy. Fishing line out of stick and string because it's simple. Want us to drift in the boat or canoe and catch another half hour of sunset. Want us to suddenly get fogged or rained on but close to shore and dripping wet. Want us to dry off in the house, cottage or bungalow and start to make love by that fired-up fireplace again while, just as we were, or something, about to put our clothes or robes on. Want us one dusk to plan out our lives together in that drifting boat with the sun half-past setting and mackerel or some other fish jumping and things in the air buzzing and loons crooning or wooing or whatever they're doing in the water and maybe a lobsterman's boat from far off motoring and a buoy from not so far off bonging, but other than those and some other unimposing sea and sky things I can't think of right now like cormorants diving, nothing. Want the water to be clear, don't want any biting bugs out there. No water skiers, moving or moored speedboats or low-flying planes. No planes. No beer cans, oil slicks, human feces, toilet paper, cigarette butts or filters from filtertips floating past. Want perfection in a setting other than in one with just clouds and sun or as close to one as I can get. Then I want to row or be rowed back and beach the boat and tie the line to a shore rope with a lobsterman's knot and walk up to the house, cottage or bungalow though no tent, don't want no matter how roomy, protective and complex a tent, and the house, cottage or bungalow not to be more than a few hundred feet from the beach and the path to it if it's uphill not too steep and this structure should be wooded outside and in and shielded by tall shading undiseased trees and in the bedroom a little breeze and I want us to make love on top of or underneath a bedspread or quilt or just to throw the covers off and do it on a clean bottom sheet. Want her to later say she wants to have my baby. "I know you do or at least want to have one too," and I can then say, could, could, and I would "Very much so, and maybe this'll sound silly when I say it, though in some other way how could it? only with you." First time it'd be for me too if something like that happened, other than with—but with her I was never sure it was true. Believed she conceived for sure but not for sure from me. Some woman other than May, Lale or Sue who said she was having and then had had mine but who was living with her husband and year-old child at the time and said he knew but because he'd become involved with two other people and one she intimated a man, even encouraged her to, but of course not to have another man's child. So both he and I wanted it aborted but she'd always wanted two and close enough in age where they'd play together almost like twins which she said would take some of the drudgery of motherhood off her hands, and after she gave birth to the first her husband couldn't get erect whenever he did join her in bed. In fact, saw them all together, and only time I met him, at a party when she was visibly pregnant supposedly from me and I was still seeing her once a week, something I regret now and would never do again with any man's lover or wife no matter what the circumstances between them, unless let's say they got married just so he could get U.S. citizenship or a work permit and weren't living together as husband and wife, simply because, well, life's tough enough, that sort of stuff, don't want to hurt the other guy when he for certain doesn't deserve it and I can so easily avoid it, and having no cohabitational sex for weeks or even months doesn't mean as much to me as it once did. But he said after he'd said "I think we should have a little chat about the burps and beats," and taken my arm and clapping me hard on the back though by his face to anyone else it must have seemed goodnaturedly escorted me into an empty room, that I mustn't think unhighly of him despite anything Penny might have said, that he's always had a very high opinion of me from everything she's said including some of the things she said she dislikes about me, though she was only twenty-six he urged her to have this pioneer amniotic fluid test but only to see if anything was amiss with my genes, and he's pleased as probably I should be to report I'm a hundred percent clean, that finally they've decided they never want the child to know its genetic father was anyone but him and hoped I wouldn't do anything in my life, or help anything from happening after it like putting my paternity into possibly publishable poetry or fiction or journals I might keep, to crimp their plans. "I wouldn't, why would I?" I said and that I think he's a fine fellow and Penny's never said anything but the nicest things about him and I've never written nor do I ever intend to write poetry, fiction, journals, plays or an autobiography of any kind so along those lines he has nothing to fear too. Then we shook hands, I think he asked what had been in my glass and got me another drink, called it a night for both of them though Penny wasn't in the room, and I never saw her again though she did call a few months later to say she'd had a healthy baby in the last five days and that Marc, that's right, Marc, as much as he liked me didn't want her to see me again or at least for the next ten years if they stayed married that long. When I asked what sex the baby was she said "If you have to know, it rhymes with whirl," and when I asked what name they gave her she said something like, well, it's all something like, "I'm sure you'll hate it and mock us for such a floricultural name so I'm not saying, goodbye." For a few years after that I'd write and this except when forced to in grade school was the only time in my life and only when I was lonely and drunk some nights, long lonely drunken nighttime paragraphs I then called poems and later threw away in one trash bag because they were so stilted, formless, derivative, just bad, and I don't write poetry, about my weanling I'd never hold nor see and who'd never know nor unknowingly pee on me. . . my year-old, two-year-old, three-year-old child who could resemble but would never tremble at my paternity. . . my little no-good nudnick kid whose folks should know my folks are prone to neurofibromatosis and diabetes. . . my young alloy, whose gender rhymes with ploy, whose name might be Troy or Roy, whom I'll never live to enjoy or destroy, noy woy I knoy whether it ever reseeds my soy. . . my mine me moans thy mind I phones thine line chimes drones. . . all starts or parts of some of my "Me my poems." Penny had the girl around eleven years ago, they emigrated to New Zealand the next year, one of their friends I bumped into a couple-years back said he'd heard Marc had drowned in the Pacific but wasn't sure where or when and didn't know anyone who was and even forgot where he got the information from or what when I asked were the children's names. And Penny? I said and he said for all he or anyone else she knew knows she was still living somewhere in the South Seas with her girls, but she cut everyone off when they left and no one if anyone was going to the Pacific and wanted to look her up remembers where in Canada Marc was born and her parents were long dead. Some nights, when the drink's gone to my head and I'm feeling sentimental and a bit self-pitying, I think this girl's going to ring my doorbell one day and say something like "I just wanted to see how your nose and earlobes stacked up against mine." Also thought if I ever wrote another poetical paragraph or paragraphless poem it'd be about a man who falls in love with this daughter without knowing who the genetic father is and maybe even gets her pregnant, even if the theme's been done and done and for millenniums before. But Helene or whoever it might be though for now she seems my best remote hope. Want her to get pregnant on the bedspread, quilt or sheet or if we do it in front of the fired-up fireplace then on the floor. To teach school while she's pregnant if it is Helene with me that summer and whatever summer that'll be though I hope some summer soon. This one, at least the next one. Want my mother to visit us for a week that summer wherever it'll be though I hope someplace uncrowded and Northeast and near but not on a secluded but unhumid shore. Her parents or mother or sibling to come for a week if she wants or friend or student if it's Helene and she has favorite students and if it isn't then if this woman's also a college teacher, and to have the time for all this she'd almost have to be or a self-supporting artist of some sort, to come for a night or two. Want to move in with whoever this woman will be when we return. To vacate my place the previous June and go to France with her for a month and then Maine for the rest of the summer or just Maine or someplace secluded and cool for two months since we probably couldn't afford, I know I couldn't by this summer, a trip abroad. Want my name on her mailbox if it's her place I do move in to. Not taped onto it but stamped if her name's also stamped into the nameplate. And maybe not for her to be pregnant this summer in Maine or wherever it'll be but reasonably soon. I can also see where some to a lot of this could happen or something comparable to. No, ridiculous, all of it, I don't know what it is, sure it is, maybe it's not, because I think she gave me a look and said some expression that suggested some of this could start happening and not unreasonably soon. Something like: not tonight, give it time, I'm talking about us, don't rush, you seemed a bit interested in me, I seemed a bit interested in you, so? no harm there, just don't ruin. I don't think I'm fooling myself. Ask yourself if you are. Are I? Am I? I don't think so. So no. Because I really do think I saw and heard things from her that suggested he's a bit odd, that guy, or maybe spontaneous is the word or extemporaneous to be truly fair, but I think I could get to like him if it got that far, so I hope he calls but if he doesn't then he didn't and it wouldn't be I don't think because of anything I did or didn't do. But I won't call him if he doesn't me, since that's not what I do. Least not with a man I just met and am not bowled over by. But if— This how I think she speaks? Not quite but go on. But if he calls I'll see him I guess unless he acts drunk or moronic, vulgar or worse, for that sort of behavior's another story, one I quickly put down with a vow never to pick up again, no matter how short. But if he does call and we get together and I'm right about him, it might turn out to be a good thing. For I like a man who's straightforward and just a bit aggressive but who still stays at the beginning and maybe for all time somewhat ungainly and shy. I think that was him. I liked it that he pursued me, continued to eye me, getting up close and just as he was about to say something, backing off, then catching me at the door. He could have let me leave, got my phone number from Diana or got Diana to phone me to say she has this friend who'd like to meet me, or just forgotten it. Party fantasies usually end when the party fantasized goes out the door. Wish I had a little more of that go-after-what-you-want stuff. But men are men—that's what they do, are good for, trained to from puppyhood—the hare is loose: release the hounds—no matter how shy and ungainly or up to a point. Eyed me a bit too desirously sometimes but I liked it in a way for it said "I'm interested and if you are you can say so by looking at me from time to time in a certain though certainly less interested way," or I at least didn't mind his occasional desirous look or not that much. He didn't at least goo-goo his eyes and lick his teeth for all to see and say absolutely the wrong things and too loudly, embarrassing me. Ah, but that balcony scene—he couldn't have spared me? But he wasn't that physically attractive to me, which isn't to say I didn't like his face. It was all right, nothing great, nothing to lob my eyes back to him and think "Hmm, quite the striker that guy," but that's okay. Better the looks most times, worse the insecurities and ego, or that's been my experience, not that I wouldn't see a man just because he was extremely handsome as long as he had many of the other qualities I like. And he seemed to have an adequate physique—adequately slim and straight, for his age, no pot or blobbiness or weightlifter's stuffed muscles and sun-stiffened skin or with no ass which, unkind, limiting and even shallow as that might make me, I'm afraid I do mind, but I guess I could live with the big biceps and that kind of skin and behind. He was also at least two inches taller than I when I don't wear shoes. I like that difference and to be taller than the man when I want to too. His hair was okay, not entirely gray, not a mop or blown-dry, which makes even the most gifted Latinist look like the most nitwitted TV sportscaster, and sufficiently trim and seemingly clean. But the way he spoke. It at least wasn't a dull and dumb voice and one where I had to tug out my ear to hear. Smart but not arched is the best way I'd put it now. None of that "Now that's good for a laugh, haw haw haw." I think I'm remembering this right, but the history of my considerations and positions, though much less in literary things, tells me I can be quite wrong. But there had to be something I liked about him to propose when he said he'd like to speak to me again that he call me and I think it might have been a couple of things but particularly his voice. I didn't do it just to later shake him off. Diana did seem chummy with him and she's said she never becomes friends with any man who isn't interesting, talented, lively and bright. She sends the others packing, she's said, to forestall boredom, and not just lovers, unless they can do something immediate for her career and books, and even if he looked the helpful type, it seemed he was having a tough enough time keeping afloat on his own. But if he was up there at that colony of theirs he must be doing something fairly interesting in whatever field his is. Did he say? Don't think so or didn't hear, but then our talk was so short. What did he speak about? Nothing to give much of a clue what he does when he isn't shooting down drinks and food and scrutinizing the calves and backsides of girls. We talked about the wedding reception I was off to. The kind of work I don't do. How long I've been at the party. That I don't like going to weddings or their receptions and he does. Mostly because he likes the accompanying food and booze? That we both thought it'd be nice to speak to the other again, but me a bit less than he and he since he first saw me, which could have been when I came in. At least I noticed him then, but not looking at me. What was he doing? I forget. But we first looked at the other when? Near the food table and bar again, when I was talking with a friend and he was with some people but seemed infinitely more interested in me. Each of us had a wineglass in hand. He stared at me I don't know how long, seconds, then looked away. Why didn't I look away first? Well, someone has to look away first, but why didn't I? Wanted I believe to give him the incentive or excuse to walk over and speak to me or meet me at the food table or some place if he was too bashful or reserved to say "How do you do?" or "Do I know you?" or "Rooty-Kazoo says kerchoo to you too" while I was with someone else. Caught him staring at me the next time I looked. He smiled, I smiled, or maybe we smiled at the same time, but now I remember I smiled first. Why? Well, why not? No, wanted to let him know the first time wasn't a mistake. Then it was my turn to look away but hoped I'd made my point and one I wouldn't make again, which was to speak to me before I leave even if I'm with someone to the end. I also couldn't just continue to smile and what expression do you make after you stop? So I had to look away, but while I was smiling. Why didn't he first? I suppose because I smiled first and he didn't want to be impolite. Besides, I was still talking to someone, while he was alone, so it was easier for him to hold his smile on me than it was for me on him. We also talked about marriage: that he'd never been and that I'd gone to my friend's wedding under false pretenses. Did I get in my pitch for the institution? Maybe my face said it, for it's how I feel. So he's been single for all of his around forty years. If he's over forty or even right on it, and he didn't seem to be doing anything not to look it, that would put him in the oh point five percentile of his sex. He's either lived a number of times with women, would be my guess, or for a while was strictly gay, but everything I quickly took in about him makes me doubt that. But just by the way he so eagerly and almost desperately followed me to the door makes me believe he's the type who gets involved with a woman too fast when it's clear to nearly everyone including the woman that he shouldn't, and suffers a great deal when it doesn't go the way he wants, which usually turns out to be the case. Therapy? Why'd I bring up that? Why even go into why, for I don't want to once more go so far off the track. But I'm sure he scorns it but seriously feels he needs it and has been told so by most of his old girlfriends the last ten years, which could be the main reason he scorns it so much. Why do I think I know? Oh, some theory I have about men his age who do relatively little to enhance their appearance and in fact do what they can, short of drawing even more attention to themselves, to detract from it, as he seemed to, that makes me think they've not only never been in therapy, which if anything would increase their self-esteem, but also repudiate therapy, because they fear the changes it would bring or are just too lazy to begin or can only think of the long-term financial cost of it, which is justifiable within means, and of course several other things. Now that's a psychological headful but what I've come to believe after knowing a number of men pretty deeply over the years, though my own therapist disagrees with my theory. What does she say? She says her male patients come in all sizes, colors, faces, ages and shapes and some wear five-hundred-dollar suits and go to beauticians twice a week for their hair and nails, and others cut their own hair with nailclippers they never think to use on their nails and bathe every third week and have never bought a sports jacket in their lives. Mothers, she's said. Some men dress like slobs because their mothers always dressed them like princes and others dress like princes because their mothers dressed them like slobs. Or some dress like slobs because their mothers always dressed them like slobs and they haven't much changed their ways and others dress like princes because when they were young their mothers dressed them like princes or they want their mothers to be drawn to them in some other than normal mother-son way or because, unprincelike and self-reliant as these men might be in every other way, their mothers still buy them their princely clothes. And women? I said. What makes them dress like princesses and slobs? and she said For all the same reasons, though substitute fathers for mothers for them, and in some instances you can also substitute fathers for mothers for the way men dress and also mothers for fathers for the women. Anyway, I like a man better dressed than Mr. Krin and a tie would have been right for Diana's party what with he should have known would be a preponderance of properly dressed people there, and what the heck, being suitably dressed for the occasion does more for you than not I'd guess. But I'm sure he has good reasons for dressing the way he did and I suspect the overriding one is his lack of means. Still, there was something I found sensual about him too. In the eyes, and I haven't yet gone on about his smile, in that he didn't footsy around and try to reach me by phone through Diana, in that he committed himself somewhat by pursuing me into the hall and saying right out his wish to speak to me again, but I don't know or am not quite sure if sensuality and perseverance necessarily correlate. My experience, not vast but I think comprehensive with men, tells me they do, but that can't always be the case. Of course it isn't always or even very often and in fact they don't, that's all, so what am I talking about?—but that shout out the window of his, now that needs some thinking into. Really, if there was any one thing anyone I'd just met could do to make me immediately recoil from him, that shout was it. What was on his mind? I don't know. Give it a try. Impulsion, self-destruction, sudden liking, perhaps desire. Perhaps deep desire. Or he needed attention, from me on the street and perhaps the people at the party, but I don't think that was it. Then what? I give up. It probably wasn't that embarrassing to me only because I was in too much of a rush to get to the reception to think about it, but he couldn't have known that. Rush he knew but not that I couldn't think that much about his shout. Anyway, looking at it in a different light, that shout could also mean that here is a man who will suddenly, and this I usually wouldn't mind with someone I really liked, grab you on the street when you're walking with him and hug you till you almost can't breathe. Or kiss you squarely on the lips because he also suddenly feels like it—on the street or in a movie theater or even at a party filled with familiar people and that he's also a person who screams when he squirts. Who twice a year or so despite his age will lift you off the bed with him in you and walk you around the room making these crazy carnal sounds, all of which I might like, that's not the problem, but bounce you up and down in that standing-up position till you have to shout Put me down, you idiot, you'll get a heart attack or trip and we'll both be seriously hurt. Who doesn't turn away from you after—I felt that. Who in fact turns in to you after. Who wipes the sweat off your face and chest after. Who keeps a handkerchief by his bedside for each of you to wipe his own pubic area with after, though the woman first. Well, I don't see how I can say that. Who falls asleep with his arms around you after. Who when he does turn over loves it when you turn over too and press your body into his back and backside and squeeze his penis briefly and cover your toes with his and stroke and hold his thigh. Who you can talk to before and after and he'll listen and his comments about most things about you will be reasonable too. Who jokes. Who always carries a pad and pen with him which I bet he also keeps by his bedside for sudden knocked-out-of-sleep thoughts about his work but not about his life. Someone who can quote a thousand poems. Who probably has a few interesting interests and friends. Who brings his interests and problems to his best woman friend and lets her share the interests and help solve his problems too. Forget the last, but someone I can have some fun with. Even be kind of dippy with—la la. The window incident showed that. Nuts as it was, to me it did. Let's face it, he's probably a bit lonely too. How do I know? Well, he just seemed to be. By what he said and did there and after, but I can't be expected to remember everything or so early go beyond much more than how I felt. But he came with no one, didn't seem to know anyone there but Diana, didn't seem to have the greatest success meeting anyone there but me, and even there he nearly flubbed it when he had a much better chance of meeting me than I think he knew, and I bet he also had no one to go home to in anyone's home so I bet he also wants to ultimately have a long-lasting something with someone and in the long run share an apartment and get married and have a child some day with that long-lasting someone or even sooner than that and when he does, well, this is pushing it of course, but when he does, well, by that time if things have gone as well as they can sometimes when both people are ready and available for it and what have you—when the timing's right, that old standby—I think I'd want one too. All that too. Yes, I'd really like that: living with someone, a second marriage and first child. I don't want to wait much longer. I'm at an age where I've got to begin thinking I can't afford to. That the baby can't afford to wait much longer too. No, things happen like this. This is how they really happen. You go to a party you don't especially want to and certainly don't have the time to, but you go and maybe you do actually want to but you most definitely don't have the time to, or you do have the time, maybe an hour, not much but enough to have a good time at the party or get a feel of it and what you'll miss by leaving early or what you're glad you'll miss, but you meet someone you at first don't want to, though that isn't what happened to me, and even if he does act a bit odd at first—when you first speak to him, not when you first see him—well, that can show shyness and reserve, but you're often a bit shy, reserved and nervous yourself, though you weren't when you met him, so, well so what, you meet someone briefly, you're somewhat attracted to him in a strange way you can't quite explain and you give him your phone number or let him know how to get it, all of which is normal, and you see him again for a drink or coffee and if it still feels good and goes well between you you see him again and again and then what do you know but you're in bed with him, which shouldn't come as a surprise with a man you've seen three times since you first met him and whom you've been continually and maybe even increasingly attracted to, and all that's very nice, you like to sleep with a man you like to sleep with but not one you think might just want to sleep with you once or twice, so all that's quite normal too. In fact all that is great, just great, what you want and said for a long time you've wanted. Or you even, or rather he even kisses you as he leaves the apartment the second time you see him since the party, and your apartment of course, he couldn't be leaving you in his. But he could if he was going out for something he or you or you both thought one or the other of you or you both needed—a bottle of wine, a loaf of bread, a bar of soap or roll of toilet paper—but this happens as he's leaving your apartment for the night, so your apartment that second time you see him since the party, which probably was for dinner at a neighborhood restaurant—your neighborhood, his, no real difference—he picked you up at your apartment or you met him at his or some outside place like one of those neighborhood restaurants, but he escorted you home—and then he's gone, you've kissed and he's gone and you know something's happened between you but you don't know what or you do, you know what's happened but you can't quite explain what or you can and you look forward to the next time you see him which just a few minutes ago you arranged, and then almost before you know anything else the next time and which you sort of expected or knew would happen he's in bed with you and it's quick, the two of you getting into your bed or his is quick, for you invited him to your apartment for dinner or he invited you for dinner to his, so maybe you didn't finish dinner or you did and getting into bed wasn't that quick, and you drank wine with it, maybe too much wine, but you didn't have the dessert you or he bought or made or got from either of your mothers or you did, you ate everything, appetizer if you had one and main course and side dish or dishes and salad and dessert and even these little cheese or quiche things with your pre-dinner drinks, and you drank nearly everything also, hard liquor drinks before and wine with dinner and brandy after or just a bottle of wine or two before, during and after dinner if neither of you that night wanted hard drinks, and then you're kissing for the first time since the last time at your door, and holding hands and squeezing and rubbing fingers and he runs his free hand up your back or whatever he does and you run your free hand along his side or whatever you do and he says "Is it all right if we go to bed?" or you say "Why don't we just go to bed?" or "take off our clothes and go to bed?" or just "go to bed?" for it's much more exciting the first time taking off the other's clothes in bed and you do, or neither of you says anything, you just take his hand if you don't already hold it or he does that with you or you or he points a free hand or a head and you both go to your or his bed and you're in bed that third time you meet since the party and next time you see each other or even the next morning if one or the other of you stayed overnight and no reason why you or he shouldn't, since I don't like, and not many times have I been in bed with someone for any other reason, when I'm in bed with someone I really like and have to leave it early the next morning and especially after the first night or he feels he has to leave mine, but anyway— without even a brief breakfast or just toast and coffee I mean—but anyway, next time you're with him, either the next time you meet or the very next morning after you wake up together or when you're having that first breakfast, you know there are going to be some problems with the relationship, there always are, so that's no real problem, but that it's going to be a long-lasting one—how long? well, maybe, no, it's impossible to say—and a good one too. No, these things happen, they have happened, with me with my ex-husband and later with several men including my ex-husband who I thought might be my second, and I wonder if it hasn't started to happen with this man too. I suppose I should just wait and find out and if it does, of course just wait and find out, but if it does prove to have happened or just happens, simple as that, well, all to the good. So far it seems okay. I'll call Diana tomorrow or the next day if she doesn't call me, but what will I say? First of all, since she has had a number of involvements with men I never knew of till they were over with, "Just how friendly are you with this man?" No, I'll save that for later if it doesn't come out in our conversation one way or the other or she doesn't volunteer. If it comes out she's seeing him now or had been and is still a little to a lot serious about him or it isn't quite over with but is getting there and my seeing him would hurt her or compromise our friendship or complicate their breakup further or the situation between them in any way, I won't see him till that's completely over with or resolved in her mind and maybe not even after that, depending on how he acted to her if he was the one who broke it up or just in their relationship. But if none of that comes out I'll say I met a man at her party, "You know who, one at the door just before I left, and he said he'd call, hasn't yet, not that I'm worried he won't, he doesn't he doesn't and it's quite possible he had a change of mind, though it didn't seem he would, but if he does, call I mean, what can you tell me about him, I'm of course talking about Daniel Krin, and if he calls you about me I won't feel put off in the least if you keep our call just between us, though don't hesitate to tell me of his if you wish, because for the brief time I said 'Hello, got to go,' he seemed okay." If she says don't go near him, he's a flirt, worse, wants to slip it up every third skirt, even worse, mean and periodically very strange and even deranged, and that's not just hearsay, dear, what will I do? If I ask why she thinks he's strange and possibly deranged and mean, since being a flirt and so on about skirts could be interpreted several ways and if it's just that he likes women and sex with them more than most men, that might make him even more recommendable to me, and she gives good reasons for everything else she said, well, Diana's proven to be no liar and fool, so I'd take her word. But if it's just that he's an unreliable or moody person, for example, or occasionally acts half his age but not in an endearing way, or he's temperamental, weak, cheap, petty, insincere and so on. No backbone—haven't heard that one for a while, nor "cold as ice." Solemn, introverted, old-maidish—flip-flops from this project to that. Finishes most of what he starts but has to know beforehand what almost everyone else seems to know afterwards that although all his works or the ones I've read or scanned, since I have only known him for a few months, are worthwhile to a degree and done competently, none are that dislodging or completing or advancing to make them important or exciting in even a tiny way. What am I saying? you could say. That he never shoots for anything monumental in the themes and authors he selects so he can at least wind up with something relatively original and big. Has brains and good intentions to spare, I'm not saying no, but also considerable self-defeatism. But, to finish up with him, since you did ask, didn't you? he sometimes lives like an indigent too, which, if you're a person like me who likes to split a check down the middle rather than feel called upon to pick it up, can put a hitch in your friendship. Not that he isn't always clean and well fed and neatly dressed, though I suspect most of his clothes, even if I've nothing to base this on except their ampleness and style, come from his late father's closets and drawers and much of his nourishment and even some of his income come from his mother, little as he's said she has to live on herself. But maybe in this day and age, and excuse me for the cliché but this is only a phone conversation, of haywire mass-consumerism, if that is the right phrase, and imagine not being able to quote a simple cliché correctly or even quasily, and don't tell me because I know I just did something not unconscionably but nonsensically wrong there neogeologically or what have you—and I honestly forgot that noun ending in ism with a hyphenless neo as its prefix for neo-words—he's to be, and I hope you're still able to follow me, congratulated and perhaps even emulated for living such a thrifty, stripped-down unupwardly mobile existence, if that last one, turned around a tad, is what they say. He does though have this awfully polished way of ticking people off who could do useful things for him if he'd only pay them the modicum of respect they think they deserve because of their professional status, pull and accomplished work, which leads me to believe he's a mite jealous of other people's success and their adeptness at living rather well off their teaching, reviewing, readings and books. But he says he's plugging along on the project of his life now, but to me it sounds like another losing calling, so maybe things will improve appreciably for him the next few years. I hope so, because despite everything I might have said about him, I like the guy, so of course wish for him the best. As for your seeing him, and I care much less than you what gets back to him if you two do ever get close enough to confide and confess, he seems the type who has one affair after the next because, and I've a good idea what the reasons are but don't think either of us has the time, he can't sustain one for very long, and I'm referring to his affairs. Or else, or perhaps in addition to, he's able to charm the pants off women at first if they don't happen to be wearing skirts, and everyone should be permitted one poor joke per long phone call, though for all I know I might have succeeded there when while I was making it I thought it was bad, but can't hold them because after a while they see straight through his delusions and the inadequacies I mentioned and know he doesn't want a stable or permanent relationship. Having one would mean he'd have to change the kind of life he's been used to for going on thirty adult years, which would put a damper or hamstring or even a diaper, and I'm sure that joke was bad, on all his excuses for the brevity of his affairs and his lack of professional success and other unhappy things. Now if you only want to go out with him once or twice because you've nothing better to do, I can't see the harm. He can be very pleasant, appealing and entertaining, but don't drag the evenings out too long. If Diana says some of that and at the end suggests I don't see him but says nothing about him being mentally ill or socially or emotionally repulsive in any unmistakable way or a devastating combination of those defects, I'll see him for a coffee or a drink. So far he seems reasonably interesting and okay. Not my ideal man in looks but not that hard to take. Besides, it'd only be for an hour or so one afternoon or night, and I also liked his smile. Maybe that more

than anything, open and something else, and also his height, build and once
he got over the jitters, his straightforwardness. But it's way too early to be
considering all this and I should do just what? Forget it for now or forever if he
doesn't call and definitely not call Diana unless he calls me and if he doesn't,
well, think about calling him. What would there be to lose? He could say no,
I'm busy, engaged, about to be, lied and am actually married with child, have
children, we do, two, three, she does but I'm her faithful live-in, I'm afraid I
can't see you because I'm this, I'm that, I'm the other thing, some new element
recently arose in my life or just today or yes, I'm sorry I didn't call, I was going
to, this very moment in fact, you won't believe this but I had my hand on the
receiver just now and your number on my lips, receiver to my ear and had
dialed the first five digits but forgot the sixth, phonebook open to Winburn,
Windbreaker, Winermiss, was just running my finger down your phonebook
page, so you could say that in a minute or so, but really now since that's about
how long we've been on the phone since you called, you would have heard my
rings, now what do you say to that concatenation of events? I dialed you just
before you rang but your line was busy, possibly because you were dialing me,
now how about that for some kind of simultaneity of minds? I dialed you but
hung up just before my call got through, if it would have which is to say if your
line or even your exchange wasn't tied up or momentarily on the fritz, because
I thought you'd be out—I don't know why, just something that popped to
mind and seemed right at the time—and I can't stand talking to anyone's
answering service, something I seem to have in common with half my ac-
quaintances and friends including half the ones with that kind of service.
Look, I couldn't get myself to even fetch the phonebook to look up your name,
though let me say straight off before you say anything more, if I haven't already
said it a dozen times, and of course I haven't since this is the first time we've
spoken since we met, first time unless you've kept since then a rigorous
speechlessness, how much I wanted to open my phonebook and look up your
number, wanted to dial you and have you answer, speak to you and ask if you'd
like to go out with me and soon, and I'm not putting or trying to one over on
you, but just thought that well, after my yelling out Diana's window at you I
felt, well, after my messages to your answering service that night I felt, well,
even after we finished speaking on Diana's landing and you went down the
stairs I felt, well, but I had to be wrong, right? in what I thought you thought
about me because here you are calling me unless it's to tell me, and I don't see
how this can be so but you never know for if anything hasn't happened to me
once it doesn't mean it won't the next moment, not to call you, so what would

you say—what I mean is you certainly didn't call me to tell me not to call you, right?—so what would you say—and what am I now saying?—so what do you say I'm saying to seeing me for coffee or dinner or a drink, and how soon, since I'd love for it to be an hour or two from now or at the most tomorrow around noon. That's what he could be thinking, she could be thinking. That's what I at least hope she's thinking or will. But I'm sure—not sure, but almost sure she hasn't thought of me once, and if once then I'm sure or almost sure or just sort of sure she just thought of me briefly, and if briefly, then very briefly, almost subliminally if what I think is subliminal thinking is right: she saw the D in the Don't Walk sign for instance and for a subliminal instance the D in the Don't stood for Dan—since about a minute or so after she turned away from my waving at the window and went up the street to that wedding reception she said she was going or wherever she was going to—possibly to a friend's apart-ment, perhaps to a lover's, maybe directly home to be with a friend or lover or sick pet or just alone, not that anything I've done or find out about her is going to stop me from calling her at least once and probably in the next few days, not that I'm going to do anything more such as trying to find out anything more about her from now on till that call, simply because I've done more than enough already to snuff out what I suppose could be called a potential rela-tionship, though she didn't at all seem like the kind of person who feels she has to lie in any way to get out of an uncomfortable situation, if my stopping her on the stairs and talking to her was one, of that I'm, well, almost sure.

CHAPTER FIVE

The Car

Up. Still that car commotion, but now just a half block off and smaller. I start for it but get just one step.

"Dennis?"

"Yes, uh, excuse me?"

"Dennis? It is Dennis. Dennis, it's Harold. How are you?"

"I'm sorry, you have to have the wrong number. Person."

"Dennis, stop it, I said it's Harold. Tell me. It's been—but it actually hasn't been that long. By the tone of my voice, I'm saying." Grabs my hand and shakes it. "How the hell are you? Your hand's cold. Really, I want to know."

"Listen, it's possible I might look like this guy—"

"Look like him? What a laugh. You're more than the spitting image of him. You've never in fact looked more like yourself. You look wonderful. But Dennis, you want to forget, go on, forget, forget. I won't mind. In the past— well I'd be the last to admit you occasionally treated me like that and did I mind? Did I ever say it at least? At least, that much? All right, I minded a little—said it and minded—complained a little you could say—kvetched, but that's about all I did. You might say I did more, but let's have a drink and talk about it."

"Honestly."

"Honestly what? Or talk about anything but that if that's what you want. All that's elapsed. For instance, how you could look even better after so many years. Because when really was the last time? My memory, not good then, is now a has-been."

"My name . . . You see, when you said Dennis, because my name's—"

He laughs, grabs my arm and starts walking me to the street. "Cab," he shouts. "Taxi." One stops. I slip my arm out of his. A very beautiful young woman and a man are walking toward us, woman saying "New-Age entrepreneurs. You know who they are?" They're about even with us. The man stops, shakes his head, takes her hand and kisses it.

"Thirty seconds," Harold says to the driver. He holds up a finger, crosses it with another. "Sí—you got it. —Dennis, you ready?"

"They're going to turn-around America's economics and social, political and moral consciousness, or in all the hip states if we're ever so lucky. New Mexico—"

"If you say so," he says, putting her hand to his cheek and shutting his eyes.

"If I? It's not I, and besides, how am I supposed to have an intelligent discourse with all this kissy hand action. Because—" but she suddenly notices us before I can look away and stares briefly at me and then at Harold at length as if she knows him.

"Look, my name's Daniel," I say to Harold, glancing over his shoulder at the woman, as he'd seen me staring at her and stepped between us. She turns to the man.

"Anything interesting?" he asks her.

"You know that woman?" I ask Harold.

"Just something," she says.

"What woman?"

"If you guys don't—" the cabby says.

"It was the way you were looking at them," the man says.

"That absolutely beautiful one who just passed with the man," as they'd resumed walking, his head on top of her shoulder. He turns to them and then back to me.

"He's quite handsome—maybe more stunning then she. Those incredible lashes. He could easily become an actor."

"She was staring at you as if she knew you. I've seen her someplace. Commercials. Maybe a subway station ad. I don't have a TV, but I've watched them. Or the movies or stage."

"Could be, Dennis, but she's certainly not from the stage. I know the stage and she's not on it. I make a point of seeing all the showcases and plays. As for subways—never touch the stuff."

"Anyway"—the woman repeatedly looking back as she walked—"my name's Daniel. Daniel, Dennis—see?"

"Free?" a man says and gets in the cab and it drives away.

"So it's Daniel now, Dennis. So it always was and will be. So you say you're not Dennis, Daniel. So you were never Dennis we'll even say. You want to say that, we will. So, as a matter of fact, there never really was any Dennis. Not in the history of American and English stage design or of mankind. It's a name I made up out of dewdrops. So what to all that I also say. Cab," he shouts. "Taxi." One stops. "Now let's have that drink. I love the unflappable way your eyes take in everything and your mind makes split-second discriminations about people and things. And you didn't take a swing at me. Now that more than anything, because what does it say? You didn't call me this and then that when I'd say by most people's precepts and norms you could have gotten away with it. You didn't mime to that divine pair 'He your friend, for I sure don't know him.' You didn't say to me 'You're nutsy, Buster, take a powder.' Not a raised voice or fist and I more than most you'll meet appreciate that."

Cabby rolls down his window and is about to say something.

"One second, friend," Harold says. To me: "You didn't and you're not and the rest of those things. You're also sympatico."

"Sure I am."

"Come now, you have to admit that. You also have a nice face. Not model-beautiful like that dreamy man's before, and a nice gleam to your eyes. I bet you were a beautiful baby. So let's get into the cab and go to a real nice pub. Sardi's, even. I love that joint. That it still exists for one thing: everything authentic today folds. Oh, overrated caricatures on the walls to spoil your appetite, but it's the perpetual stimulating overheard talk, and because of its dress code, all those gorgeous clothes. I can get us a quiet table where nobody can see us or a noisy one where everybody can and join in if you wish. So it's what pleases you, Dennis, you. I only want to please you tonight, so is it quiet or noise?"

"No tables. I don't want to go with you."

"Please, don't all of a sudden get rude."

"Scuse me, scuse me," the cabby says.

"I'm not. But if I can't convince you any other way?"

"All the very best drinks you want on me then—food too. Anything you want. You call it. Money, even."

"No really, thanks."

"I wasn't serious about the money, of course. Took a chance saying it, but I was only seeing how you'd behave. You came off with flying colors, as I knew you would. My instincts about you were right from the start. One thing though. Yes, I think I can say it. I'm serious about wanting you to come with me and I know, beyond that hard facade, who you truly are."

"I can't stand here longer," the cabby says.

"I'm sure you do, but thanks, no."

"Ah darn. Your one fault was you were always too immovable. So I'll be on my way." He walks to the cab. "On my way, I won't say goodnight, Dennis."

I nod.

"Ah darn." Gets in cab, is looking at me through the rear window as the cab takes off. It stops at the corner for the light. He sticks his head out the window opposite the smashed car. "I can still get out, Dennis. —What's this, your devilish business? Or you can still join me. Or the 21. First floor by the door. Elegant Nick to admit us and from then on even if you go there alone, to greet you by your family name, whatever yours is. You haven't lived till you've tasted their bourguignon. They know me there as well, and it's where I've changed course to. I'm a director."

I shake my head.

"Whuh? Can't hear ya. Harold. Harold Drissac and the Barclay Hotel. I'll be there till check-out time Sunday morn. Phone."

I wave, he waves, cab goes. I walk back half a block—that'll be enough time for anyone around the smashed car to forget me—look at the traffic, buildings across the street, sky, put my collar up and walk slowly to the car. Must have been smashed by the bus or smashed into the front of the bus, as the front of the bus farther up the street's also smashed but not as hard. When I saw the bus from the distance I thought it was just doubleparked.

"For the last time—step back?" a policeman says. The three of us step back. "All the way to the sidewalk again?" Sidewalk. Phone on the corner rings. He's standing beside the booth and answers it. "Wohlen. . . . Hey, hi, how's it going, last person I expected was. . . Sure, what? . . . Ha, no, I. . . I gave the number for here. . . . Now that's a good question. After talking to you for ten seconds when it seems like ten years since we—okay, okay. Let's see. You could hear it's a street, but exactly where? Fourteenth and Sixth, northwest corner, last—now this is going to be harder. Minus thirty-four from one—six, twenty—we'll forget the seconds. Seven times sixty plus that twenty-six. Three hundred— No. The last almost seven and a half hours of my midnight to eight shift. That's putting it exactly enough. My two-way's not operating, which I'm now glad of because you called. . . . How? Tell me."

I move up to the car. Two men I stepped back with before, one who's very tall with a gray ponytail, moved up before me, so if the policeman says anything again it'll be directed to us all. But stop. Really, what are you looking for? Just like that, why else? Not your everyday happening—not enough? Got this curiosity for the morbid, and not sudden but always. I'm a born snoop and repressed meddler, that's all. Fires, brawls, car crashes, nonstop sirens and alarms, I usually stop or go out to look, even put on my shoes and turn off what's cooking if I have to, but rarely this close. Want to see what might've happened to the passengers, but why? Blood, flesh, hair, torn cloth. For a moment I want to see what it's like inside one of these so soon after the crash and before it's towed off. So this is how it is, in other words. Shit? If so, then even that. I don't know and maybe I've gone overboard. Urine, shit, vomit, guts, I want one to all of those? If that's what's there, and it's not what I want per se, then I suppose so. To show I'm not too squeamish to look right at it for once and take a whiff, which maybe will change me somehow. The attitude: what's to be afraid if it's life. So that, I suppose—no, horsecrap. Know my own mind?—you bet. Oh, I don't know if it's all horsecrap, but I am curious to see what happened here and I might find. For instance didn't I one night—when my dad was very sick—incontinent too—could hold in his urine but not his shit—and I was taking care of him with my mom—stick my finger in what I just wiped from him and put it to my nose and take that whiff—*there*, that wasn't so bad, maybe it'll make it easier cleaning him the next times, and it did. "Quite the crackup," ponytailed man says, three of us inches away from the car and looking inside.

"Sure is," I say.

"If the driver and his front-seat companion, if there was one, got out alive, I'd be surprised."

"Maybe. Because I've witnessed something like this and the driver, though very banged up at the time, survived and probably at the most ended up with a scar or limp, but not bad."

"Of course anything can happen to man, anything," shorter man says. "You can get hit with a feather and die. Or else, as in the last war—number Two—a bullet shot into my helmet and all around the back inside and came out the hole it entered but without leaving anything but a ringing sound."

"To you?" ponytailed man says.

"Pardon. Did I say to me? To one of my buddies. After the war—in factual accounts—I read of just as strange things that happened: bullets in your canteens or boots but all around and out. Bullets stopped by your dogtag and dropping down your shirt and burning off your chest hairs. Bullets up your gun barrel where nobody got hurt, but also where plenty got hurt with bullets up the barrel and lost a hand or eye or died. I didn't mean me before with that helmet. Just that as an outfit like ours was you think it's you because you're so much one knit bunch. I remember the soldier's name, even. Politskiun— Don. Every five years on the dot I get a chain letter from him saying break it and not only won't I win fifty-thousand dollars this Monday but I'll probably die."

"Please, fellas," the policeman says from the booth. "Hold it, hon. Please, fellas. The sergeant's car comes along, I'm in big trouble. So now I'm telling— okay?"

"Sure," "Yes," "Fine," we say.

"You want to see, do it from the sidewalk." We step back to it. "On it this time." On it. "Good." On the phone: "So as I said. . . Accident, car with a bus. No one killed but two nearly. And from the accordion of a car now when it's making no more music, they were very lucky. One infant not as bad—her mouth. . . I do not. . . That's not true. . . . I said—now hold it a second. . . I'm sure to the hospital, but that was before my shift."

Car door's off so even from the sidewalk we can see inside. Steering wheel jammed into the dash. Underneath it an oil and gas spill. Just what he said: accordion. Its sound run out after the last squeeze. Concertina or accordion, hanging half-opened on the wall in the shape of a U. If I have a wedding—at my wedding I'll say—I want an accordion or concertina, maybe a balalaika too. How do you spell balalaika, and with two l's or three? Playing together— Russian or Polish music—and where I, champagne-sated, champagne Churchill preferred, if I can afford it and depending on how many guests, but question of affording it won't enter it and no more than twenty to thirty guests, happiest I'll ever be in my life, or close to it, which will be in the delivery room moments after my wife gives birth to our first child, would dance crazily with my bride, whirling to no special steps, instruments un-amplified electrically and players not in native dress. But "Never invite strangers to your wedding," Hasenai says in "My One and Only Nuptial Song," "especially musicians and actors. They'll drink all your sake, eat all your sushi, try to make love to your bride at the party, maybe beat up the groom (sub-stitute appropriate food and wine for your own country and scotch for mine, unless you're a stranger whose wedding takes place in Japan)."

"Longer I look at this," I say, "more I find it incredible how anyone got out alive."

"Maybe they didn't," ponytailed man says.

"But according to—"

"What does he know? He's only interested in making hay on the phone, can't you hear? 'Oh love, mushy, pussy, beat my meat, heartpiss.' A faker."

"That's it precisely," shorter man says, "only we need them."

"We'll be fortunate—I've seen it happen so I back up with experience what I say—if she doesn't shoot down here and they don't do it on the floor of this car, rubble and all."

"Like I stated," shorter man says, "everything happens to man—the works. In our platoon an officer stepped on a land mine—this, minutes after he lectured us on how to recognize them—went thirty feet into the air, was unconscious all the while he was up there, came down on his feet without knowing it and which now had no boots on and were scorched, and suddenly was awake and walked straight into a puddle to take away the heat from the burns. Later maybe because burns get infected so easily, they got infected. And because our medic was dead and we were way off no place smoking-out Italians—people tend to forget they were also our enemies then—he almost lost both legs. Lieutenant Malcolm G. Gabert his name was. I don't hear from him ever. And I certainly, I want you to know, by my aside before, have nothing against Italians."

"Excuse me, but that lieutenant incident sounds impossible."

"I knew he'd say that," ponytailed man says.

"But thirty feet up, then landing on his feet unconsciously and walking away?"

"If he hadn't been unconscious when he landed he wouldn't have landed that way. He would have landed in a way where he would have died, like not on his feet."

"But coming out unscathed?"

"The scorch burns, this gentleman said—the infections."

"Pardon me for arguing, sir," shorter man says to me, "and I can handle this, so please let me," to the ponytailed man, "but I saw it. I wasn't him but I saw him. Other soldiers in other situations got killed standing a hundred feet away from even less powerful land mines that exploded, and also when they had some natural hard protection to hide behind like concrete or sturdy trees. So who can say about life? Take it from me: not you or I."

"I don't mean to argue either," I say, "but a bomb's a bomb. Sure, anything can happen in life, to a degree, so I'll go along with your bullets in boots and so on. But if a bomb lands smack on top of you—touches your body when it explodes or just inches away, and of the force of a mine that can send a normal-sized man—he was, wasn't he?"

"My height."

"And you're a little less than my height, and if it had happened to me—and when I'm talking of a bomb landing on someone I mean the mine below—I'd have died. Or at least would've been seriously maimed, and ninety-nine chances out of a hundred that would've meant among other things losing both legs or at least one of them or one of my feet. No, both feet. They can't survive such a blast and probably not even the legs below the knees."

"What do you want me to tell you, you're right? Because I won't apologize in a war where fifty million died. And if fifty million did—if forty million I'll even say—you don't think—or thirty, or twenty, not to say a hundred million casualties or thereabouts—there wouldn't have been even a few thousand inconceivable freak accidents, plus the fifty to a hundred thousand that at first seemed inconceivable but you gradually came around to believe in them? For instance, a three-story stone building in an area totally arid from no rainfall for months collapsed on one of the villagers in a village we shelled and she was under the entire thing of it for ten days without air, food, drink or even mud to lick and she survived."

"That's only a little more possible to believe than the lieutenant incident, but still quite impossible. In ten days she would've suffocated, starved, completely dehydrated, but *something* to have died."

"That's what I'm telling you—impossible to believe but there it was before my eyes."

"You're not claiming it was God's doing, in other words?" ponytailed man says.

"I'm saying it was an inconceivable freak, which is a combination of a miscellany of coincidences and natural life and man-made happenings. Which means it could even have been to her advantage there hadn't been rain for months, plus her own body and what it was able to withstand and the will to survive and—"

"No, it's beyond being a freak," I say. "In ten days, if she came up alive—"

"That's what she did. But she didn't walk up, you know. First of all, where were the stairs? Second of all, she had to be lifted gingerly and carried away. Now I'm not saying she lived more than an hour after that, since we never knew how the wounded were doing in the hospitals, except for our own GI's. It was a human miracle—just us, what we as people fall into and get out of and between those undergo, and nothing dealing with those big manipulative fingers with the strings at the ends of them of the Lord's. You're not a great believer by any chance, for if you are, again I deeply apologize."

"I'm not. But air pockets. Or someone could've been feeding her through a tube those last few days. I'm no expert, and you couldn't have been there all the time those ten days."

"No tubes. And I didn't need minute-to-minute information on her, since nothing had essentially changed till we reached her the last day. You see, she started out in the basement of the building because that's where she went when the village was being shelled, and for ten days she was twenty-five feet under that pile."

"Maybe you're right. I've never been to war or even in one of the armed services, and I'm getting cold out here," rubbing my hands, feeling for a coat button I might not have buttoned except for the top one. "But, come to think of it I was in a very serious car accident and nothing happened to me, while the guy I hit nearly died. But that was because my car was a big used Olds compared to his two-seater British something or another sports."

"What happened?" ponytailed man says. "They weren't drafting then and you happened to come of age between one of the police actions or wars, or you were deferred?"

"The truth is—you fellows aren't federal law officers or MP's in disguise, are you? Only kidding. No, it was so long ago I don't mind admitting it now. I was called down for a physical and pretended something was a bit more than neurotic with me—but only after I couldn't fail any of the physical tests—and they believed it. It was a good act, but I just didn't want to go in then, that's all."

"If it was World War Two or Korea would you have acted that way?"

"I think I would've gone in some other capacity than gun-holding—that was the thing."

"Someone's got to pull the trigger," shorter man says.

"True. Or not. And I shouldn't have brought it up, since you did fight, you say."

"I most certainly did; I can't speak for him."

"Coast guard," ponytailed man says. "Nothing rough, but it could have been. Florida waters, snooping for subs."

"And you probably lost buddies," I say to the shorter man.

"I already told you."

"Me, never, except through natural causes. One slips on the deck. Another talks tough to a hooker. My closest amigo had cirrhosis of the liver when he joined up—"

"Excuse me—and I know," I say to the shorter man, "and I respect that, and no doubt you still carry deep feelings about those deaths and all, so now it's my turn to apologize."

"Forget the apologies and respects to death and how chilly it is out here—it isn't to me anyway. Just speak your mind."

"Speak it. Yes. Well I'll try. Gun-holding and shooting. I could maybe to save my mother's life or some innocent's or mine. Definitely my mother's and mine, if I wasn't the one responsible, and the innocent's if it was a child. Even if I was responsible, though if my mother was responsible I would too but without any question. And even if the innocent wasn't a child, and in fact wasn't even completely innocent, but a lot more innocent than the other person, though that I'd definitely have to know. The circumstances of their dispute, I mean, before I'd step in with a gun, though I don't see any reason for my ever getting hold of one. But if I was suddenly holding one, how would I know how to use it? And if I tried to and it didn't go off or went off wrong, I'd be asking, in stepping in for this innocent, to get shot at and killed. For my mother and no doubt myself, I'd try to use the gun even if I didn't know how to—and I'm talking about a gun against gun or something comparable to one. That is, if nothing else worked before that or I could see that nothing would and I now had no time to do anything else."

"A country's the same when it's fighting the enemy," shorter man says. "You have to think of each of them as different families or separate lives. Your country's your mother, the enemy's the mugger."

"That's good—mother-mugger—but there's too much involved with countries. I can't balance it. Killing in self-defense I can. Someone comes at you, it's 'Hey, this is my life, what're you doing, lay off,' and there's a rock there and whack, you crack him. Or a gun, and if not shooting it, then with the butt. Now if it's a woman or kid coming at you, and a girl more so than a boy—I don't know. Or your mother—same thing—in defending her. 'Hey, this is my mom, what do you expect me to do no matter what she did, stand there?'—right? Really, between society's needs and mine—and I know one takes in the other, etcetera, but so do the societies which are our enemies and so on—how do you justify my needs over its? Or my country attacking theirs or not, or defending itself, and how much to if we were responsible for the dispute?—but now I'm getting all unclear, my ideas. I'd have to write it, I'm not good at expressing it. But you can see how I feel. So what can I say? That I can probably help our army in an emergency in other ways. Translating, if we ever went to war again in the Orient. But only, I think, if what the army asks of me is right. Or the policies of our country in this particular crisis or war are right, which is probably in most cases impossible to find out, just because in any crisis the army or country, for tactical reasons, probably mostly always lies."

"Oh, you know?" shorter man says.

"Not personally. But from newspapers I—"

"What, the *Times, Post?*"

"The *Times,* why not? And magazines. Not *Newsweek* or—"

"So why didn't you try that device when you were drafted?"

"I'm sorry—I said so many things. You mean asking for alternative service?"

"Others did. C.O.'s."

"Right—C.O.'s. Well. But look, what am I here, on military trial? No, I don't want to joke about it, but you're—or maybe it's just when I get into a conversation that's too loaded or potentially so—"

"I'm talking considerately to him, aren't I?" to the ponytailed man, who nods and shrugs. "Considerately, not maliciously—all you have to do is listen to my voice to know. So don't answer me if you don't want to on anything. That's the prerogative of all free people, which we should be, governmentally and on the street. Because what I like about our talk so far is that we've been so flexible, listening without friction, so please let's not spoil it."

"It has been easy," ponytailed man says.

"It actually has, and honestly, no harm meant from here either. Okay. I just didn't want to go into the army—but then, I mean, *then.* Maybe I shouldn't go on."

"Finish up," shorter man says. "I'm interested, and no more interruptions."

"I didn't say much," ponytailed man says.

"I meant from us both."

"Because who knows what one can get into? I was younger—what the hell—it was twenty years ago and I found a way out and bolted. I didn't know what to do with my life but knew I didn't want to not know what I didn't want to do with— Anyway, now I see things clearer, am a lot more confident about my life, want less, struggle more—rather I expect little than want less and what I know I'm willing to put up with for my feelings and ideas, etcetera, and so on. That was no good. I think I'd say to the army now to give me this instead of that, and take it. I would. But if they didn't give me this but that, which was gun-holding and in basic training, bullet-dodging and latrine-cleaning, and later in the service possible man-killing, I'd say no and take the consequences—I think. Though someone has to clean the latrines, you might say. We wouldn't be a good match, the army and I, or that's what their psychiatrist said after I played it to the hilt to get myself psyched out, so I suppose I'd have to be put to the test. Of being called up again and what I'd do. I don't know . . ."

"Too late for that now," ponytailed man says.

"The gray shows, eh?" fingering a sideburn.

"What about the accident where you almost died? That's one I want to hear the end of, since I've a long interest in everything automobile. It rules the universe, you know. TV's too."

"It was the other driver who almost died. And thanks for taking me off the subject—both, my hair too. It—actually, I don't care about my hair except when the sides look like feathers coming out. 'Bozo the Clown,' my junior high school students, when—"

"You see? TV. So my case is closed. Continue—don't mind me."

"Come on, you don't want me to. And I've got to go."

"You crazy? In the middle? Man dying on the road and we're leaving him there? You have to."

"Okay. Colorado—the accident. Still all right by you?" to the shorter man. He nods. "A few years after the army—psyching out. Probably shouldn't have mentioned it, but so what. And I'm driving drunk down a mountain road—coasting—I was that inexperienced with cars, having just learned how to drive, and I turned off the ignition to save on the gas—I was also that broke. Anyway, the road's dark, though I was smart enough to keep my headlights on—running the battery, if that's what it's called, and I think I also liked the idea of driving soundlessly. None of this would be so clear, by the way, if it hadn't been such an experience. But where was I?"

"Down the road—" shorter man says.

"When my car suddenly stops. No, wheels didn't lock—that's what happens, you're about to say, right? when coasting with the motor off—but my fender's been smashed against the front left wheel. Of course I had to get out of the car to see this. How'd it happen? Must've been in an accident, blanked out. But just before that I was singing to some radio music same time I'm yelling out the window something like 'Hey stars, beautiful stars, look at me, city slicker in country Colorado, yippie pippie yeh,' so not so soundlessly. But if the ignition was off, radio couldn't be on, at least in that car."

"That's what I was about to ask," ponytailed man says. "What year Olds and what style?"

"Good questions. Anyway, I'm looking at my car and think I must've hit a tree. When I see, back up the road a few hundred feet, a tiny car with its headlights pointing to the sky perpendicularly. But this is silly. You don't want me—"

"Don't start. Continue."

"Some other cars stopped. I'll tell you what kind of guy I was then. Worse than a young idiot and mistakes. I wouldn't do anything like it today. Oh, little lies and mistakes today—but then, before any other car stopped, I got back in my car and tried to drive away, but it wouldn't move. Fender against wheel. So I got out as if for the first time, since some cars had stopped behind me, and with some people walked back to the tiny car."

"Dead."

"I won't say yet, for the story's sake, but anyway, we already said he wasn't, but his sports car was totaled. Doors still closed. Windows smashed in a way where they were still in their frames but you couldn't see inside."

"Safety glass. Supposed to do that. Must have been German- or Swedish-make. For glass, that far back, they were the best."

"Door windows made of plastic and slashed but intact. Someone said 'Shouldn't one of us see what's inside?' but no one wanted to open the door."

"You blame them?" shorter man says.

"No, but I said I think I should be the one since I was the other person involved—'not that I was responsible,' I said. 'The other driver was—out in my lane, not that I like putting any blame on him now,' I said—lying, lying. Actually, since I didn't see the accident, I didn't know at the time who was really responsible, but had a good idea. But say both of us were drunk or asleep at the wheel and in the wrong lanes—it's possible. Or I'm asleep in my lane and he's just drunk and in my lane. Anyway, most of me assumed I was the only one responsible, but the rest of me said to myself at the time 'Well, who really knows?'"

"I take for granted you were the one responsible," shorter man says, "based on what you said so far. But it is possible, if somewhat implausible—two drivers on the road drunk or asleep at the same time and hitting one another's car, even if it's probably happened a couple of hundred times in America this year. What do you say, expert?"

"One I never heard of but has to have happened. But continue," he says to me. "You're guilty, but of felonious car crashing or attempted manslaughter we don't know yet."

"I opened the driver's door. There's one man there, half on the seat, half on the floor."

"His body in half?"

"From the waist down he's on the seat, the waist up on the floor, his head on the pedals but still connected to the neck and the neck to the rest. I lifted him up, though knew then I shouldn't—broken bones, that sort of thing—till he was flat on the seat. Glass in his head cut my hand in several places, but that didn't matter. In fact it made things look better for me, I thought. A lot of blood, his and mine. Made sure to get some of it, but not too much as if I intentionally smeared it to elicit a sympathetic response, on my face and shirt. He was mumbling something. I said 'What is it?' and put my ears to his lips, thinking if it's something incriminating about me I should be the first or only one to hear it, especially if he died."

"That's horrible," shorter man says.

"Not only that, if he did die—and I hope it goes without saying that I was just about praying he wouldn't—and someone asked what he'd said and it had been critical of me—I was telling myself then I'd say 'He mumbled, nothing I understood.'"

"Even worse."

"It was. But I'll stop. I've said too much, besides all your time."

"What'd the near-dying guy say?" ponytailed man says.

"Yes—momentum—go go go ahead—what?"

"He said 'Other car did it, was on my side of the road.' I said into his ear very low 'No it wasn't. You were, on his side, try to remember that, and we think driving without your lights.' Sometimes since then I've thought—as I also thought with a Denver dentist I ran out on the bills around that time—that I'd call him and say 'Listen, I was drunk and in your lane, so what can I do to make amends?' And to the dentist say 'How much do I owe you plus interest over the years?' I did say I was sorry then to the accident guy, but inside more sorry it happened to us both and me the inconvenience of going to court and time away from paying work and losing my car in a car-required state when I was strapped for cash. But I never admitted to him my fault in the crash, and to the dentist—well, when I got a lawyer's letter in New York I wrote back under a different name that I was the executor of my estate and that I'd died."

"I don't get that."

"I'll explain it later," shorter man says.

"I used the apartment number and address of a not-so-willing friend and said the man he'd sent the letter to about the bill had died and if there was any money left after the settlement of a very negligible estate, his client was seventh in line. He sent a letter every half year asking if the estate had been settled, but I ignored them, so even to a few years later I was still irresponsible, since by then I had enough to begin paying the dentist back on time. Anyway, the accident guy shook his head, shut his eyes and looked dead and I held his hand—till the police came—while several people patted my back and rubbed my neck. I got a summons—that was automatic in an accident that bad, the trooper said, just as the other guy would have got one if he was even half alive at the time."

"Wait a second," ponytailed man says. "You got a summons at the accident?"

"I think so."

"Colorado? Give me a second to think. No, on that there's almost strict uniformity. You would have been told to expect one, if he didn't arrest you on the scene, and then got it through the mail. So what the trooper might have told you was that the other man would have also got one if he hadn't been near death and if you didn't seem the main cause of the accident. Do you recall him measuring your tire tread marks on the road?"

"Really, I forget. Anyway, I showed up in court hangdog and without lawyer, since I thought the judge would be favorably disposed to that. And pretended, as with the psychiatrist, to be, despite my university connection, which only involved student-teaching to a master's degree I never completed, a bit weak-minded and oversensitive to the point a few times of doing my sincerest best to repress real tears, and very unorganized and alone. I was living with a woman then but left her a block from the courthouse and told her not to give a sign in the courtroom that she knew me. I also saw there the man I hit, still with Band-Aids on his face and walking with a cane. I never asked nor found out if he'd walked with one before the accident. I wasn't questioned in depth about driving while drunk, since I was able, when I got out of the car the second time—and because they also didn't give me the balloon test, since the drunk driver they'd picked up before me got so incensed at what she called a divestment of her civil liberties that she punctured it with her fingernails. Anyway, I was able to make all my alcohol mannerisms and breath disappear. 'Get stark raving sober,' I told myself when I left the car, 'you're in trouble up to here.' Impossible, I know. But about drinking, I said to the judge when he asked, 'Yes, had a wine and a half at that party up the hill, but some yogurt before and a glass of milk after to coat it.' Also, after I said I'm sorry to the guy for what had happened to us, he asked if I'd said anything to him when he was in the car—he seemed to remember it. I said 'No, except for "Don't worry, you're gonna be all right," while I held your hand and dabbed blood from your eyes.' 'Okeydoke,' he said. 'This is the Wild West so accidents like that can happen, just so long as your insurance company takes care of it.' The judge advised me to plead nolo contendere and I got a twenty-two-dollar fine and they didn't even take my license away for a day. That was it. I walked the two miles home alone in the rain because I wanted to save on the cab fare and not be seen with my woman friend. Story has a rather unuplifting ending, but what can I say? When I got back she called me a louse for everything I'd done that day, wouldn't even run a warm tub for me and soon after that moved out, but more because we were broke and she'd just turned thirty and wanted to get married and have a child right away, while I—"

"You'd think they would have slapped something more than a small fine on you," shorter man says.

"You're right. But after all my lies to the trooper and judge, I certainly wasn't going to ask for it. Besides, I couldn't afford to go to jail or pay a big fine. Look, I was lucky."

"Did you watch a lot of TV in those days?" ponytailed man says.

"No, why?"

"When you were young then. Were you affixiated, I like to call it, to the TV screen?"

"No more than most kids my age. Howdy Doody at five every afternoon. There weren't as many stations and programs then. Mostly test patterns and Gorgeous George and Ralph Bellamy as a private eye I think and maybe not even Uncle Miltie yet. But you think there's some connection with my lying and conniving to TV?"

"I've theories, but nothing proven in the lab. But the art of getting away with things or thinking you can—that can be too much TV. That jail isn't real, for instance, but that wouldn't apply to you, since you wanted to avoid a sentence. You said you were lucky. Well, then Mr. Lucky perhaps—a character in the early days of TV."

"I don't remember him."

"Flipping a coin? Dressed sharply? Always led off with 'Hello, suckers—life still thrilling?' No? If you do go back to Howdy Doody days, tell me—the early Howdy or the late?"

"You mean the one before he had plastic surgery on his face?"

"So, if you go back that far—"

"Hey, you too—his operation right on TV—right? right?" and I slap his palm though he didn't offer it and say "And the doctors in masks working over him and his convalescence for weeks after with bandages covering his face. And he was so *ugly* before, but interesting, remember?—but much worse after because they made his face so cute and telegenic with too many freckles. And the Peanut Gallery and Bob Smith too?"

"I sat in it on TV one day."

"So did I. Sent away for the seat. I wonder if we were in it the same day."

"I'm sure not. And I only went as a chaperon for my younger sister, so I have to be a lot older than you."

"I don't know—I was a late bloomer. My family was afraid I'd never come around."

"That's surprising to hear. Still, getting back—but I've lost track of what I was going to say, and I have to apologize about Mr. Lucky. He was in the movies, even if somehow," tapping his head, "it still registers TV. But I'm also starting to freeze out here, so no further questions."

"I've only one," shorter man says. "Maybe you won't like it, but we've proven we're civilized here without the other person immediately thinking we're full of disapproval, yes?"

"Fine by me," I say.

"Good. Then what made you change? Conniving to the army, lying to the judge, that injured man, because you say you're much different today."

"Life—the maturing process—the over and over again—ideas. Gradually realizing what I was doing and did. You know—the repercussions—on me and others. I mean, I still lie—little ones to get by, to others and myself. But the big ones—well you know, they're more obvious and harmful, to me and to others, so if you continue to do them—if I do—cheat, bullshit—well you know, it's increasingly obvious you can't. But if you do after you know how obvious it is and that you shouldn't, then it's also increasingly obvious to others or should be—yourself included—that they get bigger and bigger these lies and just acting like a prick, and some more obvious and harmful than others—no, that's not it. I know what I want to say but can't articulate it, though it should be obvious what I mean by now, or fairly."

"I think I see. Okay, I can figure out the rest myself, so my case is closed too."

"You'll clue me in later if we're still here together?" ponytailed man says and shorter man says "If you don't freeze as you said, yes."

We've inched up—at least I didn't know we had—to the car and I'm about to say goodnight to them when the ponytailed man says "Look—on the floor by the soda can—a quarter."

"You saw it first, you take it," I say.

"If you believe in good luck finding coins, that one's bad."

"Oh, I'm not superstitious and you never know when you might need some extra change. You guys first? Sure? Sir?" to the shorter man.

"Not me. This time I agree with my new friend completely."

"Besides, talking about being unsuperstitious, I've a lucky coin jar at home—even have a five-dollar bill in it—but I didn't tell you this?"

"Not tonight."

"It's a stupid reference—really, unrelated. Not unrelated, just stupid. Anyway, money I've found over the past ten years, not that it's brought me good luck, but who knows? According to you two I could be dead right now without it, and for ten or fewer years. And then—well I wonder what you two would be doing now if I were. Everything else would be the same, though of course my shadow wouldn't be here and footprints if there are any, and other small to smaller things: cigarette butts I might've squashed with my shoes and so on—carbon dioxide in the air or a little less oxygen because of me, but I know next to nothing about those. But the car would be here, bus, weather, etcetera—that policeman, with maybe just the slightest of faintest chances my absence of from an hour to ten years would've changed any of that. Probably, even without me, you'd be looking at this car and possibly from this or a nearby spot. Or more probably, since you'd"—to the ponytailed man-- "have ended up just as cold and I wouldn't be keeping you here with my yakking, you'd both be inside somewhere talking about the car, or on your respective ways home, if they're not in the same direction. Or maybe they're even in the same building or on the same floor for all you know, though that's much less likely, unless it's one of those twenty to thirty apartments to a floor buildings, if they run that large. No? All wrong?"

"I'll go along about the shadow and dioxide," ponytailed man says. "As for this guy living in my building, except if he moved in today or had been hiding all this time—"

"Okay. But after living so long with this jar, I don't have the heart to stop putting found money in it or empty it out to use the money or even just to use the jar." They stare at me. "I mean, it's an old pickle jar with a wide neck—quart-size, so really good for storing things—so the money I'd store somewhere else, if I didn't use both at the same time: money and jar. I knew I shouldn't have brought up the subject of good luck." Policeman has his back to us, talking on the phone. "But I can be compulsive about not passing up found money, though not to the point where I think it'll bring bad luck if I don't. That someone first had to point the coin out to me—well, that variation of finding lucky money hasn't come up till now, so I'll deal with it when I get home or along the way, but how can I deal with it realistically if I don't have the coin? Anyway, coast seems clear enough," and I reach in to get the quarter, blow off the glass bits. Try to put it into my change pocket, but this pair of pants doesn't have one, so I feel for an empty pocket, back right one first, is none, take the comb and keys out of that pocket, which is where if I have no change pocket I put found coins, stick the keys into the less crowded left back pocket, comb into the left side pocket, quarter into the right back pocket where I'll know where it came from if I want to drop it into the jar. My notebook and Hasenai's book of poems in Japanese—and I tap the two side pockets to make sure they're there. Wallet's in the right side pocket of the pants, pen in the other. Smaller notebook—which I'm not afraid to lose since there's nothing much in it, and its metal tip has ripped, even when I've wedged it under the spirals or taped it, a couple of my pants pockets or other parts of the backs of my pants—in the left back pocket, handkerchief also in the side coat pocket, so everything's there. Subway tokens? Have none. Other coins—can't feel or find any, unless they're at the bottom of one of these pants or coat pockets. Nail clipper, I find, when I thought I lost it weeks ago, also in the right side pocket of the pants. "So, that was my Colorado car crash yawn and selected confessions. Call it a night, gentlemen?"

"We all do kooky things when we're young," shorter man says.

"Really, I'm much too cold to listen," ponytailed man says.

"A moment. Last tale. I did with you both for more minutes than I enjoyed, and if you want I'll stand you to a real drink after—worth the wait? So everyone sit. In the army I threw—on German land but Allied-held territory—a live grenade at my best buddy ever when I got overwhelmingly sore at him for something he did, of what I won't waste your time with, but it was dirty. Fortunately—that it wasn't the advancing enemy with fixed bayonets charging—it was a dud, or I'm sure, for penal reasons, I wouldn't be here speaking to you now. Though after so long and because I was born in the Village and my family would still have been here for sixteen years—my mother the last of her kin to die and in the same apartment I still live in. The same bed, in fact—I switched to theirs after she went—and please, I don't give a blink to what people say about extremely close mother-son relationships—I loved her!—maybe I would be speaking to you right where we're standing and same time, give or take."

"They also broke the mold after my mother was born," ponytailed says, "but I never did anything as angry as you. Sure, once tossed a man overboard but knew no sharks were around and he could swim."

"All of us Peanut Gallery émigrés," I say. "Wound up so peaceful and, well I was going to say 'loved our mothers,' but you couldn't have watched it too."

"My baby brother did. And you can't be too sure sharks aren't everywhere around but in your bathtub," to the ponytailed man. "Right from the piers over there I've seen them—when I fished as a kid and now just to sit and think—frequently."

"We had safety nets to keep them out—for swimming."

"Then if they weren't in the swimming perimeter before you set up the nets, true."

"So," I say, "—great talking," and I stick out my hand.

"Same here," ponytailed man says, "without reservation," and shakes.

Shorter man smiles, is about to take his hand out of his pocket, says "Doubtful as I was at first when I saw you approach that it could actually happen—for I'm usually a keen judge of character and I had you down as odd and troublesome, especially after you walked back a block after your screaming-fag incident, it was a pleasure," and I say "Thank you, thank you both," pat his shoulder and pass the corner, policeman still on the phone but now facing the street and nodding to me as he listens, carefully pull the little notebook out of my back pocket, flip through it to make sure nothing of interest's in it—"'Free speech,' the orator said, batting his adversary over the head, 'and also freedom of action'". . ."kasha tonight—make it!!" . . ."dahlias: 366: 4182". . ."pick up ticks to Bunraku by fri and dont let May give any excuses shes not going". . ."Parnassus 205 w 89 10024". . ."military court of national salvation". . ."dovecote". . ."Grossingers mocha apricot or praline". . ."trichloroethane at hardware stead of regular typewriter cleaner—savings 4-1 Di says". . ."tissues, al foil, lemons, limes, Times, cake plates 24 white". . ."May's folks: demitasse set; Mom: subscription to New Yorker"—and rip it apart and drop it into the trashcan and walk uptown.

CHAPTER SIX

Helene

I'm dancing and the band's too loud and been going on too long and I'm also starting to feel sick, so I say "Really, I'm getting dizzy, mind if we stop?" and the man I'm dancing with, I don't know his name, he told me it and I forgot, his name's Allan or Aaron or some name with an A and I think an an or on at the end of it, well Adman I'll call him just for the heck of it, since he said he was one or was that the last man I danced with, says "Anything you say, Miss Helene—just a-kiddin; too many old movies. But what is it? You're not feeling too good?" We've stopped. People dance around us in twos, threes and groups plus a few snapping their fingers and with their eyes shut doing entranced oohing solos. "Too much champagne. —Watch out for the whirling whale on your left—we'll get rolled over. I always drink too much at these damn affairs. Not damn. It's a nice affair and not Dorothy and Sven's fault I don't know how to drink. One glass, that should have done it, while I must have had three, maybe four. And this music. Excuse me, but you don't think it's God's gift to modern ears, do you? *Ears, Ears,*" when he looks at me as if he didn't hear, "because that's exactly what it gives you, hearing problems. I find it too loud, fast, for children—give me Piranesi—*Palestrina,* if not to dance then just to listen and sing to. But I used to be able to dance furiously to this—liked it better then too. Eons ago, but now—I hated to be Miss Killjoy but if I had danced another few steps, and God forbid another big swirl, I would have thrown up."

"Please, no excuses necessary. I'm in fact gratified," bowing, "knowing the physical effect it would've had on you, since I am wearing my new party shoes and only renting this—but why am I being so gross?" He takes my upper arm, holds out his other hand and says to the dancers he parts us through "Pardon, scus-e moi, happy man, hapless damoiselle," and we walk back to the dais where I have a seat next to Dorothy's. Pleasant man, clever enough tongue, but so unattractive. And what an awful affair. From the bagel tree to the champagne fountain. How could she have let her mother throw it? Reminder if I ever marry again: take the ladder route, toots, even if I am eight flights up, then to relent to those insurmountable—unsurmountable?—whatever it amounts to—parental forces. "Thank you very kindly, Mr.— I'm sorry, my champagne head, and last names."

"Arthur Rosenthal."

"Arthur, right. With an A."

"Vut den? The only way."

"No, it's just— Oh, out with it, girl—no more dissembling. Do you know who Satchel Paige was?"

"From what I read, still is. A great old baseball pitcher."

"Well I had a friend who loved to repeat—"

"A male friend?"

"Yes, a man. Loved to repeat what Satchel Paige said about lying. He said, Paige did—oh God, what did he say? His mother— Something about if you're going to lie— I wish my friend was around, but only to feed me the line. Anyway, I knew your first name started with A and while we were dancing I raked my brain to remember it. But the champagne again. Out goes memory, in goes whatever goes in. A headache tomorrow. But, don't know how I would have made it back here without you, so thanks—Arthur? Artie? Art?"

"I prefer Arthur. Mind if I sit with you? Till Dorothy gets back?"

"Where is Dorothy? There she is. Hi, Dots. Great party. Dance it away, me lady."

"She looks miraculous, doesn't she? Brides. Boy, they all do, even the ugly ones, though she wasn't ugly before. Till now she was near to being beautiful. A borderline beauty I'll call her. Not a natural beauty I can say—not like you, if you'll excuse me—tut tut, got carried away," and he slaps his wrist. "But tonight—you do excuse me, don't you?"

"Sure, but no more—for my own reasons."

"What are they?"

"Please, my own reasons. Reverse egotism, which sounds like the reverse of it, but what do you want me to say? Tonight Dorothy what?"

"Tonight she's truly beautiful, which isn't merely her dress and happiness but is also very much tied up with her knowing we all know she's a beautiful ecstatic bride."

"I'm sorry, you lost me there a little. And sure, sit if you like; at least don't stand. Don't know how much chitchat I'm good for. I'm a bit tired tonight."

"No problem, honestly. I usually don't talk this much too." He sits. "So, what do you do?"

"What do I do? I didn't say so on the dance floor? I'm a dance instructress."

"Of course you are."

"Really showed. Stepped a few more times on your toes than I should have."

"It wasn't that. In fact, you were extremely graceful."

"Graceful I'm not. And *extremely*? Would you believe I once studied to be a dancer? True, true, and people—ballet instructors, older dancers—said I had a gift for it too. But I lost the body for it. Got too top-heavy for one thing and a bit too bottom-heavy too."

"You've a fine figure."

"Fine, maybe—I don't know—but for classical dancing?—no. By the time I was fourteen the figure had filled out too much, despite what I did to stop it—you just can't reduce bones—and I couldn't, well, float the way I wanted to over a ballet stage. I was devastated."

"So what kind of work did you end up doing?"

"You still don't believe I'm a dance instructress? No, we went over that."

"Champagne?" the waiter says, pouring more champagne into my empty glass.

"Not for me thanks, really. Take it away."

"It's a wedding reception. Drink, be gay. It's luck for the bride and groom if you do. You don't and then he and next everyone here, this'll all go to waste. It's paid for and the barmen will hide the unused bottles as if they been drunk."

"That's the wedding couple's problem," Arthur says, "—the mother."

"It should be ours too. Sophie should know."

"Don't tell her I told," the waiter says. "Anyhow, it isn't so. I only said it to get you to drink. Tell folks something'll only go to waste and they stuff their faces with it, but nothing like a happy occasion. I love it when all my people I serve get drunk. They get zonked enough—hey, they don't see me knocking down some too. Not serious. Yours?" he says to Arthur.

"Why not? Any one of these glasses. In fact, I'll drink hers, mine and yours."

"Hooo, bad guy—candy from babies. But it's people like you who make for great parties." He fills all the glasses on this side of the dais, says to Arthur "Persuade her," and goes.

"Crazy guy," Arthur says, downing his glass. "So, after all that, what *do* you do?"

"Really, it's all sort of boring to me now, my work. But you're so interested in learning what I do—no, this won't make any sense. —Hi, Soph, dance a jig, kid, 'cause tomorra you'll be broke. Not serious, as the waiter says. I'm not. —Oh God, what did I say? —Sorry, Soph, but it's your champagne. It's too good," and I try to roll my eyes while I roll my head. She waves, puts her fingers to her ears that she didn't hear, foxtrots to the middle of the floor with Sven, people crowd around them clapping in unison, Dorothy taps Sven's shoulder and cuts in to dance with her mother and the clapping crowd cheers them. "I'm so embarrassed. To bring up the cost of this overpriced garish party. And the cake hasn't even been wheeled out yet. I'm supposed to—how am I going to?—stand beside them while they cut it, with its three different-colored tiers and the edible naked couple standing on top right down to the pink nipples, detumescent penis and Dorothy's dark and Sven's yellow pubic hair. Arthur, I've got to be crocked, or close to it. Say something that will make me think I wasn't that crude to Sophia or that she really didn't hear."

"I don't see how she couldn't've."

"Great help."

"What do I do did you start to ask me before?"

"Right—good. I was. Then I don't know what. Just answer. Pay no attention to what I say."

"Lawyer. Tax law. Might sound boring, but it's fairly exciting if you're interested in psychology and people and petty—and, you know, right on up the ladder—thievery."

"Doesn't sound boring. Doesn't sound too exciting, but everyone has to do something. See how smart I am? Ready for more painstaking cerebration and fancy wording? It's nice to make a good living. I'm sure you do or enough to leave reasonably well on—*live* on."

"I don't complain."

"I do because I don't make enough to leave or live on. But I'm not really complaining either, even if it might seem, with my comment about how I can complain—forget it. Anyone for tied-up tongue tonight? Not quite on the menu. I don't know why I even unconsciously suggested it, since I get paid well enough for what I do in the time I do it in. Yes I do, and health insurance, and I love my kids."

"You're married?"

"What do I do do you mean to make such an uncomplaining living and have such good kids? I teach. American literatures and languages. That was supposed to be amusing," when he looks mystified. "Russian literatures and languages?" Still doesn't get it. "Romance?" He smiles. "Ah, la love you understand. And maybe there is such a department in some university— American L and L—but I'm not aware of it. —Hi, Sven. Do her the big dip again." He does. Dorothy waves to me as her hair brushes the floor, then is upended again and I blow them a kiss and they each blow me one back. What will he think when he sees his pubic hair on top of the cake? Dot got it at the Erotic Bakeshop as a surprise for him. Good thing Sophie talked her out of having the couple recline postcoitally in bed, but I hope he scolds her for being so goddamn *New York* magazine.

"Dance with us, Helene," Dorothy says.

"Too many bubbles. I'll fall on my face."

"That's what you're supposed to do at a wedding reception," Sven says.

"And that's what everybody's been telling me to. But I have to grade papers and write a review the next few days, so I need that face. I'm enjoying myself just fine from here. And I danced on my face before just fine with Arthur."

They dance away. Rock music's been playing for thirty minutes straight. Flowers. Smell of so many of them makes me think of summer, Cape cottage, student-free.

"I'm really not a good dancer," Arthur says, "but you simplified it for me. However much you say the alcohol affected you, you danced as gracefully as I said. Not like a gazelle, mind you, with dancing shoes on, but one without them. You carry well."

"I carry well?"

"You let me carry you well, the few times I held you, and lead you well too. It felt, those times, as if I were dancing with a feather—it's true."

"Did I tickle you? Sorry. So, tax law, huh? Actually, my father used to be one. But just a plain lawyer."

"You're kidding. This is unbelievable. On his own or in a firm? Where, New York? Hey, we were made in heaven, and what's your original last name?"

"In Vilna before the war. He was too weak when they got here to study for the bar, and the piddling hard jobs he took to keep us alive quickly did him in."

"He died?"

"He didn't, no, just got very disconsolate and sick."

"I'm glad to hear that. Not that he got sick, and I didn't mean to pry. But he was a lawyer—well, let's say he eventually recovered and went back to it or was very successful in anything he did. Champagne," picking up two glasses of it. "Moments like these we need it, as the beer commercials say." He offers me one, I shake my head, he drinks it down and sips from the other. "You do forgive me?"

"Whatever for? Depression, the rest—I'd blame the Germans again ten more times before I ever would you. But then, hadn't been for them, my parents never would have fled to the Soviet Union and met in a camp. So now I'm going to say something I've thought a lot about and really feel about the order of life. Never—"

"Helene," a man says. I turn to him. Don, Ron, non—Lon. "Lon Friedensohn?"

"How are you, how are you, how are you? Haven't seen you since Diana's birthday party around this time a year ago. Schopenhauer, Stradivarius—remember? If I'm not stopping anything, would you like to dance? I love this number. From sixty-six. The Stones. *Beggars Banquet.* An abominable rendering of it—or was it sixty-seven?"

"Got me. And I'd like to but I'm exhausted. Too much champagne besides. Besides that, other things. I'll collapse the moment I'm out there."

"You're expected to. Minimum of five times for everyone under thirty-five or the wedding's not been sanctified. It's in the Talmud—look it up. And all night I've been dying to dance with someone who'll collapse with me to the floor and then just lie there laughing. Dance with me, Helene, dance with me, dance with me," he sings as he dances in place.

"Wish I could, but thanks."

"Say. Later."

"You're so admired," Arthur says, "and desired. I never saw anything like it."

"Only when I've drunk too much. Then, I must look like an easy mark and a good dancer."

"No, it's obvious. Everyone's magnetized by you. Women, men. Strangers. The way the waiter spoke to you. He's probably a sour fucker normally—excuse me—to most people, but you lit him up. I can tell: people are naturally pulled to you. I was, this Lon, and just the way half the men here look at you when they go past—even the little kids. It must get very distracting at times."

"If it's so, I don't really notice it. If I do notice it, what's it mean? It's your face they're looking at—or your body. Half of them are only thinking Oh boy, would I like to—what was the word you used?—fuck her. It's not just to me, it's to most of the younger women here. We've all touched up our faces, done our hair, shaved our armpits, put on our prettiest clothes, so what do you expect?"

"Not so, with you. It's also your intelligence they're seeing. And that particular complex of characteristics—your personableness, for instance—that distinguishes you from everyone in this room."

"Really, except for minor variations, I'm no different than anyone here, woman or man."

"What are you saying? You know, you need someone to make you believe more in yourself."

"I believe plenty in myself, no problem there. I look at myself clearly and regard myself fairly and don't think of myself excessively and that's the extent to which I want to deal with myself that way. It's because I don't respond with open arms to cajolery and compliments that I don't mind beating them back with self-deprecating jokes or something to discourage further flattery and complimentary attacks. Oh, compliments and the accompanying gushing attention can sometimes be all right, if in moderation and short order and, when the timing and setting's okay, come from someone you really like. But not when I'm pooped, sweaty, bit of a headache coming on, little stomach-ache already there, diarrhea probably next, and I'm slightly grumpy and somewhat tight."

"You're absolutely right. Say, how about a dance?" and he gets up and dances in place.

"No, really."

"I was only doing an imitation," sitting down. "So, been teaching long?"

"Long enough. And you? Tax-lawyering long?"

"Twelve years. What grad school you go to for literature? I'm assuming you did. Ph.D., I betcha, and Yale, because it has the best. I went to Yale Law and while there audited several literature courses."

"No, didn't go there."

"Where did you go?"

"Honestly, Arthur, I don't want to talk about my schooling and job. It's simply that the way I feel—but food, yes. Excuse me, but food should help me. A ladies' room too. Water on my face, maybe soap and water on my face, and to retouch up my face, redo my hair."

"You have absolutely—pardon me for coming right out with this—"

"Then don't."

"Glorious hair. I've never seen such hair. I can't believe what it'd look like loose. The color looks like the inside of a fireplace. The fire, or place, when lit, I mean."

"I was wondering."

"The orange inside the fire when there's lots of carbon in the wood, I think it is. But not red flames, just orange-red. It's both eerie and unearthly."

"Thank you, but plenty of women have the same color hair and plenty of pussycats too."

"But it's so smooth. Smooth like a real eating orange almost. It makes me want to reach out and touch it, but I won't."

"It's really messy and dirty. It should be combed."

"Suppose I said—no, I shouldn't say it."

"Fine. Now let's forget my hair. It's just a slightly untypical mop."

"It's highly untypical. I've never encountered a woman with that particular color orange whose hair was so straight. Usually that orange is on a kinky-haired woman or at least one kinkier-haired. Yours isn't kinky at all."

"That's because I washed it tonight, but now it's full of smoke. Really. I should go to the ladies' room. I also have to pee. Excuse me." I stand up.

He stands. "I'm sorry. I pushed you away."

"No, I'll come back if you want. Stay here or go to the food table, better. Have some champagne while I'm gone. Go on. I'll meet you over there because I think some smoked fish—they have some, don't they?"

"About a dozen different kinds, but only three or four are left."

"That's what I'm sure will help sober me up. The Russians use it. One of them told me at a party I went to earlier tonight. They'd never drink as much as I did without lots of smoked fish. So I'll see you over there."

"I'll be very surprised if you do come over."

"Shoot, what am I going to do with you? Are you a friend of Sven's?"

"Yes. Are all of them as unself-confident as I?"

"No, just wondering. Sven's a lawyer, so it makes sense. I don't recall Dorothy mentioning you, but maybe she did."

"We're not in the same firm and he's not Yale. We served under the same district attorney."

"You were an assistant D.A. too?"

"In Queens. I can't say we're the closest friends, but we're evidently on friendly enough terms where he thought to invite me. Were you at the ceremony?"

"Sure, how could you have forgotten? I was her maid of honor."

"I wasn't there. That wasn't what I meant. I wasn't invited. I was very happy for them, of course, but anyway, I was out of town then on a tax case."

"I see. Okay. At the smoked fish table. If you're not there, don't worry about it—I'll know you found someone else to talk to."

"Never. Why would I?"

I nod and smile, think Poor guy, and head for the ladies' room. It's at the entrance to this room and I have to walk around the dance floor to get to it. A man grabs my hand and says "Show me how to jitterbug. You look like you know how to do a great jitterbug."

"I'm sorry, I don't."

"You're the best lady, be my best lady. You've got to be good if you're Dorothy's best, since she's the best, so be good to me. Don't be annoyed with what I say. I'm smashed, best lady."

"Thank you. I'm a bit smashed too. Now please let me go."

"Jitterbug one solitary jitterbug step with me first."

"Leave her go, Teddy," the woman he was standing with says.

"When she jitterbugs one solitary step with me."

"I don't know how to jitterbug," I say to her. "Really, Teddy, I don't."

"I'll show you." He puts his arm around my waist, continues to hold my right hand with his left and walks me forward, walks me back, quickly switches hands and flicks his right leg around his left and faces me again.

"There, I did what you said, now let me go."

"We have to do it once the same way from the other side."

"Not fair," Lon says, dancing by.

"It was an accident."

"No accident," Teddy says. "The best man gets the best lady wherever he goes, always."

"Sven's brother was the best man," I say.

"So I'm Sven's oldest cousin on both sides, so that's why I'm here and who gets the best lady."

"Leave her alone, Teddy," the woman says. "Can't you see you're too old for this girl and a disgrace?"

"God," I say, "is this what happens when everybody gets drunk? What have I been missing?"

"Me, sweetheart. Marry me tonight, best lady. My wife won't mind."

"No, I won't mind," she says, "but I don't think she wants to. Leave her go Teddy. I'm sure you're hurting her."

"Release me, sir," I say commandingly.

"By your leave, best lady." He lets go, gets down on his knees, cups my shoe between his hands and kisses the tip of it.

"Ouch," I say. "Really, get up, this is terrible."

"What's happening?" Arthur says. "Make another conquest? You're too unbelievable. Still want to meet at the food table? You don't, my turn to understand."

"I want to go to the bathroom, Arthur. Lead me there?"

I put out my hand. Teddy jumps up and takes it and whispers into my ear "I'll ball you silly, you whore, just give me half the chance," and I say to him "You son of a bitch. Go shit in your hat," and stick my nails into his hand and he jerks it away. I walk to the ladies' room.

"What the hell was that about?" Arthur says.

"Where's that man now?"

"Still where you left him, staring at you and not too nicely, and showing a woman his hand. What he say? Should I have done something?"

"What a schmuck. And violent? That bastard hurt my hand. Ah: Ladies'."

"Want me to wait outside?"

"No thanks." I go inside, go into one of the stalls, put paper down in case I happen to graze the seat, squat above it and let go. Where's it coming from? Usually I'm so regular. Once in the morning after exercises and that's it for the day. Must be the food. The drink—what am I thinking of, the food? Maybe it'll make me feel better. I stand up, wipe myself, get a sharp stomach pain and squat above the seat and more comes, worse than before. This is going to make my anus hurt. I stay that way for a minute. Then my thighs can't take any more and I rearrange the papers so they're all in place and sit. Smell is awful. I flush the toilet but don't get up. Someone comes in. Sorry, ladies, who from the sounds of their handbags opening, apparently came in to fix their faces and hair.

"It smells like a pig factory in here," one says.

"Wasn't me," another woman says.

"I wasn't saying that. I know what it was."

"It's from one of the closets," second one says much lower.

"It's me and I apologize," I say, "but I'm not feeling too well. Believe me, it doesn't smell any better in here!"

"I'm sorry, I didn't know anyone was still in there," the first one says. "I should have, by your door. You have any perfume on you?"

"I left my bag at my table. Brilliant. It'll probably get stolen."

"I have some," she says. "I'll spread it around," and I suppose she sprinkles toilet water in the air, because I begin smelling it. "Also, flush your johnny."

"I did."

"Flush it again and again if it's not too uncomfortable for your rear end. Just getting the new water around freshens up the area and it also assures the stuff of going all the way to the sewer and the smell of it from backing up."

I raise myself off the seat a little and flush twice.

"That isn't Ginny Scoletti in there, is it?" the second one says.

"No," I say.

"There was someone by that name suddenly missing from the next table and people were worried, that's why I asked."

"No."

"You from the Tallin bar mitzvah?"

"The Nustermann-Baker wedding. Please, if you don't mind I'd prefer being anonymous right now, and silent. My stomach."

"By all means," the first one says. "But you're not throwing up also?"

"No, it's only from one end. Excuse me, I'm going to be silent."

"By all means. Take care. But if you need help, yell. Just because we don't know you doesn't mean we shouldn't help. Men are comrades like that to perfect strangers all the time."

"Are they?" I say. "I suppose."

"Well, how about it?" the first one says to the second. "You haven't said yet, because I thought little Mickey this morning sang like a dream."

"He sang it beautifully and read it well."

"And Lillie looks so lovely. Does she look like the mother of a sixteen-year-old bar mitzvah kid?"

"He's that old? I thought fourteen."

"Sixteen. That's why he sang so well. His voice has already changed. Mostly those kids sing awful, and at thirteen the worst. Cracked voice, like a cracked bell. Bong-g-g," and they both laugh. "Here, take a whiff of this."

"I'm high enough."

"Go on, it's the best. If you're worried about Miss Anonymous inside, she won't mind. She can even join us. Want a whiff, Silence-in-the-Closet?"

"Whatever it is, no thanks."

"Whatever it is, I promise you will like. It'll pacify your problems and make you dance like it was your last chance in your life."

"That's very generous of you, but I don't touch anything but too much champagne. At least not for years. Drugs, which I suppose is what your whiff is, make me tired and dumb, which I already am."

"This will make you feel lively, honey, and as for feeling dumb, feel dumb. That's what you're supposed to do. You're supposed to feel high. You're supposed to feel weird, cracked, bats, uninhibitively loose and detached and dumb. Every now and then, I'm saying."

"Every now and then she's saying," the second one says, "but look at her: she isn't giving. Here, might as well—for it smells too good."

I'm all done, nothing else came, and I don't want to stay in here any longer, nor do I want to see them. But I wipe up, pull up, push the paper in, flush the toilet, and leave. "Hi," I say. They're around my age. I wash my hands, say "Thanks" to the one with white powder on her fingertip she's extended to me, "but I don't want any, good as it looks. I once tried that stuff and everything felt and looked so cold for half an hour that I thought I was in a huge icebox. Enjoy your party," drying my hands.

"And enjoy yours," the second one says. "Maybe we'll hop over for a visit. Any nice-looking guys there?"

"Some. All looking for women it seems, married and unmarrieds alike. Chances should be a lot better there than at your party, I'd think."

"Tatlin, you said?"

"No, you said, and Tallin. I'm Nustermann-Baker."

"There's so many parties on this floor. It's hard to know where to keep track where you are unless where you come in here."

"You dummy," the first woman says. "You're so high you can't speak straight."

"Speak straight where? What are you speaking about, and about me? Freaking-A right. This shit is strong. Where in world am I? Ich, don't tell me—I see. Think you better help lean me up against something for I'm gonna take a spill."

"Does she really need help?" I say, grabbing the high woman's arm.

"I'll take care of her, honey, thanks," snapping her powder tin shut and putting it in her handbag.

The high woman sits on the floor against the wall, head between her knees, crying. The other woman rinses a paper towel and pats it on the back of the high woman's neck.

"Sure she'll be all right? I'll help, or get someone if you need."

"That rag's too cold," the high woman says. "Warmer. I'm getting better but want a rag not so cold."

"She'll be okay. I'll see to her. She talks a big game but she can't hold anything."

I leave. Arthur's outside. "You were a long time. Two women walked in soon after you and I bet myself you all started chatting about hair waves or whatever women do. I never know what goes on in your toilets but always wanted to."

"Dress in drag."

"Ideally, I'd like to get a video camera and set it up in a woman's room and watch it live off a monitor for a day. Or tape and record it—just like this one one night—but naturally when you're not in there, or if you are, then when you know you're on camera and you're maybe even the star. And I'm talking about potties and tampon dispensers and anything else you might have in there that we don't. It'd make a good thirty-minute movie, don't you think? I'm serious, because I'm sure there'd be plenty for me and every man to learn from it."

"Ask me anything. We shit, we pee, we get sick, we brush our teeth, and sometimes we even wash our hands and comb our hair."

"Someone will do it before me, you'll see, and make a small fortune from it and get all the awards. Some smoked fish?"

"What?"

"The smoked fish table. I was just there and they're now down to two of them, though one's sable, so we better hustle."

"I don't want anything to eat. Fact is, I'm about to go home."

"You're still tired. That's too bad, because I was kind of getting used to you here. Listen, before you go, could I ask if it'd be all right if I called you."

"I guess, but I have to tell you I'm a bit tied-up with someone these days."

"Every woman is and every man isn't, it seems."

"I didn't quite get that. But more to the point, the reason I'm not more than occasionally tied-up with someone is that I don't want to see anyone regularly these days."

"If the right guy came along, you'd see him. I'm not him. So it is. Believe me, sometimes I even meet someone who's attracted to me and once in my life I even had to turn a woman down."

"I'm sure you do. I think I even suggested as much. Look, Arthur, I don't want to get into it. I wasn't feeling well in there, which is why I took so long."

"I'm sorry, I didn't know."

"I didn't say it for sympathy, just stating a fact."

"I can still say I'm sorry, can't I? That's common human courtesy and compassion."

"Please, Arthur, don't argue with me. Because you are arguing and it's too damn silly to. We don't know each other."

"That's why I want to call you."

"Call me—I said for you to if you want—but I don't think I'll be going out much with anyone for a while, even that occasional friend. I have things to do. I don't mean to hit you with it, but papers, class preparations and exams, references to write, which can take a long time. Besides all that, my writing work, and not only reviews."

"What other writing?"

"No other writing. At least no other right now. To talk about. You're pressing me again and it's not right or fair."

"I'm sorry, I shouldn't do that. Sorry, sorry—an unbreakable habit I'll break. But if I do call, you can always make it for a single drink, can't you?"

"I suppose so if I'm not tied-up with work or friends."

"Or a coffee or lunch some weekend afternoon."

"Even there, you'll just have to call. I work weekends too."

"I'll call, you can count on it. Can I see you to the door?"

"I'm not leaving this moment. I have to say my goodbyes first. I'm not even that sure I want to go yet. Look, I'm hungry. I guess my stomach's better. Why don't we go to the food table after all? Not the smoked fish. Too late to make good use of that one and I doubt I could take it for pure eating pleasure now."

"Something more substantial? Potato salad. I'm serious—the oil in the mayonnaise should bind you. And the meatballs looked solid, simple and good."

"Maybe just a plain cheese sandwich if they have."

"They've got to. With all the meat, cheese and bread, I could prepare one for you."

We head for the food table.

"Hi, Helene," Agnes says. "Super reception, hm?"

"Super."

"The band—who could afford it? I'm still waiting for you to get on the floor again. You were walking off when we came in before."

"You saw all there'll be. Hello," I say to the man she's with. "Helene Winiker, an old friend of Agnes's. Arthur. . . Oh God, Arthur, help me out."

"Arthur Rosenthal, like the china. That's how people remember it."

"Excuse me," Agnes says. "My husband, Jim Walsh. We were all at P.A. together. Dot, Helene—you were already dancing at City Center then. The kitty corps, or one notch above."

"So it's true," Arthur says.

"Why, she ever lie to you? I'd be surprised. Mademoiselle Truth, we called her. Signorina Social Conscious, if I have it right."

"Not true," I say.

"There, I lied. Never even fib in front of a preternatural like—a predestiterminally—just a superhuman truthspinner when you're hip she knows the truth. Funny, but I was always so good at making up bombastic maxims. Anyway, I was telling the truth, so don't make me out a liar. And I think Dot and I were the only ones who stayed in theater of our group, true?"

"Shawn too," Jim says.

"She didn't go to P.A. I'm talking of my city high school friends."

"She didn't? I thought she had. And how'd I know till now Helene was a classmate of yours?"

"We're off to the food table," I say. "How's work?"

"You know how it is, since it never changes. But Jim, the rotten dog, gets every TV commercial available. Every actor hates him, including this one, he's so gorgeous, talented and lucky."

"I am neither. I happen to have the looks and mannerisms of someone who genuinely seems like, when he's lathering a product into his scalp or splashing it on his skin—"

He's saying this to her, so I wave goodbye, nudge Arthur and we go.

"So you were really a dancer," he says. "How about that. I bet you still dance exceptionally—classical steps. When I was a boy I wanted to be a poet. I was one. Won all the poetry prizes in school and some for money, making out a lot better than most poets today. I'd stay up nights with a flashlight writing that stuff. Then it just leaves you—it did me. My family said business is what I should be interested in—money, position and a sensible intelligent wife to go along with it, but one with her own burgeoning career so she won't get bored and she could bring in something, and they were right. I love money. I can be honest about it—does it bother you to hear?"

"I already said money's okay."

"I love what it brings. Cars, vacations, any book I want to buy. Even a boat once, and an island last summer—rented one, didn't buy. And I don't do well compared to a lot of the lawyers in my graduating class. I'm satisfied with a hundred thousand a year—this year—who needs more? Uncle Schmuel only gobbles it up when you only have one deduction besides yourself every other year and no cooperative or house. I'm buying one though."

"You have a child?"

"A boy—eight. Lives with his mother. She's one who was in my class and nowhere near me in grades or on the Review and makes more than I. Corporate law, that's why. And because she works harder and doesn't like to play as much as I. No boats, only business trips. —There, told you we should've hustled faster for the smoked fish. They always run out of it first. I can take you to a great restaurant if you crave some—even now. It's open till one. Has the best smoked sturgeon and salmon in town."

"Thanks, but this will do fine." I help myself to a slice of bread and cheese and several slices of turkey and tongue.

"Cranberry sauce?" a man behind the food table says. "Homemade, not canned." He plops a spoonful on my plate.

"Aren't you eating?" I say to Arthur.

"Too full—I'll just drink. Good champagne like this you don't get every night. Though I always have champagne in my fridge. Right this moment, three bottles of Taittinger's brut on the bottom shelf, but I have to admit I don't pour it as freely as they do here."

"You ought to throw wedding parties at your home. Then you'd—no, sorry."

"Go on, what?"

"Really, for the time being I have to continue to be the judge whether what I'm about to say will make sense or not and then if I should stop."

"Who are your favorite American authors, contemporary and late?"

"Wait. Let me eat first."

"Quiche lorraine?" the man behind the table says. "It's the old quiche lorraine, before all the rage. French recipe. The real McCoy."

"Sure, a slice, please. Thin." He does.

"And our curried veal? You won't forgive yourself if you don't."

"My appetite's got better but not that much, thanks."

"Tomorrow or the days after your friends here, when you discuss the party, will ask if you had it. It's the house speciality—one of a kind."

"Go on, be brave," Arthur says.

"You be brave. Grab a plate."

He gets a plate and holds it out. The man gives us a portion each.

"Now, how about a côtelette de mouton? It'll melt in your mouth. I won't even ask your permission." He puts a piece on my plate. Arthur sticks out his plate and gets a piece. "Now you'll have eaten our best except for the chicken breast l'orange."

"No room for it," I say, "in my stomach or on my plate."

"Mandarin oranges flown-in for us expressly from Valencia, Spain?—Very well, but sit down while you eat. And drink a beverage with it. I don't want you coming back to me saying I made you choke on the small servings I gave."

"I promise I won't. Thank you." He bows and we walk away.

"That guy was another who had an instantaneous crush on you. And his language, when he was alluding to food to you, was so subtly erotic."

"He was only being nice while doing his job."

"How come he wasn't as nice to me?"

"You really want to know?"

"Yes, I do."

"No. As I said I don't know you that well and I have a way of either being too much of everybody's therapist or saying too quickly how I feel, which makes them think they or I need one. I just want to eat."

"How *do* you feel? Well, do you think I need one? Then can I get you some Perrier or wine?"

"Perrier. Thanks. I'll be sitting over there—give me your plate." I go to an empty table and put the plates down. "And napkins, Arthur," I yell. "There's plenty of everything else here."

"You betcha, Helene," and he blows me a kiss. He blew me a kiss. I don't want him blowing me those. Oh, let him blow all he wants to me, but I won't give him my phone number when he asks. I'll tell him it'd be useless. Not useless, but something. Pointless, because I know he's so infatuated with me when I'm about as far from that to him as I can get. Like that other one tonight I told how to reach me, then shouting out the window at me like a goof. If that one calls I'll tell him he truly embarrassed me. No, I'll say I'm too busy to see him and then put him off forever. No, but I'll be blunt. "Can you take a dose of truth? After I left Diana's I immediately knew it was a mistake to have encouraged you to call, so that's the way it is, goodbye." No, I'll tell him I'm too busy and put him off forever or maybe I will be that blunt. I have some veal. De-lish. Sublime. Quiche. Divine. I should have somehow made room on my plate for the breast. God, I love feeling and eating well. Then I see Peter. Last man I wanted to see tonight and maybe also the first. Be honest with yourself—no. Dorothy said there was a slight chance he'd be here but nine out of ten he'd be in Lucerne. Heading straight to me. Hello, Peter—why Peter, hello. Hiya, Peter, didn't think you'd be here—Peter, what a surprise, even if Dorothy did say you might show. Oh, just let him say what he wants to say and I'll say whatever comes to me too. I slice off some lamb.

"Helene, nice to see you," and I look up and show surprise and say hello and stand up and stick my hand out to shake and he starts shaking it when he says "Shake? Come on now, I need a kiss. It's been more than six months since we've had one—between us, of course," and holds onto my hand as I give him my cheek to kiss and he kisses it and straightens my chin with his other hand and pecks my lips and lets go of me, steps back and says "What's there to say?—you look great."

"So do you—very good. Like some food?" pointing to mine.

"I'll get my own later."

"Mind if I continue?" and I sit and he sits at Arthur's place.

"This somebody's?" meaning Arthur's plate.

"Champagne?" a waiter says, holding a tray of filled champagne glasses. Peter takes off two.

"Not for me. And there is someone I'm sitting with, but I can move his plate to one of the other chairs."

"No, wouldn't want to disturb anything," and he gives me a glass, goes around the table and sits opposite me and says "And come on now, we have to drink to Dot and Sven."

"All right, for them. I think I'm feeling better. I wasn't before."

"That-a-way." He clicks my glass. "Oops, should have first made a toast. To Dorothy and Sven. May they have a long life together and a fruitful marriage with much abundance, which is redundant, but what a marriage often is. Well, came out of that one okay. But let's drink," and we click glasses and sip.

"Now," he says, "—and eat, don't let me stop you. What have you been up to lately? Much the same?"

"With minor backflips and minuscule variations. How about you? You've been to Cologne, Zurich, Lucerne—"

"Lausanne, not Lucerne."

"Lausanne, Lucerne, Lorraine, Laraine. Excuse me, but just for a moment there I thought I had a private joke going between my fork and me. Dorothy said for a curators' convention and then on a buying-selling trip for your museum, but she didn't think you'd be back in time."

"That could have been cause for jubilation."

"Why, what's it to me? You're here, good. Was it a good trip? I'm sure it was,

so, good again. A third good coming up might be my own going to Europe next
summer for a few weeks. Italy. Maybe France. Maybe just Italy."

"Remember ours? I still have dreams of us—real dreams, when I'm asleep—
of the barge we stayed on, the canals and frogs. It kills me when I wake up."

"So? Go back with someone, or alone. That's how I plan to do it: solo."

"Greetings," Arthur says, putting a glass of bubbling water with a lime slice
in it in front of me.

"Peter, this is Arthur Rosenthal, as in the china. Peter Gray, as in the color,
spelled the American way. Sorry I went at my food before you got back.
Couldn't resist."

"I can see. This my seat?" He sits, pushes his plate away.

"Arthur's a lawyer. We just met here. He's an old friend of Sven's."

"Sven and Dorothy's, and not old. Served in the Queens District Attorney's office with him. You in law too?"

"No," Peter says.

"So, tell him what you do. It's not fair not to."

"I didn't mean it that way."

"You still haven't told him. What is it with you? Peter curates for the Met.
The new primitive wing."

"Being built. An assistant curator. One of."

"And you're an assistant or associate professor," Arthur says to me, "or just a
lecturer. Not that I've anything against lecturers. I want to see if we're all
assistants here tonight or once were. Sven and I—assistant D.A.'s. But Dot
wasn't one that I know."

"I'm sure we can make her an assistant in something," Peter says. "Assistant
organizer for this wedding. Wait. Wasn't she an assistant editor for a theater
mag before she—"

"Associate," I say. "Maybe assistant. Anyway, I'm an assistant. Listen, I'm
not feeling too well again and I have to leave."

"I'd take you home," Arthur says, "but I actually would like to stay. I have no
excuse for going."

"Why should you go? I'll grab a cab downstairs."

"I was about to go myself," Peter says. "I know—I just came—but I only
drove down to do my courtesies, since I've a long workday tomorrow. And
you're on my way home."

"I'm twenty blocks north of you."

"I'll drive you—you're not feeling well."

"Go with him. This time of night—who even knows if cabs come down this far?"

"I'll say my goodbyes and get my coat," I say.

"First, someone has to make an official toast to the bride and groom," Peter says. "Has anyone done it?"

"Several."

"But a wedding toast? I came all the way down here to hear one. I'm a minister's son, what can you expect? Doesn't reinforce my argument, does it? But with the band on a break, it's the best time for one." He stands up, clinks his glass with a fork and says "Attention, everyone—please. I know several toasts have been made, but I haven't heard them. And being a minister's son, I feel called upon to make at least one official one. Another toast—what the hell, right?"

Most of the room of about a hundred people get quiet. A few people near the food table are still talking and laughing.

"Shh, shh," some people say.

"I won't make a toast till the room is totally quiet."

"Boy, this fellow really takes command," Arthur says to me.

"A toast, everyone," Peter says louder. "Everyone has to be quiet. A toast, everyone." The room's now quiet. "Waiters, please see that everyone has a fresh glass of champagne or fresh champagne in their glasses."

"I can't believe this friend of yours," Arthur says. "No let-up. What's he think the waiters are, his slaves?"

The waiters bring in several trays of glasses and bottles of champagne. In a couple of minutes nearly everybody's holding up a glass of champagne.

"Dorothy and Sven," Peter says. "Please come to the middle of the floor." They do. "Join hands."

"Hey, get on with it," Arthur says in a disguised voice. "We're thirsty; our hands are getting heavy."

"Maybe I should," Peter says to Arthur, who looks around as if someone else had yelled it out. "Thank you, sir. —Dorothy and Sven. I'm not good at toasts—not even at making toast. I burn my toast half the times I make it. Maybe that means I should get a new toaster. But even a halfway good toaster doesn't blame his bad toasts on his toaster. But it is true that while my toaster's dial is always aimed at 'light,' my toasts, if I don't watch it, always end up dark. I don't like dark toasts. But my toaster also doesn't pop, which is another reason why my toast is usually hard and dark. But the champagne tonight certainly has popped. And months before tonight one of you must have popped the question to the other and the other accepted that pop. And maybe one day not too far off one of you will be a pop, and the other will be what in most traditional families goes with that pop, as in a mom and pop store—so, what's in store for you. You might think this is funny"—Dorothy and Sven are laughing—"but it's very serious. But one thing neither of you will ever be is seriously burned, unlike my toast, nor will you be roasted by this toast. You were made for one another, like toast is made for breakfast and roasts are made for supper. You are bread and butter for each other, one spread on top of the other, but which of you will be the bread and the other the butter nobody can say, since those rolls are transposable today. As far as putting rolls into my toaster, that's out of the question and one that can't be popped. Since how can the rolls pop if they can't fit into the toaster? And if they can't fit, they also can't be burned or toasted and certainly not roasted, since nothing gets roasted in a toaster. But I'm sure both of you will always fit together and keep the other toasty—something on the order of a perfectly functioning toaster. So, I toast to your order of that perfectly functioning toaster and the bread that won't be burned that goes into the toaster. And the butter that will be spread but won't go into the toaster, though will be closely associated with it after the toast—perfectly toasted, the way you love it and each other and the way toast and bread love butter—pops out, but not to the floor. Pops out for you both to handle easily and without it burning your fingers. So here's to all of those and lots of rolls and no more toasts tonight at least from this imperfectly functioning toaster and especially to you both, Dorothy and Sven Baker— and I swear only now do I see the connection between your last name and my toast—sip sip away."

Almost everybody says "Sip sip away," and drinks up. Peter drinks up, puts the glass on the floor and crushes it with his foot. There's lots of applause, he sits and says "Drink. You haven't touched a drop." I drink a little.

Arthur says to him "I might have been a smart-ass before but only because I'm jealous of any guy who can take over the way you did. But that was without doubt the best toast I ever ate. I didn't want to like it. In point of fact I hate all toast: dark, light or roasted—but I liked yours. It was palatable and kosher and I now think you ought to send them a real toaster as a present, maybe one that can take rolls. If you don't, I will, but not your old one or my toaster-oven-broiler. I drink to you, sir—you're a clever sonofabitch as there ever was one."

They click glasses and then mine on the table. I drink all my champagne, say "Excuse me," and go over to Dorothy and Sven and kiss them both. The music's started. They take my hands. "No, I couldn't." We start dancing, just holding hands, sort of a Jewish dance to Jewish music. Other people take our hands and soon twenty to thirty people are holding hands in a circle and doing this dance. Arthur breaks the circle, takes my hand and the hand of the person I've been holding and dances around with us. Peter takes my other hand and the other hand I've been holding—Sophie's. Soon about half the guests are part of the circle and the other half and most of the waiters are clapping in rhythm to us. I see the two women from the ladies' room in the circle. The one who was sick drops her hand and waves to me and I nod and she takes back the hand of her friend and kisses it. The music stops. I'm panting from all the dancing. Sophie hugs me and says "My darling, all the same for you," and I say "One day, maybe, but no rush." Dorothy and Sven kiss Sophie and then me and then one another and Peter puts his arms around their shoulders and squeezes them into him and then hugs Sophie and then me and kisses my cheek and says "Why can't I stop thinking about you? This is no b.s. I'm such a fucking fool. Can't live with, can't without, that's my problem."

I get out of his grip. "It's all right, please, and stay. You're having fun. I am too, but too much partying tonight."

"No, I promised, and my work tomorrow starts early."

I tell Dorothy and Sven I'm leaving. "Peter's driving me home." She raises her eyebrows. My look back says "Not what you think."

"Before you go," Sven says, "have you seen the view?"

"I've looked outside. We're very high up."

"But from the outside? Half of what Soph's paying for is the balcony view. It's memorable and I want the party to be remembered. You too, Peter. Arthur. Nils. Who else? Everybody who can fit out there, come with us to the balcony. Sophie, you too."

"I can't," Arthur says to me. "I'm phobic when it comes to heights. They were lucky to get me up here, but I haven't looked outside once tonight and did you notice how I stay away from the windows? Minimum of fifteen feet. I couldn't get near the crudités table because of it, and I love those things, so someone had to bring me over a plate."

Sven takes my hand and Dorothy's and leads about twenty people out to the balcony. It overlooks the Staten Island ferry station and Statue of Liberty and New Jersey or Staten Island and some ships in the water and a liner all lit up heading out to the ocean.

"A cruise ship," Dorothy says. "That's what Sven and I should be on. Instead, what? A posh hotel here and tomorrow Atlantic City."

"I like to gamble," he says.

"Listen. You can even hear the music from it seventy stories up. Let's dance," and she grabs Sven and dances one turn around and lets go.

"I don't hear anything," Sophie says.

"I'm a little cold," I say to Peter. "I'm going in."

"No, all of us," Sven says, "me and mine included, stay and don't make jokes or start dancing—just look. It was a lot nicer the night we came up here to see if we wanted to rent it. Clearer, more stars, the skinniest of quarter-moons, but you can't predict the weather months ahead, and all the nights that same-sized moon was due, the room was booked. Look—the plane up there. Cloudy and all, it's still a remarkable sight. Only in New York."

"I think Chicago has a catering place like this on top of one of its lakefront office buildings," a woman says. "And taller, but with different type food. But it is very nice indeed. I'm glad you brought us out here—I would have missed it."

"And no comparisons, if you can. Experience it for what it is, if I can sound vaguely familiar—which is great. I also, while we're out here in front of this view, want to make an announcement."

"You're getting married," a man says.

"No, and not that I love Dorothy and she loves me and we shall cherish each other forever, which is all so, but that we're going to have a baby. That's something else I wanted to tell you, my best friends and relatives who braved it out here at my behest. Sophie, did you hear?"

"What am I supposed to do now—say no? Dorothy told me."

"Snitcher," he says to Dorothy. "But did she tell you it's going to be a girl and we're calling her Marina Claire?"

"I knew and I'm thankful. Girls are better than boys."

"I didn't know any of it," I say. "It's wonderful, what could be better?" I kiss them both.

"But is this the fantastic place to hear that kind of news?" Sven shouts.

"Unbeatable," Peter says, "and appropriate. The heart of the New York harbor and with Brooklyn in the foreground and Manhattan in back and a jet going west overhead and the two rivers splitting up and going their own way. And my mom and pop store speech was pretty prescient, eh?"

"That's what I whispered to Dorothy on the floor. 'Does Peter know?' She didn't answer. Why didn't you answer?" he asks her.

"Now I really have to go," I say.

"Of course," Peter says. "Goodbye to you all. It's freezing and gorgeous out here and the news was a knockout. —Wait up," he says to me.

"Marry her," Sven yells after Peter. "Don't be a boob not to."

"Sven, that's an awful thing to say," I say. "People have to work things out their own way."

"But you're a terrific couple and two of my favorite people and I'm deliriously happy, so what else could I say? I'd love to see you married and in a family way, which is my next big fantasy for you two and no doubt another one I should have omitted saying, but that's just tough titty on me."

"All right, I hear, and probably at your wedding reception you should be allowed to say anything you like." I go back, kiss him, he's been crying, says "Forgive me, Helene, I get too enthused and emotional," say "Bye Sophie, many thanks," blow a kiss to Dorothy and say "Hope I didn't dampen things," and she says "Pay no mind, nothing but a nuclear holocaust on us could ruin this day," go into the room, Peter says "Truthfully, I had nothing to do with that marriage-fetus wish, but you handled him right," and goes to the men's room, get my coat and sit on a bench by the elevator to wait for him. The rooms to the other parties are at the other side of the elevator bank and lots of laughing, music and chatter are coming from them. Arthur comes over. "Oh, I'm sorry," I say, "I forgot to say goodnight."

"That's what I thought I forgot. And, I'm not sure how close you are with this curator fellow, but if it isn't too close—even if it is. . ."

"We can always have lunch. I'm in the book. Only Helene with a Winiker at the end of it. W-i—"

"I know. I asked Dot about you already and she gave me your number. Six-six-three, two-five, three-six. An easy one, but I've a way with numbers. I can still remember my selective service card number and army rifle registration number and all the combination lock numbers from high school and college. Phone numbers? You only have to tell me them once. I've got a regular rolloflex—but what do you call those rolling things that have a thousand phone numbers and addresses on index cards and you spin?—well that's my head. I also want you to know I'll gladly do your tax returns this year if you want. As a favor, and I bet I get you back seven hundred more than if you do them yourself and four hundred more than with a professional accountant, but maybe not a competent CPA, and all legitimately: I do nothing to jeopardize the reputation of my firm or my own personal name."

"Sounds good. I do them myself, so I might take you up on it."

"Great. So, it was words-can't-say tonight, Helene."

Peter comes over, has on his coat, says "Nice to meet you, Arthur; see you around," rings for the elevator. Elevator comes. "Hold onto me if you're still not feeling well," and he presses the lobby button.

I hold his arm as the car descends. He kisses the top of my head. He's about six inches taller than I and has put aftershave or men's cologne on his face though I don't know where he'd keep it. Not in his pocket. Maybe for men there's such a thing as overnight cologne packages I'll call them. More likely the management provided some for the men's room, but why wouldn't there also have been some in ours? Maybe there was and someone stole it. Could be he devised his own traveling package. He was always very inventive and liked to smell good. "You all right?" I nod. "Elevator not going too fast? I can slow it down." I shake my head. "This might seem dopey, but why—" The car stops at the fourteenth but nobody gets on. "Why did you object so strenuously to Sven when he came on with that marriage talk?"

"Because he knows that that's what mainly broke it up for us: your not wanting to. Even if he was drunk or stoned, and who knows what those two are into these—" The door opens, a guard in the lobby nods to us and Peter salutes him and we head for the door. "I also don't go for that shoot-from-the-heart crap in a crowd he's also been into these days."

"Hold it. About that particular time we're talking of, it wasn't so much marriage I didn't want but that you wanted to have a baby then and at the time I didn't think I wanted one."

"I wanted to get married and have a child eventually. Why else get married or at least if you can have kids? But what does your 'at the time' talk mean? That now you think, to the woman you eventually do get married to, that you would have a child? That'd be interesting."

"Did I say that? I suppose I sort of did. Yes, I very definitely think it's a strong possibility that one day pretty soon I'd like to be a father."

"I'm sure of it."

"Be. Because with the right hypothetical woman—someone I love very much and so forth and who I think would make a wonderful mother as well as a wife—it's very possible."

"Nah, you have too many important interests and aims, which I'm not knocking, but they and you come first. You'll get married again—eventually—but you won't let a kid come into it."

"Don't be so dogmatic about me. People change. I've my rigidness and routines, but I surprise myself sometimes too."

"All right. I believe that marriage-mit-kit is a very definite strong possibility for you pretty soon."

"Pretty soon. Reasonably soon. Because—" I step inside the revolving door, but before I can push it he squeezes in behind me and we move in short jerky steps. "One more spin around?" when we're outside. "I was just getting started."

His car is parked near the entrance. A man's standing next to it and says "Pardon me for a moment, folks—" Peter takes my hand and backs us up a few feet and looks into the lobby. "Now don't be alarmed. I mean no harm. Besides, look at you, sir. You're practically a giant, so who'd mess with you, not that I'm that type in any shape or form. All I'm politely asking for is enough change to put me on a public conveyance home."

"I think I have a quarter."

"That'll put me almost halfway. Thank you. And the lady? —You couldn't contribute something too?"

"A quarter's plenty from us. There are other people to ask. I've a lot more change but that's all I feel like giving. You don't like the quarter—give it here."

"Peter."

"No, he doesn't think it's enough, let him give it back as I said. Fuck this shit. I'm not letting us get harassed on the street every other day."

"Pardon, no offense, I don't want to get myself killed by this guy," and he walks away. "Didn't mean to cause any trouble," to himself or for us to hear.

Peter unlocks my door, I get in, unlock his while he's putting the key in, he says "Thanks," gets in and shuts the door.

"God," I say, "—quiet. I can't believe it. I've had so much chitchat and bullshit tonight starting from the minute I got to Diana's party that I think—"

"How is she?"

"Please, give me a minute. There must be something else we can talk about, if we have to talk for the next minute. Or music. Maybe you can put on public radio or NCN if they're not the same. One of them should have something nice." He starts the car and turns on the radio. Station he was turned to has country music, one he turns to has a busy Brahms serenade with too much wind and brass. "Not that." He turns it off. "No, you can leave it on." He turns it on, low. "I'm acting so spoiled, but what I wouldn't do for a solo flute. Bach, just Bach. I don't even know if he has one for solo, but someone like him. Maybe I should just pray." I close my eyes, clasp my hands and pretend to pray. All I really want is quiet or sleep. To wake up, as I used to, in my father's arms, with the car parked and the family home and my shoes off and my body being lowered into my bed. He leans across me—I jump back because I think he's going to grab my leg—opens the glove compartment by my knees, pulls out a number of tape cassettes, slips one into a hole by the radio and turns the dial up and Brahms has become flute and harpsichord music and I think Bach's.

"Close enough?" He buckles up, helps me to and drives off. "And low enough? Loud enough? Sorry for the harpsichord obligato, but it is obligato. But whatever's your pleasure, ma'am, this nifty sports job will supply."

"Everything's fine, thanks. And before? To clear up a possible wrong impression? I didn't mean that chitchat's so bad. Just I've my saturation point. It's like knickknacks, chitchats. Though I have those too I also have my saturation point with them. No more than five knickknacks to a radiator cover I say. What *am* I saying? Believe me, I was fine at the start of the evening, but now I've become ridiculously chitchatty myself."

"No you haven't."

"Have to. So goddamn condescending. I crit others what I myself do. Because chitchat and bullshit have their days too. Just right now, for me, they're— This music's also too chatty. If only we could speed it up to a slow part. Mind if I shut it off?"

"Slow part's coming, but I can speed up the tape to it."

"No, no music. I don't know what I want. But same way? The radio dial? Never saw anything like this," shutting it off. "What else can it do? Record, take in, give change? Oh, shut up, Helene, till you get home, and then, if you have to chitchat like this, do it in your sleep."

"You can't. You have to keep the driver talking so he doesn't fall asleep at the wheel."

"Then let's talk about something interesting. But you start, I can't. But let's see if we can talk about only one thing till I get home that keeps us unwinkingly stimulated and our minds unmoronically—oh my God, that man!"

"Where, what? Don't startle me like that. You'll run us off the road."

"But that man we just passed. On crutches—I think being robbed." I look back. "It still seems the younger one's going through the pockets of the older man. Turn around, go back."

"Come on, you couldn't have seen all that so fast."

"But I'm still watching it—now no more—too far back. Slow down and make a U at the next left." He slows down but passes that left. "Peter, we can't drive by knowing someone's—"

"And I'm saying, if you did see something, you don't want to get involved in a possible dangerous robbery. Because suppose we go back—then what?"

"We can get near enough to see if he is being robbed, and if he is, we can drive past slowly and honk and wave our fists. If the man's already been robbed and the robber's gone, we can drive him to a police station or stay with him till a police car comes. If he hasn't been robbed, I want to find that out by asking him so I know I didn't drive past anyone being robbed. And if it's only what I think is the robber who's there, then we'll quietly drive past."

"All right. Okay." He makes a U-turn at the next left and slows down at the first red light.

"Don't stop. No car's coming, go through."

"And if a cop—"

"All the better. That's who I'm looking for now."

He goes through the light. "I hate going through red lights." The older man's leaning against a lamppost, two canes, not two crutches, at his feet. We stop, I roll down my window, "Excuse me, but were you just robbed?"

"You undercover? If you are—"

"We're not. We thought—"

"Still, he ran up that sidestreet and you can still catch him but you'll have to go against a one-way."

"We don't want to try to—either thing—and get hurt. We saw you from the uptown side and thought we could help with a honk and shout if he was still here, or help you in any way. You're not hurt? Did he get anything?"

"My wallet. Fifteen dollars. That's what you have to carry on you today in case you get robbed. My watch two other punks took last year, so I don't wear the new one when I'm out."

"What are you doing out alone so late?" Peter says. "This neighborhood's deserted."

"I like to walk. If I get that itch, I take it. There are just so many directions to go. Last night I went the other. But I don't go far. My place is two blocks down."

"Can we do anything?" I say. "Take you to a police station or wait with you till a patrol car passes?"

"It's not worth it. Fill out a report, nothing happens. If I made a bundle it might be worth having that report as proof for a big loss on my taxes. I'll go home."

"We'll drive you."

"I don't want to drive him," Peter says.

"We have to. We came this far, let's see it through."

"No thanks," the man says. "I can't get hit twice in one night ten minutes apart. It doesn't happen."

"It's disgraceful, someone stealing from anyone—but from you? I wish we'd stopped sooner."

"Good thing you didn't. He came out of nowhere, didn't look playful, might have panicked and done something to me worse. Thanks," and he picks up his canes and starts downtown.

"Some night," Peter says, passing the man and signaling a left.

"Wait, back up to him."

"What now?"

"Just back up. —Mister, stop!" I open my bag. "I only have ten dollars," I say to Peter. "Loan me a five."

"Ten's enough."

"Please, I'm only borrowing it. You've nothing smaller than a ten, I'll give you one of my fives."

He gives me a five. "On me, no loan."

"Here," I say to the man. "Don't ask questions. You went through too much tonight, you don't want to be stopped by anyone without your fifteen, and we've plenty." He takes the money. "Now can we drive you home?"

"I'll make it."

Peter drives off, makes the U. "That was very nice. I think a little excessive, but okay—nice."

"As if it isn't bad enough for him, and then to get robbed? But maybe I shouldn't have said it to him like that."

"How?"

"'Disgraceful for someone to steal from you.' But to be so deformed? Did you see the way he walked?"

"Saw."

"It's got to be so painful. Going every step like that. I'm not talking of only the threat of being robbed, but just getting up and down curbs and I'm sure falling every so often because of the canes in the street cracks and so on. And if you're out of bread and want a loaf—what a chore."

"He goes out nightly, so maybe he's more mobile and not in as much pain as we think. But look at it this way. If you have an affliction like his you have to make adjustments and other arrangements. That's what you have to do in life; that's what everyone has to do."

"You might be right. But so many people in the city and everywhere like that man. In my neighborhood especially, and which I can never quite get used to. Even someone who walks a three-legged dog. The dog does well—compensates—but he has three. But there's a one-legged baby in a baby carriage and always on Broadway that destroys me every time I see her."

"A three-legged dog, sad; a one-legged baby—that's tragedy."

"Sometimes when I'm feeling very sad about people and animals like that—which can last for minutes to hours after—I think, and usually soon after I felt that way, that I only felt this for myself somehow—but it's not true or not most times."

"Of course it isn't. Probably never, or only rarely. Your response is authentically sympathetic rather than self-pitying."

"And I'm not saying this to have anyone think better of me. But why can't we feel these things for these people—forget the three-legged animals; what can I do for them?—and help them when we can? Not just what we did before, but sort of."

"Now you've lost me."

"If they need assistance across the street. Reaching for things for them in supermarkets they can't reach. And I guess for dogs if they're lost or starved no matter how many legs—feeding them or helping them find their way home."

"No, those are good things to do. And if you mean *sorry, pity*—feeling those—sure, that's what we have to do—fellow human beings, all that. Public spirits—because those words are still good words if accurately employed. And giving to charities—good charities if we can—ones that don't squander all the given money to keep the administrators administrating them. Just as any public institution—museums as well as any—shouldn't squander its money that way. Because it's all given, that money, by individuals or some larger public or private institution. And the truth of it is that no institution or government or private company should squander its money, and museums should probably be the first ones to exclude themselves from that type of administrative abuse. I believe in that."

"There, we discussed something interesting and stayed with it for once. We needed the robbery of an old crippled man to catalyze the discussion, and let's face it, nothing that profound was said and maybe only a baby-step past knickknacks. But we could always bullshit well."

"That wasn't bullshit."

"I know; just trying out something new for no reason: depreciating what I said if it made the littlest bit of sense."

"That was real talk, real feelings. Maybe not the deepest, but this is only a car conversation to get us safely home. But I'll tell you, a lot of what some people say sounds false to them isn't. So it doesn't mean you should hold your sentiments in check because of what they don't feel. And we could do plenty else—plenty—besides bull and serious talk."

"What besides what I think you're thinking we used to be able to do well, which, all right, we did, but so what?"

"Oh that? We could still do it well—believe me—no sweat."

"Let's change the subject?"

"Or with lots of sweat. But let's change it. Getting too grownup for me. Wait, that's not the remark I wanted to make."

"We used to cook compatibly together."

"You're referring to what else we used to do well together besides bullshit and serious talk and that other subject before we changed it?"

"Yup, cook. We complemented each other in the kitchen."

"We did, and we were also great summer tourists in Europe together, with lots of European sweat. Real sweat, from the sun and lots of jaunting, not that changed subject. And when I had a motorcycle you were a great passenger behind me and then rider when I taught you how to ride it and I was the passenger, so we rode well together in various ways too. And what else well? Well, not do but attend and-or enjoy: opera, dance, occasionally the same book. And we once painted your living room together."

"Not compatibly."

"I bellyached, true. So we didn't do that so well together, nor your foyer. Like to stop for a bite together? Empire Cafe on your right."

"No, just want to go home and go to bed."

"Mind if I ask how your work's going, just to keep us compatibly on the road together?"

"Enough already with together. And fine. Curating fine?" We've stopped for a light. He didn't answer. I look over at him. He's looking pretty seriously at me. "Yipes, what's coming next?"

"What do you expect? You're so fucking great looking."

"Now now."

"Now now nothing. Fucking exciting great. I have got to kiss you. This is a long light. I know it from other nights. This one and another on Riverside and Eighty-third. I have got to, Helene."

"Not to distract you, but did you put aftershave on in the men's room?"

"Okay, why?"

"Just curious. You carry it in or was some left there?"

"On the sink shelf. The manufacturer of it put a few atomizers there as a test of a new scent, a note said on the mirror. I was supposed to take a prestamped card and send it in as to what I thought of it. You like it? I don't mind it but I won't ask for it at the store, which is what their real intention was."

"It's all right. Not alluring, not repelling. But I don't especially like fake scents on men as you might have remembered, nor any strong work scent either, though I can appreciate the latter more."

"I don't remember. I should have, shouldn't I? What I actually thought was that you liked men's cologne. I couldn't have been thinking of anyone else. But what about it?" and he makes little kissing noises. "I want to, mucho."

"Then don't make a big thing of it or hit me with the dirties or chipmunk sound effects. But do it before the light changes."

"You're not doing this just to keep the journey safe?"

"Oh sure, some safe journey. But I'm not. I'd like to kiss you." A car honks behind us. Light's changed. "Too late. I knew you were stalling. Next red light and no blab about how you have got to and my exciting nothingness. Just lean over. I'll be here, maybe a few inches closer, and ready."

"We should also go to bed."

"Now stop. One thing at a time and now's not that time."

"If it leads to it?"

"What's got into you? You were never so unwilling to just kiss nor exacting for future promises from it. So let's at the next red and if it leads to that other thing, it does. I could do it. I'm pretty ready for that too. Truthfully, it wouldn't be because I was in any but maybe an old memory way touched with unfulfilled feelings for you. You're still attractive to me. And I know what we could usually do once we got around to it even in some of our worst moments, and that you wouldn't make a big deal of it. And you wouldn't, would you? That is, if we did ultimately do it—because that wouldn't be like you. It's not smart to sleep with ex-boyfriends if they're going to put you through things after you've slept with them again for one night."

"We were almost engaged."

"The light coming up is about to turn red. Are you still game for just starters?"

"There won't be a problem." We're driving along the alternative road for the highway. River's on our left and not too far ahead an enormous liner is docked, with all its lights on it seems and one of its smokestacks going. We're a few blocks from the elevated part of the highway if that part hasn't been torn down too. Didn't a moving truck sink through what became its razed part somewhere around here which started this whole multibillion dollar removal? Light's red. We've stopped, he moves closer to me, I stay still, we kiss. Feels good. "Nice, huh?" he says. "You always had the softest lips existent, except when you got a sore or two on them. Mind?"

"Another kiss? No."

He kisses me harder, tries to pry my lips open with his tongue and I fight him. Oh let him, so I let him. We go at it like that, his hand on my thigh, mine on his, both stroking, lips not parting, my skin jingling and head back to boozy. Honks, like a boop-boop-be-doop, behind us. He releases me and the handbrake and we drive on. "Come to my place," he says when we're passing the liner and going up the highway ramp too fast for me to catch its name. I always wanted to see the QE2 up close, and maybe I just did, but only with a bit of rummaging through today's or tomorrow's newspaper about ship arrivals and departures will I know. "You don't have to stay the night, but stay if you want to. In fact if you do come you should stay. But come—that's the important thing. Helene?"

"I'm here; I was just thinking. Was that the QE2 we passed?"

"I didn't see it."

"It was several blocks long and had three smokestacks and a dark hull."

"I once sailed on the Queen and in the six or seven days it took to Bremer-haven—seven, since Le Havre was six—I don't ever remember observing how many stacks it had. But sounds right. Most liners have two. Huge ships like the Queen, probably three."

"I'd love to sail on it, but only to Europe. I've never gone by ship."

"We could this summer. Fly one way, return by ship, or the reverse. The Queen still does."

"Please, we will not. And your place? Also not a good idea. I don't care what I said about old boyfriends or even near-fiancés, it's different with ones I loved, and I loved you, you jerk."

"And this jerk loved you. So it stopped for us both. But we could still fuck tonight, because look at that kiss."

"You have to say it that way? I've nothing against curse words, but that's all acting on your part. Turning-me-on talk that's turning me off."

"Pigshit. Scumbags. Fistfuckers. Cocksucking. It's a great idea, not a good one, and you have a great body, not a good one, and I want to fuck it. I want to fuck you. I want to screw you and lay you and perform the act of love with you and grab your ass with me on top of your ass and big tits with me on the bottom and I want to suck, fuck and pluck and really plow you. I want to very badly. So, that's so bad? Fuck it and too fucking bad, for that's what the fuck I feel and want to do."

"Thank goodness there are no red lights on this."

He pulls over to the right, puts the hazard lights on and starts coming to a stop.

"Don't! That's insane! You'll kill us!"

"Sorry," and he pulls into the driving lane. "And I'm a dummy and also sorry for my talk if it repulsed you."

"It didn't repulse. It—"

"Whatever, I'm sorry, and you know what I still want to do. We'd do it for the pure kicks of it and because we once loved and now very much like and respect one another, at least you can be assured I still do with you and even if that respect part sounds contradictory after my fuck talk. Or for no other reason but—no, no reason at all or not one we—"

"Oh—"

"Please, Helene."

"Oh, I'll come up. I can't seem to—oh, I can but I don't want to argue, because why not?—sure. But only if you promise to give me a good back massage and a glass of seltzer."

"I'll massage you anywhere and all night if you want and I only have club soda."

"I thought I could always get seltzer at your place."

"Maybe I have some. I probably do, put away for special occasions."

"And just my back. Don't get so enterprising. I doubt my body could take more than that tonight. Now I'm going to doze off but not so deeply where you can't wake me when we arrive."

"You want to have a baby badly, don't you."

"Whuh?" My eyes had been shut five seconds.

"Not by me, but you really still do. Just answer me, then doze."

"Why that out of nowhere?"

"Like that. Had a feeling, had to say it. If I didn't I would have lost it. Infantile attitude á la friend Sven, but you want to get married to someone very unlike me—someone who wants to get married but *really* and have a baby soon. That's why you were so, well, sad at the balcony announcement, and later pissed off at Sven, besides what that Arthur fellow would make anyone feel."

"My, you have quite the head on your hat, old buddy. You sure do."

"Don't have to get cynical."

"Then why try to get me to say what you already know and what is probably still a sore point between us? That's even worse turn-off behavior and talk than that turn-off talk from before. Maybe you had a change of mind about my coming up."

"Most certainly not. I thought I was getting into something deep; I obviously wasn't."

"If you were saying has my attitude changed on the matter in the last year—"

"Maybe that's what I was saying."

"It wasn't, but I'll answer anyway, bluntly, not deep. It hasn't. I still do ultimately want to have a baby with someone I care for very much, and I feel confident I will. And because of my age I should be thinking seriously about having one fairly soon, not so much because of the increasing risks of conceiving an unhealthy baby but because I want to be frisky enough to take care of it and play with it and continue to know it over a long period of time. But it's not a serious problem with me. I'm not, in other words, if Mr. Love doesn't come along, going to have one as a Miss Mom or jump into marriage with a loving schmuck who also wants to have a baby, just to have one. And it's not going to stop me, your talk—at least what you've said so far, so this is a sincere petition not to say anymore about it—from making love tonight, if you still want to and we're not too tired to, since right now that's what I'd like to do. If I've broken your balls a little just now, I apologize, since that's not what I wanted to do at all. Now give me my three-minute doze."

"Granted."

He taps my shoulder. "We're here. Got a spot in front. Everything's working for us. Not a mugger in sight. Even the moon can be seen and a number of meteorites knocking about in the wrong half of the hemisphere for the night. You're not too sleepy?"

"Why, do you want me to be?"

"You harp back on that so much I think it's you who wants me to be immediately asleep."

"I don't, so let's get it over with. No, that isn't nice or what I mean, so let's put it this way: we're kind of using one another tonight, but that also has to be the way it is sometimes if nothing better is around. No, that's not nice or right either. How can I say what I have in mind to without irritating you and gumming up the goal?"

"I never heard you talk like that before."

"You have so. Selective forgetting. Let's go up."

The doorman has to unlock the door to let us in. "Hey there, Helene."

"Russell? Hi—It's been so long I didn't recognize you. You lost weight but it looks good."

"Couldn't feel better. Have a good night? Good." He holds the elevator door open till we get in, presses the button for Peter's floor. "Goodnight."

"You don't know how lucky you are having such wonderful doormen."

"He had a bypass in his thigh this year that nearly finished him. Did I set the Chapman lock in the car?"

"You pushed something in under the dashboard."

"That's it. He even took last rites."

"Then what's he doing working this shift?"

"He sleeps, rests. We might be the last tenants in. If you had no wife, kids, education or skills, you'd be fighting for his job."

He holds my hand and whistles something from a familiar aria as he watches the floor indicator flash the floors, kisses me when the door opens. I don't know why I'm doing this. I'm not excited anymore. He's not attractive to me anymore. His breath stinks from alcohol and some egg dish when it didn't before. Mine probably does too but from another food. He's handsome and slim and a good lover and I'm almost sure I'll be able to lose myself making love with him, but everything I said before except my wanting to have a baby with someone I care for and who's a permanent live-in was all wrong. False and fairly high and fagged-out champagne talk, if I wasn't feeling so sharp and sober, so don't fall for those excuses. But I do want to make love and after it's over he's a quiet guy to sleep with and he'll let me leave with no big scenes at the door, no fake promises for more, just both of us appreciative of having some of our immediate needs met, and maybe after some late-morning love-making if I want and even if he doesn't, because that's what he was also good for. For not once would he admit he couldn't or didn't want to get an erection, and what a struggle sometimes when I'd have to say "It's okay, we'll try in the morning or another day or some other time tonight—I'll wake you if I get the urge," and he'd say "No trouble, lady," and play with himself or me or whatever he'd do till he got one that stayed. But go through with it, since it's been a few months and lately I've been feeling something very important and explicable has been missing from my life which no amount of masturbating or work can make up for.

First thing in he turns on the lights and record player. "Your eighteenth-century German flute, plus or minus a century and nationality, which I was listening to before I left—I wasn't expecting you here. Sure no wine or beer?" No, so he goes. I look at the primitive sculptures and masks he's acquired or has on loan since I was last here. All to some extent phallic or oral-anal-vaginal phallic-receptive. Though a few do have procreative or foreplay subjects and one's of a bearded naked woman standing on a stool—what's that mean?—and another is of a clothed young man strumming what looks like a lute, plus a five-foot high mask of an insane shaman with his mouth closed but two tongues coming out of his nose. I bet he's had thirty different women here since my last visit. He used to keep a spermicide in his medicine chest for sudden conquests. Condoms too if he had to, which he ordered through a coupon in *Playboy*: specially ribbed. He comes back, says "Sit over here," I sit on the couch, he sits beside me, I drink the club soda, he some wine, he kisses my neck. Good, it's begun. "Why don't we take off our clothes and go to bed," I say.

"Sure, we should, but here. It'd be too unshipshape, undies all over the bed and floor." He takes off his tie and starts unbuttoning his shirt. "Actually, want me to take off your clothes?"

"That'd be nice. No, let's take off our own clothes, wash up and go to bed." I stand.

"I've washed. Did you come with anything?"

"I'm like you, or as I remember you. I always keep one in my medicine chest," holding up my bag.

"Interesting. You must be getting laid a lot these days. What do you know—said the wrong thing again."

"Truth is, I'm not, and I don't have anything with me—that was just a tease. I thought you, much as I hate the smell of those things, could use an ordinary condom at the last moment."

"At the last moment I can't."

"Doesn't matter. I've been feeling my period coming on for two days."

"Is it absolutely safe-positive-sure?"

"Always has been. I already got a few blood drops in my underpants. One go at sex and it should begin to flow."

"Should I put a rubber mat under the sheet?"

"I'll give you plenty of warning."

"You have a tampon with you?"

"That I'm prepared for," shaking the bag.

The phone rings. "Who the hell could that be so late? Maybe I shouldn't answer it."

"Don't look at me."

"I have to answer it. It could be bad family news and sometimes has been this late. I'll tell you after about my sister. Excuse me."

He runs to the bedroom, shuts the door. I go into the bathroom, undress, open his medicine chest to look for a box of Q-Tips to clean my ears. It's an awful habit, never buying a box for myself but only using Q-Tips I find in other people's bathrooms. But it's only two to four Q-Tips a person and I try not to hit the same medicine chest twice. It's just something I do—some intentionally aberrational part of me I don't question or want to change and perhaps my last link to a mediumly renegade life. I'll probably do it even after I'm married, unless my husband already buys Q-Tips for himself, but not after I have a baby, since I suppose it's necessary for a number of reasons to have them around for a child. And so far every time I've wanted to clean out my ears, which is about every second week, I've found a box of them or one of its inferior equivalents in other people's bathrooms.

I take two Q-Tips out of the box and start to clean. Door's locked, so he can't walk in. Lots of wax, some of it quite hard and dark, so it could be three to four weeks since I did this. Most times two are enough. Now, after five—maybe a record number for me—the cotton nib comes out clean from both ears without digging too far in, and I flush the used Q-Tips down.

I wash my crotch with his washrag. I bet it's a woman on the phone, wanting to come over or Peter to come by. So be it if that's what he wants, but don't be silly: he can be with me tonight and tomorrow with her. Though I'm still not sure why I'm here. Sex, yes, and the only reason, but by now I don't even know if I can get into it in any way. Sure I can. Lights out, blinds down and shut to keep out the street light, close my eyes, open my legs, feel around with my hands, and it'll easy and easier still if I can work my way to the top. The pressure of my weight usually slowed him down by half and my control up there speeds me up considerably, making us about even. Then sleep, morning, coffee, goodbye. I wash under my arms with the same rag, wash my face, rinse the rag, brush my teeth with his brush, brush my hair, fold up my clothes, run warm water in the sink and one at a time stick my feet under the tap, pushing out any recalcitrant lint between the toes, dry them and put on his bathrobe. Soft and so long on me that I feel like a girl in her father's coat. I leave the bathroom, set my things on a chair. Forgot to look for the spermicide. I did see a box of condoms. No hiding them under the T-shirts in the dresser for him. Bedroom door's shut. I knock.

"In a minute."

I go back to the living room, turn over the record, look at the two walls filled from ceiling to floor with books.

"No, you listen to me once this year," he yells in the bedroom.

Something new: each bookshelf is labeled. Poetry, Novels A–D, Novels

E–J, Short Stories, Antiquities, Literary Criticism, Deutsch und Franzo-
sisch, and half a wall of just art books: cocktail-table size, regular size, minia-
tures, some with spines hundreds of years old. Must be five hundred of them,
and half it seems on primitive art. I should ask him why so many Cycladic
pieces—my favorite period ever for stone—have women with their arms
crossed over their flat stomachs. Good guess would be fertility or breeding, but
I want something more than my own spec. I pull out an enormous book called
Dubuffet, whom I've taken-to lately—what was it he recently said in a newsmagazine comparing art to literature: that art is a hundred years advanced
over lit, or was it lit over art? But poetry. Dubuffet goes back. Too bulky a book
to put on my lap and turn the pages of so late. But that's what I'd like right now:
a simple pastoral nineteenth-century English poem to go along with my
lightmindedness and the guitar and flute. I start on the top poetry shelf, but
a book on the short-story shelf above it catches my eye. Krin. Daniel. By.
Translated by Daniel Krin. I can't believe it. I take it out. *Modern Japanese
Short Stories, translated and with an introduction by Daniel Krin.* Reputable small
press. Softcover. How'd Peter end up with it? Same Krin? I turn it over. Two-by
two-inch photo of him in a crewneck sweater, looking a little balder than he
did tonight, hair windblown or just uncut, homecut or messed up, what look
like West Side brownstone terraces behind him, so taken from a terrace
several stories up, trying to smile but looking as if he's squirming on the pot.
Photo by Rena Moscow. Not one of the well-known literary photogs. Probably a good friend at the time or a cousin or niece. Krin: Moscow. Both could
be Russian-Jewish names, Krin for Krinsky I'd think. Nothing much about
him under the photo or anything inside. NYC's public schools and CCNY, but
no mention of a postgraduate degree or university teaching, which could
mean he has none or never taught or no place he's especially proud of or this
press thought would help sell the book if it listed it, but whom would the NYC
public schools appeal to? Among his other works: *Songs of Ancient Korea: an
anthology of poems in the sijo form,* whatever that is, but one of the best
university presses published it, and by this same press: *Poems and Tales of the
Northwest American Indian* and *Pueblo Ritual Poetry.* So he's an orientalist of
sorts, with a side interest, because of the Mongoloid linkage and frozen Bering
Strait, in American Indian literature, or maybe the reverse, last one first, and
poetry over fiction. How old is he and his book? Copyright page. 1935 –
Older than I thought by about six years, though the photo makes him look
fifty, even if it had to have been snapped more than four years ago when this
book was published. Probably has had a book published since and got a

teaching job and maybe his doctorate. Dedication page. "To my mother Pauline Saffner Krin, who helped support me through this & other works." I look through the short-story shelf and the poetry and anthropology shelves, but there's nothing else by him. I wouldn't have taken him for a translator or anthologist or even someone much interested in literature. More as what? Because of his wide chest and bull neck and that Diana met him at an artists' colony: a sculptor; an erector or puttogetherer of monumental steel-crossbeam constructions through the use of pulleys and tackles and an acety-lene torch, or perhaps an action painter a little late for that scene. In other words, a moderately intelligent laborer or spontaneous stroker of artworks rather than an artful definer of them. I turn to the introduction. "Modern, in modern Japan, seems to mean—"

Peter comes in. "Good, you've kept yourself busy. Sorry about the phone. Find a book you like?"

"That's what I want to ask you. Just bought it because you were interested?"

"Let me see. —That one. Was going with a very wealthy Japanese journal-ist—I'll tell you why I mention her wealth—a short time after we broke up, and she gave it to me. Along with a book"—he pulls one off the Gallimaufry shelf—"on how to teach yourself Japanese in three easy weeks, as she wanted to buy us tickets to Japan together soon as I could fit it into my work plans. Didn't work out." He hands me the language book. "Got to know one word, but not from that. Soshi. *Small.* Or toshi. She said she was a little above average height by Japan's standards, but here was considered tiny, and com-pared to me, a pygmy, so she gave herself that name for me to use. Not toshi or soshi. Something else, and I think the feminine version of it. I called her it once—was very embarrassed doing it—and though I told her it was thought an insult to be called that here, bright as she was she didn't mind and she even laughed. Moshi. Skoshi. I think the last one's it. She also gave me a book of Japanese poems—"

"By the same translator?"

"Who's that?" Looks. "Never heard of him. The poems were done by the famous one. Been around for years. A very dear old geezer who once did a catalogue intro on Japanese rock gardens for the museum."

"But it's so bizarre you have this man's book. I met him at Diana's tonight. I thought he was a sculptor or lumberjack."

"Take it then. I read one story and got bored. I'm not saying it was your friend's fault. I simply don't like Japanese fiction, modern or otherwise. Take the language book too."

"Why would I want it?"

"Did you talk to him much? Is he married? There was no chance of his calling you—nothing like that? It was just routine cocktail party hooey?"

"No, he said he would call, but—"

"Then he will. Why wouldn't he? So take the language book—take both books and anything else here that's Japanese. Not the art books and dolls. Then when he calls, say a few words in Japanese to him. Maybe to perplex him or as a joke. Or say hello in Japanese the first time he calls, then switch to English. And why not some Japanese art books? The ones made there, no matter of whose, are as beautiful as anything the Dutch produce, and I can always get replacements at fifty percent off. First that poetry book." He goes through the shelves. "Right—she borrowed it because it had the en face originals on some poems she was suddenly dying to read, and then we broke up and she never returned it. No great loss. But the art books—"

"This is silly. I don't want any."

"But I want you to have them. This is our Japanese night. I'll even get out sake and warm it. I have the special cups."

"It'll make me sick again."

"Then beer. Japanese is the best for an upset stomach or to keep one away. Very mild, made from rice. I have some in the fridge."

"Still from those Japanese journalist days?"

"No, though I did learn the upset stomach remedy and preventive from her and I got to like their beer even more than I had before I met her. Japanese and Dutch beer. Never made the connection between beautiful art books and great beer before, but there it is—though I never dated a Dutchwoman for more than a night nor heard of a Dutch wine made from cheese. Have you?"

"I'll take the Japanese stories but that's all," and I put the language book back on the shelf.

"But I insist. And a painting book." He pulls out a book that must be two feet long and three inches thick. "This is for you. Astonishing color reproductions. Now you can't refuse a present. Serendipity call it. You meet this Japanese man—"

"He's not Japanese."

He takes the anthology from me. "He doesn't look Japanese to you, and the name?"

"Not at all. And *Krin?*"

"I know of several Daniels who are Japanese. The Hawaiian senator for one. Anyway, you meet him and it leads to your owning a hundred-dollar book, and after December 31st, a hundred twenty-five. And the language book." He gets that book out. "I want you to be a hundred percent Japanese

tonight. Language, painting, literature, drinks. I even have a Japanese pleasure book, hand-illustrated about seven hundred years ago. I should keep it
under dehumidified glass. I'm getting a beer, you get the pleasure book.
Oversize shelf, green binding, *so* thick, looks old. I also have Japanese champagne."

"I'll share your beer."

"No you won't. I want my own." He goes into the kitchen. I follow him.
"You're supposed to be looking for that book. It has a few practicable things in
it we can try, for most are for a couple supple as pizza dough and the man hung
like a horse."

"For now, let's stay occidental and modern, except for the beer. If I can ask,
who phoned? Family or more personal?"

"Someone I don't see anymore, but hear her?—oh boy. Right after the one
after the journalist. Too crazy and young. She once wanted to come over
when I had someone here, and when I said 'Not possible, I'm very tired—'"
He opens two bottles of Japanese beer. "Pilsner or regular glass?"

"Bottle will do."

"Bad for your tummy. Something about all that air through the neck." He
gives me a glass, pours, clicks glasses and says "To the land of Japan which has
given us many Daniels, one or two indirectly, and you, circuitously, a beautiful book," and drinks. "I have to get out of this toasting rut. I can't lift a glass of
milk—"

"So the woman?"

"They let her in downstairs, since they knew her from before, and then she
knocked and knocked on my door after she rang it to death. I finally said 'Go
home!' and she sat on the doormat and started crying. A neighbor phoned
me. I let her in, but hid the other woman in the kitchen. I thought I could get
rid of her in a few minutes: take her downstairs, put her in a cab, after
promising to see her for lunch the next day. But she wanted to stay over.
Finally I said I'll have to get the cops to drag her out or do it myself, and I
actually grabbed her arm and dragged her along the floor to the door. The
other woman—I'd met her that night—came out and said 'Here I am, peeka-
boo, that what you wanted to see, Doreen, or maybe you're still here because
you're hot to make it a threesome? Well get lost, you screwed-up bitch,' and
Doreen fled the apartment. I should have been more honest with her at once,
introduced her to the other woman, which was this woman's advice, but I
thought she'd get hysterical. I even thought she might have a gun. She once
ran over an old boyfriend but the jury decided it was a legitimate gripe. I'm

through with messy relationships. The woman who chased her out turned out to be almost as bad. Manic dieter. Doesn't work, affairs with unstable women. Just levelheaded from now on—scholars, professional women, and minimum age of twenty-five. I know I was occasionally drawn to the unpredictable erratic type because there was no chance of anything stable and sane developing with them. But you didn't come here for a barrage of self-analysis from me. Though you're the kind I need: peaceful, sensible, doesn't willfully throw up good food. To you I can also say I shouldn't be a satyr too. I can say it without your thinking I'm too egotistical, which I know I am. Unstable too, but I'm improving in both categories. I'm in analysis these days, but you probably know that."

"You, the original anti-analysis man?"

"Dot didn't tell you? Strange. And she says, my analyst, to be as open as I can when I can and the situation legitimizes it, not when it's pure self-obsessive talk. So I'm going to tell you something which I hope won't kill it for us tonight. Drink up."

I sip.

"More, more—take a big gulp. And probably we should sit on the couch for this one—not the bed yet."

"Maybe you shouldn't say it. You might be ready but I might not be to hear it."

"It's important you do. I might let this go with someone else—a pickup, if there's ever another one—or maybe I wouldn't. I might be less egotistical and unstable than I was—my analyst thinks so—but I don't know if I'm any more self-sacrificing and well-intentioned, except to someone I respect as much as you."

"You have crabs."

"Herpes. Good guess. It's dormant now, but let's not chance it flaring up overnight. If we use a condom it's impossible for you to get it. And before, you said—"

"Hold it, hold it, hold it."

"You don't like them, or didn't used to, and how could you?—but unlike some women, you don't refuse to make love if I put one on."

"Would you really even think twice about not telling a pickup you have herpes?"

"Yes. No. Wait, let me get your syntax straight. Would I really not? Would I really think twice? Be aboveboard, Peter. Since analysis—it's actually been since analysis that I got herpes, but not from my analyst. Maybe from Yatsuko.

She swears she doesn't have it and there's nothing I can do but believe her, since she's back in Japan. Doreen perhaps, but I'd never approach her about it because of what it could start. She'd claim she got it from me, if she doesn't already know she has it. Or even if she doesn't have it she'd then think she did and say I gave it to her to cripple her. Wasn't the pickup because she made me wear a condom that night and the few times after. She was afraid that every man she knew, except for her regular boyfriend, had herpes. As for some others—it's difficult to pinpoint whom and sometimes to locate them again, and what will I gain by it? A lesson's been learned from my screwing around. And it would be sheer magnanimity on my part to help the woman know she has it, something I don't feel inclined to being to the person who gave it to me. But if we use a condom—"

"Still too risky. There's this cesarean business if you get pregnant no matter how many years after—"

"I know about that. I can't get rid of it. I'll have to hang around for the rest of my life with it unless some genius comes up with a cure. It's a pain in the ass."

"So, since we're not going to sleep together—"

"We could still fool around. You don't get herpes through the hand, though I wouldn't want you to do it with your mouth unless you—"

"I'll talk to my gynecologist to see what I can do in the future with a carrier. Now I better go," and I start for the living room.

"Then just sleep over. I'm telling you, you can't get it unless I stick my dick in you. I'll wear pajamas. I'll wear my bathrobe in bed and keep my underpants on or change into a fresh pair."

"I'm going home. All I'm asking from you now is to help me get a cab."

"Damn. Fuck it! Piss! Oh hell, I'll drive you home."

"You have a good parking spot. Is it good for tomorrow?"

"I think so."

"Don't lose it. Just put me in a cab."

"And if I hadn't told you I had herpes?"

"And if you hadn't?"

"I would have felt lousy. Worse. Suicidal to the point of kicking myself. Okay, get dressed. But take all the books I gave you. My one condition, or no cab."

I change in the bathroom. He has his coat on when I come out and is holding my coat and bag and a shopping bag with the books in it.

"My umbrella!" I say. "I left it at the reception."

"Want to phone them from here?"

"No, and I'm sure I'll never get it back." I look inside the shopping bag. "Looks like more books than before."

"It was supposed to be a surprise when you got home. I found some other Japanese books—beauties, one only on cats in Japanese art. Nobody loves cats more than you and maybe no people but the Chinese painted them better than the Japanese. You even have two Siamese. Sammy and Sue. How are they? I miss them. Getting off your couch with my pants plastered with their hair. Fish. I remember those long white sausages of slightly digested fish I'd step in early in the morning on my way to your john. And your temperament is practically Japanese. Soft—I'm talking about stereotypically Japanese—and your voice mostly softspoken and your attitude so polite and deferential in company, so it's perfect these gifts."

"You don't know what you're saying about me, but you win."

I have my coat on and he hands me the two bags. "My apologies, Helene. It's been a bad night for us and my library but not Japan. You might even think of changing fields after several close thumb-throughs of these books, so maybe also a bad night for American literature but Japan's gain."

"You never know. But there are plenty of things Japanese I've always liked. Music, food—movies, other than for the ones where dogs walk around with human hands in their mouths."

"With Yatsuko—talking about food—I never walked out of those restaurants the way most people say they have—hungry. She ate sparingly. I used to have my plateful and then half of hers. But one last time." Before I can stop him he has his arms around me and is kissing my neck, working his way up diagonally to the jaw. I try to squirm free, bag of books drops to the floor. "What are you doing? You can't get herpes from kissing or hugging either, unless I've sores on my lips or open wounds on my fingertips which I've kissed with my herpes-infested lips. But I don't. Just on my dick."

"God, was coming up here ever the mistake. What's next on your list, rape? Get off me?"

"After I leave you downstairs," letting me go, "I'm going to whack off. Put vaseline on it, which I do only in extreme cases when I need a walloping release," and he grabs his penis through the pants, "and jerk the thing till it hurts," and demonstrates.

"Why do you have to elaborate so much? Don't answer."

"I don't have to elaborate. I do have to answer. I'm disappointed, so I'm trying to be nasty as shit to you, which includes being graphic. But in the end, to myself, well—"

"Let's go." I unlock the door and leave.

"Don't forget the bag of Japanese." He gives it to me, "No, it's too heavy," takes it back, and we wait for the elevator, standing several feet apart, and take it down, two of us against opposite walls watching the floor numbers light up. I say goodnight to Russell, who says "Don't be a stranger." Peter whistles for a cab and says "You have enough money?"

"You don't think it's a little late to whistle so loudly for a cab?"

"Don't worry, they're my neighbors. And listen, Helene. Maybe in a few weeks—"

"Got ya."

"Lunch I'm talking about. Only lunch. It's clear to me now that anything but that would never work."

"We'll see." He opens the door, leans forward to kiss my cheek and I pull back my head. "As I said, let me check with my doctor first to see if it's safe," and I get in the cab.

He puts the bag of books on my lap. "You cunt."

"Bull. You brought it on and have always brought it on and will continue to bring it on yourself," and I slam the door.

"What?" he says through the window, and raps on it. "I didn't quite hear that. What, you cunt?"

The cabby's laughing.

"Don't you laugh, you moron," Peter yells, and slams the cab roof with his hand.

"Hey," the cabby says. "Hey! Hey!"

"Hundred-tenth off Riverside," I say, "and don't get out, don't fight—please."

"Okay," and he drives away.

"I'm sorry about what happened back there. Any damage done to your cab, not that much could have been—"

"Is nothing. Not my cab. Forget, forget," still angry.

He has an accent, kind of a high Russian voice, I look at his hack license: Jascha Papinsky. "Vy—excuse me—vy Russki, da?"

"Da," smiling, "you speak?"

"Just those few words I learned at a party tonight, which I think are the same few words I learned at this same person's party last year. There were a number of novy Amerikanets there. You the same? New?"

"No understand."

"The Soviet Union. Have you recently come from there?"

"*Novy*. Here. Yes. One year. Engineer. Too bad you not speak. I want to speak Russian for hours, but all Russian émigrés in New York is drivers of taxi, no riders. And old Russians many years here no more take taxi or look my name and to me not speak. Ah, my English very bad. A big problem. *Adres*. Take."

He drives me to my building. For the whole ride from a tape deck beside him is some slow old jazz which I sit back and listen to and get to like. "Please wait till I'm in my building," I say, paying him. "And if you could also be so nice. Since this neighborhood sometimes isn't safe. Wait till I wave to you from inside my building before you go? Understand?"

"Sure thing. Glad to."

I have my keys out and leave the cab, unlock the lobby door, go in, look around, let the door close, ring for the elevator, and when it comes, look at the convex mirror on its wall to make sure no one's hiding inside. I wave to the driver, who beeps once, and take the elevator to my floor.

Sammy is speaking to me from behind the door second I step off the elevator. Sue had to be put to sleep because the pain from her terminal cancer was getting too great. I didn't tell Peter because he knew how close I was to my cats and how close they were to each other and by that time I didn't want his sympathy, genuine or false. "Okay, Sams, I'm coming—don't fly out the door." Elevator closes, so even if he does run past me he can't get into the elevator, which he did once and it took me a while to find what floor he ended up on. I open the door, he's scratching the floor that he wants to jump up. I put down the bags, wiggle my fingers for him to come and he stares at my stomach while he hums and then jumps at the spot he stared at and making squealing sounds runs up my chest till he's lying across my shoulder, purring, head against my cheek. I walk into the kitchen with him, set him down, he's finished his food and is pushing the plate with his forehead for more. I open a jar of strained-veal baby food and spoon two globs of it onto his plate, leave the spoon on the plate because he likes to lick it, drink a glass of seltzer, undress, shower, take two aspirins, brush my teeth and floss them and massage the gums with the brush's rubber tip and get into bed. That's it with parties for me, at least for a month, even if it is the season. Write that down. I jump out of bed—Sammy, sleeping next to me, gets startled and jumps off the bed and runs out of the room—get my appointment calendar and write on December's four pages a letter a day with "onth" on the 31st: "No more parties for me at least for a month." And at the bottom of the last page: "Meet people instead for breakfast or lunch, read for and outline spring term, finish 30pp of the book, just finish the book! try not to even see a man after 5 except maybe new year's eve, and even there, but who'll that be?—Oh, no woes if you stay home alone that night and on great wine and black forest ham and poached salmon fillets get high."

I'm reading a student's paper on "Postconstructionism and Morphology in the Postmodern American Novel"—I'm sure he has the first term wrong, if he's not sending up that critical school, and even if he is, the entire department by now, students and teachers both, has to know how I hate those words and themes, even parodies of them, since there's rarely anything in them for me except material and writing to help put me to sleep when I can't sleep— when the phone rings. Answering service closed more than two hours ago. I don't like answering it, as at this hour there's a good chance it's a crank. "Yes?"

"Then you got home okay. Good. I was worrying."

"Who is this?"

"Excuse me, because why should I have thought you'd recognize my voice? Arthur Rosenthal. And excuse me too for calling so late."

"Thanks for your concern, Arthur, but it's too late to even talk about it being too late."

"Now I'm very sorry I called. I didn't think it'd be that late—late italicized I mean. Because I called only fifteen minutes ago—"

"You couldn't have. I've been home more than half an hour."

"I did. And a half-hour before that, and a half-hour before that too. Maybe I just missed you the second half-hour ago and you were someplace else the last half-hour—in another room, am I wrong?"

"It's possible I was in the shower then and didn't hear it, so all right. Still—"

"Anyway, I certainly called, but that's not to say I couldn't have dialed the wrong number and that number didn't answer. But I don't often dial the wrong number no matter how late at night. Maybe five hundred to one. I can't even recall the last time. A year ago—two."

"But you do often call late at night."

"No. I only called you to see if you got home okay, and when you didn't answer, half-hour after that and then this call. When you didn't answer the first two times I called, I assumed you weren't home yet and that it'd be safe to call now."

"Did you ever assume I might not have answered deliberately and that each time you rang you were disturbing me more and more, waking me up each time?"

"I should have assumed that. But it wasn't what happened, was it? Because you said that a half-hour ago—"

"No, it wasn't, but still. To me any call after eleven at night and before seven A.M., and maybe even eight, except between very close people—forget the early morning calls, let's concentrate on the late. But people very close to one another—lovers if you may. And even there the caller should think 'Do I know, if I know this person is up, if he or she would be disturbed by my rings or is too tired to answer the phone?'—should be for emergencies only—for physical or emotional help or something like that. And after midnight even lovers should hold off their calls unless it's an extreme personal emergency, between them or very deeply affecting them and where the caller is sure the called lover would at least tolerate the call. I didn't put that well—and I didn't mean to exclude calls from immediate family, since my thoughts about those calls are about the same for nonfamily—but it's one of my rules."

"You put it well. And I'm sorry I didn't know your rules, even if I suppose every intelligent person should have the same rule. And no question it was wrong of me to call. Even if I was only concerned about you, and more concerned each time you didn't answer, which was presumptuous of me. But also because—what the heck; I've come this far I might as well say the rest—I didn't especially like this fellow Peter—may I speak openly?"

"I don't want to hear about him now. And Peter is or was a friend of mine, so it's not right, at any time of the day or night, for you to—"

"I disliked him thoroughly. I've never seen anyone so caught-up with himself—so, so . . . who gave the impression of—he's a born bastard and good-for-naught, that's what. I was almost afraid for you with him, and that if he were there with you when I called, which would be your own affair, but if someone called he'd know that someone else knew he was there and that if he was planning any harm—"

"You don't know how wrong you are. You're going on like this only because of some resentment you must have towards him because of me. But you're blowing this thing way—"

"I know, but that was my fear. Not out of jealousy. He looked capable of doing anything heinous. I don't care what kind of sophisticated work he does and how brilliant and dynamic everyone says he is, he's a goddamn snob and peacock and I bet even a chiseler and heel of the highest order—not a chiseler, I've no basis for that—but that's what I believe. I've never believed anything so much and so fast as that without utterly knowing that person or the facts, but you just tell me he's not. Of course you'll say he's not, and why shouldn't you? That would be the loyal and right thing to do."

"Please stop about him."

"Of course. But if you can believe it, except for that I wanted to make sure you got home safe, all that's not even why I called. I won't keep you another minute. I only wanted to say that tomorrow's Saturday, neither of us has to go to work, so how about lunch, say one o'clock at The Library, which is on Broadway and Ninety-second, halfway between your apartment and mine. It's even less than halfway for you, and no splitting the check. After opening my trap the way I did, I should stand you to two straight lunches and at a place a lot better than The Library, which for what it is is very good of its kind."

"Thanks, Arthur, but I just made a vow—"

"Is it because of what I said about him? Even if I shouldn't have said anything, I wasn't too far off in my assessment of him, was I? Excuse me, but what about your vow? It can be broken for an hour or two, can't it?"

"You're not taking me seriously. What I vowed was not to see anyone for an outing for the next month, since what I have to do first is crank away at finishing something and also prepare for the spring term. I'm carrying two lit courses and a composition, which can't sound arduous to anyone not in university teaching—"

"It does, I know what it is. But the next month you said, which is December. It's still November. Five whole days left. So you've five more days to have lunch with someone, so how about it? Lunch—an hour or less—no more."

"Tomorrow at one? No, I can't."

"Yes you can. I'm sorry, I know how valuable your time is—but an hour, sixty minutes to the dot. And The Balcony, not The Library, which is a five-minute walk for you—you must know where it is. Next door to the Olympia, which is a lot less than less than halfway down and sometimes live chamber music there and always a decent lunch. I'll even pick you up by cab—you can be waiting downstairs at twelve fifty-five."

"Don't pick me up, and can we make it at two? That way I might be able to get some work done, since I know I'll sleep late tomorrow and maybe even wake up with a slight hangover."

"What's sleeping-late for you?"

"Just answer; I have to go."

"Two it is, you kidding? Anything, even two-fifteen. And I'm glad you got home safe—you did, didn't you? You're not going to tell me tomorrow about any of tonight's hand-to-hand skirmishes and battle wounds?"

"I'm safe. Don't pry. Goodnight."

Didn't want to but how else? Not true, because— Damn, just should have said "Listen to me, it's not only audacious of you to"— Not "audacious," but— Oh, no big deal, and he's looking out for me, isn't that a laugh? No, it was stupid of me. Should have said "Call me another time, I'm bushed, goodnight," and hung up. But it's just lunch, falls in with my new directives, and though nosy and a bit nutty he's a sweet enough guy and was he ever on-target about Peter. But I'll establish right off with him— Already have a dozen more friends than I can hardly see even now and then— But come December— Clever—five days left in November—he caught me on that one—guy's fast. Wait, do I have a luncheon date tomorrow? I look at my appointment book. No, and it's only tomorrow, so I should be able to remember without writing it down. But I don't know how groggy I'll be in the morning or how much drink makes you forget overnight, so I write "Arthur Rosenthal, 2, The Balcony," in tomorrow's box. But come December I'm putting the kibosh to any frivolous social-going. Get a special phone-gadget installed so when I press a button it'll keep the phone from ringing when I'm busy or sleeping and the service is closed. Heard of those.

I pick up the student's paper. Why not put it off? Because I want to get all of them corrected so I can get to things I really want to do. "Morphology" again means what? It means morphine. It means latrine. I write on the paper with an arrow aimed at the word "Leonard, no more big words for me like this—I'm too lazy to look em up. And what's with this postdeconunstru—? What about supercacographicexhibitionism? (Did I spel it rite?)" Phone rings. Now he's blown it. Much too late to call twice the same night even if the last call was ten seconds ago and he was my husband-to-be and most loved lover. Whatever he has to say can hold till the morning and late into it. Stop on your own accord. Doesn't. Shameless schmuck. I pick up the receiver. "Arthur, this better be good."

"It isn't Arthur, and I know it's extremely late, but it's Dan from tonight— Daniel Krin—is this Miss Winiker?"

"Who? Oh, I'm not going to pretend—I know who. Are you out of your mind? What could you want when it's after two?"

"I'm sorry, but the clock, and this is no excuse, I'm looking at says it's one—few minutes past—but it's a bank clock, on a seedy street corner, and since I haven't a watch or another clock to compare it with, it could well be wrong."

"Whether it's two or one—"

"You're right—by all means—please believe I'm not disputing it. And you can't know how sorry I am to call. Nor how I tried everything under the sun—sun's hardly the word to use at this hour. Everything under the street light, perhaps, to resolve—and I shouldn't make light of it—neither of those lights—beforehand the reason why I did call. But I couldn't and it was an emergency which—"

"What kind of emergency, Mr. Krin? And let's make this quick. So tell me, what kind? Because at this hour I don't take emergency calls from people I've just met."

"Please hear me out. You're just about my last chance on this. The timing of my call's all wrong but I don't think the reason I called is. And by 'last chance' I meant, to help me out of a bad situation. And for the last fifteen minutes—you're still there?"

"Make it quick."

"For the last fifteen, because it was so late—and at the time I thought it was ten to one, so for a Friday not the latest of lates to call but still much too late—I debated with myself and thought 'No, don't call, too late, much too, I don't know her, just met, etcet, spoke fifty words to her, hundred, tops, and maybe a hundred-fifty between us.' But then, when I didn't see any alternative, which I'll get into, and I decided to call, but even then undecidedly, your phone was busy—a few minutes ago. So I thought 'At least she's up and at home, so if I call a minute from now and the line's free, I won't be waking her.' Of course you'd be home if you were up."

"Not necessarily. If someone dials a number the same time that phone's ringing because someone else dialed it first—"

"That'd produce a busy signal for the person dialing a little behind? Didn't think of that in relation to this. And 'dialing a little behind.' That could be misinterpreted, but please don't. Should've kept it to myself. It was un-intentional, but repeating it wasn't. Though the repeat was just my surprise at my unintentional line, not said to be suggestive. And now I guess whenever I dial someone late—which I don't normally do; I don't like getting calls myself after eleven."

"Same here."

"Even after ten. I occasionally go to bed early just to get an early start the next day."

"Between ten and eleven's all right, even from someone I just met, but never a call around two. Or if your clock's right and it wasn't that it stopped—"

"It hasn't."

"—then five to ten minutes past one. Never. But where's my watch? I'm looking at the alarm clock right now—hold on." I go into the bathroom, get my watch off the shelf under the medicine chest, put one of the pearl ear-studs back into the cockleshell on the shelf from which it must have rolled out of but got stopped by my toothbrush, put the toothbrush back into the wall holder, go back. "Your bank clock runs slow or is still suffering from an outage of an hour and a quarter some time ago, because both my watch and clock says it's twenty after two. And earlier tonight I set my watch by my clock and then checked my watch against the wall clock at that reception I told you I was going to."

"If I'd known it was past two I probably still would've called you. It's that important."

"I can imagine. You want to come up."

"Not for the reason your tone says. Please, give me a little credit. You see, I'm locked out of my apartment. If I started to tell you the scenes that led up to it—and I'm sorry, by the way, for my calls to your service, which happened way before I got locked out. I was a little drunk then. Now I'm not. I'm stoned sober—stark sober—very stark but what's—"

"What calls to my service?"

"They didn't tell you?"

"I didn't call it."

"You're the first person I know of with one who doesn't call it every three hours. I'm not saying there's anything wrong in calling it that—"

"I got home after it closed. Even if I got home before that I wouldn't have called it till tomorrow. I really only need it on school days. I'm a teacher—"

"I know. I spoke to a couple of people about you at the party. Casual. I didn't probe. Oh, so I probed. I was interested in you after you left—you must have known before you left how interested I was in you. In fact we both spoke about it—our mutual interest—so of course I'd be just as or more interested in you after I left, which caused that brainless yelling to you from the window, for instance, or helped cause it. All the drink I drank at Diana's didn't hinder it, not that I'm not responsible for how much and then how I act under it. Nor do I want all this drink talk to downplay the interest I felt without drink before or after the window incident."

"Less said about that window—"

"Thank you. The very least would be the best, but it's good it's out and that you know it's also not something I normally do. But I was interested so I asked a couple of people, Diana, mostly, 'Who is she? What does she do?' Nothing detailed, not *personal life*—but that has nothing to do with why I called now and my emergency."

"Excuse me, but since you knew I had a service—and I hope you didn't insult anyone there. It's a good service, nice hardworking people work there—"

"I didn't. I forget what I said but I know, because I was still a little drunk—and I also hardly ever drink that much or get the way I'll describe—that I must've sounded drunk and perhaps unrefined to them the two or three times I called—I hope not. So next time you speak to them I wonder if you could apologize for me. But you were saying?"

"The service is called Lip Sinc, with an i-n-c. Why don't you look up the number tomorrow and call it to apologize?"

"I will. Lip Sinc. I'll remember it since I don't have a pen. Now can I tell you about the spot I'm in and why your reasons for thinking why I want to come up aren't the ones why I do, or should I just forget it and quietly hang up? And I would very quietly hang up. For I know I'm disturbing you—I just hope I didn't get you going to sleep."

"You didn't. But let's say your reason is you've been locked out. So what's that got to do with me?"

"Maybe I should say the rest quickly before you hang up or we get cut off, and you won't, will you? You've every reason to, but this was my last dime. I even had to borrow it—or beg for it, really—but I suppose I could always borrow or beg another one. It's probably not that mortifying to do after the first time, though later it gets, fewer people to borrow or beg from and less inclined they are to stop. So before we do get cut off, and my tried-and-true mental timeclock says we're long overdue, maybe I could give you my number here and you could call back. It's kind of a long story why I'm asking to come by and, just for a few hours till daybreak when my landlady gets up and I can get my duplicate keys, sleep on your floor."

"The answer's no, naturally, to any coming by tonight. If you just want to tell the story why you think you have to come by, you can't make it short?"

"I could but not effectively. But I probably couldn't because—oh shit. . . excuse me, but my head just then."

"What, hangover or something like that already?"

"Hurts, from being hit in the head before. On the head. I was. With a phone receiver but one cut off. I don't mean to be confusing. I wasn't cut off, on the phone, but the receiver was, from the phone."

"If it's that bad, go to a hospital."

"It's not. A scratch on top and a bump, and now a little dizziness and pain, which probably accounts for my sporadic disoriented tongue, though I got that out all right with the words I wanted. And I couldn't begin to tell it—from before—because our five minutes are more than up. And the phone operators who cut in these days to ask for another coin—well, you can't speak to them as people, you know, since their voices aren't even recorded anymore, much less real or alive. They're—they come from some new kind of computerized phonetic machine that creates operator voices or what we've been used to, and with the right regional inflections for whatever region, to respond to the multivarious situations they've traditionally had to deal with on the phone, though I'm sure the machine's tinkered with periodically to let new situations in. You want a real live operator's voice you have to dial Operator, and I heard that soon—ooh, wait. I'm a little lost there—my head again, which might be worse off than I thought. I wish I could sit. And lost you a little there also, I think."

"Not if I got you right. I'm sure—but you all right?"

"Yes."

"Anyway, my experience has been that if they don't get you once your five minutes are up it's because of some telephonic malfunction and not generosity on the company's or any operator's part, and you can talk on that dime long as you like. But do me a favor—get to a hospital immediately for that head?"

"Why? They'll tell me I've a hairline fracture at the most and to go home and rest and that's what I can't do now. And let's not chance the operator coming in. Once one does I won't have time to give you my number, so please take it now."

"Why didn't you call Diana?"

"I did but nobody's in or answering. And the five other friends in the city I could, who either didn't answer or his answering machine did. With that one I gave the number of the booth phone I was calling from, but have since moved on. My mother I couldn't—though I actually could. She'd forgive me for anything, as good mothers do. But I didn't want to, as she lives alone, would get scared, doesn't sleep well—only a few hours a day and usually at this hour, and I didn't want to wake her."

"No one else? No old women friends, a brother, sister, aunt who sleeps well?"

"Out of town or living out of town or impossible for the women friends."

"Even so, there'd have to be twenty, fifty people to call before me, and a locksmith."

"Locksmith I already tried, but I lost my wallet tonight, have no cash at home and I don't have a check account."

"Who doesn't have a check account?"

"I pay three bills a month: rent, utilities and phone, and the last two every other month, so really two a month, average—all with money orders made out from money in my savings account. That way—though here, for the first time, it's hurt me—I get my interest and also don't impulsively spend money I don't have. As for the other tenants in my building—nobody to go to. Either much too frail or old, one's a dealer, another's a man who illusorily accuses me of dumping garbage on his car and door, and one woman's a drunk and, as my junior-high kids used to say, mental. I just don't know that many people, many people as I know, and some I know I wouldn't go into their apartments for any reason. And, impulsive as I am on money matters, or at least sticking to a system so as not to be, I was impulsive in calling you, in spite of the time I took to think about calling—what can I say? I, maybe because of the big lump and minor gash, but again, I don't want to depreciate the main reason by giving neurological excuses, saw myself sleeping, with my head in an old clean rag, bleeding, on your floor. I shouldn't have but I did, and with my last dime, not that it wouldn't take another hour or two, which'd get me closer to daybreak and my keys, to borrow or beg another one. But I thought, it being my last dime would help persuade you to let me use your floor. But look, spilt head or not—split—if I'm anything—and that was an interesting slip—I'm—"

"All right, give me your number. Then tell me quickly this time how you hurt your head. A fight?"

"Stopping a robbery. And the number on the phone's not clear. It's—shit, who'd want to scratch out the number on a pay phone? Sorry, but it's demented. Plug up the coin return with gum if you're desperate to make some pocket money, because then at least the caller's made his call, if he didn't get a busy signal or Information. Though if he got Information and Information, after she gives him the number, sees his coin didn't reach the coin tray, she can hook him into a live operator who can dial the number for him. But don't, I'm saying, destroy the phone so it can't be used for emergencies or scratch out the number so no one can call the caller back."

"Are you telling me there's no phone number there? Please, Mr. Krin."

"It's also my eyes, which is just part of the story, and Daniel or Dan. First my glasses got scratched. That was nobody's fault but mine. But then, along with my head before and my wallet and keys going with my coat in addition to my valuable notebook, though only to me, is the only copy I own and perhaps in the whole country of one of the books of poems I'm to select from and translate to put into one big book of this particular poet's selected collected—collected selected poems."

"Who?"

"Jun Hasenai. Around my age. But you probably haven't heard of him."

"I suppose I should have, but I hate when people say that about writers I've mentioned and they haven't heard of. I can't read or hear about everyone."

"No reason you should. He's unknown here—few poems I've managed to place in little mags over the years—but pretty well known in several Eastern European countries. He's major, style to get excited by, sensibility and themes to move and brood over and possibly transmogrify. I talk like a jacket blurb sometimes, but I really admire the guy's work. I also like it that he's lived fully but not maneuveringly and to keep his modest family life surviving he writes essays that are, well, eloquent and inciting and I eventually want to translate too, and translates Spanish and Portuguese novels and poetry and teaches Western literature in a high school for the physically handicapped and deformed. He's a mensch and can be translated—he doesn't only come across in Japanese. I just hope when I call him for another copy of the book, if one isn't in a library I don't know about here, he doesn't think I'm a terrific bungler and assign his work to someone else."

"I'm sure he won't—not after the work you've no doubt put in and the feeling you have for it. But why not call his publisher for a copy rather than him?"

"Of course—thanks—I just hope it doesn't get back to him."

"Then have someone else call and give his or her address. But you shouldn't be so worried. You have a book contract for it?"

"No, they all want to see the whole work first, intro also."

"I'll still look for your book when it comes out."

"His book, but I shouldn't minimize my own part that much. Sounds fake and is, since it's not what I feel at all. But the glasses—what's that?"

"Sammy my cat. Just jumped into my lap. He likes to speak on the phone."

"Sounds like a baby crying. Siamese?"

"Yes. I'll get him away. No, say something else, Sammy—show him you're no kid; he's twelve." Sammy says nothing. "Never talks when I ask him to. Gurgles, sometimes moans or hums. Okay, Sammy," and I put him on the bed, where he rolls over on his back, stretches, wants to be petted. "What about the glasses?" rubbing Sammy's stomach.

"My eyeglasses. Got scratched, so I couldn't use them anymore along with everything else going—wallet, keys, etcetera. Good thing I wasn't also schlepping my one and only typewriter tonight or—"

"If they got your keys and wallet—"

"Only one man did and he wasn't connected to the two who clubbed me, or receivered me, since that's what it should be called. While one man held my arms back the other hit me with a receiver that had been cut from a pay phone. But the man who stole my coat with most of those things in it was just standing there—I thought another innocent observer who was going to watch me get receivered to death—after I'd stepped in to help this newsguy in his stand who was being roughed up and robbed."

"Still, aren't you afraid he's not right this moment unlocking your door? He has your address and keys."

"That's what I told the policemen. They said to get a locksmith, but the phone numbers of all-night locksmiths they gave me and some others in the phonebook either didn't answer or were answering machines or the two who did answer said they'd only open my door if I paid them cash on the line."

"Then you shouldn't have told the second one you had no cash till he opened it."

"He might've got mad. You can't get away with something like that in this city at one or two in the morning, and you ever see the tools locksmiths have? I've nothing to steal anyway except an old manual typewriter, twenty-dollar radio, lots of classical records with no player, and those other books of Hase-nai's and what I've already translated of them, which he'd never take or any of his pals would if he gave them my keys."

"They won't know you've nothing to steal till they get there. Then they'll turn over your apartment looking for what you don't have or they think you're hiding and all the translations you've done could be destroyed."

"I doubt anyone will come. Why wouldn't they also think I got in with a spare key someplace and then bolted the door or had the money to have the lock changed tonight? And the guy who grabbed my coat off the sidewalk, where I threw it to defend myself more easily, was an elderly derelict and saw how furiously I defended myself once I got receivered on the head, so I'm sure he'll be happy with just the coat and the wallet he didn't expect to be in it."

"After all you've gone through tonight, or say you did—"

"I did. If you saw me you'd know."

"You're a mess?"

"Worse. But nothing spilling out or that hasn't dried by now, so I'll live if I can find a place to bunk down."

"I'm sure you will. But the police. They can't take the door off for you or the lock?"

"The lock cylinder and they couldn't because all the proof I had on me that I lived there was in the wallet. And to get the proof I have inside that I lived there, I needed proof on me that I lived inside."

"Then this. You can't expect me to do more. I'll loan you enough cash to pay a locksmith to open the door."

"Too late for that now, but thanks. Because 'all-night' doesn't mean all night for them or to the two who answered."

"I'll make other calls for you. Meanwhile, you should start getting up here. I'll find one, but you can't just stay on the street."

"Excuse me," the operator says, "please deposit ten cents—"

"Miss, Miss," I say, but she keeps talking and then begins repeating the message. "Give me your number there, Dan, quick."

"Three-two-six, or eight—got that?" he says over the recorded voice. "One-zero, eight or nine I think it is—yes, eight or nine, and then eight. Thirty-two, six or eight, ten eight or nine. And then eight."

"Give it again. I think I have it but—"

We're cut off.

"326(8) 108(9)8," I wrote on Leonard's title page. I pick up the receiver, put it down. It's too crazy. And he's got to be lying. Head, phone, locksmiths, newsguy, coat snatcher, numbers scratched out, one and only book and so on, and I drop the manuscript and pen on the floor and shut the light, hoping he won't call back. He does, I'll say "No, goodnight," hang up, pull the plug out of the jack and go to sleep.

But I can't leave him waiting. It's raw out, or sort of, or was, and if it wasn't all a story he gave just to come up here . . . I turn on the light, go into the living room, see out the window it's not raining but is very windy, tree branches and some trees—not just the leaves—swaying, thermometer reads 45, but could be ten degrees warmer where he is since I'm sure he's not on the river, and get his book out of the shopping bag. All this fast. Looking for some sign he's real and no fake. He's the one who said he could be but didn't want to and that's the time I really start believing someone's one, but doesn't always have to be so. Jacket photo's real enough. No pose, eyes caught in the act of wanting to avoid the camera. Fine, but if he was faking it, then again trying to present himself as he wasn't. But photo was at least four years ago. His actions at the party. Seemed real and honest enough. He was attracted to me, came over— all right, at the last moment, but could mean he was shy but could overcome that shyness if he thought the person he was attracted to was about to leave, or that he's not so shy but wanted to give the impression he was because a shy person was what he thought I'd be attracted to. Could also mean other things, but don't forget my actions to him. I was attracted too. He knew that. Only man I was like that to at this and maybe my last five parties. I was looking at him on and off for half an hour before he stopped me at the door, caught him looking at me several times, hoped he'd come over and then gave up he would. Right before I left I thought I'd ask Diana about him in a few days and if she said he was available and all right, maybe try to get her to encourage him to call me. I also thought of going over to him and saying "Odd as this familiar approach must sound coming to you from a woman, or maybe I'm a bit out of date and don't know what approaches women have raised themselves to make to men today, but you look familiar—do we know one another from some place?" But I find that hard to do to a man even when I do know him from some place. But fast, he's out there, waiting, it's got to be cold, might start to rain, so what's it to be, call or not? Maybe he intuited I wouldn't call back and has left. Thinking right now, block or two from where he called: "Knew it would never work; clever girl, can't be conned." But if his story's real? "Stinking bitch, knows my head's aching, maybe bleeding, I've no money, and in this freaking weather? Least she could have done was call to say she didn't want to keep me waiting out here and she's turning in." Fool, go to a hospital if your head's really bashed, but if your story was bunk, then bad try and goddamn gall, calling so late.

I open the book to his introduction. ". . . But no matter what I say about these stories, some readers are still going to think, 'Of course you're saying that, praising the work up and down, it's in your interest to, being the translator/introducer/anthologist, so what else could you say: "The stories stink, the writers are no good, this was the best short fiction, bad as it is, I could find written in Japanese in the last thirty years"'? Because not only do you stand to gain financially from it, you'll in all probability land a good teaching job or be elevated in the one you have, if you're up for renewed contract or tenure and your department chairman or the school's ad hoc committee thinks you need one more book.' But not so. If this book nets me $1000 for the year's work I put into it, I'll feel lucky. As for a university position? Sure, I'd love one, as long as I didn't have to teach bonehead Japanese four times a week, but I don't expect to get one from this or a half-dozen books like it. No, I translated and put together this anthology because, and please don't think I'm trying to hoodwink you into buying or reading or thinking more seriously about either of those by first coming on in such a strong nonintroductory way and then compiling a list of negative rhetorical reasons why I might have anthologized this. . ." No, call. Only decent thing. If only to say I'm sleepy and have nothing more to say and I'm very sorry what happened to him tonight and concerned for his head and because of the wound his future well-being, but I barely know him—I don't know him—and there have to be several other people he hasn't thought to call who could help him, even if he has no more dimes, which really, isn't my responsibility, but if he wants to call me some other day at a much earlier time, fine.

I go into the bedroom and pick up Leonard's paper and dial the number without the numbers in parentheses. Phone rings seven times and I'm about to hang up, thinking "Great, one down, few more to go and maybe the most likely one down also, though if he did leave, after waiting for my call, he has a right to be ticked off," when the receiver's picked up and a man says "For godsake's what?"

"Daniel Krin?"

"You want to speak to someone, on this floor, now?"

"Is this a public pay phone?"

"Yes. In a public hallway. You didn't know when you called?"

"Is this three-two-six, ten eighty-eight?"

"It's a senior citizen home, lady; you almost now made me break a leg answering this. I thought it was an emergency the way you rang."

"I'm very sorry. Someone gave me this number for a Daniel Krin."

"Maybe on another floor. Because I know all the first and last names on this one and Daniel and Krin aren't it. This is the fifth."

"Really, sir, I'm sorry for waking you up—"

"You didn't. I was out walking; I couldn't sleep."

"I'm still sorry, but please answer me so I won't have to call back and possibly disturb you again: is this three-two-six, ten eighty-eight?"

"I'll say this much to you. You call that number again and I'm not in as good a position to answer it then, you'll wake up everyone but the deaf and almost dead ones on this floor. The walls and doors are that thin, even if they were supposed to be built as, catch this, self-contained soundproof apartmentlike units. I know because I was one of the original tenants to move in to this papier-mâché house, but you can be sure the owners never thought I'd live this long to tell it."

"Thank you. Goodnight and sleep well," and I hang up.

I write on Leonard's page, under the original phone number: "326-1098, 328-1098, 328-1088." Only four? Thought there'd be more. I write all four numbers this time, original one first, which I cross out. Only four. Which should I dial next? Start with the second and if no answer or the wrong number, go down one more. I dial. Phone's picked up on the first ring.

"Helene Winiker?"

"Hi. What took me so long was I dialed two of the other possible numbers—"

"Which one it turn out to be?"

"Twenty-six, ten ninety-eight."

"That would've been the second number I called. But everyone's got his own system. Yours next time might work on the first shot while mine would hit it on the fourth. Not that I'm complaining, now that you're here."

"The first number was always busy."

"Then I would've gone right to the next one—and this is also no complaint—because the busy number never would've been mine."

"I thought you might have found another dime in your pocket or borrowed one and were calling me or someone else. Anyway, I called the second number, but it didn't answer, so I thought the second one not answering might be because you stepped away from the phone. So I called the busy one again and when it was still busy, called the one I thought you might have stepped away from—"

"Why would I have? I was waiting for your call."

"I thought *for something;* I didn't know for what. Hot coffee because you were cold."

"I have no money."

"I forgot. And it shouldn't be me apologizing. Not you either—*maybe*—if you're really in a hole. But still, when someone you don't know calls you at two o'clock—"

"I know. I apologize. I didn't mean to have you explain—I thought I was doing my best not to—"

"Anyway, the person who didn't answer the first time, now answered, so I was right calling that number back. But he kept talking. It was a nursing home and I'd waked him and now he wouldn't let me go, nor would he tell me if you were at this place—in the lobby, not in one of the living units upstairs—so that's what also kept me so long. He was such a sad old man that I didn't have the heart to hang up on him."

"You were right. And I shouldn't expect anything and I didn't, but do appreciate that you called back. And you mentioned something about my being cold? Here comes my next big pitch for sympathy."

"You are cold."

"I'm freezing my life off out here, or the last two-fifths of it. It's an enclosed booth, thank God—a relic of a distant civilization that still works, which won't stop it from being torn out and made obsolete and maybe with me in it—but it's still very cold. It'd be very very if the policemen hadn't given me an old sweater they kept a few of in their car for such occasions. If it were up to me—if there were no disturbed souls out here—but I shouldn't go on so holier-than-sanctimonious-thou about it. I won't."

"No—what about the disturbed souls?"

"If there were none out here, or homeless, myself excluded, I'd heat them—all these booths. Even if there are these people here—hell, let a disturbed homeless man sleep standing up or huddled on the floor of one, and even provided with a night's food rations and a tissue packet with a space blanket in it and a Wash and Dry for an extra bit of cleanness and warmth."

"And the vandals? All you need is to make those booths more inviting than they are. Not that I don't sympathize with what you say, half serious as it was, and that we couldn't talk seriously about how there should always be free homes for the homeless and food for the foodless and so forth. But let's not. You're cold and keyless and I'm exhausted and maybe to you heartless. But why didn't you go inside to make your calls, if any places are open now?"

"Some are but I didn't think they'd appreciate my receiving calls there if I had to—especially when I was so unkempt and wasn't even buying a coffee from them. And the subway station here—Twenty-third and Sixth—you have to pay the fare to get to the coin phone on the platform, the token-booth clerk said. So I chose, over jumping the turnstile or walking back to Fourteenth Street or going to one of the other Twenty-third Street stations to see if there was a nonplatform phone there or to Penn Station where I know there are plenty, this outside phone on a well-lit though I think fairly dangerous corner, but in an enclosed booth. You see, I also lost my heavy sweater—"

"Wait—back up a bit. Also a sweater? What else?"

"My raincoat in the fight. And an umbrella in the wind in Washington Square Park, right after I left Diana's. The umbrella couldn't keep out the cold now, but it would have the rain before which, dry on me now, for a couple of hours kept me chilled."

"I forgot about the raincoat. Shows how tired I am. But go on. You're cold, so I shouldn't interrupt further."

"I left it on Diana's hallway rack, the sweater, when I left the park drunk. The party, but I also left the park drunk. But maybe all the alcohol I drank at the party is now keeping me warmer than I'd normally be without it, though without it I wouldn't have forgotten my sweater or gone into the park and lost the umbrella. Or even gone up to you at the party—no, I hadn't had much to drink at that time nor when I yelled to you from the unmentionable. It was only after, though I certainly wouldn't have called your answering service without the alcohol, because by then I was loaded. But the alcohol had nothing to do with my losing the raincoat and its contents. By that time I was sober."

"About the alcohol, by the way, I heard differently."

"About me?"

"Alcohol and the cold. That when you think it's warming you, it's really doing the opposite, but let's not waste any more time. If you come to my building—the vestibule, which you don't need a key to get into—I'll have the money in a special spot above the bellboard, plus some change and the name of a locksmith I've managed to find who will be expecting your call. Forty dollars should be enough. If I can't find a locksmith, use the money for a hotel. I'll add another ten for a cab ride here, and at this hour a cab's all you should take. That's about all the cash I have on me, which you can pay back when—"

"Listen, I'm not making this up and I appreciate to the utter utmost everything you've offered, but a locksmith you're not going to find. And the way I look—they're just scratches on my face and head, bumps you can't see under the hair, some dried blood, torn-to-expunged for clothing—no semi-decent hotel would let me in. And anything less than semi-decent I don't feel I can take going to tonight, nor waiting till morning with a bunch of madmen and bums in the waiting room at Penn Station or Grand Central. The train cops don't even let you do that anymore from midnight to seven. Incidentally, you mark which number you got me at? I already forgot it."

"I know which one. And I called you, so we can't be cut off."

"You're right. My head. Suddenly thought before was now. Not that. After? But—and I'm not talking like this or pretending to be confused for the sake—"

"Enough. Just come here. Money will be in a letter envelope in a metal well in the wall behind the bellboard. Reach up and finger around and you'll find it. Do what you want with the money and I don't care when you pay it back, but sometime would be nice."

"Please, all I want's a floor. I'm safe. I'm good-natured. I'm very clean other than what came out of me or got stuck on me from tonight's knockdown. I'll only ask to wash up, maybe have something warm to drink—hot water, even, with a lemon slice in it if you got—and several aspirins and dabs of iodine. Nothing if you don't want or have and no washup if that's what you want also, and a blanket or coat over me on the floor and a towel or coat underneath me if it's just wood there with no carpet or rug, and that'll be it. Or just the bare floor and no body cover or anything under, and I promise, my word against anything, you'll never meet anyone more peaceful and quiet when I get there. Sure, maybe by now Diana's home or someone else from before, though we've been talking so long that it's probably really too late or too early to call anyone now. Even if it weren't, I don't have the energy and maybe not the memory nor another dime to make another call."

"Okay. How would you get here if you came and stayed on the couch or floor?"

"No couch. The floor."

"How would you? Cab?"

"I can't walk it. But I don't want you going downstairs alone or in any way to put you through anything more. I'll try to borrow the subway fare or jump over the turnstile."

"Don't jump over anything. You'll get caught and then you'll be calling me to come to the police station to bail you out. Are you sufficiently presentable where a cab would—oh, this is silly."

"No it's not. I'll do what you say. A cab. I'll spruce myself up enough so one will take me. Could you leave ten dollars in that envelope behind the bells? Or maybe, so you don't have to come downstairs alone, wait till I ring your bell."

"I'll leave it behind the bellboard now. Ten dollars—one five and five singles—I know I have those—so you won't have to call me from downstairs for change or for more. But remember, I don't know you, but we've mutual friends and you're cultured and a scholar—"

"Scholar? Not me."

"I have your Japanese story anthology, or one of them, and it lists—"

"How'd you get that prize? You weren't one of the approved three hundred something people and libraries who were licensed to buy it?—that would be too much."

"However I got it, I'm doing you a favor beyond the call of mutual friendship and professional fellowship and at an hour way beyond my deliberative decision-making and common sense time, so you will be on your best behavior?"

"The absolute best, bar none, of that I double-swear."

"You have the address?"

"From the phonebook."

"Then at this hour, despite how you might look, cabbies will have to see something of the noncombatant on your face and they go hurting for fares, so I should expect to see you in about thirty minutes—try not to make it later. I'm dead to the world."

"Thanks. Thanks. Thanks."

"Please get on with it then. Apartment 9B. Just ring it and I'll buzz you in," and I hang up.

CHAPTER SEVEN

The Apartment

He hangs up, smiles, slides the door open and goes outside, slaps his fist into his palm and thinks I can't believe it, says "She's done dood it, damn woman's come across. Not 'damn,' but I'm seeing her, maybe in minutes, hot dog." Looks around, nobody around, no good gabbing out loud to yourself on the street at any hour, not that in this city you could be put away for it. Put away? Hey, where'd that one come from? Not his but was his father's expression, along with—well whatever along with, but "Talk back to your mother or me like that and you could be put away." Oh dad, just look at me now. Holds out his arms, looks up at the sky and smiles. No, don't want to act odd either. Looks around, nobody around, sounds of someone whistling sweetly from somewhere—an Irish air—rather, Stephen Foster: Ginny, *Jeanie*, shiny orange-red hair (what did I decide on?)—but can't see him and now drowned-out by traffic. Traffic goes, no music. Though he first thought worst possible don't-even-think-of-it thing to do was call her, but had a hunch she would. "Best behavior"; you bet. Now and forever, or to whenever, till hell freezes over and life ever after and I can't exaggerate any further; for sure. Ah! "If I've one thing in life to teach you it's don't work for anyone: be your own boss." Okay—eyes to the sky and arms out again—so I'm my own boss: now you proud of me? But he meant becoming a dentist, doctor, opening up my own law office. But now to get there. How to get there? In his head: "Tweee!— Taxi!" and first one to come stops. New roomy Checker. Slips in, flips the jump seat down but keeps its backrest folded, legs up on it but feet hanging over the seat so not to sully it. "Where to sir?... Turn the heater up for you some more, sir?... Switch the radio station to something more to your liking like choral music, sir? . . . Wait for you in front while you get the fare from behind the what, sir? Bellboard? Of course, but sure you don't mean the apartments' intercom?" He steps into the street. Watch. Two-to-one none comes and if one does, five-to-one it won't stop. From now on on damp cold nights, snowy or otherwise and maybe daytimes too, going to carry in my back pants pocket an extra pair of socks.

She thinks, bringing the phone into the living room in case he calls, Why did I let myself be convinced into it—to say "Yes, oh do do come up"? I didn't say it that way, but hell. Oh well. Oh, probably not so bad. Bad, how can you say it's not? But it's not or not so bad. So he'll come over. Not "so he will": he's coming over. So he will. And let him. Let him? Nothing now will stop him. So what? Really, so big deal what? Let him even take a shower. Let him even wash his shirt and anything else he wants to wash and hang those wet clothes up. And if they're not dry by the morning I'll even iron them for him. Because what was I trying to say by my being so anxious about his coming here—that I can't take care of myself? It's just for the rest of the night. And I can quickly gauge people okay—some friends even think I have an acuity—and he seems more than all right. Story was a bit hard to believe, but he won't do anything more than have a hot drink, clean himself, go to sleep, toast and coffee when he wakes up and leave. So set him up—blankets, sheets, pillow and case—on the couch. "Just take the cushions off and"—he'll know how. Convertible couch is universal to just about everyone over thirteen. "Need me to make the bed for you? No? Good; I'm too tired to anyway, so goodnight." He wants to chat, say "I'd like to, but tomorrow I've two tons of work." And fresh bath towel; for one night he doesn't need a washrag. Worse comes to worse, let him use mine on the sly that's in the bathroom. No, with his linens and last week's I'll be doing a wash soon, so what's a little washrag? And cats; hope he's not allergic to them, but even if he isn't I'll keep Sammy in my room. If he has to wash his underpants and his trousers are wet and he has nothing else to wear—what else could he have?—to and from the bathroom or in bed, I've an old terrycloth robe androgynous enough where he won't feel uncomfortable in it and big enough to fit him snug. Say "Anything in the refrigerator is yours," and then go to bed. Suppose he's a drinker? I'm really too tired to think so thoroughly about this. But don't be shiftless; it's in your interest: suppose he is. A real drunk, not just a once-a-monther or every-time-at-a-party overindulger, then what? He was knocking them down at Diana's. So were we all. But if he is? Yes? Well, if he is? Damn, nothing but work for myself. She goes into the kitchen. Cabinet has a bottle of dry vermouth for someone who liked to make martinis for himself when she cooked dinner for them. Roberto; she couldn't stand them herself. Literally like piss. Gin is finished. Why didn't I throw the bottle out? and she shoves it to the bottom of the garbage bag and covers it with part of a newspaper so he won't think she drank any of it tonight. Oh, get rid of the whole thing long as you're at it, and she opens the service door to put the garbage out. Note's on the door. Now what? "Mice have been sighted"—she looks down at the name; it's from her next-door neighbor at the service entrance—"on the floor below and several above (10th, 13th, PH). Please dispose of your garbage (we will too, starting tomorrow when we get them . . . the market left them out of the order it delivered tonite) in plastic garbage bags that seal up with ties. Thanx. This is a very difficult note to write, as I'm for certain not blaming you for the mice. PS. Daitch's has an excellent generic bag (2 ft x 2 ft 6 in x 1.2 mil) at half the price of the brand names, and it's 2-ply. Best, Audrey Chang, 9C." What can I say? She's right, at least about plastic-bagging the trash, something we should have done long ago to cut down on roaches or kept in lidded pails out there, and she sticks the bag of garbage into a plastic shopping bag, knots the handles on top and puts it outside her service door. The Changs, with three children, his mother and a dog, usually have two huge paper bags of garbage and an empty carton or two by the service elevator, but just a doll box is there tonight. Back to the cabinet. Vermouth bottle is a third-filled and would take five more bottles of gin the way Roberto mixed them. She's used a lot of it for cooking scallops or in a last-ditch gravy when the food cooking lost all its juices and got not irredeemably burned. Sherry in the cabinet to cook with also but not cooking sherry. She brings all these bottles—half-one of vodka, unopened one of Zubrovka her father brought back from Poland last year; she should put it in the freezer and take a sip of it and tell him how it is; nearly full bottle of sour mash or bourbon if there's any difference—liquor she has just for guests—and two bottles of wine and a tiny one of cassis, to the pantry closet next to the service door. "Hello, Sammy." Puts them deep into the lower shelf. "You want to help hide them? No? Yes?" He scratches his front paws on the service door. "Feel like skedoodl-ing? Have to wait till summer, Babes." She grabs his tail at the front and pulls it upwards, then tweaks the tip. Lots of white hairs float around them. "God, do you need a brushing." Puts the ice bucket she got as a wedding gift—they got, get that straight, kid; Harris and she, Helene and Harris, the 2-H club at one time, another finer thing he refused her to use once he got so insurrectionally left-wing—tarnished, needs polish, tomorrow, along with Sammy's brushing and nail clipping—and unopened box of wineglasses in front of the bottles. Unless he got down on his knees he couldn't see them. She gets down on her knees. Even then. Nice job. And where'd she get the glasses? Ice bucket was from Diana—their first gift, delivered weeks before the ceremony. Glasses were from the wedding too. Got four to five boxes of them from different people and two or three boxes of brandy snifters. Must have been the gift to give that year or month—March, nice and icy—for we didn't touch the hard stuff then and weren't in any way real wine tipplers. Down to the last five wineglasses in her kitchen cabinet and this box she didn't know was here. "So thanks, Mr. Krin, for being instrumental—well, just helping me find them," and she winks at the pantry. He wants the two beers in the fridge and what wine's left in the bottle in there, he can have them—they won't do much to get him high. But they could keep him high. She opens the refrigerator. Pulls out the produce bin, snaps a carrot in two and chews it and drops the other half back into the bin. Better than a couple of her mother's Mandelbrot that are in a coffee can in here or the ice cream in the freezer. *Freezer*, and she starts for the pantry. No, dopey, do it tomorrow when he's not here. And four cans of beer, thought two. Puts three of them into that same pantry shelf. So, can of beer and maybe a glass of wine which by now is probably vinegar—won't do much to him, but might make him think she's not trying to hide any alcohol, and on the phone he seemed hurt from a head wound as he said and not high. Takes the linens and cushions off the couch. Wait a minute. He's supposed to do this. Just do it, it'll save time, no explaining: "Bed's made, you know how to pull it out, there's the kitchen, bathroom's past that door, if you need a clock, there's an electric one above the kitchen table, and have a good night's sleep and goodnight." She opens the couch into a bed, makes it, should she keep it open or closed? Close it, it'll just look sloppy open and make movement clumsy when he gets here and make him think she's insisting he get to sleep right away, closes it so it's a couch again, puts a pillowcase on her one extra pillow, boils water for herb tea. Heck with it: she can afford a dozen Mandelbrots, and all this waiting and doing at this late hour is making her hungry. Whatever the reason for it, hunger is hunger and to be avoided before sleep if she can. She eats one, eats two more, re-covers the coffee can and shuts the refrigerator door. I don't know how she does it. Works a normal workload as a caseworker, reads another twenty hours a week the most recondite books and magazines, sees a movie and play a week and goes to several of the art galleries around town and some concerts and all the new exhibitions at the art museums, yet still spends lots of time with my father and her friends and around fifteen hours a week in the kitchen making things like these. One day I'll follow her around the kitchen while she makes them. I'll have to follow her around three or four times before it sinks in, but I will. But maybe later on, when she's dead, perish the thought, but everyone has to die, though if there was only some natural way I could live a full long life and still go before them, but when she is and they are, perish the thought, maybe the memory of her Mandelbrot and breads and cakes will be infinitely preferable to the actual stuff even if I'm able to bake almost the exact kind. Enough. What's the point unless I want to goad a good cry? Great, right, what an only child has to share? And if it ends up childless, damn, hope you get a lifelong mate you love, bub, cuz if not it could be a lot to bear. Water's boiling and she makes tea and sits on the couch with it. Now get here soon, Krinsky, and don't for christsakes be cheap with my money and decide against a cab. Yipes. If he made good connections he could be downstairs. He'd ring the bell. She gets into pants, sandals and shirt and gets a five and five singles out of the dresser. Always tries to have that amount around the house in those denominations in case she has to take a cab from here or knows she'll be taking one later in the day after she leaves. Doesn't like drivers arguing they haven't change for a twenty or ten or even a five, and then if she makes a stink, oh wow they suddenly find it, but if they don't—to then have to give them one of those bills with no change back if she doesn't want to wait. Gets her keys, lets the door lock and rings for the elevator. She has a police whistle on her keyring and holds it near her mouth. If he's ringing her bell now, she'll get to him in time. And hates, hates like anything to go downstairs alone at this hour, but nothing she can do about it.

Maybe I'm not doing this right. He steps back to the sidewalk, tucks the back of his shirt into his pants, wipes what dirt he can off his pants and sleeves, sees through the shirt-rip his elbow's cut and dried blood he didn't know was there. Feels his pocket for his comb. Must've been in his coat. Runs his fingers through his hair to smooth it back. "Aie yie yie," don't do that. Stands in the street and signals an approaching cab. Off-duty sign's on he sees as it passes. Another cab comes. Getting lucky: two in a minute. "Cab," he yells. Passes, no off-duty sign and no passengers inside. Cheek hurts, right one. Maybe only now getting unfrozen. Feels it. "Ah, oh," very sore, and coasting over it, swollen. Better when numb, but maybe it's only now begun its natural healing process. Doesn't remember being hit there, and what he'd do now for a few aspirins. Four he'd take, and then just to lie back on a bed and rest the back of his head on a pillow. But the guy was on top of him slamming away with his fists—nobody could say what he did with the phone receiver—while I was on my hands and knees, head still echoing from the phone receiver blow, so who knows where I was hit on the head, though bystanders said everywhere. What a scene. "Beware of adrenalin, gentlemen," a Hasenai line with a little help from me. But what am I saying? There's always been a bit of the hothead and tough in me. "Cab! Cab! Go screw you too. You want to be so selective in whom you take, put on your off-duty sign." Half block away by now, arm still out the cab window and middle finger raised: "Asshole!" But said to himself then: "It's now or never, this guy's going to beat you on the head till you're brainless, so do something, don't be lazy now of all times," and still on one hand and my knees, grabbed one of his legs—both straddled me—and started bucking the guy with my back to put him off-balance and maybe to shake myself up a little and also I know so I could have time to think what else to do and then thought "Strength, use your fucking strength," and turned around on my knees and lifted him up as I started to stand up and standing fully up threw him into the air. He must've weighed two-fifty but I just threw him and he flew back a few feet, tried to land standing up but landed on his behind. Then I got over him as he started to get up and grabbed his head with both hands and banged and banged it on the ground till his eyes started to stay less open than closed and then worked him up to one knee by pulling on his hair and head and still holding that head but now by the forehead and chin, lunged it at the phone booth a foot or two away, but there was no glass in the bottom panels to ram his head through—it had already been smashed out. "Cab, cab!. . . Thank you, got the message." Guy's head went through the part where the glass had been and then he just kept pushing him into the booth from behind till the guy was entirely inside except for his feet, which he shoved in. Then he ran around the booth and tried to lock him inside by keeping the door shut, not thinking the guy could crawl out through the empty bottom part, but the guy stood up, forced his way out the door though Dan pushed back, and said "Now I'm going to finish you." The crowd surrounding them—must've been fifty people by now, men and women, some kids even, thirteen, fourteen years old—started to make boxing crowd noises, whistles, cheers, saying "Give it to him, fatso," saying "Let him have it good, slim," which I suppose was me. They thought it was just a fight. Who knows what they thought. Where was the news vendor? I felt I needed help. Later the vendor said— Cab's coming. Get set. Nice smile. Waves, says "Hey," but it turns into the sidestreet before it reaches him, no directional signal on. Vendor later said "Thanks," when he shook Dan's hand, and told him to take any newspaper or magazine for free, and that he was too afraid during the fight to do anything but run across the street and call the police from the booth there. Police came. But not before the guy, just out of the booth, walked toward Dan, saying not only was he going to finish him but "I'm going to kill you, you'll see." Guy's friend—who'd pinned Dan's arms back when the big guy said "Oh, you don't want to go away?" and Dan had said "How can I when you're stealing from this newsguy and about to break his glasses and beat in his face?"—now wasn't around. Then the guy started to take something out of his back pocket. This was before the fight, when the friend held Dan's arms back, and what knocked Dan to the ground. Dan first thought it was a handgun—it was black—and his chest got cold and heart was beating hard and he thought "What am I to do? This is the end," and then when this thing in the back pocket was up a few inches it looked like a knife handle and he thought "Oh no, he's going to stab me," and strained to get free but the friend held Dan's arms back and then the big guy pulled this object in his pocket higher and took it out and it was a phone receiver and with a blow Dan didn't see knocked him down and kept pounding his head with it and then he was only using his fists, so maybe the receiver had flown out of his hand or he'd thrown it away. So there he was. After that: fighting back and the phone booth scene and the guy coming at him again saying he was going to catch and kill him, he'll see. Where was the guy's friend? Every so often he looked around for him, so the friend wouldn't jump him from behind. Later he learned that another man, who left right after the fight, so Dan never had a chance to thank him, stepped in front of the friend when the friend tried to join the big guy in beating up Dan on the ground and said, this short but very muscular man with only a T-shirt on people said, "Let the two have it out—it's only fair." Dan said to the crowd when the big guy was coming to finish him "Listen, help me stop him. He tried to rob and beat up the owner of this newsstand, who I don't see now but he could tell you, and I stepped in to help the newsguy and that's why this big goon's fighting me." Nobody made a move to help. He didn't see the friend in the crowd at the time. Later he did, when he first heard the police siren, but only the friend racing out of it and down the sidestreet. Several people said "Kill him," either to Dan or the big guy coming at him or both. The big guy got closer, though Dan stepped back a step to each of the guy's forward steps. The people behind Dan moved aside and he was backed up against a parked car. Jump over it? Could be done. But he didn't want to run. There was his coat for one thing—how would he come back for it if the big guy and his friend were still here? Besides, he felt from the smells when the guy threatened him that he was fairly loaded and if he could dart around him fast enough he could grab him and knock him down. He yelled "Hey hey, look at that," pointing behind the guy, but he didn't bite. Then Dan jumped around him, grabbed him in a bear hug and threw him against the car. The guy bounced off it and fell to the ground on his back. Dan said "Now I'm going to beat your stupid head in, you sonofabitch, so you won't forget this," and sat on top of him, grabbed his shirt at the collar and wanted to punch him in the face but couldn't. He had his fist raised and the guy said "Do it, go on, do it," and seemed serious about it and Dan said "You're crazy." "I mean it, don't be a jellyfish, hit me, you won a ticket to," and Dan released his grip. He stood up, looked for dog shit to step in and put in the guy's face. Looked only around him—gutter, on the sidewalk, few feet into the street—since he felt safer being near the guy while he was on the ground than he would farther away from him where the guy would have time to stand and maybe go after him. Was none. New dog-litter law this summer—something, seemed to be working, for usually it would be there every ten to fifteen feet. Then the police siren. Now he doesn't know if he would've stepped in it and put it in the guy's face. Probably not, but he can't say for sure. He was that mad, so he could've, but the guy looked so stupid and for a few seconds after he said to hit him, pathetic, that he kind of doubts it. At the most he might've stepped in it and kept his foot raised a couple of inches above the guy's face. Then two sirens from police cars coming from different directions. "Hold him for the cops," someone said. He stepped back when the guy started to get up. "Get the hell out of here," he said and the guy didn't look at him but ran alongside his friend who'd just run out of the crowd shouting "Z-J, here, follow me!" and they ran up the sidestreet. When Dan first stepped in for the vendor and they said "Better stay out of it, sucker," and he said he couldn't unless they left the vendor alone and they said "Then we'll bust you instead," he felt there might be a fight—nothing much, more like a scuffle with Dan eventually talking them out of anything rougher—and took off his coat so he wouldn't rip it, even if he knew this might seem to them as if he wanted his arms free to defend himself and was even keen on a fight or just not doing enough to avoid one or to show he was afraid of one or them—and threw it to the ground, though right away he knew he should've just dropped it, and told a man closest to it "Look after my coat, please," said this softly so the two guys would know from his voice and the words he used that he was a peaceful and polite guy, and after the fight the man he'd told this to was gone with his coat. Maybe he thought Dan had meant for him to take it. Course not. Police came. About twelve of them—they kept coming, several in plain clothes—all in regular and un-marked cars. He gave a report of the fight and a description of the two men—"One was tall and dumpy, other tall and wiry, both around my height, maybe an inch or two taller—white—and wiry one with hair on his face, trim beard and mustache, dumpy one with ungroomed muttonchops, and actually the dumpy one about three inches taller than I but because of his bulk looked shorter than he was, wiry one inch or two shorter than I, and dumpy one with bright blue eyes and thin light hair covering his bald spots and wiry one with lots of thick dark curls beginning in the middle of his forehead and extremely white teeth, compared to the dumpy one's rotting ones, but I never got a good look at his eyes"—and said he'd lost his coat with a few of his most precious belongings in it—"Book of poems in Japanese I was working on that will set me back a few weeks." "Write it down, title and writer's name," a policeman said, "just so if it's turned in," and Dan said "Who will? Nobody," and the policeman said "Just take the time, all of ten seconds, and if you do get it back through us, remember that I had to break your arm," and Dan thought up an English title for the book and wrote it and the Japanese title in Japanese and Hasenai's name in English on the report. "The Hungry Landowner?" the policeman said. "Which one of these means hungry?" and Dan said "None." "Is the book about a hungry landowner?" and Dan said "I've no idea why the author called it that, since not only isn't it the title of any of the poems but it's not the theme, even stretching the point, of the book in general or any group of poems in total or any of the individual poems too, but maybe I'd have to think about that last point more." Just then a man of about eighty came over, raised his arm with his fist cocked to Dan and said "Good for you, brother. I saw it all from the start and would have jumped in to help but you looked like you could handle it yourself, and did he ever? Officer, it was a real joy to watch the good guy win in real life for a change." "I don't know if anybody won," Dan said, touching a tender spot in his head and the man said "Sure you did, don't let anyone ever tell you otherwise. Can I look at the descriptions of those two bullies, sir?" and the policeman said "Anything you can add to it, do." The man looked at the report, said "What's to add? This's what they looked like, right down to the fat one's eyes, except I'd also say both were on drugs or drunk," and Dan said "He's right. The wiry one I'm not so sure about but the big guy, which is how I was able to throw him to the ground, I'll tell you." "You never know what your strength is at times if something gets you going," the policeman said, and the old man said, "Strength? In circuses you see such strength. Lifted him like a feather"—"Anyway," Dan said, "the big guy definitely smelled from booze, though I don't see how that's going to help you unless he passes out from it on the street," and signed the report and said yes, he would bring charges against the men if they were caught, why not? even if the news vendor wasn't sure he would since they ended up not taking anything or hurting him. The policeman said "Want us to take you to the hospital?" and Dan said "Think I need to?" and he said "You don't seem that hurt, but I don't want to tell you what to do." "Let me see," the old man said and the policeman said "You a physician?" and he said "No, but I've seen accidents and know what stops cuts," and the policeman said "So do we and all his cuts have stopped—just get lost," and the man walked away with his fist cocked to Dan again, saying "That a way to go, Mr. Krin—I got your name off that report— that a way to go, good show." Policeman left. Crowd broke up. Vendor was closing up. "Usually all-night or least till four," he said. "Not tonight. Too something in the air tonight—the sky. And truly, any newspaper, two of them, or magazine is yours." Dan said "Instead of a magazine could I have a token or enough change to take a subway—someone stole my coat during the fight you might've heard and all my money and other things were in it," and the vendor gave him eighty cents, said he wished he could afford more. "No no, this'll be enough for fare and a couple of phone calls and if I need more I'll try to borrow it from someone else," and then used some of the change on phone calls from the booth he'd shoved the big guy in. Vendor locked up the stand, knocked on the phone-booth door while Dan was listening to a lock- smith on an answering machine say he wasn't in this minute, said "I'm going now—your name is what?. . . Mine is Shafik, Dan, and anything from this day I can do for you but give you more money, because I can't, I do, and you always know where I am, ten hours a day every day starting at five. Before that and weekends I work at a place where there's no phone," and Dan shook his hand and patted his back, said "I really appreciate that, thanks." Shafik left. He had a brown bag with maybe his dinner in it he didn't eat or maybe his change. Dan made more calls from that booth and booths a few blocks north, borrowed a dime on his first try by saying "Excuse me, sir, but I was robbed of my wallet tonight and all I need now is a dime to call my wife from this booth if you'd be so kind," called Helene. He tries to flag down a cab. Passes. Two right behind it. Same. What? All the empties afraid or maybe through for the night and going back to the cab garage or going back to it for gas or repairs or else their gas tanks are low and they're looking for a gas station or going to one they know of or on call or on their breaks but haven't their on-call or off-duty signs on. "Fucks. One of you could've taken me." Walks back to Twenty-third, goes into the subway station and up to one of the new bulletproof-glass token booths and says to the clerk through the gridded speaking hole "Excuse me, but do you know the news vendor upstairs, Shafik?"

"The evening one, Sandy?"

"He said Shafik. Little guy, dark, glasses—"

"Everyone calls him Sandy. He's an Arab. What's up, he hurt?"

"He almost was. I don't mean this to boast, but he could've been hurt a lot worse if I hadn't stopped two men from mugging him an hour ago. He's gone home. But someone took my coat when I jumped in to help Sandy, and all my money—"

"Can't let you in without a token. Borrow from Sandy if you helped him so much."

"I already said. He closed up early, was afraid something worse would happen to him and went home. He gave me enough change for the subway, but I used it all on phone calls from the booths upstairs—to get a locksmith, to call friends—since in that stolen coat of mine were my house keys. Remember I—"

"All that's not—"

"But remember I came down before and asked if I could use the phone here because the ones upstairs were so cold and you said I'd have to pay a token to use it because it's on the platform and I said—" He's shaking his head. "What are you shaking your head for? I said I couldn't pay for a token and use the phone booth because I only had enough change for a token and wanted to make some more calls to find a place to sleep tonight."

"I only came on a half an hour ago. Want to be exact?" Looks at his watch. "Twenty-seven minutes ago. It had to be Morton, if it was this station and entrance—the clerk before me. Bald? Scar across the nose?"

"I don't recall any clerk with glasses."

"I didn't say glasses. Scar across the nose. Bald. Elephant ears."

"I'm sorry. It was this station entrance and I thought it was you."

"We don't look anything alike. He's tall, I'm not, but you can't tell that because we're both sitting—okay. But I'm much broader in the chest and no scar on the nose and a different face and ten years on him and no big ears or bald."

"But you know Sandy. And my coat stolen's no lie, because you don't think I'm wearing this smelly summer sweater because it's my choice and garishness is my style and I think it's summer out, do you? The police gave it to me to keep me warmer than I'd be without it. And I finally found a place to stay tonight—

Hundred-tenth and Broadway—the subway stop is—and the person's given me thirty minutes to get there at the most. I called her from upstairs with a borrowed dime. 'Mister, can you spare a dime?'—I did that. So what?—but my chat with Morton before is true."

"I can't let you on either. I do, which I'd love to, but am seen doing it—fired on the spot."

"Then I'll have to sneak on. Not 'sneak,' just climb over the turnstile in front of you. Because I tried getting a cab—person I'm going to said she'd leave the money for one in her lobby—but none would pick me up because of these torn clothes, I suppose, and messed-up physical condition, all of which I got protecting Freddy."

"Freddy?"

"Sandy. I don't know why I called him Freddy. Who the hell's Freddy anyway? I'm very tired and a bit slaphappy. Was hit on the head by Sandy's muggers several times. The Lebanese. Dark, small, but big in the shoulders and arms. I only noticed that later. Looked like he lifted weights. Truth is he could've helped me more than just by going for the police. Maybe he has a lead plate in his head or, young as he is, a heart or some other condition. Or afraid. And why shouldn't he be? Or in that job, in that outpost and late at night and probably with a wife and kids at home, the ironclad rule 'Never fight back.' But glasses, Sandy, thin mustache, sweet voice and face, heavy lips, he called the police and they came promptly and muggers ran. But you weren't around when it happened."

"If it happened after I came on I still wouldn't have heard it. This box is soundproof except when you speak into it or I want it to be, which, if you don't mind—pardon me, okay?—will be now," and he unhitches a disk to cover the hole and looks at the newspaper on the change counter. Morning *News,* BRIDGE SPLIT IN STORM, photo of freighter's front rammed into a suspension bridge, car dangling off the side, caught in the cables, "2 die, 7 hurt as supertanker *Ignatius's* prow," he thinks the caption begins, clerk's eyes on him every now and then, "—Tampa Bay."

"Then I feel free to jump over. Cop comes, I'll explain. I have to stay someplace tonight and I'm sure they'll have the mugging report or I'll ask them to call in for it. They'll see why I tried beating the fare, if I'm caught, and they'll look at you as if you're nuts. Not nuts but just wrong for carrying out your job so much." Clerk, without looking up, points to his ear and then the closed hole while shaking his head. Dan goes to the turnstiles. Climb over or crawl under? Each seems an effort. Looks back. Reading the paper. "Come on," rattling the gate, "buzz me in." Clerk looks at the clock behind him. Nearly three? Dan can't quite see. Once—Fiftieth and Broadway stop— watched unobtrusively from the platform—late afternoon last week—fare beaters sneak in by slipping through the turnstiles. Started counting and one of every seventeen people got in that way though a few by going over or under. He try it, one of the arms will pin his waist to the stile's side just when the police come. Would seem easier to go under and goes under and over to the platform edge to see if a train's coming. None. Looks back. The paper. Who's he fooling?—he's looked at me. Platform pay phone. Had a dime he'd call Helene to say "Complications—finally on my way." Do and she might say "Forget it, much too late." Come on, train, come on. Hopes it's the local which he'll take all the way to a Hundred-tenth. Looks back: paper, clock, stair exit, never me. Hole where the train could be coming: dark as far back as the next station. But this is Sixth, so at the Seventh Avenue stop or even Forty-second or Thirty-fourth, just to throw the police off if the clerk did call them, he'll change for the D, if the train that comes is the E or F, but if it's the D, take it to Fifty-ninth, though maybe changing cars along the way, and change there for the Broadway local.

Suddenly has to pee and walks toward the other end of the platform. "I've reported you now, striped sweater," clerk says over a loudspeaker somewhere, "so you better pray a train comes soon and on it isn't a transit cop, which at this hour every train's supposed to be." Takes off the sweater and pushes it through a trashcan flap. Has to pee badly. Men's room locked, but he wouldn't have used it, and hates to do this but does, zipping down his fly just in time, with a train coming into the station on the other side and his back up against the last pillar on the platform onto the tracks.

"You there, you filthy slob," a man shouts from the downtown platform after Dan turns to pee against the pillar because he can't stop. Train goes, nobody over there or on his side, zips up, train on the uptown track's in sight but don't get your hopes up as it could be at this hour the train to pick up money from the token booths or one to collect the trash or clean the tracks.

Now this is going too far. Should have just said to him, well whatever I should have said I didn't, and now look at the time. He's never going to come. Maybe he's a great practical joker. Say, that what you are too, Mr. Bum? Well if so, last time. But he seemed truly desperate. "Oh I have to, oh I must." But stop making a big fuss. Go to sleep. Can't do yet. Then give it another five minutes, ten, fifteen at the most. That's more than anyone should expect from an almost total stranger, but cut it off at fifteen. Even if the downstairs vestibule bell rings a split second after his time is up. Starting from—clock—now. Good. So, sweetie, what to do till then? Yesterday's morning coffee? No, I'm up. Maybe something's on TV. Turns it on. Ad. Switches channels. Ad. Ad. Then nothing on, nothing, and then an Abbott and Costello movie or TV short. Watched these on TV as a kid and thought them senseless then. Who would have thought so many programs at this hour? The wasteland never sleeps. UHF? Too many channels to dial. Cable. Switches around and only thing on but tomorrow's cable listings and today's final stock-quotes do they call those is a nude videotape movie or scene in one. Two men and about five women rolling around together and engaging in real or simulated copulatory and oral sex on what looks like an enormous waterbed in an overlit cheap motel room. A TV's on the bed or is that the monitor of what the video camera's recording? Very violent rock music interlarded with human sucking and smacking sounds as a soundtrack. Then the sex and sounds stop, couple or triples uncouple, whose-is-it Adagio for Strings comes on faintly as background music and a man wrests himself from the others, stretches a leg as if he's working a cramp out of it and walks to the camera shaking his semierect penis. "See this," he says to the camera angrily. "Yeah," the nude people say behind him, looking at the monitor, women shaking their breasts or behinds at the camera and the other man his penis. "I'm fucking crazy angry," the man says to the camera, "and you want to know why?" "Yeah," they say to the monitor, shaking their parts harder. "Not you nymphozodiacs—you already got it all. But those sexcrazed viewing mothballs out there, hellbent on blowing up this sensual globe, that's what it is, sensual, with one and one-half tons of TNT per human person in the great U.S. of anuses. I'm fucking craziness angerness because this mother-eating lunacy hypocrisy frustration world, inside and out, and this is the truth inside the troot so you cockcruncher mothballs out there better be listening to me or I'm gonna shit on ya, gonna shit on ya, is—" Turns the TV off. Even if people want this rubbish and pay for it? I'm no prude but— Makes you wonder about the extras in the scene, not the lead himself. He's hopeless, but they think they need an acting credit that much where— But I'm getting away from my— I can't even begin to assimilate why— What if a youngster's up now and turns to that channel? My folks should see this. No, they'd still say this is the greatest country and the greatest city in it and the reason is the freedoms you have in both and though some things might seem to go too— So what's my main objection? Not just the selfcongratulatory fatuity and vulgarity— And the Albinoni, if that's whose it was—not even a nod at cleverness— Oh a nod, yes, but just because you play serious music, quote unquote, that's supposed— Why even think of it? And my feelings that such bilge shouldn't be on has nothing to do with censorship. Just that— If I had to argue the point rationally, in other words, I'd say— In other words it's not that anything about life shouldn't be brought into the open, though whether everything should be seen on TV is another— Not "another"—everything shouldn't. That was made-up life, antilife, vomit-manure to make tons of money out of life— Good God, I like to fuck as much as the next person but— So what if it's past three and only a few thousand onanists are watching this— What I'm saying— Hell, I like to play with myself as much as the next person too, but— Maybe not as much— No. What's that biblical quote about how many good or just men or just good just men each civilization needs— No sense is going to come from me tonight on this or any half-serious— And nothing to do with fatigue, I believe, and it's possible that quote comes from the Talmud. Just that I'm too darn— I'm so damn mad because— Just shut your eyes and do away with it. Shuts them, slashes her hand through the air, opens her eyes to the *Times* and turns to the TV page. Ten just men was it? If so why does "36" appear? Sex times sex? Some other day. Say, supposedly great movie is on, one she's wanted to see for years. Terrific critical reviews and one of the few movies her mother didn't walk out of in twenty minutes, and the hookup of those two was usually a good recommendation. Turns the TV on to one of the channels from before. Ad. Turns the sound off but picture stays on and reaches for the book of poetry by her bed. Opens it to her marker and reads "Lights are like a lot on fire/ From somewhere far-off doomed to zoom into your—/ The city, the city, someone speak to me about the city/ Tell me what could be more important, far-off or close by?/ Speak to me about manholes and women's bones/ About the surfeit of noises, smells, indirect touches and sights/ Lights, gloom, lots, afire/ Burned-out hearts and backyards of barbed wire/ Speak to me if you can and please, in the city/ of the city/ Where the rich don't even speak to the next-door rich/ Both so thin as the poor but from slimming drinks/ and diet creams/ The poor, groomed to be entombed to tumble and tumefy/ Rooming sights unseen to multiply/ Swooning sores unsettled to—" Tosses it to the floor. Tell me, am I just dumb or is this just junk? Movie's on. Even if she's my colleague and sort of a friend and had her publisher send me an inscribed copy, I feel cheated having spent half an hour with it. But I'll say in the Monday note I'll drop in her office box "Thanks loads, am enjoying your book I can't say how much, and lovely cover, beautiful type, acid-free paper and sewn instead of gummed? it'll still be around when the rest of ours and us have moldered to dust, overall the publisher did a bang-up job of putting it together and you must be awfully proud of the production, I know I'd be, though wish you would have given me the chance to buy the book, which I will anyhow and always do when I get one on the house, and present to a metromaniac friend—maybe he'll see what he's up against and just buy poetry instead of writing it for a while and start taking care of their kids," which should get me off the hook, because I'll never finish it. Then give it to the library on a Hundred-fourteenth. Librarian says he appreciates any gift, since if he can't circulate it he can sell it at their annual book sale. Or destroy it. Done it with others. Into the trash pail and out with the garbage, vanity-press works and textbooks on how to write and publish and potboilers so I should spread the serious word I somehow get through the mail or sometimes by messenger. The library, don't be such a Nazi, and poet lives in Rockland County, so little chance she'll find out.

Turns the sound up but movie's so good that she'd rather risk seeing it in a revival theater some time than see it now, and turns it off. Clock. Six mins, Mr. Krins. Then it's lights out in this gritty city, far-off or nearby, to tumble into the night where I hope my tumefied dreams will multiply. *Say*. Not good but bad. Should buy a shade for this window, I keep saying, and not for the little bowlered man across the river and his superhighpowered telescope.

Marietta, talking about telescopes. Superhighpowered for sure—what a dandy idea. One great thing about having your best friend in California is she can call you before eleven A.M. at the maximum overnight discount rates and you can call her when you can't call anyone else in the city because it's too late.

"Marietta, Helene, it's not too late?"

"Is a bit, but it's okay. Great to hear your voice, but past twelve, Helene— anything wrong?"

"No, and darn, damn time difference again, because I thought it was just eleven where you are. And me, of all people, after this big long debate with myself tonight—not with myself but somebody else—"

"Who dat?"

"Oh, no one. Boy, stupo, stupo," tapping her temple with her knuckles. "But what I meant was that I've always been such a stickler about phoning people at a reasonable hour. I'm sorry. And I know I'm overapologizing in excess of and above and beyond that, but I'm sorry. Listen, before I completely don't make any sense, I'll—I only wanted to hear how my only godson's doing, but I'll call tomorrow at a decent hour."

"Nah nah nah, we's up. And it's not that late. Just that I'm in the mist of breastfeeding it—he, him, little Nick—sorry there, butch—so I won't be too clear myself."

"I'll call back when you're finished. How long?"

"No guarantee. Could take twenty minutes, could take two times twenty if he still wants what I seem to too quickly run out of and he has to go on form. Just that it's tough to talk when I'm breasting. I'd give you Bob but he seems to have conked out. —Bob? Bob? He's really gone this time, not just a-possuming. He's done it before—snore, snore—when Nick's ready for the bottle or to be burped, since he thinks they're the most monotonous jobs possible next to reading Freshman English comps, right there, Bobby? —Really out. We're both so beat since Nicholas was born. Ech, now he wants me other breath. When he latches on sometimes, watch out, sport. But here's the big tunity for you two to talk. Say something to your g-mother, Nick. Your other mother, not your udder mudder. This will be his first phone talk if he talks. He's bound to howl when I switch jugs on him and keep him off the dug for a few secs. He digs that dug. You do dig dat dug der, don't ya, ittle Ick? See the usage I've reduced myself to. I can't speak to adults no more and particularly colic per-fects. Here, speak to godmamala Helene."

"Honestly, you don't have to—"

"Say hi to the old boy. You don't, he'll feel rejected and won't sup."

"Hi, Nicholas Erasmus sweetheart of mine, how you doing, honey?"

Baby cries.

"There, his first words," Marietta says. "Let me get them down for post-puberty. 'Whaa-whaa,' or was it 'ya-ya'?"

"'Ya-ya,' I think. What do you think he said to me?"

"What did you say to him? He was only responding. Six weeks?—sheet, you can't expect much more than that from him for a few more days."

"I said 'Hi, Nicholas Erasmus' etcetera."

"So he was saying 'Hiya baby, etcetera' back. Now I have to switch breasts. He's right between us in bed and I have to be careful Bob doesn't flip over during one of his Ph.D. exam dreams and thrash and crush him. Phone receiver will be right above my head on the pillow, so tell me what's been happening with you lately and every so often I might be able to divorce myself from this formidable pleasure and say a syllable or two. Cracked nipples and engorged mammae and all, sometimes I feel so sunny and voluptuous doing this that I think I'm the one being held, musically mobiled and fed."

"Sounds nice."

"Here comes Peter Cottontail."

"What the mobile plays?"

"Mmmm."

"You're gone."

"Yuhhh."

"I don't know what to say."

"Work?"

"Going well. Nothing new. Book too. Working hard."

"Ten?"

"Chairman's made gestures but I won't take if offered. Don't want it. I'll either try something new, get a better book contract for the next one and live rather penny-pinchingly for two years, or go to another school."

"Daft."

"Why? I don't want to be screwed into the same school the rest of my life or even teaching or the East Coast or maybe even America, I think."

"Sab."

"Sabbatical? No, I want to do something different or the same thing in a different place, but not take a year off on the university when I might never come back. It'd seem like cheating and also would be keeping a needy scholar-teacher from getting my job."

"Bob?"

"Way ahead of you. Months before I leave I'll tell him and then recommend him to my chairman."

"Years."

"Been looking?"

"Two."

"Delaware."

"He'd even take a job in Delaware."

"U. of. In the last MLA listing. And you?"

"Too. But Bob best. Rest. Me. You just talk."

"My folks are fine. They've sent Nicholas something. It's extravagant, so don't send it back."

"Yes."

"No. They love you and only wish the same for me."

"Two."

"Two babies? You're already planning to have another?"

"Me too for you. Rest."

"Boy, I'm really getting it about that tonight. If and when the time comes, all right?"

"Now!"

"Stop?"

"Man?"

"Hey, wilt, will ya?"

"Well?"

"Several. Nobody special. This one and that. Part of the reason I called. One I met tonight, not even a this or that, is on his way here—"

"Yeah?"

"Nothing to get excited about—he got himself locked out of his apartment and that's that. But I'm waiting and waiting. Met him at Sven and Dot's wedding reception."

"They?"

"Okay."

"It?"

"Glittering. Grim-visaging. Wanted to commit partycide. What the hell. Their affair. But this man there—met him for a minute—no, that was at Diana Salter's earlier homier affair—Dan, and what do you know goddamn, he called and is coming over to sleep on the couch because of that lockout and I'm waiting and have nothing to do, not that I don't always love talking to you, except when you're pressing me to get wed—been, remember? been—so thought of calling you."

"Glad."

"After this call—even during it if he rings from downstairs—not answering or letting him in. The phone, the door—heck with it, it's already become something of a joke."

"Do."

"What, let him in?"

"Do."

"Why?"

"Why? Want some honest but for a change good advice? No. Can't. It'll still the mill. Rest."

"I'm curious though. Just take a few elucidative secs."

"Feel."

"Feel isn't to see. Because he doesn't seem that interesting. Nothing I said made him out to be. Locked out—what's that? Translates lits—hot stuff? Just a nice nervy and slightly flaky bright guy who's kept me from sleep too long. And if he was that interesting or more interesting than I see and interested in seeing me again and I thought him interesting enough to want to see, he could always or I could always, call me or call him, but another day next week."

"Do. Ohhh—"

"Sounds incommunicable."

"Is. Then painful. Then is. And not just the engorgement and cracked teats. For when it comes down sometimes, pain like knives needling the breasts. Ever hear about that before? No nonmilker did and mixed up the knifing needles likening a twit and I'm not the only feeder to feel this. What, some collusion or my illusion about eternal women where we milkers are only allowed to talk about it among ourselves? Worth it? Yes. —Had enough there, schnooky? No. Got its mitts up and wants me to stick it back in. But that tit can't take anymore and other's temporarily out of the running. No. Shakes his head. Wronged face. About to grief. Okay, got some drops left in both but gonna talk while you're bleeding them. —Hear him? Whale of a wail Bob's said. My mind's felt like pudding since but oh this is so incommunicable having a kid. —It's Helene. —Bob just woke up. Rolled over. Missed the kid. Scratched his butt. Squeezed his nuts. Seemed to say hello to you, so hello from Bob."

"And hi," Bob says from afar.

"Hi and hello, Bob."

"You hear the baby say 'hi' too?" Marietta says. "An imitative hi but a hi. You say impossible. Well, you can say 'impossible' because you've some days on him, but so far he can only say 'hi,' and twice an 'oy.' He really did twice oy, but almost anytime I want, a 'hi.' Say 'hi,' baby."

"Hi," the baby or Marietta imitating the baby says.

"You hear? Amazing, no? Ah, now baying, so back to the breast. It's . . . what can I say? How can I put it? The—help me, Helene—what would be the words to best express what you say's the incommunicable, although you were referring to Nick then on my breast: we both just love the damn kid to death. Helene, you must have a baby. And no differing or quibbling with me either: what I said's a command. And you want to see your husband cry like a baby, have him there in the room when you give birth. And you want to be as close as you've been and maybe ever will be to someone and then two people, have him in the room for those reasons too. Yes, without question, you have to have a baby. With a man you're stuck on and who's stuck on you and who'll stick and I want you to have it soon. It'll be the second happiest moment in my life. No, the third. First was having this baby and Bob crying like one, second was when Bob and I said our vows, fourth will be when I'm standing beside you at your wedding again and holding the ring you'll slip on him, the third when you have the baby. Fifth will be when your amnio-C results come in and they say all the tests turned out negative. No, fifth was when we got our results, so sixth when yours come in. No, fifth was when I took the E.P.T. and the doughnut showed. So fifth was the doughnut, sixth the amnio-C results, seventh will be when your results come in negative and maybe eighth when you phone and say your E.P.T. showed a doughnut. So what do you say, Helene? You'll be the *mère* of *mères*. You are this moment depriving yourself of everything incommunicable we spoke about and your unborn child of your maternalness and milkiness and everything else you'll give it and each day you wait, the world another day of your great child and what you gave it and— rest. Sor. But do. Give birth."

"When the time comes."

"Now."

"I can't just grab any man and say—"

"Now, damn you, now. This is important enough to take Nicholas off for a minute. Little trick. Stick my pinky between his lips while I pull out the tit. —I know, wail. Wake up daddy. —Here, Bob, hold him for a minute. I don't care if Mrs. Larkin from downstairs— Give him the bottle then. On the side table. Has my milk in it anyway, expressed."

"What's that?"

"You'll find out. I'll in fact drive East after you give birth and bring you everything you need—clothes, crib, carriage, changing table and my breast pump. But listen. You're my dearest friend and have been for years. We're as close as close only-sisters. I know times are tough for some women—even most. Anyway, they've been complaining more than usual lately about men—the shortage and also the sexuality of potentially good ones. But you? Men have to be scratching at your windows no matter how many flights up you're up and purring and panting behind your door."

"Not so."

"*So.* I know. New York's just a holler away. I heard about ten wonderful men at least over the last few years, two of them nonpareil and childless and who wanted kids, who fell for you or would have at the slightest sign and you for a while with two of them, although not the peerless ones of course. But for your own reasons none ever quite stacked up to your—"

"Once."

"Okay, him, once. Tried to forget him but okay, him, once. And the man you were married to—let's not forget that winner long as we're at it. Anyway, all these other wonderful recent obtainable champing-for-children men, your reasons you dropped them, one dropped you—let's bless him—but— hey, can you really afford this call, late as it is to ask that?"

"It's ultradiscount time, and even if it—"

"Drop, drop, except for the one you wanted to marry and am I glad he didn't. But reach out for someone—not off the street, but if that happened to be, go with it: you never know who you'll meet leaving the movies—and let the thing happen again. Fall freely and deeply and get married in a year and go off on your honeymoon a month pregnant. And I want it to be a girl. I want our children to have children together. I want us to grow old together as related in-laws. I want you, past all kidding, to be supremely happy again as you were with your first husband when we all should have known better, and I know the only way you can. Forget books, forget teaching—they're all great and worthy but secondary, and you can always go back to them. And the—"

"Okay, enough. And maybe the phone bill is running up too much."

"And the man who's coming by tonight—"

"Mara, let her alone," Bob says.

"The two of you—let me finish—get your hand off the phone, for I see an opening here that could change her life. —And the man who's coming by—don't turn him away just because the time's long passed when he should have been there and so on. Maybe the cab he caught crashed and he's crawling this moment to your door. Think of that."

"Will you stop being silly," Bob says.

"Or the subway he might have been on caught fire and he's now maneuvering his way to you underground through pillows of smoke and will probably end up coming to you from your building's basement. Or the helicopter he took exploded in midair and he's now parachuting to your building's roof and, if he can get the roof door unlocked, will walk to your apartment downstairs. Or the—or, picked up for suspicion while running to your place, he wanted to get there so fast—"

"Pay no attention to her, Helene," Bob shouts. "Once she starts in—"

"—and this will happen right after we finish talking. He'll call you from the police station, in his one allowable call, to set him loose. Who can say in your city? But I have good instincts, and a rather adolescent imagination—too many movies and maybe living in movieland too long and maybe also too deep a belief in down-to-earth romance. But anyone who'd get himself locked out of his apartment, if we can believe him—and if it's not true, then that's saying a whole lot about his feelings and determination for you too. But anyone who would and then phone the same night he met you for only how long did you say? Anyway, you know what I think would make you the happiest, and Bob, for all his criticizing my silliness, agrees completely with me. So we hope you do it—with the one coming over or some other man you take the plunge for, and now you can hang up on me if you like. Wouldn't blame you the slightest, but first tell me this fellow's name again, in case I maybe know him and can warn you against him if my instincts about him were a hundred percent wrong."

"The name of the man who's supposed to come over but never will? Daniel Krin."

"Krin. No. Well, we beat the band for Dan."

"It won't be Dan but—"

"Seriously, Helene, you can't know how wonderful almost everything is in having a baby. Even to doing it in one room while the kid's sleeping peacefully in another. I mean, he sleeps in our room at night, but sometimes, in the afternoon, when Bob—"

"I'll consider it if at the time we have two or more rooms."

"And breast-feed it too."

"At the same time or different? Anyway, if the man comes, baby comes and then the milk comes, I will."

"You'll be such a relaxed mother, it'll just spill. I'll start saving the money to fly in for your wedding. Not with Dan-the-man so much, but you know what I mean. If you gear yourself up for it to happen, it'll happen, listen to me. Before Bob there were plenty just as highly desirable and a couple even more so—I don't kid you and I never did him. But I wanted to go to grad school, travel, work, kick it up a little and so on—you know me—till I said it was time to, since I was approaching thirty-five and beginning to risk Down's for the kid and along came Bob. Whups—sleepytime yawn. And look at this. Bob— and it seems to be a straightout nonfake—fell asleep holding the bottle to Nick's lips and Nick's asleep too, on Bob's chest. So it's one big sleepy family. But he has to be burped. Minimal ten minutes or we get a magnum of gas. But before that I'll get my hard-wrung expressed back into the refrigerator, get the Polaroid and flash attach and snap a few pictures of these two. So, my dearest dream of a generous friend—refrigerator, pictures, burps, then rock Nick in his carriage a bit and probably one more diaper change—I've got a lot to do so really must say toodle-ee-oo."

"Much love to Bob from me and a big kiss on the tuchis for Nick."

"That a way to go."

"Hey, come on there, get this wagon moving—move it along," man in the subway car says into his newspaper. He stands up, slaps the paper against his leg, opens the window by his seat and sticks his head out of it and says "Hey, come on there, get this—conductor. Hey, conductor there, what's going on? We've been—hey there, you. The one in the blue coat. Yell to the conductor there we've been parked in this station for the last two days. . . . With the Parka—that's right, the blue one, you. Yell to the conductor there I want to see him. That we—damn it. Conductor, hey, conductor. What's with this train? Get it moving, get it moving. When are we supposed to be here to, next Thanksgiving parade?"

"Any minute," a man yells from where this man's yelling to. "We got a light up ahead to stop and haven't got one to go."

"Then get that light. Call them up and tell them to put on that light because a mistake's been made and nothing's in your way. Get that light and go. People like me have to get to work or lose our jobs. Jesus," and he sits, looks around, realizes he's sitting on it, pulls his paper out from underneath him and starts reading it.

"Will you please close your window?" a woman across from him says.

"What are you worried for? The doors are open and not going to close."

"When the train starts the doors will close. Will you please be so kind as to close the window you opened?"

"It's only a little fresh air."

She gets up, says "I knew you wouldn't," makes sure the four shopping bags at her feet are positioned against one another and the seat so they won't fall, says "Excuse me if it's no trouble" to the man, he moves over a couple of feet, and squeezes the levers at the top of the window but can't get the window to move. "Mister," she yells to Dan sitting at the other end of the car. "You're my last hope here and not because you're the only one left. Could you please help me close this window—it's stuck."

"If it's stuck I don't see what I could do to close it."

"Give it a try. It might be my strength."

"A try then." He goes over to the window, says "Excuse me" to the man, who's moved back under the window and now moves again to the side, presses the two sets of levers in, window won't budge. "Seems really stuck."

"Now you see what you did?" she says to the man.

"What I do? Fifty years of this train going down the drain and you're blaming me? And you got heat—feel it," and he puts his hand on the seat. "*Heat,* so you won't freeze."

"I'm an older person. My bones are brittle. I get frozen faster than you."

"Then move to another car. There's actually too much heat coming up, making me want to take off my sweater, so it's nice mixed with a little fresh air."

"But I like this car. It's cleaner than most and who knows what's in the other cars. And this one was the perfect temperature for me without the window opened, which is why I walked through the whole train before I came back to sit here. I have a long way to go."

"What else can I say? I pulled a window down, now it won't go up. Point of issue has to be finished, for if he, a big strapping man, can't close it, there's nothing more anyone but a train mechanic can do."

"Maybe you have a special way with those window clickers."

"I don't. I put my fingers on them like you did and him."

"Ask him to try to use his special touch again," she says to Dan.

"I'm sure there isn't any."

"There isn't," the man says. "But what's the difference? This train's never leaving here, so we should all stop crying. It'll be another one they'll tell us to get off of and then it'll roll out to wherever they go, probably to the next uptown station to pick up passengers, who'll think 'Hmm, why's the train so empty?'" He stands, yells out the window "Hey there, we've been here fifteen minutes if you want to know the exact figure—either tell us to get off and you get another train here to take us, or get this one moving. Conductor there—I talked to you before about it . . . oh go to hell with yourselves, you're all a pack of meat and never gave two craps for the next guy," and he leaves the train.

"Maybe you can give it a last good try," she says to Dan. "Sometimes the first times unloosen it."

Dan shrugs, tries the window again, strains and gets it up two inches.

"That'll help but not by much. That all it'll do?"

"That's it." His fingers are black and sticky from some crust on the levers and underneath the top window frame. "Maybe this is the problem," showing her his fingers. "A grime, like glue. Probably down the sides of it—where the window slides up—too."

"I'm going to another car. I know of one almost as warm if no one there opened the windows. Want his paper? It's Saturday's."

"He might come back for it."

"With all he did we don't deserve his paper?" She crams it into one of the shopping bags, picks up two in each hand and a long umbrella and plastic raincoat that had been behind them and goes into the next car. Odor about her. Lots of junk in the bags. Small pots, rolled-up clothing, wooden hangers, loose toggles, stacks of letters, tied-up twine and string.

Conductor rushes through the car holding a flashlight. "Anything wrong, sir?" Dan says.

"We'll be moving in a minute," and goes into the next car. Dan sits, shivers, tries the window, rubs what grime he can off his hands under the knee-part of his pants.

"Hold the door," a man shouts, running down the stairs. He runs into the car, "What luck it was still waiting," pats his chest, "This isn't good, I shouldn't be losing my breath like this," sits.

"Someone, will someone please help me?" Man in the middle of the platform, turning around in one spot, tapping a white cane on the ground.

Dan looks at the man in the car. "Not me," his face says, takes his wallet out of his side pants pocket and puts it into the back, puts his athletic bag against the window and leans his head back on it, curls in his feet, pulls the ends of his coat down over his knees and shuts his eyes. Dan gets up and stands by the door nearest the man on the platform. "Sir, what is it?"

"Good—someone. Thank you. First I want to make sure of one thing. Are we at the Seventy-second Street station?"

"Ninety-sixth and Broadway—the uptown platform."

"What I thought. Were you here five minutes ago when the uptown express left?"

"Five minutes ago? If it did, it went completely by me."

Feels a watch on his wrist. "Five and a half minutes ago exactly. I was on it and meant to get off at Seventy-second but fell asleep. And a woman, when I woke up between stations, said the last stop was Thirty-fourth when it was Times Square, which is how it happens I'm here. Could you help me get to the downtown side?"

"Excuse me, but you *are* blind, correct?"

"Yes."

"Well you see, I'm standing inside the local, waiting for the doors to close. So I'd like to help, but I have to get to someplace which if I'm any more late for—"

"Thank you. Someone," he shouts, turning around, "will someone please help me get to the other side of this mess?"

"Wait—listen. The stairs are over there—stop turning—*now*, you're facing them. Maybe fifteen feet in front of you at the most. Walk straight—I'll stay here and guide you, and if the doors close, guide you from the open window here long as I can—feel for the bottom step with your foot or cane, grab the railing on your right and go upstairs. The stairs to the downtown platform are to your right about thirty feet once you get up there."

"I don't know this station. I'm also very tired, so for that reason also I'm being extra cautious."

"I can understand that. But much as I truly want to—and I truly do—"

"Hey," the man from before, head sticking out the window of the next car, "get this thing going. You maybe already made me lose my job. My supervisor can't believe when I say these trains are always breaking down—he uses a car. So move it—stop your stalling."

"If the train doesn't leave before I see a transit cop," Dan says, "I'll call one over for you or someone else who seems safe and is waiting here—"

"Help me out now?"

"Believe me, you can't believe how late I am for where I'm going. And I'm freezing here. I lost my sweater and coat tonight. So I just don't want to lose my train."

A man approaches, heading for the stairs. "Sir," Dan says, "could you take this gentleman here—he can't see, as might be obvious—up the stairs and deposit him—"

Man's past them, never made a sign he saw or heard, hurries upstairs.

"Thanks a lot. That's where he was going. —And when I mentioned your sight, sir, I only thought— Wait, I'll do it. This train's never going. Should've done it before and I would've been back by now." Steps out of the car, grabs the man's arm. Train motor starts up. "I have to get in. Ah, I don't know what I'm doing." Doors shut. "Oh well, *macht nichts.* If this one's been here so long, another should be close behind it."

"Whatever it's costing you, I'm—"

"Finally," the man in the next car says. "Hurray," and pulls his head in and shuts the window.

"No problem whatsoever," Dan says. "That's not so, but let's try to do it quickly without either of us tripping. I won't rush you though." Doors open. Dan walks him a few steps to the staircase, says "Wait a second, maybe I can have both," walks him to the car, wedges a foot against the part the door slides out of, says "Don't worry, I'll get you over there one way or the other without much more delay, but maybe in the next few moments someone will come who can take you. Hello," he shouts, "but is there anyone here who could take this man whose sight is bad to the downtown platform? I can't. My uptown local's leaving. —Don't worry, I will if no one else does," he says to the man. Two men a few pillars down the platform look at them, then seem to look away. "If one of you gentlemen is waiting for the uptown express— I just thought of something," to the man. "Come with me to a Hundred and tenth—the stop I'm going to—and once there I'll take you around to the downtown platform, stand with you till the local comes—I don't care how long it takes—and then you can take it all the way to Seventy-second without getting off. Four stops. Hundred-third, Ninety- and Eighty-sixth, Seventy-ninth and then -second. Five. It's a fair compromise. I'm going out of my way doing it that way also, but that's okay—I don't mean to sound begrudging or guilt-making. I want to help you, but you also shouldn't have been out alone this late and on the subway in the first place."

"I work downtown—baking, my living. I've never had trouble or missed my stop. Just take me—"

"Here, feel my arm," and puts the man's free hand on his arm. "Just one long-sleeved shirt. A thick cotton but not sufficient and no undershirt underneath." Motor starts up again. Doors close except for the half-door his foot's holding open. Man inside the car says "Make your move, in or out, but let the door close."

"In a second. I'm trying to get someone to take this man to the downtown platform here."

"I'll get someone myself," the blind man says and takes his arm away from Dan.

"Come with me, really. Two quick stops—Hundred-third and -tenth, and the downtown train you'd eventually get here will probably be the same one you'll get at a Hundred-tenth. If one leaves as we get there, I'll stay with you till the next one comes. You ask me, that's more than a fair compromise."

"I'll manage."

Conductor comes into the car.

"Have to go," Dan says. "How about it?" Man steps farther back.

"Hey," conductor says. Yelling man from before's right behind him.

"Watch yourself and take good—ah, said all I can say," and steps into the car. Door shuts. Conductor and yelling man from before turn around. Dan goes to the open window as the train starts moving and shouts "Will someone please help this man get to the downtown platform? Someone—you," to a man running downstairs. "You missed it so help that guy with the cane there get to the downtown side. He's blind, could use help. I tried—" but train enters the tunnel.

She goes to—beer? no, stops, then what? Doesn't know—to bed, that's it, for the last time, do what you said. Turns around, bedroom, bed, clothes off, here, there, heck with it, on the floor, chair, tomorrow she'll pick up, clean up, whole place, her weekly mess, also one of these weekend days, clean the stove, but before that defrost the fridge—covers back, light off, radio on? No, enough, plenty, too much, sleep now, that's what she needs. Lies back, sighs deep, feels good, covers up, pillow's not right, leave it. No, leave it and she'll never sleep tight. Light on, both pillows still up for reading not sleeping, down, plumps them, once, twice, light off, lies back, deep sigh, covers up, burrows in, pillowcase smells, tomorrow, also the laundry, or Sunday at the latest. So? So what? Go to sleep. Shuts her eyes. Thoughts pass—what a day, some day, night, whole day, part, party, parties, Dot and Sven, seeing Peter again, Arturo wasn't his name but what it should be, though what's that mean? "I don't know, I don't know." Sounds so odd, voice in the dark. But she should, this Arturo business, be allowed to—it's night and very late so she can make as many meaningless observations and statements as she wants till she falls asleep. Make another. Can't think of any. "Hello, hello?" Still sounds odd. "Mama I'm cold." Maybe always will sound weird while the light's out. Alone's probably why, while with another person, dark or light, he'd say "What's that you said?" and she could say "I don't know, just testing, testing, one, two, now back to head, so pretty please pay no mind," and neither would think much of it. Pleasure of company, safety in numbers. Thinks that's right, doesn't care if it isn't. But make another meaninglessism. Abracadabrafagab-rahachoo! "I love you." Very odd, maybe the mostest. Talk shortly and marry a Swiss miss—at this age, his age, versus Ms. Rage—now she's making no sense. So what and what if she is or isn't? For good, more meaninglesspish, quicker to sweep she'll get. And this other guy. Coming by. You bet. But don't forget if he rings—no way, late sir. Goodnight or good morning but a newer knowner day. Enough, pointy, too much—stop that, in fact. What? Any thought goes, quicker to deep. But something Diana said—hole back the tide. Means Marietta, means hold, means pellucid, means lucid, about chillen, she in relation to them—as daughter? mother?—but forgets. That she should breast-feed? At least on one breast? Which one—right? left? Sure, tanks, but getting much too much late. Not to conceive but to keep from sleep. What's Bugs Bunny doing in her predreams? Scat. Where's Tom or Jerry the cat to chase him away? Never liked Bugs or that cat: too mean, tiger-toothed and wool of wiles. Opens her eyes. That usually does it and did. For when she closes them right after, people or things she doesn't want in her predreams disappear. How-do mom and dad. Stepping out of the front seat of a car, circa 1960, both doors going bang. Why? Neither can even drive. Who knows how these rings bed in here. Some conglomerate conjectural connection. What? Electrica, that's all. Electrolux—the best—puff puff. Sheep sleep. Folks gone. For no one or thing stays for long. Friend Cecily from golden tooth days comes on stage. Make cents? Haven't thought or seen of her in these predreams or from what I can member from regular deeper dreamers for years. Hi Cec me friend—Cecily, hi. She waves. Long brout cigarillo in her mout when she never cigaretted before. Then all of a sodden's in a big, kid's balloon skying flyward till she's gone. "Bye." Smoke burnts to dust. Dog runs on chased by many mangy dogs. Tease the real country. Wobbly dirt road with wheel pebbles in it, tall green fluffy trees round wed apples on them on either wide of the ride, blue shy, white shouds, green operas on the trees also and yellow forwards in the hills, clear day, all day, all the dogs' talls raving, then nice sleek chased one barks. At me. Hark hark. I smile. A god, had one as a girl, but a different breed, ran away, posted rhymes up on every lamppost every day, visited all the city pounds, cried for nights, didn't want Granada, Rolph! Rolph! by now gods and countryside have disappeared. Sailing ship in empathy dark seas. Coffee brewing, moo cows, nightleak rain, and ship sinks. Now sunshiny and tree talking pigs painting a two-story mouse. Pigs with overalls on, from come comicbook or cattoon, housepainter's hats. Fuss me getting slippy. Nice we slice wheat thins the. Feels it humming on. When the cattoons come and all that sleep speak, it's only minutians away. Slap slap. Up and at. Don't go yet. Want to have some fun. Force someone on. Who you want to see? Could also force lovemaking if I hunted two and have done so in these seams with sexsex seferal times. Grandpa, that's who. Opposite of thef. Grandpa, come on Grandpa, come on looking just as he looked when she last looked him a week before he dired. Reddy face, thin freame, straight postique, thick spectators and that wonder bread smile. Daying Hiya darling, meyer darlink, my riddle sweetheart—how ya truly doing? "I'm fine, Grandpa, sleepy but mine, and you?" Knew. Disappears. Forgot what I wasn't supposed to tak long aloud in my pregleam dreams. Grandpa, bag on stage, wall in, say huddough to me again peas. Does, same suit, hat on now though. Quarter times she saw him he bore a half. Hi Grandpa—Grandpa, if knew you would do it anyruddy could, and hi. Hell me mo beautiful grandchild. Miss you, Grandpa. Me too to you, my child squeet. Miss you so much, Grandpa. Me me to too, my toot sweet. Miss you that much and am more glad I not falls into deep before I liss how much I say you, Grandpa. Me ma, ah-goo, sweet child. Wiss I had you round to isk about lots of doorbell rings. He's gone. Eyes open. Grundpepere's gone. Downstairs bother's binging. Downstairs bell's ringing. Don't answer it a night song. Only could be key. Won't let Kin in. City. Minsky. Who's he? She's too lazy. He was too late in coming. She doesn't want to see anyone now. Too sleepy, not lazy, go away awhile and maybe. Again. Downstairs buzzer's buzzing, no downstairs ring or bell. Just take the money and understand? Plenty. Or let him in or speak. Show him the courtesy, give him the couch and a wishrag and trowel and go back to sheep. Kidding? Buzzer's rebothering. Gets up, turns on the light, hasn't been in bed long, runs to the kitchen, pushes *Talk* on the intercom and says "Who is it, Dan Krin?" and he says "Yes, hi, and I know it's much later than I said but could you ring me in?—this lobby's cold." "Listen, it's—you see, well, I'm distressingly—painfully—just plainly sleepy, so I don't think I can." She still has her finger on the *Listen* button. Presses *Talk* and says "Hello?" and presses *Listen* and he says "Still here, but can you let me in?" *Talk:* "Did you find the money?" *Listen:* "Money, money—forgot all about it. Yah, it's here. I didn't need it but thanks. Is anything wrong?" *Talk:* "Take it anyway to get wherever you have to, but I really—I'm very sleepy—so if you wouldn't mind, okay?" *Listen:* "I promise no problem. On my hands and knees, and it's not just this lobby. I've only a shirt now, no sweater, so just to get warm. What I'm saying is—just as you've been too generous as it is—but don't leave me stranded down here. Really, it's too cold and I haven't the right clothes—so a few hours sleep anywhere in your apartment. Even, as I said on the phone—and I'm not joking—I wasn't and I'm naren't, aren't, am not now—on the rug." *Talk:* "You through?" *Listen:* "Yes." *Talk:* "All right, since I suppose I can't go back on what I promised. And no rug. Just come up. Ninth floor, first door to your left when you get off the elevator, which is directly ahead of you past the lobby door, but don't whatever you do get detained along the way," and buzzes him in.

Funny girl, sounded mad, can't wait, just to get inside some place, what'll he say? aiee, aiee, at this hour the apartment can't have much heat, only don't get playful, just Hello, thanks—play it straight— Don't want to trouble you any farther—further— So just. . . eighth. . . . . seventh. . . show me the rug or couch or whatever it is I'm to rest on, and if it's still okay a shower first if you don't mind, as you can see I really need it, and a towel in any state of dampness or decay would be much appreciated, so you just go to sleep, night-night, don't worry about me, and much more than my thanks, you've been, what can I say? divine. . . second. . . . . first. . .

Bathrobe, something for underneath, just a pair of panties from here or there, like to put up her hair but hasn't time, tie the belt tight, tuck the top in, nothing needed for her feet.

Door opens as he has his finger— "Hi, heard the elevator door open," closes.

"Hello, thank you, you startled me," holds out his hand, "—forgot my key. I—"

"Shhh—neighbors."

"Sorry, and no dumb, and besides, confusing that dumb remark when you also consider that I lost my own housekeys. But anyway, seriously"—her hair down, more blonde than orange now, how's that? could be the ceiling light—smooth, shiny—"I don't think I should leave my shoes here, do you? They're not wet and I wouldn't want to lose them."

"Why, is it raining?"

Big breasts, thick thighs, small waist, under the robe, what he can detect—"No, why? Don't know why I even said it, I mean," cute little feet. "I'll leave them on. They might be dirty, I guess that's why. Said it, I—"

"It's all right, this isn't a Japanese household. Come in."

"Thanks." She steps aside, he shuts the door, she locks, her back, large buttocks. "Nice place."

"You haven't seen it."

"The lobby downstairs, the vestibule. Which is it? The second entrance room, with all the marble. Oh, befores I forgets," gives her the cab money in his hand.

"No, I don't want—" trying to give it back.

"Please, it's not mine. —Then a dollar for the subway tomorrow, which I'll mail back," takes a dollar bill. "But I always get those two rooms mixed up or never had them straight." Face, smile, teeth, height, high cheeks, those sweet feet, almost oriental eyes, simple powder-blue bathrobe, paint, print, light fixture in this small room, all in good taste, tons of books shelved, don't let it get to. . . turn your. . . make you. . . something, what? No time.

"Lobby," she already said. Also: "Vestibule's the first one with the nailed-down floor runner and bells." Now: "At least I think—"

"So the door from the outside's the vestibule door and one to the lobby's the lobby door. That hold true for going out? Lobby door leading to the vestibule still the—well, not important, except for a translator's zealotism, zealotry—zeal for the exact word. I bet you thought with that last one I wasn't serious."

"I didn't think. Anyhow—"

"Sure: no talk; sleep. I'm sorry, and by nice place downstairs—just to finish this up, so you don't think I'm altogether bats—I meant old New World New York or something or another. Handsome. Hatful. Tactful. Those aren't it, blubber blubber, so whatever words I mean."

"You're tired."

"Us both. I've kept you up and up. Lucky you're still talking to me."

"I don't know how much longer I can." Yawns. "There"—another—"see? I'm catching a yawn, and for all I know I'm dreaming in my sleep."

"If you are, where's that leave me? Where would I be if—"

"No taxing thoughts. And maybe you should take off your shoes. How'd they get so muddy?"

"And my hands," untying the shoelaces. "I should also probably leave them in the anteroom do you call this room? The shoe room? You have a newspaper I can put these under?"

"Leave them. I'm doing a big clean-up tomorrow. And this room is my apartment's equivalent to the downstairs lobby. Or foyer. That's what this and that one downstairs is. Foyer. No, bring your hands with you. You'll need them to pull out the couch bed. I haven't the strength for it anymore."

Goes, follows. "Hmm, nice room. And nice couch. Don't worry about sheets or anything. All I need's a blanket or heavy coat."

"The bed is already made. And I'd say 'Let me take your coat,' or would have in the foyer, but you really don't have one. You didn't when you came to Diana's?"

"It was stolen. I didn't tell you about the newsstand?"

"You did. I'd ask to hear the whole story"—yawns—"as you can see," pointing to her yawning mouth. "Mine always seem to come in twos."

"Makes no differen—" Shudders.

"Ooh, you're really chilled. I can make you tea. Or a drink of something. Scotch, vodka? Somehow Zubrovka sounds medicinal—know what it is?"

"Buffalo grass. I'd love it, thanks. And look at the view. Mind if I look?" Goes to the window. "Incredible. I once knew an editor—he had me come to his endless apartment overlooking the East River in the Seventies. About a translation—first I ever published—around ten years ago—it was a literary magazine. Now he's got to be the most successful writer of other people's autobiographies in the country. Every book he ghosts he gets a quarter of a million for and he does them in a year. He also appears in an American Express Cheques ad, saying 'You don't know me and never will know the titles of the books I write, but four million of you bought my books this year,' or that's what someone told me, since I never saw it. But forgot what I was going to say about his apartment. What's that? Looks like a floating lit Christmas tree."

"In the water?"

"Moving very slowly."

"Probably a tug." Comes over. "A tug."

"Why's it alone? And where's it going upriver this late?"

"They're often alone. Picking up ships there—Yonkers, Albany—barges with concrete or coal on them, sometimes pushing eight at a time. I know that editor-writer. I've gone to his parties and seen him on TV."

"Really. When I sold him the translation I was told—it was also in a *New Yorker* Profile about him and his distinguished family—that every contributor for the year was invited to his annual New Year's Day party, but I wasn't. I was disappointed. They're known to be—were then—now he's married, has children—"

"His parties still are. Elaborate smorgasbord. Bar with bartenders making real bar drinks. Servants scudding around with the most exotic finger foods and champagne. Lots of well-known or interesting or very smart people there or all three. Quartet playing Schubert or pianist playing Broadway medleys. It's not what I like to do or have time to any other daytime day, but it is a great illusionary way to start the new year."

"He never took anything of mine after that, though it's true other people now edit most of the magazine for him. No big deal. I wanted to go to eat and drink well and, to be honest, to meet women—society girls involved in literature and literaturists, I understand, and just women writers and artists of every kind, and I'd probably want to go for the same reasons now. Maybe I would've met you there one of these last years if I'd sold one of the many translations I sent his magazine in that time and he had invited me, if he still invites contributors."

"I don't think that's how most of his guests get there anymore. I went with a friend and Sanderson talked to me for an hour about post–World War Two alcoholic writing and has sent me an invitation for the last three years, but hasn't invited my friend since the first time. I don't know how it works. I think my friend and he pumped iron at the same health club. I'm not yawning anymore but I am as sleepy. I'll get you that vodka now, if you're still interested, and say goodnight."

"Yes, of course, excuse me. And may I use your bathroom?"

Points, he goes, shuts the door. Won't stay closed unless he forces it into the frame and locks it, which he does. Smells flowery. Bloomingdale's soap. Carnation. Knows without seeing it. Woman he knew used to buy them by the box and used a red one too. What scent? rose scent, both soaps too hard to lather his shavingbrush with. Polka-dot shower cap on the shower's hot water valve, backbrush hanging handle-end up on the cold, series of enlarged framed photos along one wall of turned-over beached rowboats, photo of a cat strolling the coast of what seems to be the bouldery sea of the boats, Marin watercolor or oil of sea trees, rocks and island, thick deep blue bath and face towels and washcloth, three toothbrushes in the holder, bobby pins and antique ring in the cup stand. Washes his hands, face, hands again, then the soap under the faucet to get the grime off it. Water in his mouth, gargles, spits out, still tastes foul. Maybe she has a mouthwash he could swig from the bottle and spit out. Opens the medicine chest. Diaphragm case with jelly alongside but forget it. Mouthwash, but she'll know if she smells his breath or follows him into the bathroom that he's been inside the chest, and closes it. Water on his hair, wants to brush his hair with her brush on the sink. No, his gray hairs, but with all her blonde or orange or both, she'll never know. Three strokes—sides and middle—checks, brush is clean but for one gray, long enough to be hers, which he pulls out and drops into the bag in the basket under the sink. Pee. Picks up the seat.

Knock knock.

"I'll be right out."

"Just thought, because of your chill, you might want the vodka now."

"I do, thank you. I still feel chilled. But I'll be right out. Then I'll take it and go right to sleep."

"You don't want to shower? On the phone I thought—"

"I do but didn't want to put you through—"

"Now that you're here, shower if it'll make you feel better. I'll get you a washrag and a fresh towel."

"If you don't mind, one of these will do, and no washrag. Excuse me, Helene, but I have to urinate badly. So I'm going to break off this conversation for the moment."

"No, use it. And sorry."

Looks at the commode as he pees. Clean, outside and in. Hopes she isn't still there listening. Finished, flushes, seat down—should he?—cover too. She keeps the cover up when she's alone, just as he does, or is that assuming too much? Rinses his hands, then washes them—clean as the commode was he might've touched feces on the seat's underside—feels his fly, it's up, last glance in the mirror, unlocks the door. She's standing in the living room, stemmed shotglass on the table beside her. Wants him to go, doesn't care if he stays, what's her face say? No smile, quite blank, all in, that could be all. "Didn't mean to take so long or cut you off like that."

"What are you talking about?" Hands him the glass.

"Smells good."

"Polish, supposed to be much better than the Russian. Also supposed to be ice-cold, but I thought with a chill you'd—"

"Any way is fine and probably room temperature's better." Holds up the glass. "Everybody's got imported vodka today. Diana had Russian, I think; friend of mine has Finnish—"

"This was from my father."

"Oh, very generous. My father never even offered me a drink. Didn't like me to. Was afraid I'd become a rummy."

Rummy?

"Expression of his for me. Guzzler and juicehead and lush were others, all exaggerated and inaccurate, and a little unfair since he drank his share way past my present age till he was ordered not to. And I didn't mean that imported vodka has become a fad. If I had my choice, believe me . . . Is there an appropriate toast I should make before I drink this?"

"None I know in Polish. *Prosit* perhaps or down the hatch."

"I almost feel I should make a blessing, not a toast. I'm thankful for being here. To you for being so hospitable and kind. I don't know what I would've done, at the end of my end and so on, and as I said—" Tears come.

"You would have found something. Drink."

Drinks. "Delicious."

"If the Poles, my father says, advertised their vodkas as much as the Russians, they'd take the market away. Or maybe they think that taking business from them would only be one more reason for the tanks to roll in. Anyway, that's countries." Looks at the couch. "Towel, washrag, extra blanket . . . *bathrobe.*"

"Don't need one."

"It's important. I don't want you running around in a towel or your undershorts."

"Ah, if you only knew."

"What?"

"Nothing sinister—really, thank you. You have a robe that'll fit and won't itch?"

"And ambisexual. I'll get it." Starts for the bathroom, stops. "What were you saying 'if I only knew'?"

"Nothing. Just something about underpants. That the robe was a good suggestion. But don't worry, because nothing's wrong with my underpants or their environs or any idea connected to them in any way."

"It still doesn't sound right."

"I don't have any on. There you go. I used them to wipe my behind earlier tonight because the john I was in—it was in a bar but I only went there for coffee, to sober up, to dry off—was all out of paper."

"Are those pants in your pocket now?"

"I flushed them down—their toilet, not yours."

"Okay." Goes past the bathroom into another room. What'd she think when she saw the tears and he mentioned his environs and then his behind? That he never should've brought any of it up? That for the sake of good manners and taste, etcet. He didn't see how she looked when he cried because at that moment he looked away, quickly got rid of the tears. He was being honestly emotional she could think—a virtue? fault? folly?—or dishonest, trying to suck her in with his tears, or trying to affect or impress with his directness and frankness about his environs and behind, or just still a little drunk, which might scare her. If he were she he'd think at least What is it with this guy? He shoots the rest of the drink down. But her concern, papa who compares Slavic vodkas, soap, clean commode, woman with a river view, bobby pins and simple ring, obvious smarts from the start, affectionate to revered way people spoke about her, spryness, hair, just this pretty glass, puts it on the table—why didn't he ask how her evening went after Diana's? He can be clever but never learned to hold back enough or know when soon is soon enough or—jumps. Something at his feet. Cat, same one it seems from the photograph, a light bluish white, yanking one of its front nails with its teeth, saying Who are you? in Siamese, settling down inches away, pulling all its paws in and staring at him.

"So, Sammy found you. He must have been under the couch. Are you allergic to cats?"

"Why, am I acting like it? I like them, but takes me a while to be over-friendly." Bends down to pet it. Cat hisses, hand retracts.

"First put your finger out and let him smell it. They like to get to know you slowly, and one big hand coming down on them too fast can be hair-raising."

Squats, puts out his finger. Cat sniffs it, licks it, sits up and bumps his head several times on Dan's palm, he pets it and looks up.

"Now you're pals." Hands him a bathrobe. "Nothing else I can think of—you?" Shakes his head and stands. "You need another blanket or any toilet articles, in the linen closet opposite the bathroom. Feel free in the kitchen. Stove burners are automatic, if you want to use one, and oven you need a match, which are on top of the cupboard to the stove's right. Are you a big drinker?"

"Not at all. Why, my remarks?"

"For a while I didn't know what I was getting into with you, pre- and post-phone. Some of the things you said—they might be amusing or right for some people, and maybe any other time in my life or hour of the night I might respond more favorably to them, so what am I saying?"

"No, you're right. Fact is I was thinking the same thing before you said it. That I might've sounded too fancifully bizarre—I'm being euphemistic here so you don't think too unfavorably of me. Or am I now doing the same thing?—but too soon saying these things and maybe for any time."

"Well, let's not get down on yourself too hard. Just have a good shower and snack and a pleasant sleep. If you like Mandelbrot—do you know what it is?" He nods. "Some of my mother's homemade ones are in a coffee can in the refrigerator. I'll probably be up earlier than you but I'll patter around. I don't think Sammy will get out of my room, but if he does and ends up on your bed, don't be alarmed—he doesn't scratch. I've no shades on any of my windows, so if it gets very bright out it might wake you. Any idea what the weather report is for tomorrow?"

"No, and go ahead and wake me. Do everything you'd normally do if I wasn't here. All I want is a few hours sleep. Also, and I know it's a little late in the conversation for this, but you never said how your evening went after you left Diana's. The wedding reception?"

"I didn't. Thought I had. Anyway, you probably still want to talk and I don't. If you want to chat later in the morning and I don't feel too rushed to get busy with my work, we can do so over coffee."

"Fine. Do you have to use the bathroom, because I'm going to be in there a while."

"Give me a minute and then it's yours. Oh, one more thing and then you'll be set. Around five or five-thirty a man might yell 'Mike' from the park side of the drive a few times and possibly startle you. Either he's crazy and doesn't have a dog or he does have one and it runs away from him and gets lost every other day. Otherwise, have a good night."

"Goodnight."

She's dreamed. How old is she in it?—that's always the first thing she asks about her dreams. Same age she is today. She and Dan were on a beach. It seemed like the same beach she rents a cottage on every summer for one or two months, lots of pebbles and shells and huge smooth rocks sticking out of the sand or the water near shore. Then it seemed like Coney Island, a gray-colored sand but without people or wire trashcans or lifeguard highchairs on it, and no pebbles, shells or rocks. The sky was clear, weather was mild and the sun was setting in the East. He was in bathing trunks and a tank top, she in a light sleeveless cotton dress, more like a young girl's dress with blue forget-me-nots all over it and a big bow at the waist in back. She have one like it as a girl? Doesn't recall. They were holding hands. The Boardwalk and Parachute were behind them—still no other people—and she pointed to the Parachute and said "I once got stuck at the top of it for half an hour when there was a fire in the gear box thirty feet above me and it scared me so much I couldn't speak for a week and could never go on an amusement park ride again, not even the merry-go-round or one of those dumb bumping cars I used to love." All that happened. She also couldn't get into an elevator for months or on a plane till about ten years ago and even today when she drives a car over a high bridge her pulse speeds up. He said "Don't look at it then," not that sympathetically; "let's just count birds." They turned back to the water. Both were barefoot and her feet were sinking into the muddy sand, making her shorter and then much shorter than he. She held a finger out to point at birds and he held a pen and pad in his free hand. A bird flew past. She said "There's one—a tern. How many are we up to now?" He said "One," and let go of her hand to write the number in the pad. She said "It seems we've been here much too long for just one tern." "There's a second bird," he said; "quick, what is it?" "A sandpiper, but they usually travel in twos or schools." "Prides," he said. "Plagues," she said, "or maybe not. I can be very morbid, so you better watch out for me." He said "I'll do more than that; a gaggle of mores. I'll look out for you, look after you, look forward to you, look into you, look up to you, but I'll never look down my nose or look through you, or so I say." "Never mind," she said, "but tell me: why are we counting birds?" "We were asked to for the betterment of our environment, yours, mine and the child's." "Never mind, and look; there's a third one—a murmuration bird," and she took his pen and wrote the number and name in his pad. He hugged her, she didn't resist. He said something like "Stabilize your mouth, I'm going to navigate you," she opened her mouth wide and moved her head closer to his. He kissed her neck and fiddled with her dress bow and shoulder strap. She said "Will you get your hands and lips off me? I don't know you and I do mind." He let go, held his hands out to her in a strangulation pose. She backed away and he dropped to his knees, put his face to the hole her feet had made and screamed the most horrified scream and she thought he'd just found his child dead in its crib, and woke up.

What to make of it? The dream, if just the scream and dead child thought, certainly woke her up. But what of the rest? Multiple meanings of tern? Fiddling with her bow only in there for a laugh? All the baby talk with Marietta could explain the dead child being in, but what does that dropping-to-his-knees scene mean: child she wants but might never conceive, being stillborn? Her wanting to kiss him, then resisting, related to what happened with Peter before? Was the mud she was in primeval? The strangulation pose supposed to be what she thinks sex would be like with him? The sandpiper flying past the piper of passing time? Nothing she can now think of makes her think the dream was very self-revealing or profound. Engaging, moving, cinematic, even tragic, and her favorite kind stylistically, one that for the most part moves forward and tells a story. But when the meaning doesn't come at once or after some thought, she lets the interpretation of it drop till it pops out on its own. Now *that's* interesting.

She gets up, her mouth dry from all the drinking tonight. Bathrobe on, shuts the bedroom door to keep Sammy in. Bathroom still steamy from what must have been a long shower. Doesn't have to pee but will on her way back so she won't have to get up again tonight. Heads for the kitchen for a glass of water. Living room's dark except for the street lights but ample light to see. He seems to be sleeping, hardly breathing. She holds her breath, doesn't even hear him then. He can't have anything on underneath since his pants are folded on the floor beside the bed and he said he lost his undershorts. On top of the pants his neatly folded shirt and beside them on top of a newspaper folded in half his shoes side by side with what appear to be socks inside. Why'd he move the shoes in? Probably from some infixed sense of order or he didn't want her to feel his things were strewn all over. He's on his stomach, covers down to a little above his waist. Room's fairly cold, so won't do for his chill. She goes to the side of the bed he's not facing. He has big shoulders, fairly big back muscles which seem unusually tight for a man sleeping, even flexed. Big tuft of hair on his back just below the neck, also hair that comes up almost to the tops of his arms. He smells from her hair conditioner, so he must have shampooed. Same smell she smelled when she passed the bathroom. All right by her if it made him feel better, but maybe he should have asked if he could use them. She pulls the covers up to his neck, he doesn't move. She goes into the kitchen, runs the tap water to get it cold. What's she doing?—she has enough bottled spring water to take a bath. She gets it out, in the refrigerator light pours out a glass. Shuts the refrigerator door, drinks. Too cold to drink all at once, truck roars past. At this hour and that sound could only be a *Times* or *News* delivery truck, hopes it didn't wake him up. Thinks between sips he's a very bright guy, a terribly nice guy, well just a bright nice lively guy, that much is clear, with a tendency to get into scenes. Also a lot better looking than she remembered him, grubby as he was when he got here, with a sense of neatness and cleanness about himself, and that while he was here, big contrast to Peter, he didn't make any kind of pass. In the morning he'll ask—she'll sit down for toast and coffee with him—if he could see her again, and what will she say? Say yes, see what he's like once he gets over his nervousness about her and evening fatigue and lingering tipsiness, meet for tea, maybe the second time for a long walk and lunch, and if he gets as pushy as he was on the phone, stop him, and if he continues to be pushy after that, drop him, since that's not the type of man she ever especially liked and certainly not what she wants to start up with again, so just, and this has to be the main thing, go slowly with him from date to date and if it works it works, what more is there to say other than she thinks this is what she'll still think if she remembers it when she wakes up again later today, and sets the glass upside down in the dishrack, tiptoes to the bathroom without looking at him, pees nothing much so doesn't flush it, more not to waste water than not to wake him, gets down in a crouch and slowly opens the bedroom door, grabs Sammy just as he's about to scoot out through her legs and kicks the door shut and carries him with her to bed.

Shulumu, gutsofar. What is, with, I affir, I affir, behind me befar, so near, so nar, cower me dup tweetly, twilleries, get back there and didn't let are, wise up me for once, buf something like one like, gist wanded to see what she would do, nice, she was so noose and then some niece, covers over me, I was too tired to and thought I'd freeze, in time I might've covered myself up all right, a find kine lady, eager to see her out of mourning in daylight, now go to slip, sluff, go to, sloop, time to, eferthink fault wheret May, going fizz, fuzz, bing bomb, bye bye blackbird, how do you fly today? climb on its back, time another time goodbye, slaff, baa, shhh, ssss, sleepily, bobby go nug, not knee, pot cheese, flug dwempt tomb, tinny time, tommy too, tea for tots, sofa mat, softer than mine, wean my gloom, bridge slapped dashed on, sheet and pillowcase so smellowy clean, he and Helene in a car with two men friends, don't know whose and, catching them in the rearview, who they are, but everyone having a ding-a-dang time, yokes, laughs, "Catch this one," one of the men says, Dan in the driveler's seat steering, North is his best, South on his left, West afront, East ahind, Helene beside him speaking, silent visible words out of her mouth letter by letter: "Lovely landscape. Nice drive. Big bridge.

Why's it rise so high? Tale-telling clouds. I see a hamstring in that one, a man strung in the next one. Beautiful ocean or bay. Where are we, Dan, and where we going?" "We're crossing the George Washington Bridge—the one that's lit up like a brassiere on its back. You don't recognize the Jersey side?" "Don't reproach me," she says. "Just ask 'Do you recognize it?' rather than 'Why don't you?'" "I said it like that?" he lies. "If I did, I deeply apologize," when one of the men grabs him around the neck from behind and yells "The bridge, dimwit— watch it!" and they're all screaming as the car crashes through the side-railing and coasts over the water a few seconds before it starts to dive. "Are we in a pursuit plane?" Dan asks Helene. The men punch open their doors and make expert jackknife dives out of the car and with their arms out glide downward side by side talking about the great view. Helene's in the back seat screaming, a one- to two-month-old baby's in her lap sleeping, car's still diving straight down. Dan shouts "Oh no, oh darn, oh my dolls, we're ruined, dashed, we, so soon, nothing nothing I or any man can do," and throws his arms back to grab them in a last hug but can't reach them. Then when he reaches them his arms won't come down. Then they won't go around. Car roof's gone, blue sky and white clouds and a preschool teacher and her class flying above and below. He stands on the seat, top half of his body's outside, and yells "Help us, stop it," raises his arms, "All right, I suppercake, I beg!" is on his bed, where's he? Helene's, sleeping over, now he sees, it's still dark, orangy sky, strange window frame shadows on the ceiling, Mondrians they remind him of, sofabed, softer bed, better pillow, just a dream, mean, man on the mule mews moody night, jorst a morst a lost a florst by morning heights dive, doors, forced, birdmen's frenzed strength, bridge, scary biz, bees, buzz buzz, by, ben, aboo, "Mr. Krin?" "Yes?" he says. "Dr. Krin—Professor, nitch?" head of his department says. "No, jest a lecturer, Professor Fish." "Lieutenant Krin then, we'd like you to take a fourth class ex pes this term—physics, and on the cusp I'm a fade, since we don't have the font to pay extra, extra." "Me? Fee free? Physics gas and lab? That's good for a gaff, cost it's the last thing I could dabble in. As a unicycle student I used to freeze whenever I went into my physics and chemistry classes and I never got higher than a D." "Chemistry has nothing to do with it, Lieutenant, and do it for me. It'll help you in this apartment, Sergeant, take it from me. I gibt you ein box, privately. In it is Miss Effie's things to know how to teach your physics class." He gives Dan an artist's paint box. "Return it clean," and leaves. Dan takes an old leatherbound book from the box, thumbs through it and sees everything he's supposed to teach. *Chapter One: First Class. Chapter Two: Second Class.* All the way to thirteen. Bit book but not hard, he thinks. He takes the box to the office next door. Helene's typing a letter at her desk. "Dear sir," she says to the page as she types, "the bill must be paid." "Helene, a minute of your time, please. The chairman wants me to teach cottage physics in addition to my three languages and lit quarts this term." "Physical? What do you know about physical?" "Roughly nothing, but he gave me this monstrous book and I brushed through it and found I coo do it. It's in this box. I'm not afraid." He opens the box. Several other books besides the big one are in it, all old and bound in the same dark leather. He takes out the smallest book. It's a wooden alarm clock that looks like a model of an operating table with many drawers underneath and stirrups and straps on both ends. "I'm sure I'll be expected to explain this clock to my class, but damned if I know how it works. I'll save it for the last meeting." He puts it back and takes out another book. It's a cuckoo clock, handcarved in the Black Forest it says on it, and when he holds it up a wooden bird pops out, cuckoos twice, pops back. He tries to open the cuckoo's door, tries to open the hatch in back, both are sealed shut. "How do they expect me to teach about this cuckoo clock if I can't get into it? I know what. I'll call in sick the day of the cuckoo clock class. But I'm going to teach this course. And from elementary go on to advanced. I can make a good living this way and can use the change. People need people who can teach physics. It's an important subject. Goddamn, it's the law." "Economics is important also," she says. "For instance, in Port-au-Maine—" Someone's starting up a motorcycle outside. If she has a cat, where's the litter box? "What's that your saying, Helene? Car harley hear ya." He wants to go to the window and tell the motorcyclist to stop that noise. But he's in bed, no clothes on, it's the ninth floor and not his building, she might come into the room again thinking he's asleep and see him naked and ask him to leave. Noise is even louder now. Gets up, just to look, sees he has an erection, forces it back between his legs, tries to pull the blanket off the bed to wrap around him but it doesn't seem it'll come off without ripping. He goes to the window naked. "Mike," he yells outside, "can that damn rocket—people have to sleep." Mike, seated on a motorcycle, jams his foot down on the kick-starter several times. The motor always starts up and stops. A young woman sits behind him watching television on a small set strapped to the seat between them. "Fuck this machine," Mike says and gets off. "Mike," the woman says, "stay here. This is the best part. I've seen it five times before. Television I'm telling you is the wave of the future and maybe even now is where it's all at." Mike walks up to the window, holds his fist under Dan's nose and says "This little finger's the cylinder, this next little finger's the transformer, the middle little finger's the responder, the fourth little finger's the resonator, and the littlest little finger's the thumb that's gonna pop out your eye, screwball," and thrusts his thumb at Dan's eye, it goes through the window, glass gets in Dan's eye but it doesn't hurt. "Oh my," he says, "not feeling the pain usually signifies the last moments of the eye. I'm losing my brother," and starts to cry. He puts his hand over the eye, is in bed. Feels the eye, closes the other one: outside it's beginning to get light. Orangy sky still, supposed to mean snow. Maybe she took the kitty litter box into her bedroom, thinking it'd be unpleasant for him to be near it. Brushing his teeth and seeing and smelling those turds, maybe it would, but he's sure she keeps the box clean. Physics dream. Yes? Something like the ones when he was in school and shul and couldn't get out if not. Motorcycle drives off. Five, six, even seven o'clock? If he'd washed his socks and wrung them tight, he could've put them on the bathroom radiator and by eight they would've been dry. But she wouldn't want to see his socks when she goes into the bathroom. Kind of ugly too: black nylon, thin, frayed if not holed at the heels and toes, one of his father's pairs he didn't want but his mother gave him to wear or throw out. He likes the Christmas season because of all the oratorios the radio plays. But doesn't want to give Helene the impression he's trespassing with his socks and songs and— They're at a restaurant with friends. Really the lobby of an old unrundown hotel with tables and chairs in it, gurgling fountains and cartouches around the room. Diana and the Hungarian novelist and two couples from her party that night: Chase and Nancy, good friends of his from Hokku; Hasenai and his wife, Hasenai looking angry that Dan lost the poetry book. Dan reads the note Hasenai slipped him before: "Who do I impale whales to but you? Drink drank, roustabout. Must brake relations fast: let this've been our ship's wake." "Jun," Dan says, "I was going to call you in Japan—I know the dialing code and rates. You dial one-one. You dial two-two. You get the overseas Asian-American connection and you say 'Three-three, four-four,' and she gives you the operator on a ham sandwich island off the coast of Japan. To her you can speak Japanese or say 'Five-five, six-six,' and then the phone number which I have here in my address book." He goes through his pockets. "Ding, that book must've been stolen too." "Act," Hasenai says and goes with his wife and the other couples to the cloakroom. "I guess we're stuck with figuring out how to divvy up the chick," he says to Helene. "I think we should pay it," she says. "All? I thought half." "All," she says. "People have been paying our way for years." "Not so. Since when? Okay, let's for a change turn the tables on them." The other couples come back with their hats and coats on and Dan says "I'm picking up the check today—*we* are—it's entirely up to us." "No," the novelist says and pulls out a wad of twenty-dollar bills. "Let Dan," Hasenai says; "he's cost me the cost of more diners than I can name." "Thank you, Jun," Dan says and opens his wallet. The check comes to $53.22 including tax and he only has fifty-three dollars on him. "I think, after all, I will need about ten dollars from the rest of you for the tip." "Pay with our credit card," Helene says. "What credit card? I've no credit or cards of any kind." She pats his side pants pocket, pulls his wallet out and takes several cards from it. "Where'd they come from? And they're all in my name too. Waiter," he shouts, "waiter," and a waiter comes over carrying a tray stacked with plates of food. Dan's sitting at a small square table in the back of a delicacy store, eating off of a plastic tray. Chicken, baked potato, roll, salad, beer. Three people he doesn't know are eating at the same table. He finishes the beer and goes to the front of the store and stops at the turnstile next to the cashier's booth. "Where's your food ticket?" the cashier says. "Do I really need to go back for it?" Dan says. "I know what I ate and you can ring it up when I tell you what it was." "If you don't have your ticket, the rules of the house say we have to ring up the maximum in quality and amount that someone your size and age can eat in one sitting before we can let you leave. What's your height and weight?" "Look, I'm an old customer—everybody here knows me by now. Oh, just guess." "Six-one, hundred and seventy-eight, thirty-nine fifty and three cents." "For one small-portioned cafeteria meal without even an appetizer or dessert? I'll find my ticket." He goes back to his table. The tray with his dirty dishes and the ticket that was on it are gone. "Any of you see my food ticket?" he says to the other diners. "It was punched to about a dollar-eighty." They all keep eating without looking up. "Did any of you, then, take my ticket because it was punched less than yours?" They keep eating without looking up. "Then my tray—did you see the clean-up man or anyone else take it away?" They keep eating. "Thanks." He goes to the cashier, says "Listen, I'm even better than an old customer. Without seeming immodest, I'm an exceptionally good customer in a number of different ways. Not only do I regularly eat complete meals in the cafeteria and always pay for them, but I buy from the retail sections a few hundred dollars a year of smoked turkey legs, sliced sable, coleslaw, pickles, olives, Russian coffee cakes and pâtés. So you have to take my word when I say I only had four things—a baked potato, fried chicken-wing and two other things, but give me a second to remember what they are." Just then two black men come into the store and go into the men's room behind the cashier's booth. They look like father and son—almost the identical face. The room quickly fills up with people buying from the retail counters, the booth disappears behind several tall women and men, it's an underground garage they seem to be in but one without cars. Something awful is happening in the men's room and some of us should go inside. That young man looked sinister, the old man looked helpless. I'd go but maybe I'm wrong, as they were both so well-dressed in stylish suits, homburgs and vests, and I'd also never be able to get past all these people in time. The young man comes out of the men's room, cuts through the crowd with swishing motions of his hands, stands a few feet from Dan on top of a small flight of steps leading to the exit door. Everyone looks at him and then at the men's room when the door there opens. The old man staggers out, his hand around the handle of the knife in his chest, leans against the wall and starts crying and coughing. Everyone goes "Ohhh," but seems afraid or too squeamish to touch him. The young man points over the crowd and says "Dat man demoralized me," and goes out the exit door. I've got to get the police, but if I go out that door he might be waiting with a knife. He pushes through the crowd to find another exit, sees the old man on the ground, bends down, listens for his heartbeat, feels for his wrist pulse, breathes into his mouth several times, pulls his eyelids back and lets them drop, says to some people watching "I think he's had it. I knew we should've gone into the men's room to help." "You should have said something," a woman says. "I knew something was wrong also and I would have gone in there in two seconds if I'd had support." "Meanwhile," Dan says, "the kid ought to be caught, but it'd be asking for it for anyone to go through that exit door." "Try up there." She points to the car ramp leading to levels B, C, D and F. He runs up the first ramp. A car's speeding down and he has to jump out of its way. "Bugger," he yells after it. "Roach!" The car starts to back up. He runs up the other ramps and leaves through the roof door. He's on top of a tall hill overlooking the Golden Gate Bridge and Pacific Ocean. I've seen this same view in a movie, with the actor standing exactly where I am. He runs down the hill to find a policeman, all the time looking around to make sure the young man isn't nearby. His mother, sister and he go into the Seventy-second Street IRT station. I've had this dream before, he thinks, stopping in front of the turnstiles. His mother says "Everyone has the correct change to get in?" His sister and he hold their coins up, his mother says "Good, then let's go, but stay close." He's first and is about to put his coin in when he sees a sign on the turnstile: Exit, No Entrance. "Don't let's go in there," he says to his mother. "We'll never get out if we do. That sign. It means death's inside." "That sign means you can only leave through that turnstile, not go in, so try the next one without a sign." His sister puts her coin into the next turnstile. "Don't let her go," he says. "I'm not a dumb-ox. I know what that sign means." His sister goes through and his mother follows her. "Both of you—come back through the leave-turnstile while you've still time." "Hey, kid," a man says behind him. "You coming or going, but you're blocking my way." He steps aside, the man looks at the sign and puts a coin into the next turnstile and goes through. "Dan," his mother says by the downtown stairs. "I'm fed up with your emotional notions and tantrums. We'll wait for you on the platform. If you're not there by the time the train comes, go straight home," and they go downstairs. "Please," he shouts, "I don't want you both to die or for me to be left alone." He hears the downtown train coming into the station, pulls his cap down over his ears and runs outside. It's a nice day, sunny and mild, a faint smell of blossoms or orange juice in the air, but I have to get away from here fast as I can. He puts his arms out, flaps them, but can't get off the ground. The station's a stone house on an island in the middle of Broadway. Cars, buses and pedestrians go in all directions around it. They're making me dizzy, and he shuts his eyes and stands still till his head stops spinning. A canoe's parked at the northern end of the island. "Is this anybody's?" he asks the people waiting at the curb for the light to change. None of them turn to him, but one woman shakes her head. "Mister," he says to the man in the newsstand outside the station, "you know if that canoe belongs to anybody?—I don't want to steal." "You buy a paper, sonny, I give you change." He goes to the newsstand on the other side of the subway entrance. A sign on its shutters says *Closed because of family.* Which end of the canoe is the rear? Both ends have a seat with a paddle underneath and look the same. Get into the end that's nearest and call that the rear. He gets in. The street turns to water. He looks up: it's still sunny, hasn't rained. He starts paddling home. But why go any farther? Nobody's there—my mother and sister are gone for all time. He starts crying. Stop being a baby; be a young grown-up man. You did what you could for them and now you can't do anything more. I could've gone in after them; you never would've got out alive. I could've stopped them by force; you might have your sister if she was alone, but your mother's stronger than you by more than double. He starts crying. Stop crying; get a move on, makes no difference where, before someone claims the canoe. He paddles toward Central Park West. My dentist practices right over . . . there. He's paddling so well and enjoying the canoe so much that he paddles into the park and through it to the East Side. There's the doctor's office I went to for my prostatitis, there's the one for my baker's cyst. He paddles uptown along Madison and at a Hundred-tenth paddles west to

Broadway and then to Riverside Drive. I know someone who lives around here but I don't know who. Heck, I know someone almost everywhere in this city; I've been living here long enough. He paddles to Riverside Park and then up to Washington Heights. He stops in front of his aunt's apartment house on Fort Washington Avenue and yells up "Aunt Goldie, Aunt Goldie—it's me." She doesn't come to the window as she always did when my parents and sister and I used to come up here when I was a boy. He paddles across the Hudson to New Jersey and back to Manhattan and down Broadway. He's hungry, rests the paddle across his thighs, takes a brown bag off the floor and opens it. There are two waxpaper-wrapped sandwiches and a bottle of soda and paper napkin inside. He unwraps a sandwich and bites into it—liverwurst, lettuce and mustard on fresh packaged white bread; my favorite kind. He snaps the bottle cap off with his thumb and drinks from the bottle as the canoe drifts along Broadway.

"Excuse me—I'm sorry—sleep all right?" He nods. "Well—how can I put this?—but it is getting late and I'd like to get started sometime today, so what would you say to getting up now? We can have that little breakfast and chat, I'll loan you a muffler and heavy men's shirt I have, and then you can be on your way back downtown."

Design by David Bullen
Typeset in Mergenthaler Goudy Olde Style
By Harrington-Young
Printed by Maple-Vail
on acid-free paper